THE SPY WORE LONG
WHITE GLOVES

A NOVEL OF WW II

NEW YORK TIMES & USA TODAY BESTSELLING AUTHOR

CIJI WARE

OLIVERHEBERBOOKS

PUBLISHER'S NOTE: This is a work of fiction. Names, characters, places, and incidents either are the product of the author's imagination or are used fictitiously. Any resemblance to actual persons, living or dead, business establishments, events, or locales is entirely coincidental.

Cover design by Dar Albert at Wicked Smart Designs

Proofreader: Emilee Bowling, Perfect Pages Final Proofing Services

Additional Library of Congress Cataloging-in-Publication Data available upon request.

1. Fiction, 2. World War 2—Fiction, 3. American women secret agents—Fiction, 4. Women spies in WW 2—Fiction, 5.British spies—Fiction, 6. American spies—Fiction, 7. OSS, SOE, CIA, MI6 intelligence agencies—Fiction, 8. Female secret agent—Fiction, 9. Spy schools and spy-craft training in WW 2, 10. 20th century fiction, 11. Washington D.C. in WW 2, 12. French Riviera in WW 2, 13. 20th c. OSS, SOE, CIA, MI6 intelligence agencies, 14. Female spies in WW 2, 15. Churchill's Secret Agents, 16. Operation Dragoon, 17. Spies in WW2, 18. France in WW2, 19. French Resistance

Published by Oliver-Heber Books

0 9 8 7 6 5 4 3 2 1

book includes real life characters and events co-mingled with the author's well-researched imagination to lend a verisimilitude of intrigue, romance, and history." Rick Friedberg, TV/Film Director, *Friedberg Productions/Hollywood Pictures*

"[*Landing by Moonlight*]...has excitement, betrayal, romance...what more can you ask for! I highly recommend this book." Mary Kay, verified purchase, *5-Star Amazon Review*

"From the first chapter, I was caught up in [*Landing by Moonlight*]... Not only was this novel well written with an exciting plot, the author researched, thoroughly, the time period and the actual settings in various parts of France. I recommend this novel to anyone, who is interested in [WW II] and loves spy stories." *5-star Bookbub review*

Dedicated to

*Ellie Cabot, a reluctant Boston deb who invited
this Californian to her coming out party, loaned me
a beautiful blue satin ballgown and a pair of long white gloves,
and remained my beloved Harvard College classmate
forevermore*

... and to

*Lacy Williams Buck, a treasured friend who let me borrow
her first name for the heroine of this book and with whom
I shared a childhood in creative Carmel-by-the-Sea*

... and to

*Charles Webster Downer, Boston bon vivant, polo player,
barge captain of the Adrianne on the Seine, and the guy
you'd want next to you in the trenches.*

Fictional Characters

Lacy Farrington Forbes – an American-born operative in MI5's in-country antisabotage unit under the leadership of Victor Rothschild, 3rd Baron Rothschild

Theodore "Teddy" Farrington Forbes – Lacy's younger brother

Cecilia Holmes Farrington ("Granny Farr") – Lacy's maternal grandmother

Webster Endicott Farrington – Lacy's late maternal grandfather

June Farrington Forbes Rowe – Lacy's mother

James Gardner Forbes – Lacy's late father, June's first husband

Remington Rowe – Lacy's stepfather, June's third husband

Abigail Gardner Forbes – Lacy's paternal grandmother

Winfield Alexander Forbes – Lacy's late paternal grandfather

Dr. Charles "Pem" Marchand Pembroke III – a physician, architect, and
industrial design specialist

Dr. Noah Fischer – an internist and a Harvard College classmate of Pem's

Eddie Shaw – a Boston newspaper editor

Countess Anna da Schio – Lacy's boarding school classmate in Switzerland

Jayne Girard – an American Red Cross nurse

Dr. Roger Taylor – a London surgeon

HISTORICAL FIGURES

Nathaniel Mayer Victor Rothschild, 3rd Baron Rothschild ("Victor") – a Cambridge University-trained zoologist and titular head of the British branch of the international family banking firm. During WWII, director of MI5's Explosives and Sabotage Section, identifying in-country Nazi sympathizers and Irish Revolutionary Army infiltrators

Teresa Georgina "Tess" Mayor – a British counterintelligence deputy at MI5

Kathleen "Kick" Kennedy – American Ambassador **Joseph Kennedy's** second-oldest—and favorite—daughter

Rose Kennedy – Ambassador Joseph Kennedy's wife

Rosemary Kennedy – Ambassador Joseph Kennedy's eldest daughter

William Cavendish, Lord Hartington ("Billy") – heir to the **Dukedom of Devonshire**

Andrew Cavendish – Billy's younger brother

Patricia Parry Rawdon-Smith – a divorcee in 1938 and a friend of Tess Mayor

Neville Chamberlain – Conservative Prime Minister of the United Kingdom,
1937–1940

Winston Churchill – Conservative Prime Minister of the United Kingdom during WWII, 1940–1945

King George VI and **Queen Elizabeth** (Queen Consort of the United Kingdom) – British sovereigns

Lady Nancy Astor – the American-born wife of Waldorf Astor, 2nd Baronet Astor

Deborah Mitford – the youngest of the six English Mitford sisters

Diana Mitford – Deborah's older sister and eventually the wife of **Oswald Mosely,** head of the British Union of Fascists

Kim Philby – a British intelligence officer, MI6, WWII

Guy Burgess – a British intelligence officer, MI5 and MI6, WWII

Donald MacLean – a diplomat at the British Foreign Office, WWII

Anthony Blunt – an art historian and a British intelligence officer, MI5, WWII

Anne Morgan – J. P. Morgan's youngest daughter and a philanthropist

Ambassador Laurence Steinhardt – FDR-appointed Ambassador to the Soviet Union, 1939–1941, and one of the very few Jewish senior members of the U.S. State Department prior to and during WWII

Richard Llewelyn Davies – a hospital architect (later **Baron Llewellyn-Davies**)

Prologue
England

FEBRUARY 1944

The penetrating gaze that Victor, 3rd Baron Rothschild, directed at Lacy Forbes told her more than any words could convey.

Rothschild has never seen a German incendiary like this *one before!* she thought, her heart accelerating as it always did when they got that close to a Nazi killing device.

Standing mere feet away from the wooden crate of onions containing the bomb, Lacy felt the bitter winds sweeping cross the barren field outside the village of Kettering, some hundred kilometers north of London. Suppressing another shiver, she steadied her voice.

"Milord, how lucky no one was hurt, given the crate was shipped from the Liverpool docks all the way here to Northamptonshire."

"Quite amazing, really," agreed the tall, marginally handsome but slightly balding thirty-four-year-old aristocrat peering at the deadly explosive nestled among the plump golden-hued onions.

The director of MI5's Department of Explosives Research and Counter-Sabotage section handed Lacy the field telephone. Along with his insect-dissecting tools from his zoology lab at Cambridge University, he brought the leather-encased EE-8 to all missions like the one confronting them that overcast February afternoon. Powered by its hand-cranked dynamo, the phone had a maximum transmission distance of only seven miles. Rothschild's number-one assistant, Tess

Mayor, was on the other end of the line a safe distance away in a hotel-keeper's office in Kettering, standing by to take his dictation chronicling every step he took to render the incendiary harmless. Tess was a rare fellow female graduate of Cambridge University, where Rothschild, too, had been an undergraduate.

Glancing overhead, the baron declared, "We'd better get cracking before rain or snow makes this an even trickier exercise than it already is."

Exposed as Lacy and Lord Rothschild were to the frigid elements, Lacy placed the phone in its caramel-colored satchel on the planks of a wooden farm cart positioned near the onion crate.

Rothschild, with his degree in zoology and fine motor skills, was accustomed to dissecting tiny insects and frog eggs. As war loomed, the budding millionaire scientist had been judged by this superiors in the War Office to be dexterous enough to handle the more complicated cases of in-country bomb deactivation himself.

And here we all are four years later, Lacy thought ruefully, glancing across the open field at an ambulance standing-the-ready, part of a high-security bomb-defusing squad called in, all because of a bunch of lethal onions.

"Everything in readiness?" questioned Rothschild.

"Yes, sir," Lacy replied, hearing Tess's rapid breathing at the other end of the telephone line.

Lacy knew that if her Grandmother Farrington or her Beacon Hill friends back home had any knowledge of what she was doing today, those Boston bluebloods would consider it pure German propaganda.

Staring down at the bomb nestled in the crate, she felt a familiar frisson of fear and fatigue, no longer able to calculate how many of those special cases had been tossed to Lord Rothschild by then.

His eyes were once again fixed on the piles of pale onions stored in the crate's three compartments. It had been part of a shipment of produce from Spain, a supposedly neutral country. But Lacy and the colonel were well aware that Nazi secret agents, armed with bribes and strong-arm tactics, often persuaded dock workers abroad to look the other way when okaying imported crates to Britain that spies had spiked with all manner of mischief.

"Well, well." Rothschild chuckled quietly, staring down at the onions.

"Behold their latest ruse, buried beneath this pile of *allium cepa*," he declared with a smile, wryly employing the vegetable's scientific name.

"You've never seen this type of detonator before?" Lacy asked, confirming her earlier suspicions. Out of the corner of her eye, she noted a group of townspeople standing beside the ambulance with its driver stationed on the other side of the field for safety's sake. "It's a miracle this didn't go off en route like the one that exploded aboard the same convoy from Spain and sank one of the tankers," Lacy observed.

The baron pointed a finger at the crate. "It probably failed to ignite because of a mechanical fault with the timer." He chuckled again. "Those Nazi chaps aren't always as clever as they think they are."

The enemy's sheer malevolence had never ceased to astound Lacy —considering all the diabolical bars of booby-trapped bath soap, tea thermoses, chocolate bars, toxic children's toys, fake coat hangers, and bogus silver whiskey flasks packed with TNT and plasticine that the *Bosch* lobbed at Britain's citizenry.

Lord Rothschild gestured toward the field telephone, ordering Lacy to turn the crank hard to power it up.

"Is Tess ready to take my dictation?" he asked with his usual sangfroid that still amazed and unnerved Lacy, even after more than three years on the job.

She raised the phone's black mouthpiece to her lips and inquired quietly of Victor's top assistant, "Tess? Just confirming you're set to start typing?"

"I-I'm here, hands on my keyboard," was the instant reply.

From the tremor in Tess's voice, she sounded even more anxious than Lacy was. Tess also clung to a belief that Rothschild's previous experience dissecting not only insects but also specimens like trout carcasses and sea urchins had given him a seemingly magical touch when it came to the intricate and dangerous art of defusing Germany's latest deadly blasting agent.

Rothschild dispassionately surveyed the empty, frosty field. He eyed the waiting ambulance with a deadpan look.

"Does it strike you that the presence of that emergency crew over there expresses a certain lack of confidence in our efforts today? Well, never mind," he declared cheerfully. "Let's get this bloody exercise underway." Then he chuckled. "And let's not take that too literally, shall we?"

Lacy, having cranked the field phone the requisite rotations, did her best to ignore the eerie quiet enveloping the two of them. Her heart gave another lurch as Rothschild indicated he was ready to proceed with the next phase of business.

She suddenly recalled the first time she'd accompanied him on an assignment like that, asking with the naiveté of the neophyte "sabotage investigator" she'd been back then whether he didn't find his acutely hazardous job utterly terrifying.

"When one takes a fuse to pieces," Lord Rothschild had said that day with an absent wave of his hand, "there is no time to be frightened. One becomes absorbed in the detonator's beautiful mechanism, rather like an exquisite Swiss watch." Then he had cast her a sardonic look. "I do confess that the first few of the hundred or so bombs I've dismantled made me a bit nervous."

That particular afternoon, Lacy couldn't help but notice that Baron Rothschild's gaze narrowed in a show of intense concentration, signaling to her that the task confronting him did, indeed, present something new and perhaps more spine-tingling than usual. Lacy's throbbing pulse slowed only slightly when a faint smile slowly crossed his lips.

He announced matter-of-factly to Tess at the other end of the phone's receiver, "Please note for the record that this crate the dock men unloaded and sent to Kettering's greengrocer has three compartments. The right side, as we were informed earlier, has onions in it," he pronounced, his smile almost a grin.

Lacy nodded, extending the phone receiver as far as she was able so Tess could hear more distinctly. The clatter of her keys was sharp and clear as she took down every word he uttered to create documentation of the perilous operation—the detachment of each wire, the step-by-step moves he made—were that bomb to cost him his life.

"And I can see," he continued serenely, minutely noting each observation of the innocent-looking crate, "the middle compartment *also* has onions in it."

Rothschild cocked his head toward the other end of the field. His abrupt nod was Lacy's signal to place the phone receiver, its mouthpiece facing him, gently upon the empty farm cart positioned nearby. A second nod was the command to remove herself for safety near where the ambulance was parked on the road.

Lord Rothschild pointed in the direction of the explosive device he would soon attempt to render harmless, declaring to the phone receiver in his strong, calm voice, "Duly note that the *left*-hand compartment of this wooden crate has already had most of the onions removed, but I can see at the bottom, there is a block of German TNT the size of which I reckon was sufficient to blow up the other ship in the convoy."

Lacy, who had moved some meters away from the cart, halted mid-step. "And the fuse is still attached?" she asked over her shoulder, realizing she was holding her breath.

With mild amusement tingeing his voice, Victor replied, "I would imagine that's why we've been sent for."

He gave another sharp nod of his head, and Lacy hastily set off for the opposite end of the field. Still within hearing range, Lord Rothschild's next words rang in her ears.

"Let the record show that Miss Lacy Farrington Forbes, our delightful American debutante from the wilds of Boston in America, has left the immediate area. I will now proceed to defuse this latest and rather nasty bit of German engineering that's so recently arrived on our fair shores."

Not for the first time, she wondered how she had gone from a skinny, rebellious, dirty-blonde expat American kid, dragged around Europe by her bohemian-but-Boston-Brahmin mother and certifiably crazy stepfather, to land the position of second assistant to the head of counterespionage for the Brits.

As Lacy continued across the uneven, frost-covered ground as directed, she kept her back to Lord Rothschild. Finally, catching her breath, she slowly turned around to stare at the man in the distance whom she admired more than any she'd ever known—except, perhaps, for a young doctor whose life she had saved on a Nazi-infested train traveling from Bucharest to Venice.

Do not *think of him now! Focus!*

Standing the required distance from Hitler's latest attempt at sabotage, Lacy petitioned a God she wasn't convinced was real that the 3rd Baron Rothschild's insect-dissecting skills might save his life yet again.

Lacy gazed through the binoculars strung around her neck, focused on Victor Rothschild, and sent up one final prayer.

And may my brother find a path far from those Irish rebels and ...

Her mind went blank. It was hard to know what to pray for when it came to Theodore Farrington Forbes. Instead, she forced herself to concentrate on the figure of Lord Rothschild standing at death's door two hundred meters across the field and waited to see whether the baron's luck would hold at least one more time.

Part One
Debs Go to War

Chapter One
London

MAY 11, 1938—FIVE YEARS EARLIER

Lacy Forbes stared at her mirrored reflection in the guestroom assigned to her at the residence of the U.S. ambassador to the Court of St. James. Gazing critically at herself in her frothy white debutante gown, she was barely conscious of the motor traffic whooshing by on Kensington Road below her second-story window at Number 14 Prince's Gate. She took appreciative note of her elaborate caramel-colored chignon created out of her formerly mousy blonde hair by her host's in-house stylist. The pearl choker around Lacy's neck had been an early gift from Grandmother Farrington for her upcoming twenty-first birthday in August.

She took a step back from the mirror, taking in a view of her full-length gown filling the looking glass with its tulle skirt, tight ivory satin bodice, and lengthy organdy train, a purchase that represented three week's salary as a copy girl at the London Bureau of *The Baltimore Sun.*

Do you suppose this ridiculous rig might double as somebody's wedding dress?

She could only hope that she could sell it at a charity shop after the blasted court presentation since money was suddenly no longer easily forwarded from her trust-funder allowance in the States. She was fast learning what it meant to "live within your means," her

Grandmother Farrington's words in a long-delayed letter from Boston that had been held up by the threat of war hovering over all of Europe.

That balmy May evening, Lacy was being "presented" at court on Diplomats Night courtesy of Granny Farr's waving her magic wand at American-born Lady Nancy Astor, who'd agreed to be her sponsor. Granny's wand had also been sharply pointed at fellow Bostonian Rose Kennedy, the wife of America's newly appointed ambassador to Britain, Joseph P. Kennedy Sr. The result was an invitation to stay at the ambassador's residence the week of the court presentation.

And thus, Lacy found herself dressed to the nines, contemplating what a fortuitous fluke it had all turned out to be. Lord only knew she was definitely *not* on the prowl—as most of her contemporaries certainly were—to nab some youthful, aristocratic specimen, late of Oxford or Cambridge, who might make her a titled lady. In fact, she had no desire to marry anyone *ever*. Why would she, given her insane family situation on America's East Coast?

No, the "British Debutante Year of 1938," as London's society pages had dubbed it, was proving to be Lacy's *salvation*, much to her relief. Certainly, she'd had to attend all the endless events that went along with being a deb in England, but crucially, it had allowed her to remain in Britain and not be forced to return home by certain members of her family.

Tugging on her long white leather kid gloves, which reached exactly four inches above her elbow, Lacy began to worry about the organdy train attached to her shoulders. It stretched exactly 2.7 meters long and, if one counted in American measurements, fifty-four inches wide, as specified by the lord chamberlain's strict, written requirements. The daunting prospect of having to make agonizingly slow curtsies to King George VI and Queen Elizabeth in turn without swaying off the mark or falling flat on her face and *then* backing away from the throne, not tripping over the damnable train, didn't bear thinking about, and—

"La-*cee*!"

A voice from down the hall abruptly cut into her apprehension concerning the impending evening's obligations.

"Come in!" she called.

The door opened cautiously, revealing Kathleen Kennedy, an

acquaintance from Boston and, now, almost a friend. Kick, as she insisted on being addressed, stood in her own silk and lace finery, her slight tendency to plumpness corseted to a fare-thee-well.

"Ah, you're already dressed," the ambassador's daughter declared, looking relieved. She entered the room and closed the door. "Can you give me a bit of a zip? Mother and her maid are fussing over my sister Rosemary, so I took a chance you might help."

"Of course," Lacy replied. "Come near the window and let me see."

Regarding their two reflections in the room's tall mirror, Lacy surmised that her Grandmother Farrington must have called in every marker she had stockpiled in Boston to get Lacy included, with Kick and her older sister, on the list for that year's royal presentations, sharing the limelight with the Kennedys. The added bonus of also having Viscountess Nancy Astor to call on for support had most likely given Granny's efforts the final push required to include Lacy in the Kennedy coterie heading for Buckingham Palace within the hour.

This entire scheme of mine to stay in Britain would never have worked without Gran, bless her! thought Lacy.

She flashed a smile at Kick and signaled for her to turn around.

"Ah ... *now* I understand what needs doing up," she noted. "Ready to take a deep breath?" She placed her hands on Kick's metal fastening. "Here we go."

Kick inhaled as Lacy firmly began to tug the zipper.

"Oh, golly, it's tight!" Kick exclaimed as Lacy tugged harder.

"No problem," she murmured reassuringly. "Just a half inch more of track to go."

Once the zipper was in place, Kick took a step closer to the mirror, pleading in a quiet voice, "Do you think you have room in your evening bag for a chocolate bar? I'm absolutely starving, but Mother forbid me to eat a morsel after lunch. At this rate, I might faint in the anteroom!"

"Of course," Lacy assured her and opened her small, beaded purse before taking the contraband candy from Kick and tucking it in next to her lipstick, a handkerchief, and a five-pound note.

"Always have some mad money in case you need to escape any unpleasantness," the wise Cecilia Holmes Farrington had cautioned her favorite granddaughter early in life.

Snapping the bag shut, Lacy could only wonder at such strange bedfellows the Catholic Kennedys and the Anglican Astors made. Lady Astor was notoriously both anti-Catholic and antisemitic, while the Kennedys and their nine children were famously fans of the Pope, which only illustrated how politics, even in a world threatened by possible war, could take a back seat to the burning desires of American socialites plotting to launch themselves, their progeny, and their close friends into London's high society.

But for Lacy, the social jostling seemed trifling set against what had occurred two months earlier. The appalling fact that Hitler, in March, had invaded and swiftly annexed Austria, where she'd attended boarding school, rendered the night's female frenzy over court presentations utterly frivolous, and she felt a pang of guilt for being part of it all. But what choice did she have if she wanted to remain in Britain?

Granny Farr agreed that the one thing that would silence her family's insistence that she forego enrolling in the London School of Economics, quit her job at the newspaper, and return home was participating in England's social whirl. Thus, there she was standing beside Kick Kennedy, a fun-loving, lively American likely to be named one of the "Debs of the Year."

The simple fact was Europe felt like *home*. She'd lived longer at the posh finishing schools her mother had banished her to in England and on the Continent than she'd ever spent time with either of her parents or various stepparents. Truth to tell, she felt more at ease in London and Paris than either Boston or New York.

Lacy patted Kick on the shoulder as a sign she was safely encased in her gown. Once more, the younger woman gazed appraisingly at herself in the mirror.

"Well, I suppose this is about as good as it'll get," Kick declared.

"You look wonderful!" Lacy replied—and meant it.

The dark-haired young woman wasn't a bit of a conventional beauty, but she had turned out to be a winning companion, ready for anything the nobs flung her way. With brilliant blue eyes and a dimple in her cheek when she smiled, which was often, Kick always seemed to exude an attitude of happy expectancy that had put Lacy at ease from the minute she'd entered the ambassador's residence to prepare for the big event.

Kick glanced at the clock on the wall. "Mother said that Debo is due any minute downstairs. She and her mother, Baroness Redesdale, will be traveling to the palace in another car driving directly behind us."

Deborah Mitford, the youngest of a pack of six sisters, lived around the corner at Rutland Gate. She was also a deb being presented at court that very night and a newly minted friend of Kick's since the ambassador's daughter had arrived in London a few months earlier. Lacy could see that the two girls had become close friends during the frenzied lead-up of multiple cocktail parties, tea dances, and all-night balls that had already taken place during that year's social season.

Through Kick and Debo, Lacy had, in recent weeks, been introduced to several other young contemporaries whom she'd come to like immensely, including the whip-smart, Cambridge University-educated Tess Mayor.

"I'm just sorry Tess isn't part of all this tonight," Lacy commented, reaching for her evening wrap.

That first night she'd met Tess at the 400 Club, the petite, chestnut-haired Miss Mayor had loudly declared to one and all that she had no interest whatsoever in making a debut.

"And besides, my poor academic parents plainly can't afford it," she had added with a grin, addressing many of the friends there, including Victor, the young zoologist and recently ascended 3rd Baron Rothschild with whom Tess had attended university. "Let it be known, however, I have absolutely no objection to attending all the fancy balls, tea dances, and nights out at the 400 Club with *you* toffs, so thanks for inviting me!"

Victor had suddenly grown serious, commenting within earshot of Lacy, "Your very presence, my dear Tess, raises the caliber of all this foolishness by leagues."

Kick, with a final glance at her corseted waistline, nodded her agreement with Lacy at what a pity it was that Tess wasn't part of that year's court presentation.

"It truly *is* too bad that Tess won't be with us tonight for the big show." Kick grimaced, then added, "Frankly, she has the best of both worlds ... joining us in all the fun but not having to be trussed up like a Thanksgiving turkey or make a wobbly curtsy and possibly humiliate one's entire family if a single mistake is made in front of the cream of London!"

Lacy, grateful to think the audience in the Throne Room would hardly take note of the origins of a Miss Forbes of Beverly Farms, Massachusetts, asked, "Do you think Tess will join us later?" Kick had included Lacy in her plans to head for the 400 Club once the event at Buckingham Palace concluded.

Kick nodded. "Oh, I imagine she wouldn't miss seeing us after all this is over. She'll want to hear every juicy tidbit and then dance all night, the lucky duck."

Tess *had* danced throughout many nights, not only with Victor Rothschild but also with their mutual Cambridge University mates Kim Philby, Guy Burgess, and the Cavendish brothers, the eldest of whom would one day be the Duke of Devonshire. Lacy had kicked up her heels those past weeks, along with the other "bright young things" —the sobriquet their group had been labeled in the society pages.

Recalling the first fun she'd had with people her own age—like Tess and Kick and the rest—in eons, Lacy pointed to her unsteady headdress.

"I'm sure our friend Debo is a whiz at all this, but how are we to manage these blasted things?" she demanded, giving her *de rigeur* trio of quivering ostrich feathers a slight shake to show how they were tilting dangerously to the left on top of her head.

"Push their comb into your hair at an angle as tightly as you can," Kick advised. "Mine seems to be fastened fairly well, but poor Rosie …"

Lacy had already sensed that the inner circle upstairs and down at Prince's Gate recognized that there was something noticeably odd about Joe Kennedy's eldest daughter, Rosemary. Earlier that day, Kick had described her to Lacy in a whisper: "She's terribly sweet but a little … uh … backward. 'Slow,' I guess you'd say. It's best to just smile at her and ignore it when she has one of her … outbursts."

Shifting from the touchy subject of the decidedly off-kilter member of the Kennedy clan, Lacy gently smoothed Kick's train back into place.

"There you go. You're all set." Lacy hesitated, then asked, "Are you feeling as nervy as I am about tonight? Especially those curtsies and the backing up part with our wretched trains."

"Not so much for myself," Kick replied slowly. "But Mother insists that I'm in charge of getting my sister through all this in one piece, and actually, *that's* what's terrifying me. If either of us trips or even sways in the wrong direction, there'll be hell to pay."

"*You'll* be a sensation!" Lacy reassured her. "I guess the trick is just keeping our concentration focused on exactly what we're supposed to do at each step of the ceremony." She hesitated, then ventured carefully, "But does Rosemary seem ready for all this ... pomp and circumstance?"

Kick bit her lower lip. "This morning, I've said a rosary for her, so let's hope it will see her through." Lacy's new friend heaved a heavy sigh and reached up to give her brown curls a final pat. "Mother said we're to go downstairs as soon as we're dressed. Both cars are already waiting out front."

"Well, if this stupid headdress stays put, I guess I'm as ready as I'll ever be," Lacy replied, giving a final tug to each of her long white gloves. "Let's get this show on the road. Lead on, Miss MacDuff!"

Kick grinned back. "May I remind you that I'm a hundred-percent lace-curtain Boston Irish, *not* Scottish like you posh Beverly Farms Forbes types—but I forgive you." She flashed her dimple and pointed to the bedroom door. "Now, let's go meet the King and Queen!"

Chapter Two

Emerging from the front door of the embassy residence, Lacy recognized Deborah Mitford and her mother seated in the back of their chauffeur-driven Rolls-Royce parked beside Prince's Gate.

Kick waved at the Mitfords' motorcar and smiled as the window rolled down. Lacy took in the sight of both women awash in white satin and lace and organdy finery, their white feather headdresses bobbing securely on their crowns.

Kick had confided to Lacy as they'd hurried downstairs to greet them, "Just so you know, Debo's parents produced six daughters and one son, but Debo's the only sane one of the entire bunch."

Deborah declared through the window, "Brava! You two Americans look perfectly wonderful!"

"You do too!" Kick replied, gaily waving her thanks as she followed her sister Rosemary into the back seat of the embassy's enormous Cadillac 452 A-V. Mrs. Kennedy and the ambassador got into the lead car, a twin to the one Lacy entered after the two sisters had settled themselves in the back seat. Kick's eyes were sparkling with excitement. She swept her hand to include the well-appointed leather upholstery and the small drinks unit nestled in one door.

"Welcome to my father's in-your-face American answer to all the Rolls-Royces, Bentleys, and Daimlers you'll be seeing driving down Pall Mall tonight."

Lacy could almost hear her straitlaced Grandmother Forbes's cutting comments about Joe Sr. and his extended family's rampant desire to keep up with the Protestant Joneses.

"Those Kennedys are nothing but shantytown Irish barkeeps—and probably bootleggers on top of it all!" her father's grim-faced matriarch declared any chance she got.

Lacy carefully shifted her weight on the limousine's jump seat and marveled at the differences between the two sisters sitting across from her, their gowns creating an elegant froth of fabric on the vehicle's plush carpeted floor. Kick was aglow with excitement. Rosemary, in contrast, kept darting her eyes nervously around the car's interior while clenching and unclenching her hands in her lap. Lacy guessed the poor girl's palms must have been dripping wet inside her long kid gloves, her lips remaining tensely clamped shut.

The two embassy vehicles flying small American flags on their fenders, along with the Mitfords' Rolls, drove slowly down Pall Mall in a parade of expensive automobiles as crowds of London onlookers lined the road. The throngs waved and leaned forward, squinting at the limousines' windows to get a glimpse of the debs and their finery.

"Mother said to wave politely at the crowds as we go by," Kick declared. She turned to Lacy, adding, "Don't you just feel like a princess or something?"

But Lacy thought, *No ... I feel guilty as hell, considering what's happening in Austria right now!*

When she considered the array of young men she'd observed at the parties that had preceded tonight's presentation, she'd not been impressed. An unsettling number had been callow youths clearly in pursuit of "a little girl with a little money" to refill the post-Great War family coffers of their cash-strapped parents. Since the Great War, the British elite had been struggling to keep their grand houses from literally crumbling or being sold off to pay crushing Death Duties. If an all-out war came to Europe again, she wondered what would they do?

Lacy forced herself to push such gloomy thoughts aside as their cavalcade pulled up to the tall wrought iron gates adorned with gilded royal crests fronting Buckingham Palace. A uniformed official swiftly waved the twin Cadillacs forward and across the broad esplanade leading to the entrance that the two hundred debutantes and their sponsors were to use. A double phalanx of liveried servants in white wigs, red coats, white gloves, and knee-length buff breeches lined a long red carpet, which the new arrivals were to traverse.

Lacy managed to smile and nod, but all she could think was it all seemed a little crazy. Even so, if curtsying to the King and Queen meant she could stay in London and learn to be a genuine journalist, she was willing to play that silly game.

Once they exited the vehicles and entered the magnificent palace itself, gentlemen-at-arms, also in scarlet coats and sporting plumed helmets, directed them up the red-carpeted Grand Stairway, where the ambassador was instructed to take his place among the diplomatic corps. The women were escorted into a large room packed with nervous debutantes and their sponsors.

Lacy immediately spotted Nancy Astor standing in statuesque splendor among the other aristocratic patrons and their charges. Tall and slender, with the noble features and expressive eyes that had seduced a viscount, she was clothed in an elegant pale-blue evening gown, minus the train plaguing Lacy and the others. Three regal white feathers were balanced perfectly on the viscountess's head, encircled by a diamond coronet.

Lacy was frankly amazed that Granny Farr's long-distance machinations had resulted in Nancy Langhorne Astor, the second woman ever to be elected as a member of parliament, agreeing to be her sponsor. But then, Lacy imagined that if the social lioness wished it, she could probably get Adolf Hitler's mistress on the list of young ladies to make their bows to society.

"Ah, there you are!" Lady Astor declared, striding across the richly carpeted room. She glanced appraisingly first at the three Kennedy women and then at Lacy. "Well, you all appear in fine fettle," she addressed the young women, then turned to Mrs. Kennedy and remarked, "Rose, you and I must soon abandon our charges and go with the other chaperones to the Edwardian Ballroom." To the debutantes, she explained, "We will meet again at the door to the Presentation Chamber and drift behind you at the proper distance while you run the gauntlet, making your curtsies to Their Majesties—alone."

Rosemary looked positively stricken, and Lacy barely suppressed a groan.

At 9:20 p.m., the Buckingham Palace usher, resplendent in his Saville Row suit, white shirt, and silk tie, scrutinized the line of debutantes edging toward the entrance to the Grand Hall as if he expected gate-crashers to disrupt the proceedings.

When Lacy approached the ballroom, he said in a clipped, oh-so-posh voice, "And *you* are?" and waited for her response, his eyes glued to the card she'd handed him with her particulars.

"Lacy Farrington Forbes, Boston, Massachusetts, Amer—"

Interrupting her, with just a touch of disdain, he looked up and said, "And your sponsor is?"

Annoyed by his tone, given that the information was plainly in front of him, Lacy replied more sharply than she'd intended, "As it says on that card in your hand, *sir* ... I'm sponsored by Lady Nancy Astor, along with the wife of the American ambassador to the United Kingdom, Mrs. Joseph Kennedy."

So stop treating me as if I'm some kind of imposter! she felt like adding, but of course, she did not.

She was rewarded with an expression just slightly short of a sneer.

"Yes, I'm quite aware of who Lady Astor and Mrs. Kennedy are, miss."

She could practically hear him thinking, "Cheeky Americans!"

The usher's snooty attitude was one of the things Lacy liked least about the Brits' attitude toward her country, and she knew full well that anyone working for the palace must not have thought kindly of Joe Kennedy or anyone associated with him.

The rough-around-the-edges senior Kennedy had been a major donor to the reelection campaign for FDR's third run for president, and the ambassadorship was clearly the payoff. Upon his arrival early that year, Kennedy had made it abundantly clear that, as the newly installed U.S. ambassador to Britain, he sided with the fervent isolationists back in the States who wanted no part in yet another European war that might be in the offing.

Lacy felt like an invisible observer among the swirling crowd of white-gown-clad debs, her mind on the fact that any sensible person dreaded the thought of another conflagration like the Great War that had ended barely twenty years earlier. But while studying at a ghastly school for young ladies in Germany, she had seen for herself the deliberate cruelty of the current Hitler regime since German troops had overrun Austria, and—

Don't think about that now, she scolded herself. *Concentrate on getting through this.*

Her attention was quickly brought back to the present when, at precisely half past nine, the King and Queen entered the immense gold-red-and-white ballroom. The Presentation Chamber's gilded entablature and grand portraits on the walls were equaled only by the large golden chairs positioned side by side on a raised, red-carpeted dais.

Lacy's heart began to accelerate as she and her two companions joined the crowd of debutantes inching their way in line toward the broad doorway. As each deb approached her magic moment, Lacy saw that the court ushers gave the next deb in line the eagle eye, seizing the trains that the girls were holding over their left arms and placing the lengths of fabric on the floor, where they trailed behind each young woman as she made her grand entrance.

Speaking for the first time since their arrival, Rosemary tugged at Kick's arm and whispered, "Oh gosh, we're almost next! I don't *want—*"

"It's all right, Rosemary!" Kick replied in a hoarse whisper. "I'm right here. Hold my hand."

One by one, the cluster of mostly eighteen-year-old daughters representing the cream of British aristocracy extended their pink cards of command to a head usher. He, in turn, handed each card to the lord chamberlain, who then called out their individual names in stentorian tones. Beyond and to the left inside the Grand Hall, Lacy glimpsed rows of guests, including a large array of distinguished men resplendent in all varieties of uniforms, gold epaulets, and rows of medals pinned to their chests. Ambassador Kennedy had foregone the traditional buff-colored knee breeches and, instead, dressed for the occasion in a white tie, tails, and a pair of black trousers similar to those worn by some of the less important waiters.

Kick gave a nod to Lacy over her shoulder as she and Rosemary were motioned to pass over the threshold and advance into the Grand Hall. Lacy followed suit, moving up a place as a small chamber group played softly in the background. Gazing through the broad doorway, she took a moment to absorb the hall's soaring cream-colored walls and elaborate swirls of gold plaster filigree decorating the pillars and towering ceiling arching overhead. Kick risked one more glance back at Lacy, offering a tremulous smile.

Why, she's more nervous than I am! Lacy thought.

She shot back an encouraging grin. A second later, a booming voice abruptly returned her to the reality unfolding in the Presentation Chamber. The lord chamberlain called out, "Miss Rosemary Kennedy and Miss Kathleen Kennedy ... presented by the honorable Mrs. Joseph Kennedy of Boston and Hyannis Port, Massachusetts, United States!"

Lacy crossed her fingers, hoping that Kick's sister would make it through her presentation without mishap. Before she could silently wish them both the best of luck, Lacy heard her own name called out.

"Miss Lacy Farrington Forbes, of Boston and Beverly Farms, Massachusetts, United States ... presented by Lady Nancy Astor, the Right Honorable 2nd Viscountess Astor."

Lacy inhaled one more deep breath to steady her nerves, glancing at the sour expression on the lord chamberlain's face as she passed by. She returned a plastered-on smile, then strode into the hall, looking straight ahead at the King and Queen.

Following a stately thirty paces behind the Kennedy sisters as they traversed the grandly ornate room, Lacy admired how kind and considerate Kick always was around her sister. The younger Kennedy gently bumped Rosemary's gloved elbow with her own in a gesture of reassurance as the pair approached within feet of the monarchs.

The two stopped precisely on the little gold crowns woven into the carpet a meter from the seated King George and Queen Elizabeth. Lacy watched as the king, a slim figure attired in his scarlet-and-gold field marshal's uniform, offered the duo a faint smile. The queen, dressed in a gown of silver lamé embroidered with silver pearls and sequins, inclined her head ever-so-slightly in their direction. Lacy judged the expressions on their faces to be the well-practiced ones of royals doing their annual duty but perhaps not particularly engaged in the process.

Lacy held her breath when the Kennedy sisters smiled prettily and, amazingly enough, made equally deep curtseys without so much as a quiver. She could see Kathleen give a swift kick to her train in order to back up gracefully, as required, but Rosemary, attempting to glide backward and off to her left, tripped on the fabric of *her* train, a debutante's worst nightmare. In a flash, Kick reached out and barely arrested her sister's fall but not before a muffled gasp rippled through the hall.

Chapter Three

Just as Lacy reached the gold crowns woven into the carpet in front of the royals, she saw out of the corner of her eye that the Kennedy girls had made it out the door. Miraculously, she, too, managed deep curtseys before each monarch, smiling as best she could at the King and Queen in turn. Her relief to have made it thus far collided with a rush of adrenaline flooding her body. As a consequence, she gave a none-too-gentle kick to her train but succeeded in navigating backward without tripping. After pausing on her satin pumps for a few moments, she then executed a reasonably graceful exit from the crowded chamber.

To her astonishment, when the three young women rendezvoused with Rose Kennedy and Lady Astor in another grand hall where light refreshments were being served, not a word of Rosemary's near disaster was mentioned. In fact, Rose Kennedy treated the court ceremony as a complete triumph during which nothing disastrous had nearly occurred.

Even so, Lacy noticed that the eldest Kennedy daughter was soon whisked back to the ambassador's residence with her parents. At an acceptable moment, the second of the U.S. Embassy's limousines set off for the 400 Club carrying Kick, Debo Mitford, and Lacy, along with a close friend of Tess Mayor's a few years older than they were, Pat Rawdon-Smith, whom Lacy had also met during deb season.

Sitting up front with the chauffeur was an embassy employee acting as chaperone.

Kick let out a long sigh as she leaned back on the mammoth vehicle's leather upholstery.

"Well, thank heavens *that's* over!" She smiled broadly at her fellow passengers and declared, "I'm now officially *out*, and I intend to dance all night, don't you?"

"Hear! Hear!" agreed Deborah Mitford.

Pat Rawdon-Smith, a recently divorced friend of the group, nodded and held up her index finger to get their attention.

"*But* ... before we get to the club, let's discuss letting a flat together with Tess Mayor on Gower Street." To Lacy's surprise, Pat had leaned forward, her broad smile including the newcomer. "The place is in Bloomsbury, with room for a maximum of four or five flatmates, Lacy, so it'd be ripping if you could join us."

Kick declared in hushed tones, "I'll be lucky if I'm not sent to Hyannis Port before the summer's over. Everyone at the embassy is worried about war breaking out at any time now. Daddy says there's talk of Britain passing a military training act for single men between age twenty and twenty-two."

Pat Rawdon-Smith blurted almost in a wail, "Why, that's practically every boy we know!"

"Well," Debo scolded, "I doubt that's news that should be broadcast until it's official, so let's not think about all that tonight, all right?" She adroitly guided the conversation back to sharing living quarters: "I'd love nothing better than to share a flat with all of you, but there's not a chance in my family. We six sisters are to live at home until the knot is tied with someone in trousers, more's the pity."

Kick's tone was wistful. "Lacy here is a good roommate prospect, though, aren't you, Lacy? *She's* got an actual job at a newspaper."

Lacy's thoughts immediately fled to the diminished state of her personal account at her London bank. Going in on a flat with Pat and Tess was bound to be cheaper than even the lowly hotel where she currently lived.

To Pat, whom she barely knew, she replied with enthusiasm, "I think Tess is super. I'd love to talk to you both about sharing a place."

Just then, their vehicle pulled up at the curb.

With the sound of band music filtering out into the street, the foursome emerged from the limousine and hurriedly made their way past the uniformed majordomo guarding the door.

"Aren't you excited?" Kick whispered to Lacy. "All those dreamy boys we've met will be inside, just waiting for us."

Lacy gave her hand a squeeze and whispered back, "Waiting for *you*, you mean." Before Kick could shake her head in denial, Lacy said with a smile, "Kathleen Kennedy, my friend, you are *definitely* a contender for Deb of the Year."

The atmosphere at the 400 Club in Leicester Square was all blue lights and Art Nouveau architectural style, with a tiny, dimly lit dance floor and an eighteen-piece band playing soft, seductive music. Within the chic, sheltered walls, threats of war seemed far off. From the looks of it, Lacy imagined a girl could get in a lot of trouble, given the minuscule space where revelers' swaying bodies were "pressed together like sardines," as Kick had forewarned her.

Pat, who'd assumed the role of their leader, headed for a long, linen-covered table at the back, where Tess Mayor jumped up from a seat next to Victor, the twenty-eight-year-old 3rd Baron Rothschild. They were surrounded by a number of other young men in formal attire, all former classmates at Cambridge University whom Lacy had briefly met at various social events during the spring.

Gilded chairs were soon found for the new arrivals, with Lacy placed between Lord Rothschild and Tess. Victor's young wife, Barbara Hutchinson, sat next to him on his left side. Glasses of Veuve Clicquot champagne soon appeared, with Kim Philby, another of the young blades, raising his flute.

"To the debs of '38—may they dance long into the night!"

"To the debs!" everyone chorused, with the sole exception of Victor's wife, Barbara, a debutante in a previous year, who merely sipped from her glass, looking bored.

As various orders of food began to appear at their table, Kick leaned in and said to Tess, "You must tell Lacy about your job working for Jonathan Cape." To Lacy, she explained, "Jonathan has opened his own publishing firm." Kick turned back to Tess, announcing proudly, "And I'll have you know that our American friend here now works at the London bureau of the *Baltimore Sun* newspaper!"

Both Tess and Victor regarded Lacy with increased interest. Lounging across the table sat a rather dissolute-looking young man named Guy Burgess she'd met once at another party. He peered blearily at the new arrivals, a nearly empty glass of whiskey in his hand.

"Fancy that ..." he said, slurring his words, "a Yankee news hen in our midst who's somehow gained entry to the 400 Club."

"Guy!" Tess reprimanded. "Be nice. I *know* Lacy, and I like her very much. In fact"—she smiled brightly—"Pat and I hope she might consider sharing a flat."

"My, my," Burgess replied, toning down his sneer but only just. "Our Tess and Miss Divorcee, Patricia Rawdon-Smith née Parry, working for that Olympic athlete and Labor Party toady. What a rooming group those three would make, don't you imagine, Victor?" He downed a half glass of whiskey, adding with a laugh, "But then you Jews are known for your tolerance of the lower orders, aren't you, Vickie boy?"

Tess jumped up from her chair and pulled Burgess to his feet. "Come now," she ordered firmly, gesturing to the bottle of whiskey on the table, "you need to work off some of that Glenlivet. Let's dance!"

Pat whispered in Lacy's ear, "I never could understand how Tess stays chums with him, but I guess she remembers when he was actually amusing during their Cambridge years."

Lacy, appalled by Burgess's antisemitic zinger directed at Victor, turned and determinedly changed the subject, asking the youthful baron about his work as a scientist at a lab connected to Cambridge University.

"Yes, I'm a zoologist. But I'm much more interested to hear of your newspaper work. Tell me about it."

In the course of his close questioning, Lacy felt forced to admit that thus far, she'd found it difficult to get her editors to take her journalistic efforts seriously.

"And what would you wish to write about if they gave you a green light?" he pressed. Lacy sensed he was actually interested in her answer and wasn't just being what she'd come to call "British polite."

"I want to write about the tensions between Germany and the rest of Europe through the lens of being an American. An outsider. Someone who has lived nine-tenths of my life in Europe."

"And how *do* you feel about the possible conflict threatening to blow up our Continent?"

Lacy paused and took a sip of her champagne. "I think most Americans are ignorant of the true situation on the ground in Europe." She hesitated once more and then continued, "I went to school in Germany and Austria and saw what was bubbling up over there ... how Jewish businesses were ransacked and the local police did nothing to stop it. I want Americans to know the truth ... to know—"

Lacy looked at him, suddenly unable to speak for the lump that had risen in her throat at the memories of the casual cruelty she had witnessed there. Her mind was suddenly filled with a vision of a little girl standing beside her weeping mother, whose Jewish husband had been hustled into a police van while bystanders threw rocks through the windows of their kosher butcher shop.

Victor lowered his voice. "Well, Miss Forbes, I hope those in charge at your newspaper are smart enough to let you write what you witnessed." His smile was melancholy when he asked intently, "Did you learn to speak German when you lived there?"

"Yes—and also French when I was sent to schools outside Geneva and in Paris. I managed to speak tolerably well enough to attend the Sorbonne for two years." She laughed. "You know how snooty the French are about foreign speakers. For some reason, my German accent has been more acceptable."

"I did much better with German as well," he agreed, which wasn't surprising, Lacy considered, given that his family originated from Frankfurt's Jewish ghetto. "What brought your family to Europe?" he asked.

Lacy summoned her usual reply when that question was asked of her. "My stepfather thought he had the talent of a Keats or Shelley, so when I was six, he and my mother deserted stuffy old Boston and filed me away at various boarding schools so they could live in the Lake District and, later, France, embracing what they fancied was the poet's life."

Victor's expression telegraphed the sympathy of a fellow sufferer.

"Six years old ..." he said slowly. "That's rather a young age, even for our set's ritual child abandonment."

"At least my younger brother was with me at some of the schools," she said, flashing on the memory of the night Teddy had run away from their school in Switzerland and been found sleeping in a barn, curled up next to a farmer's dog.

"And *was* he?" Victor asked.

"Who?" she said, forcing her wandering thoughts back to Victor.

"Your stepfather. Was he a budding Keats or Shelley?"

"The boy wonder, Remington Rowe?" Lacy offered a short laugh. "Eventually, my mother thought not. After I spent twelve years at various schools all over Europe—but before I could apply to the London School of Economics—my mother and Rem abandoned the Continent and moved to New York, where he has family." She paused. Then, for some reason, she felt compelled to confess, "I was abruptly summoned back to the States to make a debut at Delmonico's, so I must admit that tonight, I feel a bit like a poseur."

Victor raised an eyebrow and offered wryly, "You have good company here, I'll wager."

Lacy smiled her thanks. "Once I found my way back to Europe, I went to the Sorbonne for those two years and then landed my job as a copy girl at the newspaper to pay my own way—which was probably a better choice than my previous plan to attend the London School of Economics. It turns out I'm dreadful at maths," she admitted with a laugh, then added, "At least that school admits women."

"Ah, yes, but I sense you were a good student, like my friend Tess here."

Victor's wife, Barbara, who hadn't said a word all evening, shot him a frigid look and abruptly entered the conversation, declaring, "Wasn't Tess more of an actress in the Marlowe Society than a scholar at Cambridge?"

Just then, Tess quit the dance floor and brought over to the table a few more of the Cambridge crowd Lacy had met before, thereby cutting short an exchange that had suddenly grown tense. Tess unknowingly filled the awkward moment by introducing Lacy to an elegant figure named Anthony Blunt, who was attired, as most of the men were, in white ties and tails. Standing next to him was a tall, handsome Scot named Donald MacLean.

As the men nodded politely and then greeted their other friends at the gathering, Pat whispered in Lacy's ear, "Tony Blunt knows oodles about eighteenth-century art, and Donald ... well, he just mostly tags along."

The newcomers quickly joined those lounging at their large table and immediately began downing more champagne while trading both witticisms and insults at lightning speed.

At a little after half past two in the morning, the embassy chaperone arrived at Kick's side, bending close to her ear and whispering loud enough for Lacy to hear above the music, "I'm instructed by Mrs. Kennedy to see you and Miss Forbes home now. The car is waiting outside, miss."

Kick sighed and looked apologetically at a tall, spare young man she'd introduced as Billy. Pat leaned forward once again and informed Lacy quietly, "That's William Cavendish, who just became the Marquess of Hartington and thus heir to his father, the 10th Duke of Devonshire. Billy and his younger brother, Andrew Cavendish, both like Kick, so I wonder who will win her heart?"

Kick, who was ignoring the ambassador's emissary, said to her companion, "Let's at least have one last dance." She jumped up from her seat and boldly led the young marquess onto the dance floor where they immediately began to glide gracefully cheek to cheek. Lacy glanced at the frowning embassy chaperone and then back at Kick, who had tilted back her head and locked intimate glances with her clearly enamored partner.

"From the way she and Billy look at each other," Lacy murmured back, "I'm betting on the marquess over his brother."

"That's probably all for the best," Tess noted cheerily, "for I think Debo Mitford has her eye on Andrew Cavendish."

The music ended, and Kick reluctantly drifted toward their table, hand in hand with her partner.

"*Please,* miss," the embassy escort urged Kick, almost pleading, as if his very employment depended upon it—as it probably did—"your mother insists that you two arrive safely inside the residence before three."

"Well, at least I didn't turn into a pumpkin at midnight," joked Kick.

Guy Burgess, who by that time had consumed the remaining

bottle of Glenlivet, declared loudly, "No need to worry about any pumpkins, Miss Kennedy ... You already *look* like one in that rig you're wearing."

"*Guy!*" Tess said sharply.

Everyone in their group fell silent, with only the quiet music playing discreetly in the background. As the deadly pall grew ever longer, Lacy could tell Burgess had gone too far, even for him. She was well aware that during the deb season, the others present had become extremely fond of Kick. They all exchanged looks that mirrored their discomfort as Billy put his arm around Kick, declaring softly, "Come, my lovely lady. Let me walk you to your car."

"Oh, now, Billy boy," Burgess complained, "don't go gallant on us and—" Before Burgess could expand on his rude barb, the young marquess turned and said, tightlipped, "*Enough!*"

A startled silence descended on the group. Burgess slouched back in his chair. Lacy stood up, anxious to escape the presence of "Burgess the Toad," as she had privately dubbed him. Debo and Pat, apparently shrugging off his behavior as "typical Guy," decided they'd stay a while longer.

Once in the back seat of the limousine, Lacy waited while Kick said her goodbyes to Billy, who seemed to Lacy a very decent young man. Leaning back on the plush upholstery, she closed her eyes while their chaperone took a seat next to the driver in front. Her mind drifted to the invitation to share the flat on Gower Street with Tess and Pat, and she found herself smiling.

I so love London ... and my job ... and now I'll have a place to live with two people I think might become good friends!

Lady Astor would expect Lacy to attend many more social events in the coming months, and by the time the London social season of 1938 was over, perhaps Lacy would have saved enough money to tell her mother and Grandmother Forbes to go to hell!

Despite the threat of war, she was staying.

The night sky had a faint pink glow on the horizon when they pulled up in front of 14 Prince's Gate. Kick put her finger to her lips, quietly hissing, "Shhh ... Let's see if we can make it inside without a fuss."

A Marine guard opened the front door as they approached. Kick and Lacy tiptoed into the foyer and were about to climb the stairs when the guard pointed to a telegram on a silver tray resting on a highly polished mahogany table near the door.

"It's for you, Miss Forbes," said the guard. "Mrs. Kennedy told me to be sure you saw it when you came in."

"Thank you," Lacy murmured anxiously.

Telegrams, in her experience, only heralded bad news.

"Let's take it upstairs," Kick urged. "You can open it in my room."

Chapter Four

Nodding to the guard, they lifted their gowns' long skirts, hoisting their trailing organdy trains over their left arms, and trod carefully up the carpeted steps and along the hallway to Kick's room.

"Well, do *you* want to open it, or do you want me to?" Kick asked as she closed the door. Her worried expression warmed Lacy's heart.

Kick may be a friend worth having.

"You're a dear," Lacy replied, "but I'd better open it."

Lacy sank down on the feather duvet cloaking Kick's four-poster bed. Slowly, she peeled off her long white gloves, setting them to one side. Then she slit open the envelope and stared at the bold black print.

DEATH IN THE FAMILY. STOP. RETURN IMMEDIATELY. STOP. TICKET ARRANGED ON PAN AM CLIPPER MONDAY. STOP. JUNE

Since the moment Lacy's mother, June Farrington Forbes, had married her second husband, Remington Rowe, who was seven years younger than she, June had demanded forthwith to be addressed by her first name only "and certainly not by that vulgarity, 'Mom!'"

As Lacy stared at the cable, her mind went numb except for wishing she could, indeed, "stop" June from inflicting the pain she had routinely caused so many. Given their outright parental neglect of both her and Teddy, Lacy had long since ceased thinking of either her mother or her stepfather as parents in the normal sense.

Kick peered over Lacy's shoulder at the telegram, murmuring, "It doesn't say who has passed away."

The same question was already whirling through Lacy's brain.

Who died? she wondered. *Please, not darling Granny Farr!* Her heart clutched at the thought of the one person who'd cared about her welfare having left her world. Or perhaps the "death in the family" referred to her late father's warhorse of a mother, Abigail *Gardner* Forbes, who invariably emphasized the "Gardner" when introduced to newcomers, as it was a surname ranked in the top echelons of Boston society. Lacy felt the fatigue of the long evening settle over her like a shroud prepared for whoever had died.

"Well," she said with a sigh, "in true Forbes family form, I guess I'll find out who departed this life when I get back to the States."

Kick patted her shoulder sympathetically. "At least if I'm sent home to Boston at the end of the summer, we can take a train to see each other."

Lacy managed a weak smile. "Believe me," she answered, "that is about the only good thing I have to look forward to."

<hr>

As it turned out, the person whose funeral caused Lacy to fly across the Atlantic Ocean from abroad was not anyone she had expected.

A haggard woman Lacy hardly recognized opened the door to Remington Rowe's Fifth Avenue apartment. Her mother appeared utterly unlike the beautiful woman Lacy had always envied, with her classic cheekbones and startlingly translucent skin. Lacy peered past June's right shoulder at the mirrors and portraits on the walls of the enormous living room, draped in swathes of black silk. White sheets were covering all the living room furniture.

Her mother reached for Lacy's left arm and literally yanked her inside, slamming the door. Before she could say anything by way of greeting, June screamed, "That son of a bitch *killed* himself in a tawdry artist's loft on the Lower East Side!"

Gone was her mother's cropped hairstyle with a mass of signature dark waves framing her heart-shaped face and sea-blue-green eyes. On this day, June's hair was seriously in need of a trim and sticking out in all directions, as if her cook had taken to it with an eggbeater. June's cheeks were marred by dark circles fanning from beneath eyes that almost seemed black and menacing. Whatever horror had recently transpired had aged her.

Lacy tried to free her arm to pat her mother's shoulder in sympathy.

"Moth—I mean, June! What in the world happened?"

June wrenched herself away and began pacing back and forth.

"He was *with* that bitch when it happened!"

"*What* happened? *Who* was Rem with?"

"What does her name matter? He was with one of his *girlfriends* when the gun went off!"

"*What*? He had a gun?" Lacy gasped. "How did it go off?"

"One of them murdered the other, and frankly, I don't care who did what to whom!" She glared at her daughter. "First *your* father drinks himself to death, and now your stepfather does *this!*" In June's other hand, she clutched a copy of the *New York World* tabloid newspaper, whose thick black headline blared,

SOCIETY PLAYBOY POET & LOVER IN SUICIDE PACT!

Shaking the paper in Lacy's face, she shouted at the top of her lungs, "He was always an absolute *lunatic*, you know! Drinking nonstop ... drugging himself with cocaine. Out of his head—and so was she!" Tossing the paper to one side, June planted her hands on her hips and uttered an icy directive. "You say you're a newspaper woman now! Well, *do* something *useful* for once in your life! If you love that disgusting journalism trade so much, find a way to *silence* this hellacious scandal!" Before Lacy could even reply, June turned away, shouting over her shoulder, "Don't unpack. I've sold this place, and we're moving to Washington, D.C. I've cabled U.S. consultants in five cities to find and order your brother to come home and I've heard *nothing*!"

Lacy also hadn't had contact with Teddy in ages, missing her brother and worrying about him every day. It was no surprise to her that he'd refused to respond to June's demands. He was past his eighteenth birthday and no longer legally under her thumb. Lacy cringed at memories of his fear and loneliness as a little boy consigned to boarding schools in foreign lands, where he'd been bullied by other children when he'd cried and told by headmasters to "toughen up" when his mother had never appeared in person or written often. Watching him grow sullen and removed during his childhood, Lacy had been weighed down by a sense of responsibility, not only for his well-being but also, at times, for his very survival.

June broke into her gloomy thoughts with the loud demand, "If you know where Teddy is, missy, you'd better goddamn tell me!"

By that point in her mother's tirade, Lacy had realized that June had been imbibing her own fair share of Rem's always ample supply of hard liquor.

"You're moving to D.C.?" Lacy called after her as June stormed down the hallway toward her bedroom. "Well, good for you! But just so you know, I'm going back to Britain after the funeral."

June spun on her heel and yelled, "No, you're not, and there *is* no funeral."

"Rem's buried already?" Stunned to hear that, she demanded, "Then why did you make me come back here?"

"Because the damn Forbes trust is in your and Teddy's names. You'll be twenty-one in a few months, and judges might listen to you if we petition the court to make me the trustee, with Teddy to back you up. You two are going to start doing what I *tell* you to do or neither of you will get another cent of allowance! At least they let me control *that!*" Her mother's last words shot like shrapnel at Lacy, who stood frozen in the foyer. "You're coming with me to Washington, and that's final. We have an appointment there with my new lawyers next week, and I guarantee we're going to break that trust!"

Lacy sank down on her suitcase, the hurricane strength of her mother's histrionics hitting her full force. June disappeared into her bedroom while Lacy absently rubbed her bruised upper arm where her mother had grabbed hold to drag her past the front door.

What number husband was Rem? she thought absently. *Number three? Or was it four if one counted that no-account Count Malinsky, with whom June had lived for three years in Malta?*

Like Lacy's mother, Remington Rowe had been a lifelong trust-funder. His overblown artistic pretensions had always given Lacy "the willies"—as her brother, Teddy, termed the effect of Rem's behavior around the two siblings. Rem had sported a beat-up beret and a scraggly goatee that had always faintly disgusted her. She'd never told a soul, but when she'd hit puberty and visited on a rare holiday in France, he'd taken to standing framed in the doorway of her darkened bedroom in the old stone mill in Normandy in the wee hours of the morning. The ancient dwelling had been converted into a romantic holiday home suitable for the budding poetic genius he'd thought he was. He and June had demanded young Lacy and Teddy ride a nearby farmer's donkeys *naked* so friends at their ribald parties could bet on the races they held.

The reality was that Rem had never produced a book of published poems, nor had he advanced past the threshold into her room, but Lacy could tell that was what he'd wanted to do. His stepdaughter had actually been grateful when June had spied him lingering there late one night during that vacation and abruptly shipped her off to yet another boarding school. Unfortunately, the girls' institution her mother had selected that time was the awful one in Austria.

Perched on her suitcase in the foyer of the late Remington Rowe's apartment, Lacy sank her head in her hands. Her mother didn't really expect a lowly copygirl, late of the London bureau of a second-tier newspaper, to have any influence in hushing up the latest society scandal. No, June was once again determined to change the rules binding the trust.

The ambition to break the trust had been foremost in June's plans since her first husband, James Forbes, had died a drunk shortly after Teddy was born. Staring into space, Lacy could only conclude that her mother had tricked her, now that she was almost twenty-one, to return to New York in order to pressure her as an adult daughter to join in a petition to the court to make June, rather than the iron-fisted Forbes family lawyer, the primary trustee.

Shock, succeeded by anger, began to churn in Lacy's gut. She'd flown across an ocean filled with prowling German U-boats and skies dotted with Nazi fighter squadrons, only to find that Rem was already *buried*! For God's sake, June had married the jerk and apparently driven him to suicide. Even more outrageous, she was demanding, as per usual, that someone else clean up her latest domestic catastrophe and hand her a pile of cash.

Well, it's definitely not going to be me!

Lacy knew enough about the estate to be concerned. Even though she would officially turn twenty-one in August, she didn't get the bulk of her share until she was thirty—or married. Could her mother actually persuade some high-powered Washington lawyer and judge to put the widow of James Gardner Forbes in complete charge of the family fortune? Did June have some secret, hitherto unknown leverage over Lacy, a powerplay she was concealing to pressure her daughter into helping her get access to the money?

She's trying to find Teddy! She knows I'd do anything for him.

Did this current uproar somehow involve him? There'd been no news of her younger brother ever since June had cut off his monthly allowance too, a recent development to not-so-gently persuade him to return to America. Lacy wasn't about to inform June he'd gone off to Ireland with some hothead friends of his. She had no idea where he was at that moment or how he was funding his adventures as war clouds gathered over Europe. Given today's bombshell that Rem was already in the ground, she had many urgent reasons to get back to Europe. Finding where in blazes Teddy had gone off to was one of them.

Out of the corner of her eye, she noticed that a shiny black phone was sitting on the hall table. Her mother had stormed into her back bedroom, leaving Lacy alone in the foyer.

"I'll call Granny Farr," she murmured as she reached to lift the earpiece off its cradle. Surely, she would rally her other grandmother on the Forbes side to mount a legal defense to guard the various family trusts against June? Who understood the former June Farrington's lethality better than her own mother?

Clicking the lever for the operator, Lacy tried to convince herself that a certain elderly woman—in her opinion, the only sane adult on both branches of Lacy's family tree—would surely know what to do about a parent who left a swath of human wreckage in her wake wherever she went.

Chapter Five
Boston

December 1938

From her desk near a window at the *Boston Globe*, Lacy gazed out at the snow flurries that had begun to accumulate a few stories down on Washington Street. Sadly, she wasn't in London, nor was she particularly looking forward to Christmas that year, but at least for the past six months, she'd escaped her mother's harangues and legal maneuvers to gain access to the Farrington and Forbes trusts.

The minute Lacy had arrived in Massachusetts, Granny Farrington had seen to that by alerting her legal banshees, as well as Lacy's other grandmother, Abigail Forbes. In a rare, united front, both women had asked their legal warriors to shield their mutual grandchildren from the machinations threatened by the unstable widow of the long-deceased James Forbes.

"As you know, I'm not especially fond of Abigail Forbes," Granny Farr had said, sipping a cup of tea one late afternoon, "but I do appreciate how she immediately engaged those assassin lawyers of hers to stop June in her tracks."

It was a mystery to Grandmother Farrington and Lacy how June could be the offspring of Gran and her late husband, Webster Farrington. Lacy had known her maternal grandparents to be two of the kindest, most civic-minded citizens of Beacon Hill. Crucially, they had always served as Lacy and Teddy's protectors whenever the elders had been able to intervene.

"Your great uncle, Clarence Farrington, was more than a bit off," Granny Farr had revealed to Lacy, her eyes growing moist. "It's all been a tragic puzzle regarding your mother's behavior, but perhaps my daughter inherited her utter selfishness and outrageous approach to life from that rather inbred branch of your grandfather's family tree."

As June had threatened, she'd made her move to Washington, D.C., but after tangling with the Forbes legal team—and without Lacy as her foil—she'd soon realized she didn't have the funds for a prolonged attempt to gain control of the family trusts, and her barrage of threats had abruptly ceased.

As for using Teddy in some way, neither June nor Lacy nor the lawyers on both sides had any idea of where the eighteen-year-old had gone once he'd left England for Ireland.

Reflecting upon the last half year since she had fled New York, Lacy was roused from her reverie by a voice that suddenly rang out in the large newsroom studded with hard-bitten reporters, desks, and typewriters.

"Hey, Forbes! In my office on the double!"

Editor Eddie Shaw waved her through his door, saying in his gravelly basso, "I'm sending you to cover a tea party with a bunch of Beacon Hill snobs hoping to recruit ambulance drivers and cash for France." He glanced at a piece of paper on his desk, then said, "I want you to interview this woman, uh ... Anne Morgan, who's heading up this ambulance thing. The US hasn't declared war anywhere, so find out if she's legit."

After weeks of proofreading obituaries written by other staffers, Lacy could hardly believe she was finally getting an actual news assignment.

She quickly volunteered, "Anne Morgan is J. P. Morgan's youngest daughter and a pretty well-known philanthropist." She was surprised Shaw hadn't heard of Morgan. But then, Lacy considered the facts: Anne Morgan had founded the American Woman's Association to help working females develop leadership skills—a subject in which she doubted Editor Shaw had much interest.

Lacy offered the grouchy newsman another tidbit she knew about

Morgan: "The French government gave her the Legion of Honor medal for her work in the Great War, so I'm pretty sure her efforts to raise money for ambulances in beleaguered France are on the up-and-up."

Shaw cocked an eyebrow in annoyance.

"Assume nothing. Just be sure she *is*. I figured that this first assignment with the snooty crowd on Beacon Hill was just up your alley," he said with the churlishness of an executive forced to hire someone he didn't consider worthy. He shoved the information sheet with the address into her hand, adding, "Gimme eight hundred words or less on this, and do me a favor: don't screw up." Ducking his head with a green eyeshade encircling the bald pate, he waved his hand in dismissal. "Afterwards, go home, write the piece, and hand it to me, eight a.m. *sharp!*"

"Will do," Lacy replied, grabbing her coat off the stand and heading for the door before he could issue any more directives.

She turned her attention to the address that her editor had scribbled down and quietly chuckled under her breath. Not surprisingly, the location of the charity tea was around the corner from Granny Farr's and two blocks from Grandmother Forbes's deserted residence, empty but for the servants who'd been left behind when the ancient widow had boarded the train for Florida before the first snow fell.

Lacy ran home, dressed quickly for the event, grabbed her Kodak Brownie camera, and rushed downstairs.

"Gran, you won't believe it! Old Man Shaw is finally going to let me write a feature on Millicent Wadsworth's charity tea for Anne Morgan!"

Her grandmother, dressed in her finest faintly Edwardian velvet attire, pointed to the embossed invitation to the same charity on her fireplace mantel.

"I'm just heading there, too, darling," Granny Farr said gaily, "and I'll keep my ears open for any juicy tidbits you might use in your story."

"Would you mind arriving first?" Lacy asked. "I need a few more minutes to jot down some questions I want to be sure to cover with Miss Morgan."

Granny nodded. "I'll just get Nora to walk me there so I don't slip on the ice, but don't be too long. Once someone starts asking for donations, the crowd tends to thin out."

Once Lacy had her notes organized, it took her mere minutes to walk down Acorn Street, Beacon Hill's old cobblestone thoroughfare, to the Wadsworth residence on Mt. Vernon, one of Granny's longtime neighbors. A biting blast of winter wind prompted her to push up the collar of her woolen coat more snugly against her neck as she mounted the brick stairs to the townhouse's front door. Pulling her slender reporter's notebook out of her shoulder bag, she rang the doorbell. She could hear the clinking of teacups and the murmuring guests inside the Wadsworth home.

As she waited for someone to answer and usher her inside, Lacy marveled, for the hundredth time, at how effortlessly Granny had outmaneuvered her willful daughter in another realm. Last spring, she'd insisted that June "or my granddaughter must immediately come to Boston to look after me as I recover from near pneumonia." June certainly had no interest in playing nursemaid to her mother and had dispatched Lacy the following day, warning her that she was to "get herself to D.C. soonest." Gran had assured Lacy with a wink that "my lingering malaise will provide a good excuse for you not—*ever*—to move to D.C."

Her Grandmother Farrington's next action had been to call an old friend formerly on the Woman's Page of the *Globe*—and bingo! Lacy had been given yet another dog's body job for a very low salary. Even so, her last months in Boston had been a miraculous reprieve.

"Having you here with me, darling Lacy, has given me such hope for the next generation."

Interrupting her reverie, the Wadsworths' front door was suddenly opened by a maid she didn't recognize. Lacy introduced herself as a reporter from the *Globe* doing a story about the fundraising event.

"Well, I'll let you come in," the maid said ungraciously, "but you'll have to wait until I find out if it's all right to have you here."

The Wadsworth servant, clad in a black uniform and starched white apron and cap, bid the visitor take a seat on a straight-backed chair in the black-and-white tiled foyer. And before Lacy could inform her that she'd known the Wadsworth family since she could walk, the servant took her coat and instructed, "Don't move a muscle while I see if Mrs. Wadsworth allows newspaper people at her party."

When the woman left the door to the sitting room open, Lacy grabbed a quick photo of the crowd milling inside. Relieved to have caught a glimpse of Granny Farr sitting in one of the chintz-covered wingback chairs, she settled back to wait. To her surprise, the red-faced maid soon returned and beckoned Lacy to follow her.

"Mrs. Wadsworth says you may come in," she allowed grudgingly, "and your grandmother said to tell you she has someone she wants you to meet."

Lacy crossed the threshold into a room that was more a library than a parlor, with floor-to-ceiling shelves jammed with leather-bound books that appeared rarely to have ever been read. Some thirty well-dressed women balancing fine bone china teacups with a cookie on each saucer were gathered around an imposing figure Lacy guessed was Anne Morgan. Tall and impressively buxom, she looked to be in her mid-to-late forties, clad in a navy suit and matching cloche hat.

Granny Farr had risen from her chair and was standing between hostess Millicent Wadsworth and a tall, arrestingly handsome man not much older than Lacy. Dressed in a well-cut suit, starched collar, and tie, he had a chiseled, fine-boned profile that struck her as wildly incongruous in a room full of women.

"Ah, here's my darling granddaughter Lacy with her reporter's notebook already in hand, I see," Granny Farr announced, nodding in Mrs. Wadsworth's direction. "Come say hello to your hostess and meet an interesting young doctor here to learn about getting medical supplies to the places in Europe where they'll undoubtedly be needed."

Intrigued by the fulsome introduction and the striking presence of the only man in the room, Lacy took a step toward the youthful physician and extended her hand. Before she could greet him, Millicent Wadsworth reminded her guests firmly, "Let us hope that America will only offer practical things, like bandages and ambulances, and not conscript nice young men like Dr. Pembroke here."

The doctor eyed Lacy for a second longer than she felt was necessary before extending his hand.

"Charles Pembroke," he said with a smile, and when Lacy placed her palm in his, she noted the slender fingers of a surgeon or concert pianist.

However, the rest of him appeared far from delicate.

Lacy's gaze traveled from their clasped hands to Dr. Pembroke's broad chest and a set of shoulders that made her wonder whether he'd been on a prize-winning rowing crew in college—or perhaps had been a long-distance swimmer like the athletes she'd seen at the '36 Olympics in Berlin. His dark hair, bordering on black, along with his even facial features and tanned complexion, added to the aura of a young man who seemed far more likely to be at home outdoors in the woods or captaining a sailing sloop than indoors in an operating room.

A dashing specimen, to be sure, Lacy thought, steeling herself to ignore his good looks and cobalt-blue eyes to concentrate on the story she was there to report. She'd known those handsome, privileged blue-bloods all her life, along with their assumptions that the world was their oyster and that deference of every kind was their due, especially from women.

Even so, she couldn't help but be impressed by his ease around the gaggle of chattering females, as well as his friendly demeanor, which, surprisingly enough, struck her as genuine.

Mrs. Wadsworth gushed over her guest as if he were her prized possession.

"I should have introduced you as Charles Marchand Pembroke *the Third*," she declared proudly and then offered a girlish laugh. Turning toward Lacy, she elaborated, "His father, Dr. Charles Pembroke Junior, was an old beau of mine a million years ago, and our families have been friends since the year one."

Dr. Pembroke the Younger smiled almost apologetically. "Yes, I made it through med school, but I'm really an architect," he said, adding, "or almost one. You see before you a recent product of the Harvard Graduate School of Design. Harvard's president, James Conant, has this idea of sending a fully staffed field hospital to England to help the British if there's a war with Germany." He offered a depreciative smile. "I'm in charge of figuring out what it should look like."

"It sounds as if you and he think a war is inevitable," Lacy said, keeping her pen poised over her open notebook while doing her best to ignore the steady gaze of his startlingly blue eyes.

"Given Germany's actions so far, many of us are afraid there's *going* to be a wider war soon. And then there's poor Finland," he said. "Russia, allying itself with Germany now, has become a terrible threat to that unfortunate country. Russian troops have been making raids across their shared border, killing and wounding the Finns, soldiers and civilians alike."

"Will Russia invade Finland, do you think?" Lacy asked.

"That's the worry," the doctor replied, nodding. "I have a Harvard classmate currently trying to raise money for a field hospital for *them*. If he can only secure the necessary funds, he wants to ship medical relief and personnel over to Finland as soon as possible."

"And then, of course, there's Austria," Lacy noted with a glance at Mrs. Wadsworth, whose downturned lips were closely akin to a scowl. "Hitler's troops just swooped in and annexed it to Germany with violent efficiency."

Dr. Pembroke's expression grew somber. *"Kristallnacht?"* he questioned, using the German for the nefarious November night the previous month when Nazis in both Germany and Austria had killed or injured many Jews and destroyed Jewish properties.

Lacy nodded. "Goodness knows what conditions are like there now."

"Exactly," Dr. Pembroke declared, as if he and Lacy were the only two participating in the discussion.

Mrs. Wadsworth's expression had shifted from critical to censorious, as if her young guests were being terribly impolite to bring up such an unpleasant subject at her lovely tea party.

Dr. Pembroke, however, didn't seem to notice. "Terrible, wasn't it–what the Nazis did there? My team designing the Harvard Field Hospital is collaborating with the American Red Cross." He nodded in the direction of Anne Morgan chatting with a cluster of women on the other side of the room. "I'm interested to learn Miss Morgan's approach to recruiting volunteers for her worthy endeavor."

Lacy flipped over a clean page in her notebook and asked, "So, you're a doctor *and* an architect? Which profession do you prefer?"

"Good question," he responded with a short laugh. "I doubt that my physician father would be pleased with my answer." Appearing anxious to change the subject in front of their hostess, he pointed to Lacy's reporter's notebook, asking, "And you work for …?"

"The *Boston Globe*," Lacy replied, adding, "features department." She neglected to inform him that her story was assigned to the lowly Woman's Page. "Your project sounds very involved. What else would the Harvard project need to send overseas besides ambulances and drivers?"

"Prefabricated buildings, a laboratory, the latest clinical equipment—and all transportable," he listed promptly, "to say nothing of medical staff … doctors, nurses, lab technicians, a pharmacy, and so forth."

"That's quite impressive," Lacy commented, wondering what "and so forth" would entail. A secretary? A reporter to chronicle the project, perhaps?

"How will it be funded?" she persisted.

Before Dr. Pembroke could answer, Millicent Wadsworth, who'd remained standing impatiently nearby, listening to their extended conversation, intervened.

"The Harvard Field Hospital project will be funded in the same way Anne Morgan's efforts are, most probably," she noted tartly. "Generous, civic-minded women like the ones in this room, whom I'd like you to meet so you can put their *names* in your story!" she declared with pointed determination before taking Lacy by the arm. "Come, my dear, and let me introduce you to Miss Morgan and the others."

Wishing she'd been allowed to snap a photo, Lacy could only nod farewell to the engaging Dr. Pembroke. Her mind was spinning with the possibilities of Americans being willing to donate money, along with specialized equipment and medical and support staff, to help Britain and France prepare if it came to a fight with the Nazis. What if she could somehow volunteer for an undertaking like Harvard's and get herself back to Europe, where she'd always felt she belonged?

Chapter Six

Millicent Wadsworth kept Lacy's left arm in a firm grip as she guided her toward her guest of honor standing across the room. Charles Pembroke and Granny Farr followed in their wake.

Lacy felt a flush of chagrin at the thought that her obvious interest in the intriguing and accomplished Dr. Pembroke's endeavors had nearly caused her to forget the reason she was at the soiree. Lacy could see that Charles and Granny Farr were engaged in a lively conversation of their own, while she, after only a few minutes of chatting with Miss Morgan, realized that the philanthropist was extremely practiced at getting her message across to members of the press. Lacy soon gathered more than enough particulars to fill several columns in the newspaper.

As she dutifully took down the names of the various women attendees, the idea that had lodged in her brain a few minutes previously burst forth with such force, she almost shouted it aloud.

I can volunteer to drive an ambulance to get back to Europe!

When there was a pause in the conversation, Lacy leaned forward and said quietly, hoping that neither her grandmother nor Dr. Pembroke could hear, "*I* know how to drive, and I speak French, Miss Morgan. I learned to do both in Europe, and I'm quite experienced, in fact. Might I volunteer as one of your ambulance drivers?"

Up close, Anne Morgan appeared even bigger boned and more

amply bosomed than at first glance. She cast an eye at Lacy's slender frame.

"How wonderful of you to make such an offer, but ... may I ask ... how old are you, my dear?"

"Twenty-one last August," Lacy replied, seeing out of the corner of her eye that both Dr. Pembroke and her grandmother had ceased their chat and were listening intently.

"Too young, I'm afraid," Miss Morgan said firmly, eyeing the absence of a wedding ring on Lacy's left hand. "We have set twenty-five years old as our minimum age for unmarried young women to join our ambulance corps. It can be brutal work in a foreign land."

"But I've lived in Europe all my life," she protested, "and I speak both French *and* German fluently. Surely, you could make an exception."

Her damnable Forbes trust wouldn't disperse anything substantial for nine more years—or until she was married—at which point, both sets of attorneys had stressed, "your husband will take over management and control of the money."

If she just had *access* to that money, she could *buy* an ambulance and insist she be the one to drive it!

Just then, Granny Farr made a move to speak up. The octogenarian smiled at Miss Morgan, pointing to Lacy's notebook filled with her scribbles from her conversations with both the doctor and the wealthy Francophile.

"I see, Miss Morgan, that my granddaughter has gathered the important particulars for the article she's writing for the *Boston Globe*." To Lacy, she urged in a sweet, forgiving tone, "I hope you don't mind, dear, but I'm a bit fatigued after enjoying this lovely party. I'd so appreciate it if you could escort me home."

Lacy immediately suspected that even Granny Farr was not in favor of her granddaughter driving an ambulance onto bloody battlefields.

Charles Pembroke spoke quietly beneath the hubbub of voices.

"I have my car outside, Mrs. Farrington, and I'm due back at my drafting board at Harvard. Please let me drive both of you home."

Lacy's grandmother demurred with her usual charm, "Oh, heavens, that's so kind of you, but we live just around the corner."

Lacy barely heard her, still smarting from Morgan's rejection of her offer to volunteer as an ambulance driver.

Meanwhile, her grandmother thanked her hostess "for such a charming, stimulating afternoon, Millicent!" Mrs. Wadsworth nodded vaguely and drifted over to her other guests.

Charles smiled at Lacy, held her gaze, and said conspiratorially under his breath, "Please convince your grandmother driving you home provides me a polite exit out of here."

Lacy gently seized Granny Farr's arm and whispered, "Do all of us a favor, including the good doctor who wishes to escape, and let him take us home."

Her grandmother laughed. "Well, then, of course you can, Dr. Pembroke."

Upon their request, the Wadsworths' maid retrieved their coats and opened the front door so they could pass through.

"Thank you so much," Lacy murmured, silently evaluating possible opportunities with American organizations like Dr. Pembroke's to not only provide ambulances and volunteer drivers but also send field hospitals to Europe. She nearly laughed aloud at the jolt of new awareness that perhaps she'd stumbled upon yet another ingenious way to catapult herself back to Britain.

Granny Farr took Lacy's arm, commenting pleasantly to their volunteer chauffeur, "Let us be off!"

Lacy glanced at Dr. Charles Pembroke, her mind's eye recalling how he'd been surrounded by a cluster of admiring middle-aged women who probably considered him the perfect catch for their daughters. She gazed at his left hand just as he was pulling on a glove against the biting cold.

No wedding band.

She wished she could tell Granny, then and there, to forget any matchmaking plots to keep her granddaughter by her side by placing eligible young men like Dr. Pembroke in her path. Charles Pembroke, physician and architect, was, indeed, quite a catch, but she couldn't see herself tending babies and hosting teas for other young marrieds in the tradition of the Millicent Wadsworths of Beacon Hill.

In fact, as of that afternoon, she could suddenly imagine herself as a *new* version of a dogs body—perhaps as a Red Cross volunteer heading for duties abroad? Surely, the Red Cross accepted women volunteers twenty-one years and older? It certainly would be an improvement over her present position as a slave to a bunch of misogynistic, all-male reporters at the *Boston Globe.*

As Lacy stood beside Granny Farr, waiting for Charles Pembroke to bring his vehicle around, the pressing question became how she would go about signing on to an American charitable organization that could fling her back across the Atlantic.

When Charles Pembroke's impressive roadster pulled up to the door of Granny Farr's townhouse, the octogenarian leaned forward with an invitation.

"Please, come in for a glass of sherry or a whiskey as small thanks for bringing us home."

Lacy stifled a groan for she longed for nothing more than to take a bath before tackling her 800-word story, due the next morning. And besides, she hated it when she was made to feel like some left-behind spinster when there were unmarried young men present.

"Granny, darling, Dr. Pembroke mentioned he had to get back to Har—"

To Lacy's annoyance, Charles Pembroke broke in. "That was a lovely gathering at Mrs. Wadsworth's, but I'm no tea drinker." He smiled over his shoulder from the driver's seat, declaring, "I happily accept your kind offer, Mrs. Farrington. A sherry would be most appreciated." He swiftly leaped out of the gleaming roadster and opened the rear passenger door, helping Lacy's grandmother out of the car and up her front steps. He said to Lacy over his shoulder, "And besides, Miss Forbes, I want to learn what you think of Anne Morgan's idea of recruiting young women to drive ambulances onto battlefields."

"And do you approve of women in such roles?" she questioned him just as Granny's maid, Nora, opened their front door.

"Why not if they can do the job?" he answered. "I'll just park the car and be right back."

Lacy was glad he couldn't see her look of utter surprise at his generous answer as she followed her grandmother into the front parlor.

"Nora, dear," Granny asked her maid, "would you please pour two small sherries and a whiskey?"

A few minutes later, Nora ushered Charles into the front sitting room, along with a tray of drinks. Before their guest could elaborate further on his feelings about women in roles that traditionally recruited only men, Lacy watched her grandmother turn toward Dr. Pembroke and flutter her eyelashes.

"I presumed you'd actually prefer something a bit stronger than sherry? My late husband did love that Glenlivet."

Charles Pembroke nodded with a grin.

"Perfect. But do make it a light one," he said to the maid. To Lacy, he continued, "I'm truly interested in what draws a woman like yourself, who speaks French and German, as I heard you say, to be willing to sign up for such an arduous job." He paused, adding, "In our planning for a field hospital, we're considering including American nurses and a few female lab technicians and drivers on the team, but we're still researching this idea to see if it's viable."

"American women served as nurses and drove ambulances in the Great War, Dr. Pembroke," Lacy pointed out.

"Call me 'Pem.'"

Lacy blinked. "People call you 'Pem?'"

He nodded. "'Charles Marchand Pembroke the Third' is quite a mouthful, don't you think? I got tired of being the butt of jokes in school, so over the years, I persuaded my friends to just call me 'Pem' and be done with it."

Lacy couldn't help but smile. "Okay. I'll make it 'Pem' ... that is, if you'll call me 'Lacy' ... but 'Pem' is so Back Bay, Boston," she teased.

"How so?" he said, feigning insult.

Lacy shrugged, indicating he should take a seat on her grandmother's Victorian-era furniture that would have made Abraham Lincoln feel right at home.

"Before I lived in Europe," she said, "I knew a Priscilla Cushing near here who went by 'Pookie.'"

Pem laughed, inspiring in Lacy a mischievousness she hadn't experienced in an age.

"And then there's my cousin, Frances, called 'Frendee,'" she continued, "and Granny's friend Diana, whom everyone calls

'Dinksie.'" Lacy paused, a finger raised. "And, of course, how could I forget Christopher Cabot Cook, who goes by—"

"'Cookie!'" Pem broke in with an even heartier laugh. "I knew him! He was in my college class at Harvard. A very nice guy."

Lacy gave him a look, arching her eyebrow. "Well, there you are. 'Pem' sounds *very* Back Bay."

Granny Farr was delicately sipping her sherry, observing their conversation like a tennis match. Lacy imagined she'd noted that their guest was definitely hoping to charm them both. *The word "flirt" might even apply*, Lacy thought.

"I must inquire, Pem, how is the rest of your family?" the older woman asked. "Millicent Wadsworth may have considered your father one of her legion of beaux, but I hold similar memories of your dear grandfather, the original Charles Pembroke Senior." Granny's smile turned wistful. "I lost contact with him when he went to Tulane Medical School. Married the stunning Alice Emerson before he graduated, I recall."

Pem nodded, and Lacy sensed his good spirits deflated noticeably.

"Yes. Sadly, Grandmother Alice and Grandfather Pembroke both died in the influenza pandemic in 1918, when I was seven."

Granny nodded sympathetically. "That was such a time of tragedy for so many. And your mother is from New Orleans, I believe?"

Pem nodded, adding with reluctance Lacy couldn't help but notice, "Yes, that's where the 'Marchand' in my name comes from. She was Suzette Toussaint Marchand. My father went to Tulane, like *his* father, but came home with a Southern belle by his side."

"And you?" Lacy asked. "Did you follow them down South to medical school?" She fully expected agreement, which was soon forthcoming.

"Yes. First Harvard undergrad—"

"Like your father, yes?" Lacy interrupted.

He nodded confirmation. "Then I graduated from Tulane Med in '35."

It seemed to Lacy that Charles Marchand Pembroke III was a typical Boston blueblood, deeply mired in tradition and a young man who did whatever his family dictated.

And I've always done quite the opposite, she thought wryly.

"I didn't practice after my residency though," he offered, as if reading her critical mind. "As I mentioned earlier—and much to my family's chagrin—after Tulane, I enrolled at the Harvard Graduate School of Design. I've been constructing things out of string and cardboard since I was a little kid," he said somewhat sheepishly. "I'll receive my diploma in architecture this spring."

"Well, *that* sounds like rather a major career detour," Lacy blurted. She glanced at Granny Farr and then asked, "How did your parents take it? That you're not practicing medicine, I mean."

"My father, particularly, wasn't very pleased," he said with a rueful shake of his head. "I still owe the bursar's office for much of my design school tuition."

"So, your parents vetoed underwriting that particular dream?"

Lacy felt a stab of sympathy. Rich people used money like a bludgeon against offspring who dared to defy the family's dictates.

Pem shrugged. "I'm happily working off what I still owe this final year as part of the staff on the field hospital project." His eyes grew animated. "It's exciting work creating the blueprints for the operation. It uses both my medical education and what I've learned in design school." He cast an amused look at Lacy, adding, "At least that's what I tell my father, who's still practicing internal medicine at Mass General."

Granny Farr leaned forward and patted the hand not holding Pem's whiskey.

"And do you still live in that wonderful old house your parents had on Linnean Street in Cambridge?"

His glance immediately focused on the crystal glass of spirits in his hand. "No. My ... wife and I have a home in Brookline."

Lacy immediately sensed Granny's surprise and sharp disappointment at hearing that news, a revelation that unnervingly struck Lacy the same way.

He's married?

And the type to choose to forgo wearing a wedding ring, she considered cynically. She inhaled a breath, telling herself the unexpected news didn't matter one way or the other.

"Then you won't be going with the field hospital when it's sent abroad?" Lacy inquired, anxious to probe him for the project's details. "Do you know, yet, where it will be based?"

Could he—or would he—arrange an introduction to his team? Lacy wondered, an idea forming in her mind. She'd willingly sign on to something like the Harvard project, even if it went to France instead of England.

At least I'd be back in Europe and—

Pem interrupted her racing thoughts. "Exactly where the field hospital will be situated is not officially announced yet, so don't quote me, but I expect Britain. Probably in the middle of England somewhere. With all the unrest in Europe, I think medical people here and in the UK are thinking and planning ahead."

"England ..." Lacy murmured, tamping down her excitement at hearing that. "Will it be sent overseas next year?" she asked eagerly, delighted to think 1939 was just around the corner. There truly might be a way she could sign on in some minor capacity, even as a secretary.

Pem shook his head. "Oh goodness, no! With German troops occupying the Sudetenland in October and Hitler's terrible actions against German and Austrian Jews in November, we'll be lucky if we can requisition the needed materials by the spring or summer of 1940. Maybe not even until 1941. You cannot imagine all the red tape involved, especially since America's so isolationist these days. Everything about this effort is being kept low profile."

Not before deep into 1940 or later? she thought with dismay.

Pem's field hospital wouldn't be operational for an age! Poor Finland had been steadily harassed by Russia for months. She wondered how soon *they* could expect any help.

A wave of frustration and resentment swept over her. Why was everything conspiring against her achieving the one single thing that was important to her: returning to Europe, where she had a chance at true friendships and her life might have purpose and meaning, to say nothing of finding out where her younger brother was?

And to top it all off, Charles Pembroke was *married*. Even a simple friendship was definitely out of the question if her two grandmothers had anything to say about it.

So now *what?* she fretted in frustration. How could she devise a socially acceptable way to stay in contact with a married man who could pave the way for her to meet other Americans like him who were dedicated to supporting projects that could help Britain and her allies? At that point, it was her only possible ticket back to London.

Now what, indeed?

CHAPTER SEVEN

Lacy was hardly aware that Granny Farr had picked up the conversation with Charles Pembroke that she had allowed to lapse into uncomfortable silence following his disclosure of being married.

"You say you live in Brookline," noted Granny Farr. "How nice for you and your wife, Dr. Pembroke. It must be delightful to live in such pleasant surroundings."

Lacy could see that her grandmother had swiftly abandoned any misbegotten hopes she might have had playing matchmaker for her granddaughter.

It's the Boston Brahmin in her ... always astonishingly polite in any and all circumstances.

As for Lacy, she'd promptly placed Pem back in the category to which she'd originally consigned him: a predictable follow-alonger. Since she'd learned he and his wife lived in Brookline, the suburban oasis at Boston's eastern edge known for its stately homes, tree-lined streets, and exclusive, top-rated schools, she could see that Pem, too, was clearly stamped out of the classic Boston Brahmin cookie mold. Its members followed in the precise footsteps of whoever came before them.

"And have you children?" Granny asked politely, consuming the last of her sherry.

"N-no ... no children," Pem replied almost apologetically. "I've been in school rather nonstop these last years."

Granny put her sherry glass firmly on the table near her chair. "Is your wife's family from Brookline too? Perhaps I know them."

Oh God, Lacy groaned silently, *the old* Who do you know? *game.*

Pem also placed his glass down, clearly preparing to take his leave. "You might know Eleanor's two families—the Aldriches and the Choates? Both have lived in Brookline or the greater Boston area practically since their founding."

Lacy found herself wondering just who had purchased Dr. Pembroke III's home in such a pricey suburb since the head of household was still working off the bills from his design school tuition.

"Ah ... yes, Eleanor Aldrich Choate," Granny mused. "Your wife was quite the debutante her year, I seem to recall." She looked over at Lacy. "I remember her photograph in the *Globe.* Lovely looking girl. Came out in 1931, didn't she? Four years before Lacy here." She cocked her head at each of them in turn. "It's rather surprising that *you* two haven't run into each other before this, isn't it, Lacy?"

Lacy nodded in polite agreement, replying, "Well, when you were in college, Pem, I was in prison at a boarding school in Austria."

"Now, Lacy ..." Granny Farr remonstrated.

Ignoring her grandmother's credo to "never complain; never explain," Lacy gave a short laugh. "After I became Reluctant Debutante of the Year in '35, I promptly returned to Paris and enrolled at the Sorbonne."

Pem regarded her soberly. "How I envy you for that."

Lacy looked at him with surprise. "You do?"

"I do," he repeated. "My French and German are atrocious, and I'm probably going to need them badly in my work, more's the pity." He paused briefly, then rose from his chair. "Well, I must be going." He fished his wallet out of his trousers pocket and rifled through it until he withdrew a business card and handed it to Lacy. "At the Morgan event just now, I heard you inquire about driving ambulances. Get in touch if you're still interested in the next year or two. We will accept volunteers aged twenty-two and above, which you will be by then." He turned and made a brief bow to his hostess. "And now I really must be on my way. Thank you for the whiskey and the good company. I'll just see myself out."

Lacy and her grandmother remained silent until they heard the front door close.

"Well, what an accomplished young man," Granny Farr commented. "An architect *and* a doctor, no less." She paused and then added, "But I do hope you don't have a serious interest in driving an ambulance around a battlefield, darling."

"I imagine those ambulances arrive *after* the battle, Gran."

"Well, at least that young doctor thinks women are adept at handling roles they're capable of, like a nurse or lab technician. I liked that about him," she said, always the peacemaker in the Farrington-Forbes family. Granny Farr sighed. "You two would have made quite a suitable match, you know, if you'd been living here in Boston—which, of course, has always been my heart's desire."

Lacy rose and collected their empty glasses to put on the drinks table against the wall. She turned and smiled fondly at her grandmother.

"Thank you for that, but as for Dr. Pembroke, you were starting to sound like the ever-scheming Grandmother Forbes," she teased. "And now that you know that the *third* edition of Charles Pembroke is a married doctor and I'm a working gal, I seriously doubt I would have been his type anyway."

Despite that declaration, she sensed that her grandmother had noticed the mild, flirtatious spark that had flared briefly between her granddaughter and the virtuous Dr. Pembroke. Actually, Granny Farr had done something quite kind in prolonging their acquaintance that afternoon because the truth was, she liked him too.

Granny noted pensively, "Such a pity he's wed to Eleanor Choate. A pretty girl—but not much else, I'm told."

"Granny!" Lacy said, shocked.

But her grandmother merely shook her head and speculated, "Perhaps surgeons tend not to wear jewelry on their fingers because doctors are always washing their hands."

Lacy made no reply, doubting that married architects had the same excuse for being ringless.

Granny heaved a sigh. "Aren't you glad I found all that out, as I think he was quite taken with you—and you with him?"

"Oh, Gran, you're being very silly, but thanks for the compliment if you think he was being anything but polite."

Silently, Lacy asked herself why a young man, married for some six or seven years with a nice, roomy house in Brookline, had not insisted on producing a Charles Pembroke IV.

Or even a Charlene.

Sipping the last of her sherry with one hand, Lacy fingered Pem's business card in her other. Printed in the corner was an embossed crimson Harvard shield declaring *Veritas*, the university's famous motto: "Truth."

It struck her that the truth was *she* was the envious one. How marvelous to be working on such a worthwhile project like a field hospital bound for Europe whose sole purpose was to relieve suffering. She'd certainly known a different kind of suffering at the hands of parents whose sole purpose was to please themselves at the expense of their young progeny. Their constant banishment to years of boarding school, even during summers and most holidays, had amounted to a cruel form of punishment.

Once again, she had the familiar vision of herself, a schoolgirl in Vienna, watching an anguished, distraught wife witnessing her husband being dragged away from their kosher butcher shop by a Nazi brownshirt. It had been an early warning sign of what the Nazis were to do on *Kristallnacht*. What a relief it would be to put aside one's own haunting memories to focus on relieving the misery of others ensnared in far worse situations than she had ever experienced.

Granny set her glass down with a clink as a new thought hit Lacy like German artillery fire.

Earlier that day, Pem had mentioned that a Harvard classmate of his was trying to raise funds for *another*, similar-sounding field hospital to deploy—"hopefully soon," he'd said—to poor, beleaguered Finland, which was constantly being harassed by the Russians.

She focused her gaze on her grandmother, a genuinely regal figure in her afternoon tea dress, her silver hair swept up and swirled in a stately chignon.

If she, Lacy Farrington Forbes, was also considered among the privileged class of Boston bluebloods, why couldn't *she* assume the role of a Millicent Wadsworth and offer to mount charitable efforts raising funds to send medical services to that besieged country bordering territory-hungry Russia? That way, she'd be an essential part of such a project. She could enroll in Red Cross courses ... make herself indispensable to the endeavor, and—

Lacy watched as her grandmother slowly rose from her chair and declared she was retiring to her room to rest. "I'm rather in need of a quick lie-down after such a ... stimulating afternoon," she said. "I'll dress for dinner in an hour and see you at seven?"

"Of course," Lacy murmured, her thoughts on fire as she rose from her own chair to bid her grandmother farewell.

Granny moved toward the sitting room door, and Lacy suddenly realized that her pace had been much more halting than usual lately. Cecilia Farrington had always been a port in the storm for Lacy. She hated to acknowledge that the only relative she had ever been able to rely upon was in the final years of her life. Lacy's one comfort was that she was certain her grandmother would, if she asked, use her stellar social connections in Boston to help her raise funds for a worthy project like a field hospital for poor Finland. And perhaps there'd be wealthy people whom her family knew in New York City and Washington she could also tap for donations? If *she* were the one to raise the funds in the fashion of an Anne Morgan and head up such a worthwhile enterprise, she could appoint *herself* one of the team members heading for Europe!

Despite her increasing excitement, she felt a clutch of guilt. Could she really ask her grandmother to help her fund a project that would send her favorite grandchild into harm's way?

At that moment of reflection, Granny's housemaid entered the room. "I'll just be clearing away these glasses, Miss Forbes," she declared softly in the lilting Irish accent of a recent immigrant.

"That's lovely of you, Nora," Lacy replied, heading for the hall stairs toward her room. "Thank you so much."

Mounting the richly carpeted steps while clutching Charles Pembroke's business card in her hand, Lacy forced herself to put her misgivings about leaving her grandmother aside and concentrate on getting in touch with Pem to obtain the name of his Harvard classmate desperately seeking to raise money for his Finland Field Hospital project. As soon as she filed the Anne Morgan story at the *Boston Globe*, she'd offer Pem's friend her full-fledged personal and fundraising support ... and then resign from her newspaper job.

Lacy steeled herself for the blast of frigid air that would greet her when she emerged out of the steamy MBTA station and into Harvard Square. Once on the street, she headed for the small café Charles Pembroke had suggested on the phone when she'd boldly called him first thing that morning.

"I imagine Noah Fischer would consider your offer to raise funds for Finland manna from heaven," Pem had replied to her request for a meeting. "How soon would you like to be introduced?"

"Today, if possible," she'd replied instantly, then added, "Of course, I know how busy you are, so if—"

"Today it is. Can you get to Cambridge by one o'clock?"

The train from Park Street Station had arrived in the square promptly at a quarter to one. By the time Lacy had walked the few blocks to the designated café, Pem was waiting just inside the restaurant's entrance. She determinedly ignored the almost-giddy feeling of relief at the sight of her host, his broad shoulders clad in a camel-colored cashmere topcoat. In his sartorial splendor, Pem stood in marked contrast to his companion, whose trench coat was wrinkled and worn. Standing next to Pem was a thin, spare young man Lacy assumed was his former Harvard College classmate.

"Dr. Noah Fischer," Pem declared, greeting her with a welcoming smile, "let me introduce you to a budding journalist-philanthropist, Miss Lacy Forbes."

The two shook hands and then, along with Pem, followed a waitress who led them to a corner table set for three. Pem served as their host and ordered a shepherd's pie for the table with a wry glance in his colleague's direction.

With a chuckle, Dr. Fischer endorsed his choice. "Best bargain in the place for impoverished scholarship students like I was in my undergraduate days," young Dr. Fischer declared, adding, "Even Pem here agreed with me about the menu at this place when he first started classes at the design school. He was quickly learning how the other half lived, weren't you?"

"I still am learning," Pem admitted with a laugh. "Funny how that happens when one is paying one's own bills." He turned to Lacy. "Even when I first met Noah, he knew he wanted to be a doctor," he pointed out matter-of-factly. "He was first in our class as an undergraduate and was easily admitted to Harvard Med. Me?" He shrugged.

"My alma mater's medical faculty turned me down flat, as they should have, given my grades in biochem."

"But you got into Tulane med school," Lacy countered, stating the obvious.

Pem shrugged his shoulders again. "Thanks to my father seriously pulling some strings. Meanwhile, Noah decided to first get a master's in public health from Columbia and *then* went on to Harvard Med. All I did was head for 'let the good times roll' New Orleans and Tulane Med and somehow managed to graduate."

With a brand-new wife in tow, Lacy thought and then wondered why that particular fact was the first thing that had come into her mind.

Noah Fischer spoke up like the loyal friend Lacy could see he was: "But you ultimately found your niche in architecture and design, didn't you, Pem? And your medical training has made you a much better designer of hospitals. What you've devised for these portable field units we're trying to build is brilliant and demonstrates how modern medicine *should* be practiced."

As Lacy listened to their exchange, she congratulated herself on having behaved "inappropriately"—as Grandmother Forbes would have judged her contacting Pem less than twenty-four hours after they'd met. But the fact was the sooner her charitable money-raising scheme went into gear, the sooner she could travel back to Europe. It could provide the steppingstone she needed to return to London, where so much was happening on the world stage, and finally get a *real* job in journalism.

She cleared her throat and waited until the waitress had poured their coffee, then launched into her proposal to become a fundraiser for Fischer's field hospital bound for long-suffering Finland.

I might even get a book out of an adventure like Finland! she thought as she continued to lay out her ideas for raising money for the young doctor's project.

As their pleasant lunch dwindled down to the dregs in their coffee cups, Lacy began to wonder whether Pem's frequent glances and smiles in her direction meant he'd concluded that her getting in touch with him so swiftly meant she'd assumed that something more than a common interest in field hospitals was possible between them.

Absolutely not! she scolded herself silently.

She genuinely wanted to help with those overseas efforts to stem the suffering already evident in Finland and elsewhere. Charles Pembroke, along with Noah Fischer, were merely the means for her to do just that.

And then there is Teddy…

She still had no idea where her "baby" brother was as Britain appeared to be lurching closer to war with Germany every day. Her thoughts often dwelled on how abruptly Teddy had decamped for Northern Ireland with those hooligan Irish drinking buddies of his. Just that week, the *Boston Globe* had reprinted an article from the *Irish Times* that described a series of attacks on British customs houses that had happened there in late November. U.K. military sources had made much of the fact that the only fatalities were the neophyte IRA volunteers, themselves, when their own explosives had blown up during the operation. It sounded like just the kind of thing those idiot friends of Teddy's might be up to … But would her brother be foolish enough to be part of such a thing?

Very likely.

Teddy was yet another compelling reason her destiny was in the United Kingdom. Even though they were no longer children, she'd probably never shed the sense that she should look out for her younger brother. She gazed at Noah Fischer and wondered what she'd have to do to persuade him that he absolutely had to allow her to be part of his Finland Field Hospital project.

CHAPTER EIGHT

A mildly insulting question from Noah brought Lacy's attention back from her worried musings about her rebellious younger sibling. "So, Miss Forbes," the young Dr. Fischer said, all business, "precisely how *much* money do you and your fancy Beacon Hill charity ladies think your swish tea parties can raise for the Finland project?"

Pem straightened up in his chair and appeared about to speak up in her defense. Before he could, Lacy quickly leaped to her own.

"Oh, for sure, there'll have to be tea parties and some 'fancy dos' with this crowd I know so well, but I applaud your skepticism, Dr. Fischer," she said, raising her chin a notch. "I fear you'll need to stomach a healthy number of those 'swish' events if you wish to squeeze money out of the tightwads I know." She cast him a direct, steady look. "What I'll require from *you* is a short, well-written, heart-tugging, and convincing description of what this project of yours is all about. I'll use it to publicize your efforts and lure people to come to events where my family connections and their wealth might add up to paying for something worthwhile."

"Hear! Hear!" cheered Pem. "Spoken like a veteran fundraiser."

If only you knew how little experience I have.

Pem turned to Noah and added, "You are one lucky man if you have someone like Lacy Forbes pulling for your project."

"Thank you," she said quietly, reveling in the feeling that someone, at least, held her in decent regard.

In the next few minutes, while Pem gallantly paid their luncheon bill, she and Noah Fischer exchanged contact information and agreed to meet in a week. He promised to give her a written report outlining the Finland Field Hospital project, listing its specific needs. In turn, she agreed to provide him with a schedule of proposed events in Boston, New York, and Washington, D.C., where Lacy's Farrington and Forbes family and friends connections would hopefully result in fundraising soirees on the order of the Wadsworth event she and Pem had attended.

Emerging from the restaurant into frigid December air, Pem insisted on escorting Lacy to Harvard Square, where she could catch the underground back to Boston. Walking along Massachusetts Avenue, with the university's tall brick walls and filigreed wrought iron gates encompassing Harvard Yard on her right, he leaned close to her left ear and said, "You're really something. Surely, you know that, don't you?" He held on tightly to her arm to steady them both on the icy sidewalks that led to the subway station entrance. "The Harvard project has the university behind it, but Noah's strictly on his own. I can see you're certainly not afraid of challenges."

Walking side by side with him down the uneven brick sidewalks of Cambridge, Lacy was prompted by an unexpected sense of camaraderie with Pem to be absolutely candid.

"I'm genuinely behind what both of you are doing," she said, glancing at him sideways, "but you and Noah need to understand that I see it as my best means of returning to Europe, where, eventually, I can try to get back my old job at the London bureau of the American newspaper where I worked. One day, I hope to become a serious financial or political journalist over there. So, the truth is, I don't relish organizing a bunch of charity events swarming with people I don't really like or respect very much, but I'll do it for all our causes. And one more thing," she added, holding his gaze. "I've never done anything remotely like this before."

"I know that," he said, staring back at her.

"You do?"

"I asked around and learned you've only recently returned from England."

"Then why—?"

"Because," he said, holding her glance, "I have every confidence that a woman like you could be very persuasive and even wildly successful at something like this. I can tell your concern is genuine about what's going on over there and the suffering that people are enduring."

"You hardly know me."

"Somehow, I think I do." He looked beyond Lacy's shoulder, as if his thoughts had drifted elsewhere. "I *hate* attending events like the Wadsworth reception yesterday. I know what it's like to long to be in the place where you can just do the work you care about. It's the same with me. Being a doc is certainly a worthy endeavor," he said, "but for me ... I just want to be at my drafting board, designing things that will make life physically better and easier for people." He looked at her strangely, as if considering his next words carefully. "I think we both recognize, don't we, that making our particular tribe feel less guilty about all that money they're hoarding by giving it away to worthy causes is about the only way we can help accomplish some genuine good in the world."

Lacy allowed his deeply felt words to sink in. Then his other statement rang a dangerous echo in her head.

"I have every confidence in you."

Granny Farr had been right: if she had ever wanted to fall in love with someone, she and Charles Pembroke III might have made quite a "suitable" match, indeed.

Putting such thoughts firmly aside, Lacy noticed that the winter wind had become even more biting by the time they had reached the top of the stairs leading down to the subway station in Harvard Square. It was time to say goodbye.

Impulsively, she asked, "What does your wife think of your switching from medicine to architecture, as you have?"

Pem was silent for a long moment before he answered.

Finally, he replied, "She thinks it's idiotic for me not to be part of my father's medical practice or join *her* father's."

"Eleanor's father is also a doctor?"

"Yes. The boxes were checked," he said quietly. "But all along, I knew I wanted to be an architect. I simply put my wishes to one side for a while and caved into the pressure."

Oh, do I understand what that kind of pressure is like.

She shot Pem a brief smile, thinking *he* was "really quite something," as he'd dubbed her, but rather than voicing her admiration, Lacy kept her tone light. "And now you *are* an architect."

"Almost. I won't have that diploma on my wall until this coming spring."

"But you're doing the *work*," she insisted, "and that's what counts."

The feelings flowing between them felt intense. He'd stood up to his father in the end ... much like she had recently with her own mother.

Lacy extended her hand. "Well, thanks so much, Pem, for arranging this lunch. I'm sure Noah will let you know if I have any success raising the needed cash for his Finland project."

His blue eyes locked on hers. "Oh, you can be sure that I'll be keeping track of what develops on that score," he replied, seizing her gloved hand in his own. "You take good care, now, Miss Lacy Farrington Forbes."

She stared at their clasped hands for a moment before reluctantly withdrawing hers. Then she turned and hurried down the concrete stairs, the sound of his last words ringing in her ears despite the roar of a subway train pulling into the platform that would whisk her back to Boston.

"*Oh, you can be sure that I'll be keeping track ...*" he'd said.

Did she really want him to do that?

She told herself she couldn't think about that now. She had to concentrate on convincing Granny Farr to be on board with persuading their rich friends to invest in the Finland fundraising scheme. The problem was she had to do that without admitting she intended to accompany the field hospital team to Europe.

A swift pang of guilt assaulted her because of that part, but it couldn't be helped.

Chapter Nine

APRIL 1940

Lacy could hardly have anticipated the range of emotions she'd experienced in the fifteen arduous months it had taken a first-time philanthropist to raise the funds for Dr. Noah Fischer's Finland Field Hospital project.

Her first hurdle had been convincing Granny Farr to endorse Noah's efforts on behalf of that beleaguered Scandinavian nation. Invited to tea to meet Cecilia Holmes Farrington, Lacy's new partner had appeared at the door of their Beacon Hill townhouse clad in his usual rumpled, well-worn trench coat and otherwise casual attire.

However, once the earnest young doctor had placed stark news photographs on the octogenarian's coffee table and made a passionate description of the suffering of Finnish civilians—to say nothing of the brutal injuries to the country's brave soldiers—Granny Farr had called to her maid, who had rushed into the sitting room.

"If you would, please, Nora dear ... bring me my checkbook."

Securing every penny after that had been much harder fought, with Lacy petitioning people in the Farrington-Forbes circle while Europe had, since September of 1939, been consumed in a full-fledged war. More Americans than ever shuddered at the thought of the US joining the conflagration.

Frustration, irritation, exasperation, exhilaration, and ultimately, triumph ... She and Noah had felt it all since the day she'd quit her job at the *Globe* and battled to secure the money, equipment, and medical personnel required for a well-developed field hospital bound for Finland.

Lacy had been troubled throughout her fundraising efforts by the fact that no one had heard a word from her brother, Teddy.

On a morning when she was about to take a train to New York for another Funds for Finns event that a Forbes cousin had been willing to sponsor, she asked her grandmother, "Would you be willing to write Rose Kennedy to prevail upon the ambassador in London to put out feelers about Teddy? Inquire as to his current whereabouts in Ireland—or wherever in the world he might be these days?"

Granny Farr set down her porcelain cup of coffee in its saucer and nodded. "That's an excellent idea, dear. I'll do it today."

On Lacy's next fundraising trip to D.C., while deftly avoiding any contact with her mother currently living in that city, she finally caught up with Kick Kennedy, who reported that the ambassador's queries had not yielded any results.

"At least *you're* doing something useful," Kick complained to Lacy when they met for lunch. "My parents ordered me to return to D.C. literally days before war officially broke out last year. All this time, the only thing I've wanted to do is get back to England to be with Billy and support him any way I can." Kick's aristocratic boyfriend, heir to the Devonshire dukedom, had joined the army, while she had been forced to play the ambassador's daughter in the endless social whirl of Washington. "Here I am doing absolutely *nothing* that means a hoot while Billy's risking his life!"

<hr>

Following Lacy's return to Boston, she finally summoned the nerve to break the news that she planned to accompany the field hospital unit to Finland. She nearly wept at her grandmother's unexpected reaction.

"I'm afraid," Granny said after a long pause, her voice tremulous, "that I was feeling a bit maudlin when you first came to stay with me. I know I haven't many more years left, and, selfishly, my initial reluctance to have you leave was because I wanted to keep close the best companion an old lady could wish for."

"Oh, Gran—" Lacy choked, barely able to speak.

"*But*," Granny emphasized quickly, pouring sherry into a thimble-sized glass for her granddaughter, "I've supported your project to aid Dr. Fischer from the outset, as it's a highly worthy effort. It'd be a terrible waste if you didn't see this mission through." She stared intently at Lacy. "You're the only Forbes *or* Farrington who's amounted to anything in your generation—or the one before you. I'm very proud of you, darling." She paused, her brow furrowed. "Mind you, I'm not *thrilled* you're doing this mad thing, but I think it's marvelous the way you've raised the funds needed from all those old skinflints we know." Cecilia Farrington flashed a rare Cheshire cat smile. "I'd have done the same thing as you," she declared, "if I'd been born a generation or two later than I was. I wish you Godspeed, my dearest child, and I promise to help here in Boston any way I can. Please, just let me know what I can do."

The next night, Lacy took the evening train to New York, where she had a ship to catch. Watching the Hudson River reflected in her window as her train approached the city, she fought a morbid feeling that she might never see her grandmother again. Given Gran's advanced age, she might well die before Lacy returned from Finland, or Lacy might encounter physical dangers being part of her field hospital team operating near or on the battlefields. Each day, she'd read about the growing casualties among British and French forces fighting on the border with Germany. Suddenly, the enormity of what she had launched surfaced the anxiety and fear that, until now, she'd kept at bay.

Her face stared back at her in the window's glass reflection, questioning whether she was in any way equipped to meet unknowns that were bound to come her way.

The following morning, up early with her Louis Vuitton footlocker on the dock beside the rusty-hulled *S.S. Drottningholm* bobbing on the Hudson River, she felt both awestruck and mildly terrified that all her hard work had finally led to their spring-day departure.

She stood silently beside Noah, watching the loading of their myriad medical supplies, three Ford trucks, two Chevrolet ambulances, cartons containing auto parts, dozens of fur-lined boots, masks and linens, skull drills, woolen blankets, and precious glass vials of medicine packed in cotton batting all being hoisted on board the ship due to sail on the evening tide.

As the last pallet disappeared into the ship's hold, Noah expressed his wonderment that their mission was about to get underway.

"None of this would be happening," he reflected, "without you and your Grandmother Farrington persuading the American-Scandinavian Field Hospital group to allow our Finland unit to become part of all this."

"Well, we also got the U.S. State Department to sanction us as a separate entity," Lacy said with a nod, recalling the horrific red tape and opposition she'd encountered even *after* they'd raised the money to fund their smaller operation. "You can be sure the key was Granny Farr and her letter that a mutual friend of hers and FDR's managed to put on the president's desk. It not-so-gently reminded Mr. Roosevelt that he needed those Scandinavian-American votes in the Midwest to win the election in November." Lacy laughed at the memory. "She also asked him to pressure the State Department flunkies 'to cut the confounded formalities!'"

Waving a letter of endorsement from the White House, Noah exclaimed, "Your *grandmother* was the reason you finally got this?"

"Yup," Lacy replied proudly. "And she did it despite all the isolationists claiming the Atlantic Ocean is their guarantee of America's safety. She just kept hammering away that it was unconscionable for America to ignore the plight of the poor Finns being beaten up by the Bolsheviks."

"Well, I plan to keep this at the ready in my pocket whenever some government official tries to put roadblocks in our path."

Lacy offered a broad smile to the young physician who had become her "partner in crime," as Noah phrased it. They'd worked as a well-oiled team in their months-long effort to organize all aspects of a field hospital.

"In the end, I guess you could say all the stars lined up for us," Lacy declared with silent gratitude for the miracle she and Noah had wrought.

"To say nothing of your wanting to serve as ... what have you dubbed yourself?" Noah teased. "Liaison officer?"

Lacy drew herself up with mock outrage. "I will be your *much-needed* travel agent, recording secretary, European guide, talented linguist, public relations flunky, and all-around girl Friday," she asserted, using terms she'd invented to define for others what her role was to be in their unique enterprise. She and Noah had become fast friends, and from time to time, Pem would drop by their office with blueprints in his hands. Each time he appeared, Lacy studiously treated him with pleasant but distant regard.

Almost as if her thoughts had the power to rally a certain someone in the flesh, Noah was suddenly waving his arms in the air and had begun to shout from the foot of the ship's gangway.

"Well, *Holy Moses!*" he yelled at the approaching figure. "I never really believed you'd pull this off! Lucky for you, Pem, I absconded with enough funds from our benefactress here to pay for your berth on this tub."

Lacy turned and gaped, open-mouthed, at the sight of Dr. Charles Pembroke III waving back at them while striding away from a taxi toward the ship they were soon to board.

Noah demanded of the doctor, still ten feet away, "I hope you managed to get all your visas issued. Otherwise, turn right around and—"

But Pem, a suitcase in each hand, was gazing only at Lacy as he drew nearer.

"I've got 'em right here." He set down his luggage and patted his cashmere coat's breast pocket. Then he looked down at Lacy, his arms stiff by his side. It almost seemed to her as if he were holding himself back from enveloping her in a bear hug, which she was embarrassed to admit she was only too ready to return.

"I hope it's all right with our liaison officer if Project Finland has added a new doctor to the manifest?" Pem asked, grinning broadly.

Lacy somehow summoned the will to control her dizzying excitement. She could hardly believe that Pem was standing right beside her. Rattling around in her brain were simultaneous peals of joy and warning sounds that her world had just turned upside down.

"You've volunteered as a *doctor*?" she gasped. "For *us?*" She forced herself to frown. "I don't mean to be rude, Pem, but you've admitted to me you prefer architecture to medicine. Do you remember *anything* you learned at Tulane Med School?"

Once more, Pem grinned at each of them in turn. "This chit is quite rude, isn't she?" he asked Noah good-naturedly. "But, yes, I've been boning up— pardon the pun—on how to set fractures and dig bullets from human flesh. Believe it or not, my father was so happy to assume I was back practicing medicine, he actually saw me off at the Boston train station!"

Lacy was dying to ask him how in the world he'd managed to convince his overbearing father to sanction his son's sailing into a war zone, to say nothing of getting his wife, Eleanor, to endorse his joining their enterprise.

Unable to resist, she asked in as friendly a tone as she could muster, "And Eleanor? Is she all right with you coming with us?"

Noah had an uncomfortable expression on his face, matched only by Pem's.

"She ... uh ... wasn't thrilled at first, I confess," he admitted, "but agreed with my father that it might be a way to push me back into practicing medicine."

"But I thought you were terribly keen on becoming a full-fledged architect," Lacy blurted. She was surprised to discover that she was mildly disappointed he'd given in to family pressure after all.

"I *am* a full-fledged architect now," he declared with obvious pride. "Got my degree last spring. And I will be right back at my drafting board when I eventually join up with the Harvard group in Britain. They'll need me if they follow through on plans to build more field hospitals there and in France, where they're so desperately needed. But meanwhile"—he smirked—"until the Harvard Field Hospital group is ready to depart, why shouldn't I sign on with the Finland project to see for myself if my building designs turn out to be practicable? If I have to patch up some soldiers and civilians in the process, I'm happy to earn my keep with a scalpel."

"May I remind you, my friend," Noah warned, suddenly dead serious, "as much as I appreciated your sneaking me some pro bono blueprints for *this* project on the Q.T., this is no lark. The waters off Britain are so thick with Nazis, Americans on board ships sailing out of New York Harbor are now forbidden to depart for 'belligerent countries'—like England. As of three days ago, as the State Department flunky recently told our Norwegian captain, this ship is now bound directly for Norway instead of the UK as a first stop."

"So is *that* why you telegraphed me to get visas for all those Scandinavian countries?" Pem asked.

"Yes," Noah replied, "and it's why I didn't tell anyone on our team you might be joining us," he added with a nod in Lacy's direction. "When you asked to join us last week, I doubted you'd be able to secure the paperwork in time."

Pem turned to address Lacy. "By the way, it was your grandmother who made a call to the president of Harvard, urging him to lend a hand in getting my visas stamped."

"*What?*" Lacy gasped.

"I telephoned her, asking her advice, since I knew *she* knew everyone who counted in the Boston area."

"And so she called President Conant?" Lacy was nearly speechless at the thought that Pem had petitioned Granny Farr for help.

"True to her reputation, she sprang into immediate action and got the president of Harvard to make some calls on my behalf while she contacted all the relevant consulates in Boston," he revealed. "She was absolutely marvelous, Lacy. And by the way, she made me guarantee I'd send you her dearest love."

On my last day in Boston, she promised to continue to help, Lacy marveled silently, *and look what she's accomplished!*

Remembering their farewell, Lacy felt her heart fill with a comforting sense of Granny Farr's presence despite the miles that separated them. Her thoughts still reeling from the fact that Pem had seemed to have magically appeared by her side, she could only stare at him, dumbfounded, as an electric silence filled the chilly air.

Noah cleared his throat and informed the new arrival, "The plan now is to land in Bergen and travel overland through Norway and Sweden by train and ferry to Finland. It may be an awfully long time before any of us circle back to Britain."

"We'll get there eventually, I'm sure," Pem said with a warm smile in Lacy's direction. "The important thing is that we're *doing* something to fight the damned Nazis, even if Congress won't."

"It'll be full-on spring in Scandinavia by the time we dock," Noah reminded him, setting his foot at the base of the *Drottningholm*'s gangway. "That is, as long as we don't sail into some German mine along the way or get stopped by the British blockade in the North Sea. We can only hope a little decent April weather might make our overland trip a lot easier."

For a moment, all three were silent, thinking about the Nazi ships, submarines, and hostile forces from both sides that lay beyond the waters east of the beautiful statue facing them across the Hudson River.

Staring out at Lady Liberty with her lighted torch soaring into a gray sky, Lacy shivered in her warm woolen coat. What they were about to embark upon was, indeed, no lark. An adventure, surely, but one she imagined was fraught with potential peril, most of which, she realized, she couldn't possibly predict.

CHAPTER TEN
NORWAY

APRIL 1940

Lacy heard the ship's heavy steel door closing and turned from the railing to see Pem walking in her direction on the swaying deck. After all their days at sea, she still marveled that he had decided so suddenly to join Noah's medical group and sail to Norway with the team.

"You okay?" he called. "I saw you leave breakfast just now. I've got something in my doctor's bag for seasickness if it's finally caught up with you."

Lacy shook her head and pointed across the railing at the heavy fog that was beginning to envelop the ship. "I wanted to watch as we enter Bergen Fjord, but look how foggy it's getting," she said. "A deckhand told me just now that the captain has posted two men on the bowsprit, trying to spot mines."

"He must think the Germans are patrolling around here somewhere," Pem replied, his gaze sweeping the horizon.

"Norway's a neutral country, so who'd be putting explosives this close to their shores?" Lacy wondered aloud.

"It's the Brits, probably," Pem answered grimly. "They want to fend off the Jerries trying something tricky in Scandinavia."

Miraculously, their journey across the Atlantic in wartime had been without any untoward incidents except for a single day of very rough seas. For a good twenty-four hours, everyone other than Pem,

Lacy, and the crew had remained in their staterooms close to the bathroom. Their time alone on the deck had only given Lacy more to fret about. Earlier, Pem had been fairly candid about the fact he'd only managed to persuade his wife and father he should go on the journey by emphasizing he would be serving as a frontline physician.

"But what if you return to architecture when all this is over?" Lacy had asked.

In that conversation, Pem had stared at the rough seas battering the ship. Finally, he'd said, "It will definitely present a problem." He'd looked directly at Lacy. "Eleanor is a lovely, very nice person, but she wants what her mother had."

"To be the wife of a doctor?"

"That and to remain in Brookline and have a life like all her neighbors."

"And you ...?"

Lacy would never forget how he'd glanced down at their hands, positioned side by side on the railing but not touching.

"I want more. Or perhaps I should say I'd like something different than that life. It's been an issue between us from the start."

And one, Lacy suspected, neither had discussed before they were married.

"So your coming with us on this mission is a sort of time-out between you two?" she had dared to ask.

"That's how I see it, but I'm not sure Eleanor does. She thinks this will draw me back into the world where she feels most comfortable."

And will it? Lacy had wondered but hadn't asked on that wind-tossed day. Instead, she'd changed the subject and pointed to the looming shape of a ship clothed in fog as they'd sailed toward the coast of Norway. All on board had been jubilant that the *Drottning-holm* had managed to slip past the British blockade in the North Sea.

As far as Lacy could tell this foggy morning as their ship entered Bergen Harbor, their captain appeared to be ignoring the pea-souper, piloting their liner dead ahead slowly and cautiously.

Pem directed her attention to the ghostly outline of a number of other large ships beginning to appear, which were resting at anchor as they entered Bergen's misty port.

"I'm amazed there are so many in here," he said. "I'd have thought these freighters wouldn't have risked being targets for one side or the other."

Shivering in the damp, Lacy could feel their own vessel powering down to a crawl. Pem called out to a crew member, asking about their scheduled arrival time.

"The captain has been ordered by authorities onshore to drop anchor until a pier can be cleared for the ship to dock."

"Darn!" fretted Lacy. "We've got to make that train to Oslo with our gear."

Meanwhile, medical personnel from their group were coming out on deck. Red Cross nurse Jayne Girard, with whom Lacy had shared a stateroom, waved a friendly greeting, drifting toward the ship's bow on the starboard side. Peering into the increasing gloom, Lacy felt fidgety and anxious to finally stand on dry land.

"Look," Pem said, sweeping his arm in an arc from left to right. "A lot of other ships appear to be in the same limbo as we are, waiting for a berth."

Lacy squinted through the fog at additional large vessels riding at anchor in the middle of the peaceful harbor. She turned to the crew member who'd spoken earlier and asked him about the ghost ships.

"Oh, I expect they're waiting to be loaded up with iron ore," the deckhand said matter-of-factly, "just like we're waiting to discharge all of you passengers."

Lacy consulted her wristwatch. According to previous arrangements, two special railcars were waiting for the medical group on the night train to Oslo, which they would exchange the next day for one to Stockholm.

"If we don't dock soon," she said worriedly to Pem, "we'll miss our train."

And miss their train they did, all piling into the one hotel large enough to accommodate their group in the quiet town of Bergen with its steep hills surrounding the bay.

In the lobby, Lacy announced to their team, "I changed our tickets to the noon train tomorrow. *Please*, everyone, don't be late."

That night at dinner, Noah spoke quietly to Pem and Lacy at

their table in a secluded corner of the hotel dining room. "The manager just told me that authorities here caught a spy three weeks ago. The guy was dressed as a woman, pushing a baby carriage along a trail that leads up to the cliffs."

"Wow, pushing a *baby carriage*?" Pem commented. "How original."

Noah nodded, continuing, "But not so innocent. The pram had a radio transmission set built into it! Its dials had been set long range, presumably to signal German vessels every time an Allied ship left this port."

With a shudder, Lacy responded, "And then I bet some German U-boat below the waters we just traversed would try to attack and sink it."

Noah nodded. "That's apparently what happened until authorities here caught her. I mean, *him*."

"Well, did they shoot the guy?" Pem demanded.

"Nope," Noah replied. "When I asked about that, the manager said, 'Oh, no! We have no death penalty in Norway.'"

All three fell silent until Lacy glanced down at her watch. By that hour, the *S.S. Drottningholm* was already steaming back out to sea. She could almost imagine the shadow of a submarine following near its keel, aiming a torpedo at the ship that had delivered them safely to Norway.

Fiddling with her linen dinner napkin, she declared, "Let's pray that our captain and that wonderful crew make it safely through the North Sea."

"I second the motion," Pem agreed, taking a sip of water as they watched their waiter pour the wine. "All I can say is we're damn lucky that *our* crew is now safely on land."

Lacy nodded. "One bit of good news is that I just had word our medical equipment and the field hospital components are now at the train station, ready to be loaded aboard the freight cars that will take them to Oslo tonight and on to Stockholm. We'll follow tomorrow. From there, it's a boat to Helsinki."

She tried to stop thinking about the *Drottningholm's* uncertain fate steaming into mine-laced waters at such a treacherous moment. Instead, she concentrated her thoughts on the enormous task ahead—

finally transporting the medical staff and equipment across Scandinavia.

"So, on to Finland!" she proposed, raising her newly filled wine glass. "And good luck to us!"

"On to Finland!" they all chorused.

Lacy peered out the rain-spattered train window, taking in her first glimpse of Stockholm, noting its impressive historic architecture standing alongside numerous functional buildings in the active Swedish commercial port. With Pem in the seat next to her and Noah across the aisle, she consulted a small map of Scandinavia she kept folded in her handbag.

Pem peered over her shoulder. "Well, that's reassuring," he commented. He traced his finger along the dotted line representing the ferry route from Stockholm across the upper Baltic into the Gulf of Finland. "The last leg looks like it'll take our hospital unit directly to where the team could actually do some good."

As the train pulled into the station, Lacy was suddenly aware of the accumulated fatigue she had built up during their long, tense journey over land and sea.

"I don't know about you two," she said, unable to stifle a yawn, "but once we get to the hotel, I plan on sleeping till noon."

Hours later, when she entered the Hotel Carlton's dining room in the early afternoon, ready to have some lunch, she looked around at various tables for Pem. On the train trip from Norway and across Sweden, he'd always managed to locate a seat beside her. Standing alone in the dining room surrounded by the cacophony of languages she didn't speak, she found that she already missed their long, quiet conversations. Their talks had ranged from describing their lives growing up among the Boston elite to sharing confidences about why they both felt compelled to take part in the struggle against the forces trying to conquer Europe. They hadn't spoken of Eleanor again, but Lacy always felt her presence, nonetheless. Even so, it had been remarkable that the two of them never seemed to fall into awkward moments, nor did their discussions ever lapse into silence.

In the moments before she'd fallen asleep the previous night, she'd done her best to convince herself that their increasingly close connection was simply one encouraged by the intimacy of traveling so far together. Wouldn't anyone have the same reaction, sharing thoughts and feelings in a darkened train carriage where they'd seemed suspended in time?

A voice behind her made her jump. "Well, you were certainly a sleepyhead."

She whirled around and shot back, "Ditto for you," to the very person she'd been thinking about.

Pem was clean-shaven and dressed in the medical team's gray uniform, which was not quite military but certainly not regular civilian attire. His dark hair still looked a bit damp from a recent shower, she imagined, and the tie beneath the cleft in his chin was neatly folded in a Windsor knot. His medical insignias were on display upon his jacket's lapels, but for once, no doctor's bag was in his hand.

"Care to have lunch with me?" he offered, and within minutes, the pair were following the Maître d' leading them to a quiet corner table.

No man should look so handsome after that many hours on a train, she thought, then immediately chastised herself. *Just cut it out! Why do you so conveniently seem to forget he's* married?

Taking the chair held out for her, she felt as if *her* officer's uniform of a knee-length scratchy wool skirt and ill-fitting jacket with a Red Cross patch sewn to its upper sleeve made her look like a "Minnie Ragbag," as her British friends would have judged. As soon as lunch was over, she was determined to swap out the shapeless, uncomfortable skirt for her pair of pleated, wide-legged gray slacks that even Katherine Hepburn would approve.

In the next moment, she reminded herself sharply, *Nobody's going to care what you look like!*

But at least you'll be comfortable, she defended silently.

Lacy and Pem had barely placed their order before the manager of the Carlton Hotel burst through the wide doors to the lunchroom and clapped for attention.

"Quiet, please! *Quiet, everyone!* I'm afraid I have an important announcement,"he said, first in Swedish, followed by English.

The chatter throughout the room subsided, and Lacy watched the manager clasping and unclasping his hands in a show of obvious anxiety.

"Something bad has happened," she murmured, her heart suddenly racing.

Without further ado, the manager announced in a loud voice, "I've just been informed that German troops invaded Norway last night and have also occupied Denmark!"

The room erupted with shocked reactions. Lacy heard her own swift intake of breath. She looked at Pem and saw in his expression the same surprise and disbelief she felt. For her, there was also a jolt of fear.

The manager waited a moment for the hubbub to subside and then added, "Also, the first German troops landed in Bergen and are now advancing on Oslo!"

"What about here in Stockholm?" someone shouted, and the manager merely shrugged his shoulders and made no reply.

Pem and Lacy looked at each other, astounded. Was it possible that the Nazis had arrived less than *forty-eight hours* after their field hospital group had landed at Bergen's port city? Lacy could tell Pem was worrying, as she was, about what all that would mean for their medical crew. For the work they had come to Finland to do.

If the U.S. State Department hadn't made them jump through so many bureaucratic hoops and delayed them by over a month, they'd have already been in Helsinki by now!

"All those ships we saw before we docked ..." Lacy moaned, "the ones just sitting at anchor in the harbor when we sailed into Bergen. They must have been *filled* with German soldiers just waiting to disembark and attack Norway!"

The thought as to how close they'd been to the enemy made her feel sick.

"And we floated right past them," Pem exclaimed. "Holy mother—"

"We've got to tell our team!" Lacy urged. She turned in her chair, looking toward the entrance to the dining room. "Where's Noah? We need to make a plan, pronto, about what we do next!"

"I left him still sleeping," Pem said, pushing back his chair. "C'mon. Let's go find him."

A radio in the hotel lounge next to the dining room, tuned to the BBC, suddenly blared. The room was crowded with hotel patrons straining to hear the latest news in an English broadcast from London.

"We'd better listen too," Lacy said, putting her hand on Pem's sleeve to halt his forward progress toward the lobby elevators.

They drew closer to the radio as the BBC announcer spoke of a traitor named Quisling, leader of a pro-Nazi party in Norway. According to the most recent reports, the man had been secretly colluding with his Nazi military counterparts and had given the Germans the go-ahead to land in Norway. The surprise attack had been met with stiff resistance by a handful of Norwegians, who had fired at and sunk three enemy ships in Bergen Harbor.

His tone grave, the broadcaster continued, "The Norwegian king and his family, along with his government, have fled to Narvik. Sources speculate that the royals will board a boat further north at Tromso. Meanwhile, reports are coming in that regular citizens are being gunned down in the streets of Oslo."

"Oh no!" Lacy cried in unison with several others standing nearby.

"As for the government of Sweden," the news announcer continued, "authorities there seem not to be offering any resistance to the German invaders."

Shouts of "Cowards! Traitors!" echoed throughout the room.

Amidst the explosion of startled and dismayed reactions to those shocking revelations, Noah suddenly appeared beside his two colleagues, his hair uncombed and his clothing disheveled.

"You've heard?" Lacy confirmed.

Noah nodded. "Half an hour ago. I was just on the phone with the American consulate here in Stockholm," he said hurriedly. "Our hospital unit has been granted temporary quarters in a church rectory just outside the city while we figure out what comes next for us. The problematic peace treaty the harassed Finns were forced to sign with the Soviets just recently appears to be holding, so no more fighting there at the moment."

Pem wondered aloud, "But maybe now the plan is for Russia to invade Finland for real."

"Meaning what?" Lacy demanded. "That there'll be no way, as Americans, we can set up a field hospital there?"

"I doubt Jewish Americans like me and a few of our team will be very welcome around these parts from here on out," Noah replied. "Let's remember, Russia and Germany are allies these days. Many Russians are well known for their antisemitism, and if either the Germans or the Russians fully occupy Finland ..."

Lacy began mentally reviewing the crushingly hard work of getting a complete field hospital across the treacherous Atlantic in order to help the poor Finns. At that moment, *they* were the ones in danger—or at least Noah Fischer was, along with several others on their staff.

Noah sank into a nearby chair and said tiredly, "The Nazis will be arriving in Stockholm at some point soon. Our American consulate is scrambling to arrange transportation for our unit and all our equipment to sail back to the States on a neutral Swedish vessel ... eventually."

"You're kidding?" Lacy protested, dreading the thought of returning to America having failed their mission before it had even begun. "Our people and all those supplies and our heavy gear are being evacuated *back* to the States?"

Pem, who'd been silently watching their exchange, intervened sharply: "And what does 'eventually' mean for getting our team on a Swedish ship to sail home?"

Noah shrugged, his shoulders stooped in defeat. "There's no telling, but I hope it's soon because, as an American Jew, I don't much look forward to the Germans interrogating me when they arrive here, as I'm sure they will."

Lacy's memory flashed to the Jewish butcher being hauled off by the brownshirts in Vienna. "Is there any way our consulate can get you back to the US any sooner than the unit itself?" she asked, feeling overwhelmed with worry.

"I dunno," Noah said, looking into the distance dejectedly. "All I can think of right now is the herculean effort we made to get here ... and for *what*?"

Lacy gave his arm a sympathetic squeeze. "I was just thinking the exact same thing." The lion's share of the field hospital equipment had already been unloaded from the train they'd taken from Norway. Three enormous Ford trucks and two Chevy ambulances were parked outside on the back streets behind their hotel, scheduled to be uploaded on the boat train that would have taken them to Helsinki. "We fought so hard to transport those tons of gear and all that medicine," she moaned. "I can't believe it's all for nothing."

"Not to mention recruiting our medical team," Pem chimed in. "Those docs and nurses left their jobs and families. At least our supplies surely should be needed *somewhere* over here."

A wild thought suddenly came to her. "What if we simply took our unit to *France*?" she declared. "As Americans, we're still neutrals with connections to the Red Cross. Surely, a portable field hospital would be welcome there. The casualties have been brutal."

"I already suggested that, and the U.S. Consulate instantly shot it down," Noah replied, his voice registering disgust. "Orders from the State Department still forbid Americans to sail into 'belligerent ports' like France or England."

"That's ridiculous!" Lacy exclaimed. "Our government's proposed lend-lease program, if Congress approves, will send *battleships* to the Allies, but we're not allowed to bring a *field hospital* to tend to the war wounded?"

"Getting Congress to approve FDR's lend-lease scheme is still a very big *if*," Pem reminded her.

"That's just another stupid decision by Washington bureaucrats who never leave their cushy offices or deal with the real world," she fumed, despising the red tape in D.C. that had confronted her efforts at every turn.

Pem shifted his gaze from Noah to Lacy. "Just so you know," he announced, "I, for one, am not going to go back to the United States."

Chapter Eleven

The three remained in a huddle in the hotel lounge while guests scurried around in the wake of the disturbing news they'd just heard on the radio. Lacy blinked in surprise as she attempted to absorb Pem's declaration that he was going to remain in Europe despite the German invasion of Scandinavia.

Almost without thinking, she blurted, "The last thing *I* want to do is to leave Europe after all the effort it took to get us here!"

She hated the idea of the three of them splitting up—or was it more than that? There was no ignoring how shocked and abandoned she felt by Pem's decision not to remain with their group.

When Pem turned to address Noah, Lacy felt even more left out of the conversation.

"The Harvard hospital unit is due to be sent over to England under some special dispensation through FDR. Maybe the best thing, Noah, is for you and me to find a way to meet up with it when they finally get it to Europe. Do you think the American consulate here in Stockholm could help us do that?"

Before Noah could answer, Lacy declared, "Well, *I* sure as heck don't want to go back to Boston. I got us here, remember, so don't you think I could be useful to the Harvard project, as well? Keeping records and doing office work for the unit? I've lived in Britain and have connections with a good number of higher-ups who might be helpful to us," she proposed, irritated that the two men hadn't thought of her usefulness on their own. "Will you cable Harvard and propose me?"

Pem shifted his attention from Noah and grinned at her. "My bosses in Massachusetts might not realize it immediately, but I think you could be *very* helpful to us, Miss Girl Friday-Liaison-Czarina!"

Lacy nearly kissed him on both cheeks ... but didn't. The plain fact was the latest Nazi invasion had tossed them all a big helping of chaos, and her emotions were a confused tangle. She found herself wondering how she'd have felt if Noah had been the one to insist on staying and Pem had chosen to return home. What decision would she have been prompted to make *then*?

Lacy Forbes, you are in such deep trouble!

After a long moment, she declared, "Well, whichever of us decides not to get on that Swedish boat to America," she declared, "we've got to move fast if we want any chance of getting the visas we'd need to travel to the UK."

"One thing is for sure: we can't pass through Germany or any of the countries they've conquered," Pem said with a grim expression.

"Definitely, for me, a case of 'Jews need not apply,'" Noah agreed. "And by the way," he continued, "when we first arrived here and I checked in at the consulate, someone standing in line ahead of me was applying for a visa to Russia now that the Finns have signed that peace agreement. Maybe we could—"

"That's brilliant!" Lacy jumped in. "For sure, no one would want to head in the direction of the advancing Nazis ... But what if we headed in the *other* direction? One of the journalists here at the hotel told me he'd heard that flights are still taking off from Stockholm to Moscow!"

Pem gave a warning shake of his head. "Since Russia and Germany are allies, won't Moscow be crawling with German soldiers, just as Sweden will be?" He gestured in Noah's direction. "That can't be good ... especially for our Doctor Fischer here."

Noah grimaced in agreement. "I doubt there are many places on the European continent that are very welcoming to a Jew these days. But either I sail home from Sweden and this entire exercise was a pipe dream and total failure, or I take my chances with you two and volunteer for the Harvard Field Hospital project in Britain, where I can still do some good. The problem is we have to *get* there."

Pem paused, and Lacy could see he was considering how dangerous the decision to head for the UK might be for his friend.

He said, "Look, Noah, it's plain risky for you not to leave directly for home while you have the chance."

"Given the German U-boat fleet, it's equally risky for any ship to attempt to sail down the Baltic and across the Atlantic if the Nazis soon take over here," countered Noah. "Maybe I'd rather take the risk that gets us a chance to see if our field hospital in England operates the way we think it will."

No one spoke for a long moment. Finally, breaking what had become an awkward silence, Lacy clapped her hands and declared, "Okay, then. What's our decision? Who's up for storming the gates of the Russkies?"

"Whoa! Hold on, there, missy," Pem said, raising a hand like a traffic cop. "First tell me where we get the money for this joy ride."

Lacy grinned and replied smugly, "Since the Finland unit is being sent home courtesy of the U.S. State Department's coffers, we've got the leftover operational funds we've raised, which can easily pay for three tickets to Britain!"

Noah laughed nervously. "Don't blab about that to our donors, okay?"

Ignoring him, Lacy said to Pem, "Making our way from Moscow via a convoluted route to avoid German-occupied territories, we'll probably have to ad-lib things as we go along. A zigzag route across Europe down to Gibraltar and then up to England will definitely take some doing, but we'd *eventually* catch up with Pem's colleagues when they get to Britain, don't you think?"

Noah cocked his head and said to Pem, "From what I hear, your Harvard crew might not pull their act together far into next year, but I suppose we could always sign on as volunteer medics in Britain until our team shows up."

"You're making it all sound fairly simple, but I know damned well it's far from it," Pem said with a worried frown. "Before any of us have a chance to volunteer in Britain, we could get arrested by some Nazi along the way or get stranded somewhere terrible." He leaned forward and put his hand on Noah's arm. "Are you *sure* you want to do this? Traveling through all these landlocked countries because we can't sail to Britain the way we came? It's going to involve a serious element of risk for all of us but especially for *you*, my Jewish friend."

Noah's expression told Lacy he also had begun to ponder the enormity of a journey through nations actively threatened by Hitler's forces poised to dominate most of Europe.

With a sigh, he said, "I guess I should give this some more thought. Just before I came to see you, the docs and nurses in our crew all voted to go home on the Swedish freighter out of Stockholm. Maybe it wouldn't be a bad idea if I went with them."

Lacy looked from one man to the other. Pem was right—the three of them should be careful not to underestimate the risks they would take if they didn't board the ship the State Department said they'd provide. But for Lacy, the thought of returning to her life in America and the ongoing family drama was a no-go.

"Look," said Pem, "each of us must make his—or her—own decision, but I've already made mine. I think my best shot to hook up with my colleagues in Britain is to do what's been suggested. First head for Moscow and then see where that leads after that." He looked from Lacy to Noah. "I'll respect you both, whatever you decide."

Lacy inhaled a deep breath and once again reviewed her main motivation beyond merely wanting to return to Britain. Like Anne Morgan and her ambulances, her whole idea was to do something to counteract the Nazis.

Pem had been clear: he didn't want to return to Brookline, Massachusetts.

"I-I want to head for Moscow too," she said softly, "but I completely understand, Noah, if you don't." She took hold of his left hand and squeezed it gently. "In fact, I'll worry every minute if you do decide to come with us—but it's totally up to you either way."

"Same for me," Pem said, putting a hand on Noah's shoulder.

"But here's the thing," Lacy reminded them. "The hordes in this hotel are bound to figure out this same exit strategy—going through Russia. If we three decide to do this, we immediately have to head for the Russian consulate and apply for the visas we'll need and get plane tickets to Moscow."

Noah glanced at his watch and said, "I'll let you know my decision in an hour."

Lacy stared out the window of their noisy small prop plane.

"Oh glory," she said, expelling a long breath as the wing dipped, revealing the Moscow Airport below. "The ground down there is a gray carpet of warplanes."

"How's the runway look for landing?" Noah asked from his seat across the aisle.

Lacy grimaced. "Well, it's *there*, but they do need to mow the grass."

Pem leaned over her shoulder to peer out, his aftershave filling her nostrils with the fragrance of lemon verbena. *It's nice and spicy*, she thought idly, then suddenly wondered what his wife, Eleanor, thought of the scent. Pem had not mentioned her since declaring his decision to remain in Europe. Why did he rarely refer to past times he'd spent with her or plans they'd made for their future together? It was odd and, for Lacy, more than a little unsettling.

Watch it, kiddo ... You and Pem are colleagues, so ignore the smell of his aftershave, will you please!

Pem's gaze out the plane's window fixed on additional rows of aircraft off to one side of their landing strip. "Pretty impressive," he murmured.

Once their plane made its bumpy touchdown and they were directed across the tarmac, Lacy nodded in the direction of the lines of aircraft they'd spotted from above. Viewed from the ground, they were battle worn and ill-kempt. The same was true for the incredibly filthy interior of the airport.

"I can't believe how disgusting everything looks," Lacy commented, keeping her voice low. "The man who checked us through the gate said this place was built not long ago. Can you believe it?"

Instead of answering her, Pem blurted under his breath, "Shit! Look! Germans!"

To their right stood a bunch of soldiers with the insignia SS embroidered on their collars. Next to them was a figure in a plain khaki Russian Army uniform gazing intently at the arriving passengers with a list in his hand.

He abruptly called out in stilted English, "You! You three! Stay there!" before striding to their side. After a perfunctory exchange of greetings, the soldier assigned to duty at the airport announced gruffly, "I have been told to inform those of you passing through from Stockholm that you cannot remain in Moscow." He pointed to the travel documents the three of them held at the ready for inspection. "See? You have only transit visas. You must immediately travel on."

"But our plane to Odessa doesn't leave from here until tomorrow!" Lacy protested, waving the tickets.

"You cannot stay!" The Russian sternly shook his head. "You have only transit visas," he repeated.

"But we're *transiting*," Pem chimed in, his exasperation evident. "On a *Russian* plane from *this* airport. *Tomorrow*!" he added for emphasis.

Slowly shaking his head back and forth, the Russian soldier pronounced, "*Nyet*! You cannot stay this night in Moscow."

Before Lacy could protest further, Noah pointed to their plane tickets. "Well, then, can we trade in these for train tickets?" he asked politely, but Lacy could almost feel the fear vibrating behind his question.

The army officer shrugged his shoulders. "I don't think so, but you go to train station and see."

Lacy was about to lose her temper, but the presence of numerous German soldiers nearby forced her to control her ire. Calling attention to themselves would endanger Noah most of all. She glanced at her companions' faces and could see that they were wondering what she was wondering herself:

What in hell have we gotten ourselves into?

Lacy waved the tickets in front of the guard once more and swiftly took over the conversation. "What if they won't let us on the train with these?" she inquired in an even tone.

"Buy new ones," the Russian replied with a shrug. With a gesture in the direction of the two SS officers, he warned sternly, "You leave before midnight or someone will arrest you."

A cold knot formed in Lacy's stomach. There they were on the first leg of what was bound to be a very long journey, and they were already in danger of ending up in a Russian jail.

"Arguing is hopeless," she said in an undertone. "Let's go. The consulate in Stockholm gave me a name at the American embassy here."

"You're right. We need to regroup," Pem said quietly, "but we can't make plans here in the streets. Let's get outta here."

The two German officers emerged from the airport entrance in their wake and continued to watch them as they gathered at the curb.

"The consulate also mentioned that the Metropole Hotel is supposed to be a fairly decent place," Lacy said, glancing over her shoulder.

"Perfect," Pem murmured. "I say we first reorganize at the hotel and figure out what we do from there." He lowered his voice, adding, "I'd prefer that those gentlemen don't overhear our plans."

Noah remained silent, casting furtive glances at the two SS officers. Lacy saw that his face had drained of color and he was clutching the handle of his doctor's bag with knuckles that had turned a ghostly white.

Chapter Twelve

The taxi driver Pem had hailed outside the airport was more than happy to accept a few American dollars plus a half-pack of Lucky Strike cigarettes that Pem had found in his jacket pocket.

"Glad our cab was the only vehicle around," he noted, glancing out the rear window. "I think we've lost those goons." Lacy and Noah nodded their relief in unison.

Alighting from their taxi ten minutes later, the trio stood with their baggage in front of the Metropole Hotel. Its forlorn, dilapidated appearance was made worse by the sight of Russian men and women wearing tattered clothing and grim expressions shuffling down packed streets.

"Just look at those poor people," Lacy murmured to her companions. "Some are walking without shoes!"

"So much for the Great Soviet State," Pem replied, *sotte voce*.

Even inside the once-ornate lobby, several women were wearing bedroom slippers and dressing gowns. Children were climbing over the backs of frayed sofas, and a sweet, perfumy scent was filling the air.

"Vodka!" murmured Pem.

"Everybody around here reeks of it!" Noah mumbled under his breath. "And so much for all the supposed happy Russian revolutionaries."

Lacy glanced at the overhead chandelier and advised, "Let's not talk here." With a nod toward the light fixture, she added, "The reporter I talked to warned me that listening devices are everywhere."

A clerk was sitting at a large desk with an outsized portrait of Stalin hanging behind him. The desk was covered with the ashes from his cigarettes, along with black specks that Lacy soon identified as dead flies.

"*Dve komnaty?*" the clerk repeated in response to Lacy's request for a double room for Pem and Noah and a single for herself. He vehemently shook his head. "*Nyet!*" He shoved a green ticket into her hand, saying in heavily accented English, "Maids quarters only available." He pointed to a once-grand staircase leading to the hotel's upper stories. "Third floor. Lift here not work."

Noah accepted the proffered key and stoically headed toward the staircase, his suitcase and black doctor's bag thumping against his thighs. Lacy and Pem followed with their own luggage and trudged up the steps behind him. With her Louis Vuitton footlocker in Pem's custody, she lugged one of his leather suitcases.

Their allotted room was basically a broom closet. It faced an airshaft and contained a narrow bed covered with a thin, soiled linen bedspread. An ornate oversized desk left over from czarist days decorated the otherwise dismal room. The doors had lost their knobs, the floor its carpet, and the basin attached to one wall had no plug to keep the water in.

Looking around, Pem said with a straight face, "'Fraid we won't be able to do much surgery in here."

Lacy didn't even have the energy to smile at his joke. She sank down onto the solitary bed, and its mattress springs emitted a loud twang. Startled, her two companions looked at her, and all three of them began to laugh, although Lacy could tell her laughter bordered on hysteria. When she finally caught her breath, she pointed to the ceiling.

"No chandelier, thank goodness, but let's keep our voices down." She pulled out their useless plane tickets from her handbag. "Once we've all had a shot of vodka ourselves, I say we locate the American embassy in central Moscow to find out what documents we'll need. From my map, I expect we'll have to pass through Ukraine, Romania, and wherever else gets us to a train that will take us to Bucharest. Maybe from there, we can fly to Gibraltar."

Pem nodded, adding in nearly a whisper, "Thank God the Romanians—thus far—have remained neutral, like Sweden."

"What are you two? Travel agents?" Noah challenged, his smile forced.

Pem grinned, teasing Noah, "Bucharest is *in* Romania, in case you were wondering."

"You know, I *am* kinda a travel agent," Lacy said, her expression thoughtful. "Even as a kid, I had to figure out how to get from some stupid boarding school to wherever my mother and her latest husband were spending the summer or a holiday. Trust me, I'm an ace at reading foreign plane and train schedules."

Pem and Noah leaned over her shoulders while she pointed at the red blob on the map of Europe she'd pulled out of her handbag. "Here's Romania," she explained in hushed tones, tracing a line with her forefinger that stretched some 1,500 miles from Moscow to Bucharest via the vast region of Ukraine. Given their experience at the airport, she didn't have to elaborate on the possibility that Nazi soldiers and Russian secret agents could be a threat at every turn.

She thought back to Noah's physical reaction to the mere presence of the two German soldiers they'd managed to elude. She wondered whether Pem, too, had started to feel the undercurrent of fear that she did, especially when it came to Noah. They'd come face-to-face with the evil that put people like Noah in their crosshairs all over Europe.

Or maybe it's more like a noose tightening around the necks of all three of us.

Pushing such a likelihood to the back of her mind, she said, "If we get to Bucharest and there are no flights from there, we could continue by train to Venice." Again, she traced a line on the map with her index finger, adding, "Once across Italy to the Mediterranean side, we could probably get to Spain by boat."

"Hmmm," Noah said, staring at the map. "Zigzagging like that—and factoring in unexpected delays along the way—it could take us quite some time to make it to Gibraltar and from there to England."

She looked at both men, managing to summon an encouraging smile. "Well, look at it this way. Going that crazy route," she whispered, "we'd never set foot in Germany or Austria at all!"

"Okay, then," Pem said, reaching for his coat. "Let's head for the

American embassy, get our travel paperwork in order, and get this show on the road."

Lacy could feel a growing sense of desperation as an antique grandfather clock leaning against the paneled wall ticked the minutes away. She, Pem, and Noah had trekked to a former noble's palace in the heart of the city that served as the U.S. Embassy in Moscow and been directed upstairs to what might have once been a ballroom. There, surrounded by faded upholstery clinging to gilded chairs and the once-glorious, but no longer highly-polished parquet floor beneath their feet, they'd been waiting for over an hour to even be seen by a low-level embassy official.

Noah whispered, "Doesn't the ambassador just have to sign a piece of paper?"

Pem agreed, asking no one in particular, "Yeah. Why is this taking forever? I'm starving!"

With increasing concern about their midnight deadline to exit Moscow, Lacy strode toward a desk positioned in front of the ambassador's inner sanctum and had a few words with his secretary.

"What did she say?" Pem demanded when Lacy returned to her seat.

"I mentioned the names of a few prominent folks around FDR that Granny Farr knows and threw in that you two are Harvard grads."

"And?"

"We'll just have to see if that does any good."

A few minutes later, the secretary walked over to them and disclosed in almost a whisper, "We do sincerely apologize for the wait, but the reason is the ambassador has filed an official demand about your exit visas with the Russian government."

"And?" demanded Lacy, echoing Pem.

"And we're waiting for a reply," the secretary replied, her patience clearly strained.

"Look, we appreciate your efforts very much," Lacy responded with as much grace as she could muster. She gestured toward Pem and Noah. "Surely, the Russian authorities should give these American doctors the courtesy of simply allowing two neutrals to leave this country with the correct visas."

Pem interposed, "And also, Miss Forbes needs the correct papers."

Just then, a door opened and Laurence Steinhardt, a tall and thin middle-aged ambassador, appeared. "Miss Forbes?" he called across the large room.

Lacy jumped up from her seat and replied, "Yes?"

"It appears we are able to provide the proper documents for you and your colleagues to make your way out of Russia."

Lacy rushed toward him expressing her profuse thanks.

"Not at all, my dear," the ambassador replied, a faint smile creasing the corners of his mouth. "You are now free to leave the country by train today instead of an airplane. My secretary here has also managed to book your tickets for later this afternoon."

Despite his friendly demeanor, she thought he appeared strained. *Why wouldn't he,* she thought, *having to deal with a country where virtually nothing works?*

Ambassador Steinhardt looked over at her companions. "And is that Dr. Fischer with you over there?"

Startled that Noah had been singled out, she answered, "Yes, sir. May I introduce you to him *and* his colleague, Dr. Charles Pembroke."

"Dr. Fischer needs no introduction," the ambassador replied jovially, striding across the room to shake his visitors' hands. "Young man, I read about you in the *Columbia Alumni Bulletin,*" he said. "Wonderful work to get a field hospital all the way to Scandinavia, my boy. Too bad Russia's allies made short work of your efforts there."

"Y-you went to Columbia?" Noah stuttered.

"Columbia undergrad," he replied. "And I received my law degree there in '15."

Lacy almost laughed aloud at realizing it wasn't FDR's or Granny Farr's name that had sprinkled the fairy dust needed to obtain their necessary exit documents but rather the old school ties among fellow graduates. She'd been vaguely aware Noah had earned a master's degree in public health at Columbia University before going to Harvard Medical School, but who knew Ambassador Steinhardt was a Columbia man? *He's also Jewish,* she thought suddenly, remembering reading somewhere that he was a prominent member of the Federation of American Zionists as well as a leader on FDR's Democratic National Campaign Committee.

Once again, it came down to *Who do you know?* Even so, she was amazed by the miracle it had wrought that time around.

The ambassador handed Noah a sheet of paper with the embassy letterhead embossed at the top. "I've prepared this letter that says you three are under the protection of the U.S. State Department." He gazed at Noah intently before continuing. "You're Jewish, aren't you, son?"

"Yes," Noah confirmed, "but not especially religious, sir."

"Well, you may have the ill luck to encounter some Russian or German border guards along the way to Gibraltar. Unfortunately, they might not like the fact you're a Jew—even though you're American and a neutral. Keep this letter with you. It might possibly get you out of a jam at some point."

Lacy was as grateful as Noah and Pem for the ambassador's kindness and generosity. The American official turned to return to his office, saying over his shoulder, "I've had our cook prepare a basket of food for your trip, as I guarantee you'll need it. Travel safe, with my good wishes." He paused and turned to face them once again. "And keep your eyes peeled. I'm betting you'll be followed once you leave here."

Exiting the grand mansion, Lacy immediately sensed the ambassador had spoken the truth. Two burly and very obvious members of the Russian secret police had taken the place of the pair of German soldiers they'd encountered at the airport. The new twosome were clad in identical black overcoats and fedoras, although the shorter of the pair had a prominent wine-red birthmark staining one cheek. The two men walked less than thirty paces behind as Lacy's group scanned the street for a taxi.

Noah said under his breath, "What if those guys try to grab us right off the street?"

"We run back into the embassy," Lacy whispered back.

She breathed a sigh of relief when Pem was able to hail a dented and rust-encrusted taxi to the train station, where yet another hurdle presented itself.

"Do you want to travel on the *hard* or the *soft*?" the train clerk demanded in broken French once Lacy had established she spoke that language and not Russian.

The embassy secretary had warned them that the "hard" were cars occupied mostly by soldiers and Russian "wanderers"—the country's word for homeless people. Each "hard" compartment had several layers of shelves "like a linen closet," the U.S. official had explained, "so travelers can lie down, side by side, like books on a shelf, to sleep. Otherwise, they stand for the entire journey."

Pointing to their tickets, Lacy swiftly replied, "We're traveling on the soft."

But the "soft" car to which the three had been assigned was like any third-class carriage, yet in their case, the upholstery was far more threadbare and torn than even the furniture at the Metropole Hotel.

"*And* it's repulsively dirty!" exclaimed Noah as the trio entered their assigned train compartment.

Lacy saw through the train window that the ever-present Russian minders were suddenly standing on the platform outside. "Well, at least the embassy cook outfitted us with half a dozen caviar-and-egg blinis, plus a bottle of vodka for the trip," she said, trying to cheer up her two companions as she took her seat by the window.

Pem put their food basket on the overhead shelf and sat down next to her. On Pem's other side, Noah sank onto a frayed section of their upholstered bench seat. A few moments later, a man carrying a diplomatic pouch stamped with the Swedish flag entered their compartment. His canvas bag was similar in style to the one Lacy had scrounged from a U.S. State Department acquaintance in D.C. before she'd left New York. She stashed hers under the seat, feeling more secure that at least their traveling funds were under their control.

As its engine fired up and the train slowly began to leave the station, Lacy's pulse quickened at the sight outside their window of the Russian government goon with the birthmark disfiguring his face. He took a step closer to the train and glowered at her. She swiftly averted her gaze just as a woman chattering in French to no one in particular entered their crowded compartment, along with a couple of Russians carrying battered briefcases.

They had barely relaxed for the first time that day when Lacy felt her breath catch. A tall, slender German officer suddenly appeared in the doorway. He had a swastika insignia on his cap, and his feet were clad in shiny black storm trooper boots that reached just below his knees. Blond and blue eyed, his smooth-shaven face was expressionless as he surveyed his fellow passengers for a long moment before squeezing into the last remaining seat.

"Oh, great," Noah whispered. "Not exactly a preferred traveling companion."

Lacy sensed her heart beating rapidly but didn't respond. Meanwhile, Pem's worried glance signaled his growing apprehension.

Why did a Nazi officer have to choose this compartment of all the ones on the train?

Pem patted her arm, urging under his breath, "Let's just close our eyes and try to sleep." Then he reached for Lacy's hand as the train gained speed.

"Ukraine sure is one big country," Noah grumbled a few days later as they were pulling into Odesa.

Lacy had nearly lost track of how long they'd been traveling since leaving Moscow. Equipment breakdowns and missing staff had slowed them down for hours nearly every day. Their ultimate destination of Great Britain felt even farther away when their coach was side-lined "by mistake" on a separate platform in a railyard twenty miles down the line with no provisions for food or water. Fortunately, their stash of funds provided the sustenance they were able to purchase once they'd walked down the rails to a tiny hamlet in the middle of nowhere. They'd waited nearly a week until a connecting train to Bucharest finally pulled into the station. It, too, proved to be appallingly filthy and barely operational.

Once their carriage was reunited with a train heading for Romania, Pem pointed out the compartment window, which was nearly opaque with dirt. "At least we can finally feel a train rolling down the tracks, even if we can't see out the window."

But Lacy's thoughts were far less cheerful than Pem's. She wondered whether she would have still chosen to go on their journey if she'd known it would involve spending so much time on a train and being accompanied by the narrow-eyed Nazi officer who had remained on board. *Traveling by slow rail in wartime*, she thought with a sigh, *offers a huge opportunity for something to go wrong.*

Like Pem, Noah appeared to be feeling more confident than she was. He leaned toward his seatmates and spoke in hushed tones behind his hand. "I guess we should count our lucky stars that there are no other Germans besides the one riding with us on this Nightmare Non-Express!"

CHAPTER THIRTEEN

"Wake up!" Lacy urged her two companions in a harsh whisper. "We're stopped at some border crossing, I think."

Noisy, guttural chatter and the sound of heavy footsteps at the end of the corridor outside their compartment served to rouse everyone from the stupor induced by their days of excruciatingly slow travel south through the Russian countryside and across Ukraine. There'd been further mechanical delays and missed connections, and much to their unease, the German officer in their compartment was still with them.

"We must be at the Ukrainian-Romanian border by now," Lacy informed Pem and Noah. She consulted the newer map of Central Europe that the American embassy official in Moscow had kindly provided her.

"It sounds like German soldiers just got on board," Noah murmured nervously.

Lacy cocked her head and then nodded, able to hear more clearly German being spoken in the passageway outside their compartment.

"From what I can make out," she murmured, "they're asking to see passports."

"Why would Germans have the right to do this if Romania is neutral?" Noah whispered hoarsely.

"Hitler's ally, Russia, invaded Poland a year ago and annexed parts of Western Ukraine at the same time," she whispered back. "I read somewhere that they've occupied even more of the country since. The Soviets must already be allowing the Germans to strong-arm travelers at the border with Romania."

Pem leaned forward and reassured them in a low voice, "Our travel visas are all in order and signed by an American ambassador. There shouldn't be a problem."

"Noah has that State Department letter in his pocket Steinhardt gave him," Lacy murmured, "and Pem's got the other one Granny Farr obtained from FDR." She suddenly wondered how much influence either document would have with a bunch of Nazis.

The German soldier who'd been riding in their compartment since they'd all boarded in Moscow rose from his seat, slid open the glass door, and disappeared. A few minutes later, a phalanx of officers entered the passageway, their uniforms sporting insignias on their lapels that matched those of the German officer who'd been traveling with them.

"Passports and visas, please," demanded one officer, repeating his request in several languages.

One by one, the passengers dutifully handed over their travel documents. When the officer inspected Noah's, he said in highly accented English, "You say you're American, yah?"

"I am," Noah replied, darting an anxious glance at Lacy.

"Your name is 'Fischer,' I see." He gazed intently at Noah's passport photo. "'Fischer' is a Jewish name, yah? Not like a fisherman who brings in a catch," he said, smiling faintly at his grim joke.

Lacy felt a stab of icy fear run down her back. Fear and a sense of guilt.

Oh God, she moaned silently. *We should never have said anything to encourage Noah to make this trip with us.*

Pem spoke up, his tone sharp. "Dr. Fischer is *American*, as are Miss Forbes and I." He gestured toward Lacy. "Dr. Fischer and I are physicians, and we're neutrals on our way to ...Venice."

As Pem finished his sentence, Lacy realized the wisdom of not revealing that their destination was Britain, which was definitely *not* neutral in the present conflict.

"Venice?" the officer snapped. "Your transit visas say Gibraltar, a British territory."

Her thoughts spinning, Lacy summoned her most charming smile before chiming in, "That was just what the American ambassador in Moscow put down."

"Steinhardt? Another Jew!" spat the officer. "Just like Fischer here, yah?"

So much for Ambassador Steinhardt's letter of protection.

Feeling increasingly anxious, Lacy hastened to lie. "We're planning to board a boat from Italy back to America." She indicated her companions, adding, "We've been on a medical mercy mission in Scandinavia, but now we're being rotated back to our home."

"Doctors, you say?" the officer said with a sneer. "So many people these days claim to be something other than they are." He cocked his head. "Can you prove it?" he rudely challenged Noah.

"We both can," Pem intervened once again. He then reached under his seat and pulled out his black doctor's bag. He nodded to Noah to do the same, which he did, fumbling briefly until he retrieved a similar leather case and rested it on his knees.

"You! Fischer! Open it," ordered the German who spoke some English, clearly annoyed the men were telling the truth. He gazed into the contents of both bags. From Noah's, he pulled out a vial of pills, scrutinizing the label. "Very strong drugs, I see," he said. "Do you have the documents to allow you to carry such things?"

"I'm a doctor!" Noah repeated doggedly. "Anyone with a medical degree is authorized to—"

"*Silence!*"

Lacy hastily dug into her handbag and pulled out a bottle of pain pills she always carried for premenstrual cramps. She'd taken two that very morning.

"Look, Officer!" she inserted herself boldly. "*I* have these strong pain pills, and I'm not a doctor."

"Why do you possess them?" he demanded before threatening her. "Perhaps I should arrest you, too, for drug trafficking?"

During her years in Europe, Lacy had observed that many Germans were practically phobic about illness and surprisingly squeamish about the details of various maladies.

"My doctor in the United States gave me these capsules because I have terrible periods," she said, producing an embarrassed smile before adding, "You know, bad bleeding and pain and—"

"Enough! No need to go into detail."

Ignoring his warning, she informed him, "There is nothing bad or illegal about medicine like this, especially for doctors whose job it is to treat patients suffering pain. Dr. Fischer here tends to wounded soldiers taken from battlefields—"

"I said, *enough*!" the officer practically screamed. He turned toward his two lieutenants. "Remove this dirty Jew off the train until he is able to prove he has the right to carry such contraband."

Pem jumped to his feet, his hands curled into fists. "Now, look here, Officer—"

In the next instant, the leader of the Nazi triumvirate stepped forward and slapped his black-gloved hand hard against Pem's chest, sending him flying into his seat with a thud. "Shut up, Doctor Pembroke the Third," he snarled, glancing at Pem's passport, "or you and Miss Forbes here will come with us as well."

The German officer pushed Lacy's and Pem's travel documents into their hands, keeping Noah's.

Lacy whispered urgently, "Show him the letter from FDR, Pem!"

"*Silence!*" screeched the lead officer. Then he ordered his two compatriots to seize Noah by both arms, with the result that his doctor's bag fell to the floor.

All the other passengers, including Lacy, froze, stunned by the swiftness with which the group hustled their prey off the train, leaving the German officer who'd been traveling with them to calmly reclaim his seat, take a steel file from his breast pocket, and nonchalantly smooth the ends of his nails. Her heart pounding in triple time, she leaned over and pulled Noah's doctor's bag into her lap.

"Hand it over!" ordered the remaining German officer, grabbing Noah's bag from her. In seconds, he'd disappeared down the passageway to join his confederates outside the train.

Within minutes of the soldiers leaving the coach car with Noah in tow, the locomotive shrieked a warning that the engine was starting up again and that the train would soon roll across the border into neutral Romania.

Lacy fell back into her seat, her body trembling uncontrollably. "Oh God, Pem ... Can't we *do* anything?"

It's Austria all over again! Hitler's bastards can just do whatever they want wherever they want, and the rest of us simply stand by and ...

Before she could compose herself, Pem leaped up from his seat and stormed out of the compartment, sprinting down the corridor in pursuit of the German soldiers who had Noah surrounded on the platform outside their train carriage. Horrified, Lacy stared through her window, watching the squad of border guards shout and beat the butts of their guns against Noah's thin shoulders and chest. In a swift move, the Nazi officer who'd been their traveling companion also jumped out of his seat and raced into the passageway after Pem.

Lacy quickly rose to her feet and bolted after him. She saw that, near the end of the corridor, Pem and their fellow passenger were already in a life-and-death scuffle on the small square opening between their car and the one ahead of it. The train suddenly gave a lurch and slowly inched forward, gathering speed as the Nazi officer drew a weapon out of a holster attached to his belt.

Merely feet away, she screamed, "Pem! He has a gun!"

Pem made a grab for the weapon, managing to turn it around and point its barrel into the officer's left shoulder. The two men grunted and pushed against each other as their train passed a worn wooden sign announcing they had officially entered Romania.

Before Lacy could even complete her next thought, Pem used the Lugar's barrel and his own shoulder as a battering ram. His forward motion launched the soldier's weight against a section of worn canvas stretched above the small metal floor linking the two cars. Lacy heard a ripping sound, and in seconds, the Nazi officer was tumbling onto the gravel train bed that flanked the tracks and rolling down the incline. Lacy hardly had time to realize his body had flashed out of view before she reached Pem's side. Gasping for breath, he clutched a metal handle on the side of their car that rolled from side to side as the train gathered speed.

"At least … I didn't … shoot him," Pem said, sucking in several lungfuls' of air. Wind whistled in the space where the officer had fallen through the canvas, which was flapping in the wind between the two cars. Continuing to inhale deeply, he managed to pant, "You know … that 'do no harm' pledge … we take as doctors?" It took another minute for his breathing to become even again. "I-I wanted to kill the bastard for pointing out Noah to those SS, but I guess that oath was what kept me from pushing his finger against the trigger of his gun."

Lacy started to cry. "I can't believe what they did to Noah! What will happen to him? Where will they take him?"

"God only knows," Pem said, appearing to be as shaken as Lacy felt.

"I'm just glad the gun didn't go off and kill *you*!" she exclaimed.

"I just pushed it *against* him with all my might."

She threw her arms around him with relief. "Thank God you're all right, but that fall off the train may have killed that Nazi creep."

"He'll be bruised plenty," Pem replied, hugging her hard against his chest, "and maybe end up with some broken bones, but the train was going fairly slowly. Unless he hit his head on a rock, I'm pretty sure he'll survive."

Lacy leaned back in his arms as the wind swirled through the space between the train cars, whipping her hair into a tangle.

"If he does survive," she said, raising her voice over the clacking of the train wheels gathering even more speed, "he's sure to telegraph a description of you down the line. He saw your name on your passport!"

"And yours too," Pem said worriedly, moving them off the vibrating platform and into the passageway of their car.

"Let's just pray we get to Trieste before he can report us," Lacy said. "Even though Italy joined Germany in the Steel Pack, Italy's still neutral in this war, as are we." Anguished, she asked, "But what will those goons *do* to Noah? We should never have urged him to come. At least you cautioned him to take the boat home."

He put a hand on each shoulder and forced her to look at him. "Noah's a big boy. Remember, he asked for some time to consider his decision and chose to come with us. All three of us were taking big chances to try to get to England with a war going on." He gently put his forefinger beneath her chin. "You and I still are. You are not to blame, Lacy. The Nazis are."

"I suppose so ..." she replied. A sudden sense of anger and frustration churned her guts. Shifting her gaze to Pem's face, she exclaimed, "Our plan was supposed to be spending a few hours on a couple of planes and maybe a train or two and look at us! It's been *weeks*! Noah's been taken and beaten to a pulp. He'll be sent to God knows where. And the guy you threw off the train is either dead or alive *enough* to tell someone our names and descriptions!

We are in a world of hurt here, Pem. What in hell are we going to do?"

"How far are we from Italy?" he asked.

"Quite a ways," she answered, adding, "and getting farther from where poor Noah is by the second."

Pem pulled her even closer to his chest and declared softly, "We had no way of predicting all this, but now that we are where we are, I think we'd better get back to our seats before a conductor or someone sees us. You can show me how far we have to go to get to Italy on your map." They hurriedly walked down the long passageway leading to their compartment. "I'll go in first," Pem declared.

"Wait!" She put a hand on his arm. "How do we explain why that goon—who obviously pointed Noah out to those Nazi border patrol guys—hasn't returned?"

"Just watch," Pem said grimly.

Pem went on ahead while Lacy attempted to smooth stray ends of her hair back into its chignon. Everyone looked up expectantly when the pair entered the compartment and sat down in their former positions. The French woman passenger had tears in her eyes, and the rest of their seatmates kept their gazes carefully averted after that.

Pem pointed first to Noah's empty seat and then to the empty space opposite them where the German soldier had been sitting. "It seems that our *other* fellow passenger decided to join his compatriots and remain on the Ukraine side of the border," he announced blandly. "Didn't want to miss the fun, I guess. The bastard!"

Their traveling companions, who didn't speak English, looked puzzled, so Lacy repeated Pem's first two sentences in German and then in French, omitting the subsequent epithet. She felt Pem's right arm encircle her shoulders once again, which only triggered a strange and unexpected desire to howl at the moon.

"I just can't stop thinking about poor Noah," she whispered, the enormity of what had happened in the last hour crashing down.

She'd be forever haunted by the vision of the German soldiers beating the man she'd worked beside for nearly a year. How would she inform Noah's parents in Cambridge? And would any of them ever know what had happened to him? Her dark thoughts nearly choking her, she fought hard to hold on to her composure.

As if Pem sensed her wave of despair, he pulled her even closer.

She tucked the top of her head under his chin and kept her face to the window to avoid the questioning gazes of her fellow passengers.

Whispering into her ear, he said, "We'll go to the first American embassy we can find. We'll tell every important person we know what's happened to Noah. This is a violation of international law, and—"

"None of that matters over here where Jews are concerned," Lacy spoke over him brokenly, struggling to keep her voice low. She leaned back and whispered hoarsely, "I saw exactly the same thing happen to Jewish merchants when I was a pathetic schoolgirl in Vienna. International law means nothing in a world where the Nazis are dedicated to wiping out Jews wherever they find them. No one in America is paying that a bit of attention. They even deny it's happening." She felt the tears she could no longer stem spilling down her cheek. "Oh God, Pem ... I can't bear to think what they're doing to Noah right now! Look at all the good he was dedicated to, and now ..." Her voice cracked before she could continue. Inhaling a deep breath, she murmured, "He's one of the finest people I've ever known, and we both know we'll probably never see him again."

She met Pem's gaze. His eyes, too, were brimming with emotion, and she noticed a black-and-blue welt rising on his neck where the Nazi had assaulted him. She reached up and tugged his collar up to hide the injury.

Pem leaned closer. "Noah's truly the best. And you're probably right," he spoke softly into her ear, gathering her against his chest once more. "We may never see him again." Pem held her tightly as her shoulders started to tremble with silent sobs. "I know, sweetheart," Pem said, his breath warm against her cheek. "I know."

They rode with their arms around each other until the morning, when they were due to cross yet another border into Serbia. Lacy realized with a start that if they attempted to exit the train at a stop near an airport to see whether there were flights to Italy or Gibraltar, they would undoubtedly be apprehended immediately.

There was no abandoning the train journey from hell until they made it to Trieste ... if they ever did.

Chapter Fourteen

Just as dawn was breaking outside their train window, Lacy stared with intense concentration at the open map on her lap, desperate to devise a plan.

She nudged Pem awake and said in an undertone so any stirring passengers in their compartment wouldn't hear, "It looks as if we have three more border crossings. At every single one, until we get to Trieste on the Adriatic, we're both going to have to hide before border agents come on the train." At Pem's look of skepticism, she insisted, "We've *got* to, just in case a message about us has been sent down the line."

"Let's pray the guy I tossed off the train took a long time to get help or find his way to a functioning telegraph office."

"Well, we can't take a chance!" Lacy replied. She kept her voice to barely a whisper. "I've been thinking about it all night. Hiding out in the lavatory is our only hope because I'm sure they'll check every-where else ... even in the baggage compartment."

"But what if they forego the niceties and inspect there too?"

"Oh, I'm sure they will, but I have a plan," she said, grabbing her purse and their locked, battered canvas diplomatic bag of money. "Quick! The train is slowing down. It'll be at the station in a minute. Let's go!"

The pair smiled politely as they exited the compartment crammed with several new passengers who had gotten on in Romania and were traveling west along their route to Serbia, Croatia, and Slovenia. Pem and Lacy ducked into the lavatory as the train rolled to a stop just inside Serbia on their way to Belgrade. They soon heard the familiar sound of harshly spoken German, as well as the thump of jackboots pounding the metal entrances between carriage cars.

"Border police!" they announced in stentorian tones. "Have your documents ready!"

"Goddamnit!" Pem hissed. "The Germans are already taking over checkpoints between countries they haven't even conquered yet!"

"But intend to," countered Lacy.

She ordered Pem to wedge himself as best he could behind the toilet in the bathroom's only stall while she stood near the doorway, ready to try to block the entrance.

"Why am I in here and you're guarding the door?" Pem protested.

"Because I know what I'm doing!" Lacy hissed. "So just *stay* there!"

Lacy strained to hear the voices in the adjacent passageway, and sure enough, there was soon jiggling of the handle and pounding on the washroom door.

A guttural German voice shouted, "Open up! Unlock this door!"

"Hello!" Lacy called back in German. "I'm in here using the facilities!"

"Open this door, I say, or I'll *shoot* it open!"

Anticipating that, Lacy plunged her hand into the front of her trousers and pulled out a soaked sanitary pad she had deliberately not changed all day. With the bloody object in her left hand, she opened the door six inches with her right and brought genuine tears to her eyes. "Officer ... I-I'm so s-sorry, but, as you can see, I'm ... well, I'm changing my—"

"*Mein Gott!*" the uniformed man cried. "Stop waving that horrid thing in my face! All right! All right! *Christus!*" he screamed and slammed the lavatory door shut from the outside.

Locking it once more, Lacy sank against its width, terrified by how close they'd come to being caught and arrested.

"Lacy?"

Shushing Pem, she hissed, "Be quiet! Stay where you are till we leave the station!" With her back against the door, she slid into a heap on the floor.

"What the hell did you do?" he demanded hoarsely.

"Shhh!" After a few long minutes, a whistle pierced the air and the train gave a lurch. "Okay ... I think we're safe," she said in a low voice.

Slowly, she rose to her full height, avoiding Pem's astonished gaze as he emerged from the toilet stall. She was embarrassed not only by the ruse she had invented to ward off the guards but also because she was still holding the bloody evidence of its implementation. She quickly tossed the pad into a trashcan near the sink, turned her back to him, and bent over the faucet to wash her hands in the trickle of rusty water spitting out its mouth. Meanwhile, the train began to gather speed as it moved out of the station toward Belgrade.

The German patrol has obviously left the train, she thought with relief, thanking the fates that they'd crossed yet another border, coming ever closer to Trieste in Italy.

"Are you all right?" Pem asked, stepping toward her.

"Not particularly," she said, drying her hands on a filthy towel near the sink. "And now you know all the secrets of womanhood. Disgusting, isn't it?"

"I'm a doctor, remember?"

"And you're married," she reminded him with a sudden fierceness. "Of course a woman having her period isn't news to you."

"No, it's not," Pem replied quietly. "But I've never seen a braver or more unique method of using what you had at hand to prevent our arrest." Without warning, he reached toward her, gently seizing her chin in one hand. "I am forever in debt to you for such a clever way to spare both of us from a fate like Noah's. You know, don't you, what it means when you've saved someone's life?"

"Not really," she replied as their gazes met.

He leaned forward and brushed a kiss against her cheek. "It means you are linked forever to that person," he whispered.

For Lacy, what they'd both done to avoid the German authorities had triggered a kind of delayed reaction of trembling, and her teeth actually began to chatter. Pem took a step back and rubbed his hands briskly up and down her upper arms.

Once she stopped shuddering, he said, "Okay. That's better. Let me wash my hands while you ... ah ... take care of ..."

"This?" she said, pulling a fresh sanitary pad out of her handbag with a grim smile. "There are certainly no secrets or taboos between us anymore, are there?"

Pem merely raised an eyebrow and turned his back to wash his hands in the sink, giving her a chance to use the toilet and "suit up," as she jokingly noted.

They were well into Serbia before they could relax and prepare to pull off the same "avoidance scheme," as Pem dubbed their hiding in the lavatory at every border crossing.

For the rest of their harrowing train journey through Croatia and Slovenia toward the port city of Trieste, Lacy took comfort in the success of their pilgrimages to the lavatory each time they crossed into another country.

After one such charade, once they were safely back in their compartment and on their way to the next checkpoint, Pem reached for her hand resting on the tattered upholstery that covered the train seat. He leaned to within inches of her ear, his warm breath soothing on her skin. "You truly are ... pretty wonderful, you know that?"

She gave a slight, negative shake of her head and closed her eyes, whispering, "Not really."

During the long nights rolling along the rails, she often awoke to find herself encircled in his arms. The first time it had happened, she'd been groggy and felt unsettled at realizing how physically close they were. She'd tried to move away, but Pem had held on.

Don't let this happen, Lacy, she had warned herself. *You'll be the one to lose!*

Each time, though, she always gave up the struggle. But with Pem's every reassuring touch, Lacy sensed that her well-guarded heart was at risk in a territory more dangerous to her well-being than even the Nazi-infested land they had so perilously traversed.

By the time they finally arrived in Trieste, just over the border from Slovenia into northern Italy, they'd continued to be each other's sole support while coping with even more endless delays and bureaucratic hurdles.

"Other than walking," Pem joked, "this has to be the longest way it's humanly possible to travel from Moscow to Trieste."

In mid-May, just before noon, they finally exited their train after what seemed like a lifetime since they'd flown out of Stockholm. Lacy's arms ached from carrying the weight of Pem's luggage while he dealt with her footlocker and the canvas bag with what was left of their traveling funds. Glancing sideways as they made their way into the echoing lobby of the train station, she reminded him, "Let's not forget a few of our most *memorable* delays."

With feigned nonchalance, Pem said over his shoulder, "Oh, you mean when the scheduled train never showed up in Nowhere, Serbia, and we slept huddled in a railway shed?"

"And then there were the nights we spent in that deserted freight car in the middle of Slovenia waiting to sneak past the guards when our connecting train finally showed up."

"Ah ... what sweet memories we share," he said with amused sarcasm, although Lacy suspected he actually meant it.

They headed for the left luggage department to store their baggage for a few hours until they boarded their final train to Venice, a mere hundred miles distant. Even as Pem locked away their belongings, Lacy's stomach clenched as she recalled their constantly being on alert for Germans who might be tracking them down in Hitler's ongoing rampage throughout Europe. One passenger entering their compartment en route had announced that the Allies were failing to keep the Germans at bay, revealing that the Wehrmacht's armed forces had swarmed into France on May 10.

From the moment the German SS officers had arrested Noah, Lacy's and Pem's reoccurring nightmare became having to race into the lavatory at each and every border crossing. Like seasoned thespians, at each stop, they'd performed their "bloody game of make-believe" to avoid German guards who might have been alerted about the soldier Pem had dispatched off the train in Romania.

Pushing such unsettling memories from her thoughts, Lacy led the way on a short walk from the Trieste train station to the port city itself, grateful that at least Italy had remained marginally neutral thus far.

At a small café near the waterfront, they were soon informed that the consulates in Venice and Milan were the only official American presence in Italy. Once their waiter disappeared with their order, Pem said quietly, "I guess we have yet one more train ride before we can report what happened to Noah."

After a light meal, Lacy stood on a dock overlooking the Adriatic Sea and deeply inhaled the salty air, struggling to summon the energy needed to face their next hurdle after Venice. They must somehow find their way to British-controlled Gibraltar, located on the western edge of Spain, where the plan had always been to beg or bribe an airplane ride to the UK.

Stretching her arms to embrace the Italian sun reflecting off the churning water, Lacy said with a sigh, "At least it feels wonderful to be away from those stinking trains—and I do mean *stinking*!" She pulled in another deep breath of sea air. "I spend all my time now fantasizing about taking off from Gibraltar and arriving in southern England in only three or four hours by air."

Pem nodded. "From the moment we exited the train today, didn't it feel as if we'd literally been let out of prison?"

She looked at Pem and tried to smile, but Noah's jailors were never far from her thoughts. She pointed at her rumpled suit jacket with its Red Cross arm patch and the stained blouse she'd been wearing for weeks. Wrinkling her nose, she said, "I think I'll make a bonfire with my clothes when we get to England!"

Pem shot her a peculiar look and took a step closer. "I'm putting you on official notice that you'll find yourself in great danger if you start describing to me any plans to abandon your clothing." His voice had grown husky when he drew her against his broad shoulders. "Lacy, I—"

She lay both hands flat against his chest and shook her head. "Please, Pem ... we ..."

"Lacy, what I'm about to say to you is long overdue, so hear me out," he insisted. He seized both her hands, and the electricity that perpetually flowed between them seemed almost unbearable to her then. "I've wanted to tell you—"

"Well, don't, Pem!" she exclaimed, yanking her hands away. "I know what you're about to say, so please stop!"

Lacy turned away from him and looked out over the water.

"You don't want me to say what we both *know*?" he demanded. "That we have deep feelings for each other after what we've been through. That—"

She turned back, held up her hand, and put a gentle finger against his lips. "We can't just fall into something casual, Pem ..."

"What's going on between us is far from casual!" he protested.

She paused to gather the thoughts that had been disturbing her sleep for days. "Well, then, we cannot allow ourselves to fall into something *serious*," she countered, trying to lighten her tone, although her next words belied her efforts. "Pem, I can't deny what you're saying. And believe me, I don't deny what we obviously both *feel*," she admitted. "We both know it could turn into something *very* serious if we let it. And you're so right," she said, her eyes glued to his, "we've been through more together than most couples experience in a lifetime. The plain truth is ... I couldn't have made it without you."

"Nor I—for damn sure—without *you*," he interrupted her, cupping her face in his hands. The tenderness in his voice nearly undid her.

"Even so," she insisted softly, sensing she was in grave danger of starting to cry, "for *me*, anyway, taking our ... closeness ... a single step further will undoubtedly end up breaking my heart," she confessed, her voice catching. She felt his hands drop to his sides, but she soldiered on. "And frankly, I don't think I could survive that. In case you've forgotten, you are a *very* married man to a woman you've told me is lovely and a very nice person." She raised her chin and declared, "This can't end well—especially for *me*—so let's just not start."

"It's already started," he said stubbornly.

"Well, I say we can stop it!"

"Lacy, please let me just tell you that—"

"Tell me what?" she interrupted. "That you and Eleanor aren't very compatible? That you two just don't match up like ... well ... like *we* do on so many levels?" she said, walking a few steps away from him, staring out over the water again, her arms hugged against her chest. "I'd believe you if you told me all that, but the simple fact is you *are* married and have been for seven or eight years now. You married long before we met," she pointed out, "and had plenty of time to have realized how unhappily things turned out for you, yet you did *nothing* about it."

"We didn't have children," he declared, as if that were his defense.

"A disappointment in that department as well?"

"No! What I meant is that I wouldn't agree to having any kids," he countered, an expression of sadness that she'd never seen before clouding his handsome face. "I didn't want to add other innocents to our lives. And you're right. I couldn't even acknowledge to myself all the other things you've just itemized. That is, until I met you. What I feel for you is so completely different than anything I've ever known. We've been partners in everything. I can depend on your good sense. Your ... I guess I'd call it 'groundedness'—if that's a word."

"I don't think it is," Lacy noted, and Pem laughed.

He put his hands on her shoulders and gazed directly into her eyes. "How could I not notice that you're gorgeous, you're sexy, you're fun to be with? And who could deny that you're beyond enterprising when it comes to evading the Germans?" he said, the smile that had charmed so many tugging at the corners of his lips.

"Well, you're pretty gorgeous yourself," she shot back, wishing his cheekbones weren't so chiseled or his eyes so blue, "and that's gotten both of us in hot water. In your case, I sometimes think that things come a little too easily for you."

"And just like now," he countered, ignoring her gentle jab, "you tell me the truth about everything. Even about *me*," he added. "Why wouldn't I have fallen in—"

"Don't say it!" she exclaimed.

But Pem just shook his head. "Before we met, I think I just distracted myself from the mess I was in because Eleanor and I never argued, even though we've always seemed to live oh-so-politely in separate orbits. Instead, I focused on battling with my father about the practice of medicine and getting my architect's degree, no matter what. I kept myself diverted by doing all that, and I didn't allow myself to—"

"To face the mistake you'd made," she interrupted, "doing what your parents wanted you to do? You simply allowed Eleanor and your parents to decide what you should do with *your* life!" She stacked her hands on her hips. "I have to say, Pem, I do not find that very admirable."

"I don't either."

Lacy shook her head sorrowfully. "And I don't think the time to sort things out on that score is during a *war*, do you?" she demanded. "Meantime, I can't afford to fall in love with you. It will just hurt too much when it all ends."

"Well, it's too late for me!" Pem retorted. "I'm *already* in love. And even more importantly, I love you beyond anything I ever imagined a man could feel for a woman."

He turned and strode away, retracing the path to their train soon to depart for Venice.

Chapter Fifteen

"I'm already in love."

For a second, Lacy began to wonder whether she'd truly heard Pem say that. With a long exhale, she gathered her wits and raced to catch up with him, plucking at his sleeve to slow him down.

"And I love *you!*" she exclaimed as he turned to face her. "I know that now." With a harsh laugh, she added, "But that doesn't solve my problem that you're *married*. The fact is you're here and Eleanor's in Boston. Do you plan to divorce your wife long distance?" She regarded him closely. "We may have fallen in love with each other on this train trip from hell, but how irrelevant that all seems under the circumstances."

"Because of the war? I disagree," Pem pushed back. "For me, what's happened with us has become the most important thing in my life. It feels as if it's now or never—to start living the truth. And by the way, that includes the truth about what I feel for you."

Lacy steeled herself to resist the intensity of the emotions that were washing over her as she absorbed how seriously he'd come to regard her ... as she had him.

"Believe me," he said, his tone threaded with compassion that touched Lacy to her core, "I am well aware how much your supposed loved ones have hurt you." He gently brushed the back of his fingers along one of her cheeks. "Before I left Boston, I asked my mother what she'd heard about the famous Forbes clan."

"I bet she had plenty to relate," Lacy retorted, unable to hide the bitterness she felt that June and her collection of men had lived their outrageous lives so publicly.

Pem nodded. "She had heard the gossip about the craziness your mother and the men who've filed through her life have caused your entire family—and you, too, I would assume."

"And did she tell you how my stepfather ended his life?"

Pem took her hand gently. "Yes ... she knew quite a bit about that very publicized scandal of your stepfather's death. I'd read all about that too," he revealed, seizing her other hand. "And I can only imagine how awful it must have been for you, growing up in that world." With a troubled look, he said, "You suffered one abandonment after another, didn't you?"

"To say nothing of parents constantly behaving badly in one form or the other when they *did* stick around," she added, thinking how terrified she'd been as a young girl when Rem's shadow had lurked at her bedroom door in the wee hours.

Almost as if he'd read her mind, he asked, "What was your stepfather like? Did Remington Rowe ... ever hurt you?"

Lacy shook her head and looked away.

"Did he ever touch you?" Pem asked gruffly, and Lacy knew what he meant.

"Not quite. The only time my mother ever did me a favor was when she sent me off to another school to get me away from Rem. But only to protect her own interests, of course."

A series of memories stormed through her brain ... flashes of her little brother, Teddy, sobbing in her arms and her being put on trains and ocean liners for yet another boarding school or summer camp season in yet another new location somewhere in Europe.

"The only member of my family who was always on my side was Granny Farr," Lacy said softly, "but my mother did her best to steer clear of her unless she needed to dip into a Forbes or Farrington trust fund."

She looked away, staring into the distance. The dirt path leading to the rear of the train station was deserted as Pem encircled her in his arms and pressed her cheek against his shoulder, cradling her head with one hand.

He said quietly, "I truly don't want to add to the emotional burdens I can see you've been carrying for a long, long time. But it might help you just to know that you are *loved*. Totally. Unconditionally. By *me*," he declared emphatically. Pem leaned back, forcing Lacy to look at him. "And I admire you for who you are and what you've done all on your own. *I* love you," he said for the second time that day. "So very much, and I will sort out things with Eleanor."

"You mean get a divorce? When?"

"When I can." He gave her a feather kiss on each eyelid. "It's a simple fact, this love I feel for you. We both know it, so you can just forget trying to push it away."

Pem kissed her then, long and deep and with both a fierceness and a tenderness that nearly brought her to her knees.

He knows *me*, Lacy thought almost despairingly, and it scared her to death.

Hardly aware she was even speaking, she murmured, "I can't deny whatever this thing between us is either." Her voice became low as a deep sadness took hold of her emotions. "But as they say, 'at another time, in another place,' we might have been that perfect match Granny Farr considered us that day in Boston when we all first met. But it can't be *now*, Pem," she said earnestly. "Not when we're so many miles away from your real life. Not when your real life includes a wife and you make it sound as if changing that isn't possible anytime soon."

"That may be true right now, but *this* feels like my real life!" he declared heatedly. "My life with you since the day we boarded the ship in New York."

In some ways, it had always been *easier* for him to go along with what others wanted for him—until he'd simply decided not to do that anymore and no one from Boston had been present to oppose him.

For me, nothing has ever been easy, Lacy mused, contrasting her youth with his. On their insane shared journey, Pem had tasted his first freedom from all the family constraints placed upon him. *And certainly, it must be a heady feeling*, she thought. But what was to guarantee he wouldn't slip back into his old habits of acquiescence if family pressure reasserted itself?

If we both somehow manage to survive this war and make it back to the States, he'll still be married to Eleanor Choate of the New England Choates, she thought, resentment coiling in her chest like a snake waiting to strike. "Sorting it out" with Eleanor might not be the easy task he'd made it sound.

She wondered how she was supposed to survive if she tasted what it was like to feel safe and secure in a life partnership with a man like Pem and then had it disappear when their real world returned. There was no doubt in Lacy's mind that Pem was not like the other men she'd known when it came to appreciating a woman with ambitions like she had. A woman who wanted a life outside what her gender or upbringing had prescribed for her. He would support her in all things.

But Charles Pembroke III had been raised in a world that had dictated nearly every aspect of his charmed life. *Until now*, she thought glumly. And why not, when he was over six feet tall and wickedly handsome with his dark hair and electric blue eyes? He'd been highly educated at Harvard, for pity's sake, fitted out with both a medical license and a degree in architecture! Pem had been born, like she had, into one of Boston's elite families. Who knew better than *she* did that the pull of obeying the rules of his class and professions could be hard to resist if the demands at home once again came to bear?

"Look," she mumbled, holding out her arm so he could see her watch, "it's getting late. We'd better dash to the station or we'll miss our train to Venice."

"You're right," he replied, seizing her hand once more and escorting her the last hundred yards along the dirt path leading to the railyard, "but don't think for a minute this discussion is at an end."

Lacy gazed out of the terracotta-framed window overlooking the Grand Canal, its turquoise-and-sapphire waters appearing much cleaner from the distance of the third floor of the Palazzetto da Schio than they had from the water taxi that had brought them there.

"*Palazzetto* means 'miniature palace,' right?" Pem scoffed, setting down their luggage on the guestroom's stone floor. "These look like pretty big digs to me! Your friend, the contessa, has been nothing but a sterling hostess."

The lovely three-story ochre-colored building with a terracotta-tiled roof was owned by a classmate of Lacy's. Anna da Schio had attended one of the many boarding schools at which the Farrington siblings had been enrolled. In the intervening years, Anna had grown into a slightly portly but perfectly coiffed unmarried woman of obvious inherited wealth with a staff at her beck and call. Before she'd directed them to the stone stairs of their guest quarters, she'd told them that her parents had recently died in a boat accident, leaving her their "little palace" and "a life to call my own."

Lacy shifted her gaze from the view out the window to Pem and said ruefully, "I'm just grateful she remembered who I was. We were thirteen years old when June banished Teddy and me to Switzerland."

"Well, thankfully, our hostess *did* remember you since desperate times called for desperate measures." He grinned.

"Well, we were pretty desperate arriving in Venice today."

Pem nodded in agreement. "I imagine that Anna da Schio likely considered you an unforgettable character in her young life. She couldn't have been more gracious when we rang the bell at her front door."

Their hostess had been utterly at ease welcoming the two of them into her home and simply assumed they would want to be accommodated in the elegant bedroom overlooking one of the most stunning views in Venice.

Now that they were alone, Lacy explained to Pem, "Italians may be Catholic, but the upper classes are quite accustomed to ... well ... you know," and then she blushed.

"Yes, I certainly do know," Pem said, his voice taking on a dangerous, husky tone. "Please realize that my desire to take you over to that beautiful four-poster bed right there actually might kill me." He took another step closer, his lips parted, his eyes shadowed, hungry. Ignoring her warning look, he wrapped his arms around her. "Face it, Lacy," he whispered into her ear, his breath a warm aphrodisiac sending bolts of electricity shooting down her spine. "Venice is for lovers, and here we are in the middle of a war. What do you think?" he said softly. "Wouldn't we be fools not to take advantage of—"

He didn't finish his sentence because Lacy, to her astonishment, found herself kissing him to blot out everything but the two of them in a world that was crashing down all over Europe. Crashing through the wall she'd built up against trusting anyone with her wounded heart.

In the end, she couldn't fight her feelings for Pem any longer or ignore the magic cast by their romantic surroundings. Nor could she resist reveling in the longed-for feeling of safety and security with a man who expressed his care for her in everything he said and did. With their luggage still surrounding them on the stone floor, Pem tightened his arms around Lacy's shoulders, and suddenly, nothing else mattered.

He eased her onto the ornately carved large four-poster bed with its sculpted gilded cherubs, their carved wings holding up yards of silk above her head, the exquisite, embroidered sheets soothing her skin. Before Lacy gave up all caution to the winds, Pem reached for a condom stashed in his doctor's bag sitting on a bedside table.

She instantly pulled away.

"Ah ... I see ... you planned ahead," she accused him, her thoughts flashing to a persuasive young man she'd known in Paris who'd been equally well equipped and failed to become more than a one-night event. "But were you sure exactly for *whom* that condom was intended?"

Dusk had turned to dark. Pem brought the packet close, as if for her inspection, and replied with a confident smile, "Oh, believe me, these only had your name on them. I knew before I even took that train down to the New York docks to board the *Drottningholm* that I was crazy about you and wouldn't want you to suffer any consequences if I were *ever* lucky enough to make love to you."

And although she was both startled and touched by his defense, in the back of her mind, Lacy couldn't quite banish what he'd said about not wanting to have children with his wife. Clearly, condoms had prevented "complications" on that score as well as they would that night.

Eleanor...

Pem paused, cocked his head, and said questioningly, "Lacy ...?"

He'd left it up to her, the do or don't.

"As you said ..." she began slowly, "desperate times call for desperate, crazy, insane, unreasonable, and impractical measures. But, yes, Charles Pembroke the Third ... Venice is definitely for lovers."

Despite the potent mix of sensuality and guilt, Lacy realized there was no denying she'd come as close as she could manage to forgetting about everyone and everything but the wonder of feeling loved and secure—and reveling in the physical pleasure she knew in her soul she and Pem would discover that night.

The morning sun was turning the waters of the Grand Canal a sparkling green. Lacy and Pem stared out their guestroom window at a scene of such beauty that the war raging in Europe seemed as far away as the moon.

Out of the corner of her eye, she caught sight of the four-poster and its telltale rumpled linen. She felt Pem's arms circle her body as he drew her back against his chest. She was glad he couldn't see her face, her cheeks flushing with a rosy glow at thoughts of the memories they'd made just steps from where they were standing, locked together as one.

"I'm starving, aren't you?" he asked, bestowing a kiss on the back of her head. "It's nearly ten o'clock. What do you say we head downstairs and see what *La Contessa* is serving guests this morning?"

Lacy breathed a sigh. "I'm hungry too, but oh ... I wish we could stay in this haven forever."

"Oh, so do I," he mumbled, brushing his lips against her neck.

He turned her around and pulled her close, the evidence of his renewed desire pressing against her thigh. She longed to give in to the overwhelming passion she'd experienced in his arms all night, but a niggling voice in her head whispered ... *Eleanor.*

She pulled back and sought his glance. "We need to talk."

"*Now?*" he murmured, reaching for her again.

"Yes," she said firmly, taking a step back and holding on to the back of a nearby chair to steady her nerves. "There's another woman in this room this morning," she said, attempting to keep her tone light and non-accusatory, "and her name is Eleanor."

Pem turned and took a step closer to the window that looked out onto the canal sparkling in the morning sun.

"I know," he acknowledged, his voice suddenly sounding husky. "I haven't forgotten either. I know what happens next is up to me, but we're a long way from Massachusetts, and you and I are where we are ... in beautiful Venice ... and in love."

"But it is your problem to fix if you truly want me in your life, agreed?" she said softly.

Pem nodded. "Yes, it's my problem to sort out. And I will ... as soon as it can be done." His sober expression brightened a shade. He turned and reached for her hand. "Don't you think we'd better show our faces to our hostess?"

Lacy nodded, attempting to assess whether Pem's answers settled the question, for her, of where the two of them stood in the mad whirl of passion and commitment they'd both finally embraced.

And, of course, part of the mix was that the world beyond that magical place awaited. The real world of war.

The two cast a last look through the window at the glorious view of the Grand Canal before Pem took her hand and led her down the stone steps outside their room for their first breakfast together in *La Serenissima.*

The moment they entered onto an outdoor gallery facing a side canal that ran the length of the palazzetto, Anna da Schio called out, "Well, hello there!" from her seat at the end of a long, elegant table.

A gentle breeze wafted through the open space, and Lacy inhaled the seductive scent of verbena. She was filled with an unfamiliar sense of delight at the sight of sunny marigolds and various varieties of trailing plants that spilled over the edges of a platoon of terracotta pots surrounding the alfresco dining area.

Their hostess smiled broadly at her two guests as they approached. Her English was excellent and had only a slight Italian lilt to it. She pointed to the sideboard under the stone-framed windows fronting a dining room and invited them to "Please help yourselves."

A radio enclosed in a highly polished mahogany case stood next to a buffet of tempting breakfast offerings. Lacy sighed with pleasure at the sight of an impressive display of fruit, delicate pastries, and silver pots full of coffee, whose delicious aroma almost made her dizzy with joy after the weeks of bad food during their railroad odyssey.

"Did you sleep all right?" Anna inquired. "You must have been exhausted from such a harrowing journey as you described to me last night."

Lacy was afraid to look at Pem or comment on how well they had or hadn't slept, so she merely replied, "You'll never know how much we appreciate being in a genuine bed after sitting upright in train compartments night after night. We can't thank you enough, and—"

"Not at all!" Anna insisted. "You can't imagine how delighted I was you even remembered me after all this time." She smiled at Pem. "Lacy was a standout at that Swiss school. I was very sorry she was there only one year."

"My mother was on to another one of her adventures," Lacy said cryptically to Pem, "and off we went to a German boarding school that time."

Anna pointed to the radio. "I've just been listening to the wireless," she disclosed. "While you were making your way by train through Slovenia and across to Venice, there was a disastrous failure of Allied British and French forces to stop the Germans pouring into Belgium and France. The situation is rather dire now, I'm afraid."

"We saw a few newspaper headlines along our way, but what's happened now?" Lacy asked as she and Pem exchanged looks of alarm.

"The BBC announcer said that Allied expeditionary forces are racing toward *Dunkerque* in a full retreat," Anna disclosed, using the French pronunciation of the seaside port.

"Oh no!" Lacy exclaimed, then explained to Pem, "Dunkirk's a coastal city in the north of France that faces the English Channel."

Anna added, "And apparently, everyone there is praying for a miracle to ferry the troops across to Dover. Masses of Allied soldiers are lined up on the sand, waiting for transport. Meanwhile, they're exposed to German aircraft diving down extremely low, their tail guns blazing, shooting at close range. Can you believe Churchill's trying to evacuate some three hundred *thousand* troops from there?"

Lacy could feel Pem's arm, casually draped around her shoulders, tighten.

"We should be in Dover," he declared, and Lacy heard the anger in his tone. "It will be a bloody mess when they land those soldiers on the coast of Britain. They'll need miles of hospital trains to take the wounded inland for treatment, and I don't think England has many on hand."

Lacy shook her head. "Well, the *first* thing we should do before anything else is go to the U.S. Consulate here and make a report to the State Department about Noah's arrest by the Germans."

They had described to Anna the terrible fate of Pem's fellow doctor and the leader of the field hospital project for which Lacy had raised the funds.

"I can ring up the consulate if you like," Anna offered. "I've played bridge with the emissary's wife on occasion."

For once, Lacy was grateful that the *Who do you know?* game could be played in their favor. But a few hours later, when she and Pem reported the story of Noah's arrest by German SS officers at the Ukrainian-Romanian border to the U.S. official, he merely promised to pass on the information to the State Department.

"And *then* what?" Lacy asked as politely as she could.

The consul, as if well acquainted with the demands of Americans experiencing troubles away from home, replied with practiced patience, "We'll begin to make inquiries about Dr. Fischer's whereabouts through whatever channels we still have ... but as you can imagine, relations with the Nazis are becoming more problematic in these troubled times."

And sadly, Lacy and Pem discovered how true that was the very next day.

Chapter Sixteen

"I've waited lunch for you," exclaimed Anna, greeting Lacy and Pem, who were just returning to the palazzetto after a morning of glorious sightseeing. Their hostess had generously provided the da Schio oarsman to scull them around the canals of Venice, where they had passed a series of spectacular areas, including the Piazza San Marco. They'd ridden in style in Anna's stunning, shiny black gondola and disembarked onto the da Schio's private dock with memories filled with the beauty of a magical city floating on water. "Everything's prepared on the gallery," Anna announced and led the way to the terrace that overlooked the water.

They had barely tucked into a delicious array of sliced meats, plump figs, and cheese when a wild-eyed servant appeared at the door. "Signorina, signorina!" he declared, his agitation obvious. "Italy has just declared war on France and Britain!" Before anyone could react, he dropped a newspaper on the table with a screaming headline three inches high and disappeared.

Lacy glanced down at it, learning from the front page that it was June 10. She'd heard earlier that morning on the wireless that Norway had finally surrendered to the Nazis after battling bravely for weeks.

"That dreadful Mussolini!" Anna fumed, setting her cup of cappuccino in its saucer with a clink. "First he signs the Pact of Steel with Hitler, and now he joins in the war against Britain and France with that maniac!"

After hearing the announcement that Italy had joined the Axis powers, Lacy was immediately assaulted with a suffocating sense that everything was suddenly closing in on them.

Pem appeared to be as alarmed as she was. "Despite America's declared neutrality," he mused aloud, "I wonder if we Americans will now be perceived as one of Italy's new enemies, given FDR's close relationship with Winston Churchill?"

Anna offered a reluctant nod. "I'm afraid that's a distinct possibility."

Lacy declared, "Well, then, we've got to find a way to get to England as soon as possible!" She put down her ivory-handled fork beside her plate. "Anna, we don't want to put you in any jeopardy. You've been more than kind to us."

Pem agreed. "At any moment now, Germans will be everywhere in Italy."

"I'm sorry to say German security police have already been seen in the city," Anna confirmed, frowning. "My servants spotted several of them at the outdoor markets this week."

"Looks like we barely dodged yet another bullet," Pem said tensely, shifting his gaze to his hostess. "Don't you think it's safest for all of us if Lacy and I begin to make our way to Gibraltar—*today*?"

Lacy shot him a look of both frustration and fear. "I like your plan, Pem, but just how do you propose we do that?"

Anna hastily volunteered, "My boatman can take you to the mainland, and then I can have someone drive you to Portofino on our Mediterranean coast." She shifted her gaze to her coffee cup, her expression somber. "Both my uncles side with Mussolini and the Nazis, so I'm afraid it's probably best if you leave before they get wind that you're here with me." She hastened to add, "It's been wonderful having you as my guests. I just wish it could have been much longer."

"Of course," Lacy and Pem chorused, both swiftly rising to their feet.

"From Portofino," Anna speculated aloud, "you'll have to find passage on somebody's fishing boat to get you across the Mediterranean to Spain."

"Why not aim for a yacht?" Pem said with an obvious attempt to lighten their darkening mood.

A man to the manor born, Lacy thought but replied only, "C'mon, Pem. We'd better go pack."

Lacy was surprised and touched to see Anna's sincere look of regret at having to urge her houseguests to depart Venice after their short stay at her palazzetto. Lacy wondered why she hadn't realized that Signorina da Schio would have been a wonderful friend when they were in school together if only her thirteen-year-old self had made more of an effort.

"Once you get to the Italian Riviera," their hostess proposed as Pem dropped their luggage near the open front door, "ask down by the water if a ship or even a fishing vessel sailing south could get you to Spain. After making your way to Gibraltar, perhaps you could fly to England from there?"

"That's been our hope," Pem said. "It's incredibly kind of you to arrange a car and driver."

"I only wish I could do more to help."

"You've been wonderful in every way," Lacy assured her, "but I suppose we'd better get going."

Anna gestured toward the canal. "My vaporetto is waiting to take you over to the mainland. There'll be a car, along with a driver named Giorgio, waiting for you there. If anyone stops you on your way, just say you were guests of Guido and Luca da Schio. My driver will back you up."

Pem asked carefully, "Those are your Fascist uncles?"

Anna shrugged. "At least they're good for something in this sad world."

Lacy stepped around their luggage and embraced her. "There's no way we can possibly thank you," she said, leaning back with a watery smile. "You've been a much better friend to me than I ever was to you."

"We were so young then," Anna replied with a forgiving smile. "I hated being sent away to school too. I always wanted to be better chums with you, but you didn't stay at that Swiss refrigerator for very long."

Lacy burst out laughing. "I don't think any of us ever took off our long underwear, day or night ... winter or summer!"

Pushing such memories aside, Lacy swiftly kissed Anna on both cheeks, European style, and then followed Pem out to the dock and their waiting vaporetto.

Lacy glanced behind at the boat's wake carving a white path back to Anna's home facing the Grand Canal's ever-changing water, which was then the color of turquoise. "I wish we could have stayed there forever," she said, hearing the wistfulness in her voice.

"I wish we could stay there forever in that glorious guestroom," Pem elaborated, pulling her toward him on the boat's hard wooden bench and briefly nuzzling his lips against her neck. "I hope whatever vessel we find to take us to Spain has a cozy cabin below deck. It might be our last time alone for a long time, Miss Lacy Farrington Forbes."

He stealthily placed her hand near his groin, and Lacy felt the thrill of his closeness and the obvious evidence of his desire.

"You haven't run out of condoms, have you?" she whispered with a sidewise glance at the boatman piloting their craft.

"No, indeed," he whispered back. "If only we could have luxuriated in that four-poster just a little while longer ... but I'm sure we'll work something out."

***

The noise from the propellers outside the plane's window seemed to reverberate several decibels louder as the craft banked steeply to the left, flying over the green-and-gray patchwork of southern England.

"Oh my gosh!" Lacy cried excitedly and then swiftly lowered her voice. "I can't *believe* we're finally here!"

"There were definitely moments on that fishing boat," Pem said in an undertone, "when I had my doubts we'd ever make it to Spain, to say nothing of finally getting to Gibraltar."

Lacy pointed excitedly out the plane's window. "Look! There's Tangmere Airfield!"

"And just get a load of all those RAF planes lined up on the tarmac!" Pem said, leaning over her shoulder to gaze down at his first glimpse of the British countryside of West Sussex.

Lacy gaily counted on her fingers, "April, May, nearly all of June.

A mere three months on trains, planes, boats, and automobiles to get here," she jested sarcastically. "Now, on to London!"

He bent across the airplane's armrest and brushed his lips against hers, ignoring the other, mostly military passengers on the plane.

"We only made it aboard this tin tube because of you, Miss Debutante!"

Once they'd arrived in Gibraltar, Lacy had managed to use her Washington, D.C., State Department connections with the British authorities to wangle them two seats on a flight to southern England.

"Pretty amazing luck you have, young woman, that some attaché who witnessed your presentation at court acquiesced to the State Department's bidding and did us a rather large favor," Pem teased, kissing her ear. "But what do you suppose will happen next since I have no visa to enter the country and *you do*!"

Lacy tried not to look worried but merely replied, "The Brit at the embassy said it could be sorted when we arrived."

"My guess," Pem said cheerily, "is he didn't want to deal with it on his end."

Lacy shrugged. "Well, I guess that our adventure just continues."

After the plane landed, Pem's shaky immigration status proved far more daunting than either of them could have imagined. They trudged across the tarmac with their luggage and filed into a Quonset hut for customs formalities. Lacy pulled out her passport and resident visa.

They'd advanced only a few steps when a British soldier accosted them before they could head for the canteen. "Dr. Pembroke?" he declared, glancing at a manifest list in his hand. "I'm afraid you'll have to come with me."

Lacy's stomach clenched at the thought of military authorities whisking Pem away less than a minute after they'd touched down on British soil.

"Please, Lieutenant," she pleaded, spotting the insignia on the soldier's uniform, "can't I just make a call to ... to our American ambassador, Mr. Kennedy?"

Lacy had absolutely no idea whether Kick's father would have any memory of who she was or that she'd even stayed at the embassy residence during her presentation at Buckingham Palace in '38.

The officer, who'd been polite up until that moment, cast her a scowl. "You must not have heard, miss. It's more than a rumor, lately, that Kennedy might possibly be recalled to Washington by your President Roosevelt. At least that's the talk everywhere, so I doubt our authorities will pay much notice to any appeal by that German appeaser on your companion's behalf!"

"*What*? Joseph Kennedy's being recalled?" gasped Lacy, although privately, she wasn't as surprised to hear that news as she made out to be.

Ambassador Kennedy had made no secret of the fact that he was an ardent isolationist. Lacy could imagine how FDR might wish to have another representative in Britain as Hitler's troops gobbled up more and more of the Continent since Italy had joined the fray on Germany's side. That had to be even truer, as German U-boats were attacking American merchant ships in the Atlantic with increasing regularity, nudging the US ever closer to siding with the Brits.

So now *who can I contact about Pem*? she thought desperately.

She blurted to the lieutenant, "What if Lady Astor called in to your superior officer? Or my friend Victor, Lord Rothschild? Would that help?"

"I'm afraid Jews don't have the same sway in our country as they appear to have in yours," he snapped. Lacy was stunned by the not-so-veiled antisemitism of the soldier's answer. During her pleading, the soldier's lips had formed a tight, straight line. "Dr. Pembroke, you are to wait here," the soldier ordered. "Miss Forbes, I would ask you to proceed to the anteroom with the other passengers cleared for entry."

Lacy had no choice but to head for the small canteen on the other side of a military police barrier and wait. The line to the solitary telephone call box was long, and before she'd even come close to ringing up a single British friend or acquaintance to ask for help, Pem came striding to her side with his hands ladened with official paperwork. As he approached, he waved the documents at her, and her spirits soared.

"They granted you a visa?" she exclaimed.

"Nope." Pem shook his head. "They granted me the privilege of either entering an internment camp for undocumented immigrants or—"

"Or?" she demanded, anxious and alarmed.

"Or accepting an assignment as a practicing physician at a military hospital in Manchester that treats seriously wounded soldiers who've recently been evacuated from Dunkirk."

"*Manchester*!" she wailed. "That's miles north from here!"

It seemed so unfair that Pem had more hoops to jump through and that, in the blink of an eye, it seemed certain they were going to be parted. Lacy felt a laden sense that nothing in her life ever turned out as she wished. She was assailed by a horrible feeling that, after that day, she and Pem might not actually ever see each other again.

"But you're an *American*! I thought we were supposed to be two close countries merely separated by a common language?" she joked bitterly.

"In the world of immigration regulations, I'm considered an alien with no entrance visa," Pem reminded her. "Luckily, though, I could show them a copy of my medical diploma from Harvard, along with my Massachusetts doctor's and architect's licenses and my passport. Noah insisted I bring copies of all important documents with me for the Finland project, and thank God I did."

"Why won't they at least allow you to go back to the States?" she wondered. Pure dread settled over her since Pem's returning to America wasn't the outcome she wanted at all!

"No dice there either," he said with a shake of his head.

"Even with the letter you have from FDR?"

Again, he shook his head in the negative. "Only Americans connected with the military or diplomatic corps can get on a plane flying across the Atlantic—at very high altitudes, by the way," he confided, "so as to avoid enemy attack. Traveling by sea these days is even riskier. So, between being locked up in an internment camp with a bunch of German spies, homegrown Fascists, and Irish revolutionaries—to say nothing of run-of-the-mill criminals—and working as a doctor in the Midlands, guess what I chose?"

"Manchester, here you come," Lacy said glumly.

Chapter Seventeen

Pem looked around at the khaki-clad crowd inside the military airport's canteen and breathed a sigh. "I've just been handed a voucher for a ticket on the overnight train to the Midlands," he declared, adding with a grimace, "and I'm informed that once I get there, I'm to be 'restricted to quarters.'"

"You can't ever leave the hospital till the war ends?" Lacy cried, aghast.

"Not that long, but I can't leave the hospital until they assess whether I'm worth keeping on the medical staff," Pem replied. "And who knows if I will be? After all, I've been practicing architecture, not medicine, for a year. I hope to God I remember enough about treating the injured to get by. At least with Noah, I would have someone to watch my back and make sure I didn't kill anybody."

At the sound of Noah's name, they exchanged stricken glances. A moment later, Lacy was in Pem's arms, holding back tears.

"Oh good Lord, what a mess we've gotten ourselves into," she moaned, her voice muffled against his chest.

Pem pulled back and tucked his forefinger under her chin. "Well, at least I can remain in the country," he said, "but what about where you'll be?" He looked over at the red call box, a long line still waiting there. "I take it you haven't reached any of your friends?"

Lacy stood stock-still, her mind revolving around the few possibilities that might be open to her. "I think, first off ..." she said slowly,

"I'll try to beg a bunk with some debs I met during the coming out ceremonies at Buckingham Palace last year. They asked me to share a flat, so they might let me stay with them for a bit. As for what I should do next …" She paused and then declared with determination, "I imagine my best bet is probably to try to get my old newspaper job as a copy girl at the London bureau of the *Baltimore Sun* back."

"Can you do that now? Work here as an American, I mean?"

"Let's hope so—if I strong-arm the right people," she replied.

Pem leaned toward Lacy. His voice low, he said, "One reason the immigration people are so touchy about 'unknowns' is that rumors that Hitler may be planning to try to invade England soon are getting stronger. Anybody entering Britain without proper papers could be considered a spy."

"Invade *this* country?" Lacy gasped.

"That's what I overheard while I was waiting for the authorities to determine what to do with me." Lacy and Pem stared at each other for a long moment. Then Pem looked at his watch. "Let me go with you to your friends' to make sure you have a place to sleep tonight. Then maybe you'll come with me to Euston Station to say goodbye?"

Lacy felt as if her breath were suddenly being cut off. She'd thought they'd feel safe once they landed in England, but then …

"I hate this," she whispered.

"So do I," he replied, grasping her hands, "but we'll write each other as often as we can. If I don't maim or slaughter anyone, that lieutenant told me that maybe I could be granted a leave by Christmas." He flashed her a crooked grin. "Thank our lucky stars Britain is short on doctors, even ones as untested as I am."

For Lacy, though, it felt like the inevitable end she'd always imagined her relationship with Pem would come to. He'd be gone for months, and who could guess how that would affect their … *what*? An affair with a married man? Was that all it was? *Maybe his being banished to Manchester is for the best*, she thought, with a familiar feeling of being left alone to cope with yet another loss.

Look on the bright side, Lacy told herself, reflecting that that way, neither one of them would break it off in some horrible drama like June did every time a man left her. Lacy could blame their separation on life and the raging war, not the fact that being in love with a legally unavailable man was predictably hopeless.

No real harm done, right?

But a part of her wanted to put her head down and cry her eyes out.

It was still daylight that July evening when the rumbling black taxi pulled up to the Gower Street flat of Tess Mayor and Patricia Rawdon-Smith in Bloomsbury, a fashionable section of Central London.

Lacy was relieved to discover that she'd jotted down their address in her diary after having lunch with Kick Kennedy in D.C. the prior spring. Kick had mentioned that she'd faithfully kept in touch with their mutual friends while desperately—but thus far unsuccessfully—plotting against her parents' wishes to return to London to be with Billy Cavendish.

When the door to the Gower Street flat opened, Pat Rawdon-Smith blinked, and her mouth formed an "O" in shock. Lacy suddenly felt self-conscious. How shabby she must look in her bedraggled Red Cross uniform. In the past, she'd seen Pat only when she was dressed to the nines in her party attire. On this day, her friend was clad in fashionable, pleated gabardine slacks and a cashmere sweater set, as if she were ready to go out for a stroll.

"Oh my God, it's *you*!" Pat exclaimed. She looked back over her shoulder and shouted, "Tess! Victor! You will not *believe* who is standing in our hallway! Lacy Farrington Forbes!" She turned back to her visitors. "Victor was literally just asking about you!" she exclaimed, directing a curious look at Pem.

"About *me*?" Lacy said, mystified. She quickly made introductions and then leaned forward and whispered hoarsely, "Why is Lord Rothschild here? Is that sourpuss wife of his with him?"

"Barbara? She's pregnant and staying at their Merton Hall place in Cambridge. Victor's taken a flat in St. James's for reasons you'll hear about, I suspect. But you and I both know that he's always been a bit smitten with our friend Tess."

"I sensed something like that at the 400 Club on Presentation Night," Lacy replied, keeping her voice low.

Pat dropped her voice to match Lacy's. "Actually, it's nothing like that at the moment. He's here trying to recruit us for hush-hush jobs somewhere in the War Office or something. He's been appointed to a high-up position that he won't even name."

"How exciting!" Lacy exclaimed. "Are you going to accept?"

"I'll tell you later," Pat whispered.

As the three of them stood at the doorway, Lacy heard the sound of rapid footsteps, and suddenly, Tess was sprinting down the hallway toward them.

"Well, Lacy," Tess laughed, "you certainly took your time about deciding whether to share this flat with us!" To Lacy's surprise, Tess rushed forward, and the slender, petite young woman with dark, curly hair gave her visitor a hearty hug, a gesture seemingly out of character for a Brit. But then, Lacy remembered that Tess's rather Bohemian upbringing by academic parents in and around Cambridge University had made her friend into a person rather different from the debutantes of her acquaintance, like Pat and Kick. "Where in God's name have you *been* all this time?" Tess demanded. "Kick wrote that you couldn't possibly still be in Finland after the Jerries invaded Scandinavia." She looked at Pem curiously. "We were a bit worried about you, but I see you've made your way back here in quite good form."

"Tess, I'd like you to meet m-my ... uh ... colleague, Dr. Charles Pembroke," Lacy stuttered.

"'Pem' will do nicely," Pem assured both women with his engaging smile.

Lacy volunteered, "As you might imagine, we had to leave Scandinavia in a rush and skedaddled off to Moscow. From there, we took an endless series of trains south and west on the worst railroads on the planet." Briefly relating the rest of their zigzag itinerary and their confrontations with the SS, she concluded, "From Gibraltar, we hitched a plane ride with the military, landing at Tangmere Airfield three hours ago."

Over Tess's shoulder, Lacy caught a glimpse of Victor Rothschild striding down the hallway. Pat swiftly made introductions. "You know Lacy Forbes, of course, Victor, and this is Doctor Charles Pembroke." She grimaced, adding, "They've just told me that a fellow physician they were traveling with from Moscow wasn't so lucky when they encountered some German border guards. The poor chap was taken from the train in central Europe somewhere. But these two made it, and here they are on our very doorstep!"

Pem shook hands with Victor and inclined his head to Tess and Pat. Lacy marveled that he seemed utterly at ease with three posh Londoners he'd never met.

Gesturing toward Lacy, Pem said, "If it hadn't been for this lady speaking perfect French and German, to say nothing of her grace under pressure in the face of a few nasty run-ins with those Nazi guards along our way, I'd be in a prison like our valued friend, Doctor Fischer."

"Well, come in, come in, you two!" Pat exclaimed. "We want to hear all about it!"

Victor, Baron Rothschild, spoke for the first time. "Indeed, we want to hear everything. And I mean *every* detail."

"And of course we have a bed for you," Tess declared, pouring Lacy a second cup of tea. "Once you get a job, we'll happily allow you to pay your share of the rent," she added with a mischievous smile.

"I just hope I can find employment as quickly as possible," Lacy replied with a rush of gratitude for Tess's much-appreciated and immediate invitation to become a roommate.

She and Pem had spent the past hour sipping a weak brew "due to rationing," Tess had explained apologetically. Lacy and Pem took turns elaborating on the trials of their months traveling from Scandinavia to Britain, including the horror of what had happened to Noah.

Lacy could see Victor was moved and not a little distressed to hear the story of Noah's capture.

"If you would like, I'll put in a report about this to the War Office so this incident is on file with the proper channels should any information about Dr. Fischer surface."

"Oh, that would be so hugely kind, Victor," Lacy replied, tears edging her voice. "Pem said he would take on the difficult chore of writing Noah's parents about what's happened. May we say that your filing a report and one of us will keep them informed?"

"Of course."

At length, Pem glanced at his watch and heaved a sigh. "I regret to say that my train is leaving London later tonight. After Lacy and I arrived in England—me without a visa—I was eventually given a ticket to Manchester, where I've apparently been assigned to the staff of a British Army hospital. Sadly, I've got a train to catch in two hours."

Victor set his teacup in its saucer, and Lacy assumed he was also planning to take his leave. To her surprise, the young Baron Rothschild had other ideas.

"Before the good doctor and Lacy depart for the station," Victor said, "I think I might be able to help with Lacy's job search."

"Oh, Victor, that is so kind of you!" she responded.

"Not kind at all," Rothschild said, "but very much in my own interest." He shifted his gaze toward the other women in the room. "Pat here insists she wishes to remain a girl Friday in her current job, but Tess, I'm happy to report, is open to becoming one of the two assistants the War Office has budgeted for my unit."

Lacy looked over at Tess, who was smiling and nodding in agreement.

Tess allowed, "Working at Jonathan Cape Publishers has been interesting, but Victor has convinced me that I really must do my bit for the war effort. Given I speak fluent French and German, like Lacy here, I quite like the idea of helping him track down rotten, home-grown Nazis stirring up trouble in their horrid meetings with swastika flags pinned to the walls!"

Lacy looked at Victor with surprise. "Is that what your new position involves? An anti-Fascism unit working within Great Britain?"

"That's about as much as I'm authorized to tell you, but yes."

Pem quickly responded, "As you probably know, Lord Rothschild, the US has the same kind of thing going on with the German American Bund, a group that's supporting Hitler's regime across the United States! At huge rallies, they're spreading antisemitic propaganda to increase support among German Americans."

"It's disgusting," Lacy chimed in.

Victor nodded. "Well, while you two were traveling from Moscow, the British Union of Fascists was finally banned here in May, but that's not put an end to the continuing sedition. My new job is to deal with the problem, and I need a second assistant in addition to Tess."

Pat interjected excitedly, "And you won't *believe* it, Lacy, but Debo Mitford's sister, Diana, and her horrible husband, Oswald Mosely, were plotting to establish a *radio* channel between Germany and Britain! Their plan was to propagandize British citizens into accepting—even welcoming—an invasion by Hitler's troops! Can you *imagine*?"

"Deborah Mitford's sister is a *Nazi*?" Lacy said, astonished that a member of such a renowned aristocratic English family was mixed up in supporting Hitler. "Wasn't Diana Mitford also a debutante a few years back, and her sister, Nancy, quite a good writer?"

"Diana the Darling Deb? Yes, she certainly was," Tess confirmed, her arched eyebrow reminding Lacy that Tess had never been shy about letting her friends know she thought the entire social coming out business was ridiculous. "Diana and that beastly traitor, Mosely, were deservedly arrested for their treachery. Turns out, they were even married in Joseph Goebbels's apartment in Berlin!" Tess addressed Pem. "The youngest sister, Unity, fawned all over Hitler until she tried to kill herself when war was declared last September."

"Good heavens!" Lacy gasped and glanced at Pem, who also appeared taken aback.

Pat reassured them, "Our dear Debo and her other three sisters were just as appalled as the rest of us at Diana and Unity's disloyalty to the country." She added, "Unlike Diana and Mosely, though, many of the British Union of Fascists leaders escaped internment and have gone underground. Like that German American Bund organization Pem just described, these holdovers are still trying to recruit kindred spirits in favor of aiding and abetting Hitler's plot to invade England."

Lacy shifted her gaze to Victor, wondering out loud, "So, is your new government division in charge of tracking down *those* types?"

"The in-country threats?" Victor nodded. "Something like that."

"And if you succeed in catching them, then what?" Lacy asked.

"We get the local police to arrest them under the Public Order Act."

"And *so* they should!" Pat declared with vehemence. "You can imagine how all this has shaken up our deb brigade. Talk about an 'enemy within.'"

So much had changed since that night at Buckingham Palace and the 400 Club frivolities.

Tess remarked, "What about those wild men from Eire who seem to think the Nazis will let them govern Northern Ireland after any war they hope to win?"

"Unfortunately," Rothschild replied soberly, "our homegrown Irish revolutionaries seem happy to do their best to damage our munitions factories and the country's power grid."

Lacy could only imagine what an exciting newspaper article or even a thriller could be written about Rothschild's work to halt those intent on undermining British national security. "What government department does this unit of yours actually come under?" she asked.

Victor frowned. "This is all supremely hush-hush," he said sternly, "so, Lacy, the little I'm at liberty to tell you, as possible recruits, must be discussed privately in my office."

Tess, Pat, Pem, and Lacy nodded, all four leaning forward, eager to hear whatever additional crumbs of information Victor was willing to share. He pointed at the insignia on his uniform.

"I've just been made an overnight colonel in the British Army, which gives you some idea of how pressed our war effort must be," he noted, downplaying the importance of his military commission. "The in-country unit I'm to head is highly classified." To Lacy, he said, "If you're interested in this work, come to my office tomorrow morning at nine, and I'll fill you in a bit more."

Chapter Eighteen

Lacy was stunned that Victor Rothschild had invited her to his office for a job interview less than an hour after she'd arrived in London. He raised his hand, though, in warning.

"Please note, however," the young baron added with a sardonic smile, "that our three-person division has so little status, it's being housed in a cell in Wormwood Scrubs prison."

"Good gracious!" Tess exclaimed. "You didn't tell me *that*!"

"Lacy rang your doorbell before I could," Victor replied with amusement. "Let's just say the challenge for all of us is to do what we can to halt the threatened German invasion of our shores."

Lacy felt an actual shiver skitter down her spine. She had finally made it to England after eluding Nazi troopers all along the way, and Britain expected the damn Germans to arrive on their island at any moment.

Victor seemed to read Lacy's anxious mind about the imminent threat of a German landing. Smiling faintly, he said, "While our RAF boys are fighting them off in the skies quite splendidly these days, as Tess said, we must all do our bit here on land."

"Hear, hear to *that*," Lacy responded, "but what would Tess and I actually *do* if we joined you in whatever hush-hush work you're leading?"

Not answering her question, he glanced at his watch and declared, "It's time I'm on my way, but, Lacy, why not come to my office tomorrow morning? I'll outline the full roster of duties of my two assistants to see if this would be a good fit. For all of us," he added.

Almost dizzy and disoriented from the rapid chain of events, Lacy could only stammer, "Y-yes. Thank you."

Victor nodded. "Tess can serve as your guide to our prison cell headquarters—yes, Tess?" Baron Rothschild then inclined his head toward Pem, who swiftly rose to his feet and clasped the baron's extended hand. "Good to meet you, Doctor," Victor said. "I wish you all the best and hope we meet again. And remember," he added, his voice suddenly steely, "this conversation never happened." To Tess and Pat, he murmured, "I'll just show myself out."

Pem looked over at Lacy and warned, "I'm afraid I should be heading for my train." He reached for her hand. "I hope you're coming to see me off?"

Lacy could only nod as she rose to join him, struck by the reality that after all those months together, she was uncertain when she would see Pem again.

"Just ring the bell downstairs when you get back," Tess said warmly to her new flatmate, "and we'll have your bed made up and ready for you."

<hr>

Lacy's emotions were in turmoil as she stood in the echoing expanse of Euston Station, with whistles shrieking warnings that trains were about to depart. She watched from several feet away while Pem waited to see whether the ticket agent would accept his army voucher for rail passage to Manchester. As she witnessed their exchange, she fought against the wave of sadness settling over her, a feeling which had intensified as soon as they'd had supper at a nearby café and come to the station.

I already miss Pem even before he's departed, and when I think about poor Noah ...

Yet, at least she had an affordable place to live and might have so quickly found a way to keep body and soul together by working for Victor now that she was finally back in London. Enrolling at the LSE had faded to the background at that point, but hadn't her main plan been to try to land a journalist's job? Chances were, though, she'd be slotted right back into a dog's body position at the *Baltimore Sun* with its lowly pay scale for women confined to proofreading obituaries, like before. At least a job in Victor's unit would mean she'd join the fight against the Nazis who'd so cruelly arrested Noah.

Vaguely aware that Pem and the ticket agent were deep in conversation, Lacy had a sudden thought. Perhaps she could make enough money employed in Lord Rothschild's unit to pay her bills while working on the book she'd been mulling over, which would describe her harrowing journey through Nazi-occupied territory in the wake of Hitler's lightening takeover of Central Europe.

"America's got to *wake up*," she'd exclaimed to Pem during the taxi ride to the station, revealing that she'd had an account of their trip percolating in the back of her mind. "Hitler's goal is obviously to take over all of Europe. Even England herself. America can't let that happen!"

Pem's positive reaction had been gratifying. "Maybe you'll get that job with Rothschild that pays your rent and write the book at night!"

Pem always looked on the bright side of life and all its possibilities, Lacy realized, but all she could think of then was that he would be busy in Manchester, preoccupied with learning to be a doctor again. Meanwhile, she'd be in London without him to talk things over with when she hit inevitable roadblocks as a fledgling author.

Would it be that old adage "out of sight, out of mind"?

Just then, Pem appeared at her side with a ticket in hand. She glanced up at the train station's large round clock dominating the departure area.

"I leave from Platform Ten," Pem announced, pointing to the large board over their heads that listed all the trains, "in ... uh ... seven minutes!"

After being inseparable night and day for so long—poof! He'd be gone. And for how long?

Maybe forever?

He took her hand, but she pulled away, her voice catching. "Actually, I-I don't do well watching trains leave the station."

Pem searched her face, raising one hand to brush away the tears that had slipped down her cheeks. "You were always the one leaving on a train, weren't you?" he said softly.

"Mostly, yes." She struggled to keep her voice steady. "Sometimes, though, Teddy and I would be brought to a station to see off my mother and a man I hardly knew departing for somewhere exotic. Once they were gone, our latest nanny would escort us onto another train destined for the next boarding school."

"Then I won't ask you to go with me to Platform Ten," he said quietly. "We can say our goodbyes right here." He cupped her face in his hands and bent his head down, kissing her for a long and lingering moment. Finally releasing her, he murmured in her ear, "I love you, Lacy, so please remember that. I promise I'll write you the moment I know what my address is." He gazed directly into her eyes, insisting, "And *you* have to promise to write me right back, yes?"

"I promise," she replied, barely above a whisper. "But you write first."

He nodded, kissed her briefly on the forehead, then turned away. Watching his receding back as he strode toward his train, Lacy found herself imagining how little time he'd probably have to maintain a correspondence.

As for her future, only Victor Rothschild could confirm whether she actually had a job.

Lacy and Tess emerged from the steps of the East Acton tube station in the Hammersmith section of London. The muggy early-September atmosphere was curling the wisps of hair that had escaped the chignon Lacy had carefully coiffed in anticipation of their joint interview with Victor Rothschild. On the one-year anniversary of England declaring war on Germany, the two young women trudged a few hundred meters toward the arched entrance of the forbidding sixty-five-year-old Wormwood Scrubs prison. Breathless from the pressure to be on time for their meeting, they entered through a set of large wooden doors flanked by matching four-story towers constructed of massive quantities of red brick, which were punctuated with tiny windows. To Lacy's eye, the pile definitely looked like a place where no prisoners ever escaped.

"Is Victor's new office truly housed in one of the prison *cells*?" she whispered to Tess in the cavernous foyer they'd entered.

"That's what he said last night, but we'll soon find out if he was just joking," Tess replied, casting a glance at the stark, stained white walls and then down at the bare cement floor as their footsteps echoed eerily. "It's just another War Office requisition," she explained, "grabbing whatever buildings they can, I suppose."

At the reception kiosk, they were met by a guard who glanced at a clipboard and then escorted them down a long corridor filled with scurrying figures clad in either army uniforms or three-piece suits.

"Not many women, I see," Lacy murmured to her new roommate.

"I expect not," Tess replied, her voice low.

After a long walk straight ahead, their uniformed companion turned into an intersecting corridor, paused at a door marked B1c, and announced, "Here we are, ducks." He gazed at the two women with obvious curiosity. "When Lord Rothschild came in this morning, I was told that he was expecting you two." He knocked sharply on the metal entrance graced with a small, barred window, waited until Rothschild could be seen approaching through the glass, and then declared, "Cheerio!" before adding, "Best of luck to you, girls," in a tone that indicated they'd need it.

Their escort disappeared around the corner even before the door opened. Lacy suddenly thought of Pem, who was undoubtedly facing *his* first day in an unknown environment at a Manchester army hospital, just as she and Tess were about to be interviewed for jobs in a government department about which they'd likely be sworn to secrecy. Glumly, Lacy figured she and Pem would have less and less in common as time went on. When she'd returned from Euston Station the previous night, she'd reluctantly revealed to Tess and Pat that Pem was married.

Tess had blinked, commenting, "How sad. The way he kept looking at you, I figured that after surviving such an incredible journey together, you and he ... uh ... were—"

"We were," Lacy had admitted, "but given the current status of things, I'm beginning to wonder if the relationship is ... well ... pretty hopeless now that Pem's ordered to Manchester for the foreseeable future."

"From the way he acted toward you," Tess replied, "I'd have more faith it might work out if I were you."

Tess is right, Lacy thought, knowing she needed to stop always assuming things would never go her way.

The prison's metal door suddenly emitted a loud click, jolting Lacy back to reality. Victor stood in the frame, nattily turned out in his Royal Army colonel's uniform but looking for all the world like the banker the Rothschild family had wanted him to be.

But he's no banker anymore, she marveled silently. He was an aristocrat-zoologist heading up some hush-hush operation fighting home-grown Nazis and saboteurs. *Who could have imagined such a thing that night at the 400 Club?* Lacy thought with a sideways glance at Tess greeting Victor as the close friend he was.

"You owe us a gold star for finding our way to this godforsaken place!" Tess announced with a smile.

"You both are entitled to one," Lord Rothschild responded, nodding his head at each of them in turn. "Welcome to my cell, which I sincerely hope will become your personal prison as well. Come in, come in," he invited, gesturing toward two chairs set opposite his desk.

Their interview consisted of Victor coming quickly to the point that his new hires would help him run a "small-but-mighty operation."

"As I indicated yesterday," he continued, "this is an antisabotage division tasked with rooting out in-country German infiltrators, along with Irish and Welsh terrorists bent on securing their countries' independence by siding with the Jerries."

"You mean we'll be spy catchers?" Tess demanded.

Victor shrugged. "Of a sort. This unit, B1c, will be in charge of tracking down British Fascists who've gone underground but are still willing to recruit others to aid and abet Hitler's desire to invade England. We've long suspected that the IRA's local bombing campaign of rail stations and telephone transmission centers may be substantially funded by the Germans—either intelligence agents they've inserted in the country by air or sea or locally grown separatists to whom Hitler is making payments *and* promises he never intends to keep."

"Good heavens," Lacy murmured.

"We're especially anxious to apprehend any Welsh or Irish revolutionaries, along with German infiltrators, to *stop* them before they can weaken our defenses."

Lacy suddenly thought of her brother, Teddy, who'd gone off to the wilds of Ireland when June had tried to order him home. She absolutely had to figure out a way to find out where he was over there. She could only hope he hadn't gotten mixed up with any violent extremists who could land a lonely boy in deep water.

Maybe Lord Rothschild could help me track him down?

Meanwhile, Victor's expression had grown serious. "We've lately gotten wind of something the Germans are calling Operation Sealion, intended as a full-fledged takeover of England. Landings by air and sea are expected any day now, with German operatives first coming in to show the way by pinpointing roads, bridges, and ammunition depots."

"Who's the 'we' in 'we've gotten wind?'" Tess asked.

"British intelligence," he answered shortly.

Tess inquired, "MI5? MI6? Or is it Naval Intelligence?"

"Excellent deduction," Victor commented dryly.

"And your work is a part of all this?" Lacy asked, stunned that she and Tess would even be considered for employment in that realm.

"I've been asked to head the domestic antisabotage and explosives division under the umbrella of MI5."

"Really? *MI5*?" Lacy repeated, exhaling a breath. "That's the government intelligence agency in charge of domestic security, isn't it?"

"Yes, antisabotage fits rather well in that slot, don't you think?" he replied rather sardonically, Lacy thought. "MI5 is much like your FBI, and as you are probably aware, MI6, the Secret Service, operates largely overseas." He paused and then added with nonchalance, "Oh, and by the way ... our little unit will also be in charge of bomb disposal if the German explosives found in Britain are types our authorities have never seen before."

"Our group could be doing *bomb* disposal?" Tess exclaimed. "You never mentioned *that* yesterday!"

"There are regular bomb disposal units being trained throughout the country," he hastened to assure them, "so we'll be called in only on the special cases when a device that no one recognizes and requires my type of expertise turns up."

"How wonderful for you," Tess retorted.

Victor wiggled his ten fingers at them. "My zoologist's fine motor skills for dissecting tiny insects in my Cambridge laboratory have been duly noted by the War Office," he added drolly.

For Lacy's part, she was beyond impressed that Victor, at thirty-three years old, had been put in charge of a laundry list of several very crucial national security matters. "So, basically," she ventured, attempting to sum up for herself and Tess what they might be involved in, "your division of MI5 is to provide in-country secret agents charged with locating German subversives and their proxies operating on British soil—as well as defusing dangerous devices not seen before?"

Victor cast her an admiring look. "Precisely." He pointed at two empty desks facing each other in the small space. "But it won't be, by any means, all cloak-and-dagger work," he noted with a wry smile. He pointed to a stack of folders on each desk. "You two will also verify a fair amount of translations of German transmissions we constantly receive to make sure there aren't nuances that other government translators might have missed. You will also have to go undercover to boring meetings of renegade groups that never really do much. Even so, you must then remain mum on everything you hear and see—including which one of you brews the tea each day at four o'clock."

He handed them each a document with an official-looking letterhead.

"What's that?" Tess asked.

"The Official Secrets Act." He cast his warmest smile in Tess's direction. "I think you'll both do splendidly. And if you'll accept my offer of employment at thirty-three pounds and two shillings a month," he said, pointing to a space at the bottom of the document, "please sign here."

PART TWO
DEBS AT WAR

Chapter Nineteen

The first few days of Tess and Lacy's indoctrination in the world of MI5's highly secretive B1c unit had proven how severely pressed the British government was to recruit people for the war effort. Lacy surmised that the fact that she—an American citizen in her twenties, who would be paid nearly twice as much as a newspaper copy girl—had been asked to join the unit told the tale of just *how* pressed.

"Don't sell yourself short," Tess had insisted. "Our pronunciation in German is far better than that of those Cambridge University secret agents who speak with their posh British accents and are arrested as soon as they open their mouths abroad!"

Near the end of the week, Lacy had received a cryptic note from Pem stating only his address at the hospital in Manchester. Since then, she'd had time to write to him only twice, as she spent her evenings after work reading intelligence dispatches about threats from invading saboteurs. There were pages detailing the enemy's incendiary devices, to say nothing of their twisted plots to blow up transportation centers, the power grid, and munitions factories. Her one genuine letter from Pem had been heavily redacted by some government censor with a heavy black pen.

Victor's first assignments for her turned out to be far tamer than his job description had indicated. Handing her a list of times and addresses, he issued his orders.

"I want you to don your dowdiest frock and find a way to infiltrate these watering holes frequented by members of the barred British Union of Fascists and to visit a few of the Irish social clubs here in London. Our intelligence says they're constantly plotting ways to disrupt neighborhoods all over the city."

"Aren't the former members of the banned BUF now quitting in droves?" Tess asked.

"Yes, but the diehards are still gathering in secret, and it's a good place to look for German spies who may have gotten into the country under the guise of being refugees. Often, they also try to connect with the IRA troublemakers here." To Lacy, he advised, "The BUF-ers and a certain number of Irish living among us will be only too happy to show our unwelcome visitors how to best prepare the way for German troops if the Krauts do, indeed, storm our shores. When you're in the pub, keep your ears peeled for anyone speaking English with an Irish or German accent."

"Do women actually frequent these places?" Lacy asked, wondering how a Yank would fit in.

In his uncanny way, Victor said, "Just pretend you're Boston shanty Irish in sympathy with the Germans and IRA supporters." He paused, his eyes narrowing. "Did you ever read the Official Secrets Act paperwork I had you sign?" he asked.

"Yes, sir," Lacy replied promptly, only too aware that she would risk hanging if she ever divulged anything about the work she was about to do for that little-known branch of MI5.

So much for writing a tell-all book about this, or even a bestselling thriller, she lamented silently.

Victor handed her a sheet of paper. "Here's a list of pubs, cafés, and social clubs where the local Fascists and Irish operatives are wont to spend time." He regarded her steadily. "You're likely to encounter some very convincing characters. Trust *no one*, do you understand? No one."

Lacy nodded, but she wondered whether she knew enough about the world of spies and secret agents to be able to spot one of Hitler's operatives bent on preparing the way for his storm troopers. And she needn't worry about telling Pem any secrets. She'd yet to receive a second letter from him after the heavily censored one. She could only imagine how busy a doctor who'd been assigned to treat those who'd survived the evacuation from Dunkirk must be.

But still …

Lacy peered through the evening gloom across the street on Queensland Road in Islington. Lord Rothschild had informed her that the pub, Hannigan's, was an establishment that had been welcoming Irish settlers living in London as far back as 1871. Even from where she stood, Lacy could hear raucous laughter and the lively sound of Irish pipes, along with "violins that might well set your feet to tapping," as Victor had teased the previous day when he'd given Lacy her first assignment.

Lacy's boss had informed her that, apparently, entire families came to hear music reminiscent of home and that in such a setting, she might have an easier time fitting in with a crowd of Irish expats. On that Saturday evening in mid-September, hers was merely a reconnaissance mission. She was to look and listen for any indications that denizens of a place like that might also belong to groups sympathetic with Irish revolutionaries bent on attacking key sites in England.

"And one or two might even be IRA operatives themselves," Victor had cautioned, "indulging in a brief respite from making mischief by downing a pint of Guinness. Best not to engage in any probing conversations, just chitchat. You need only observe what you see and report back to me."

Until that day, Rothschild had mostly had her typing up his notes or confirming the translations of German wireless transmissions piled in his inbox. Standing across the street from the pub just then, Lacy could feel butterflies begin to flutter in her stomach. After inhaling a steadying breath, she looked in both directions before resolutely approaching the entrance to the pub.

From the dim doorway, Lacy could see and smell the haze of cigarette and pipe smoke and smell the yeasty scent of beer. Slipping into the crowded room, she noticed that most of the women were clustered on one side, gossiping animatedly. Closer to the raised dais where the musicians were playing, men in work clothes or well-worn woolen garb were grouped around tables littered with empty glasses. Lacy edged along the back wall behind the women and tried to be as inconspicuous as possible, her eyes scanning the various knots of people.

A number of men appeared to be engaged in earnest, sometimes heated conversation. To her far right, her attention was swiftly drawn to a young couple; the redheaded woman was pounding her fist on the table while her companion looked away with a sullen expression. As Lacy focused more closely on the lad's sandy hair and scowling face, her mouth suddenly fell open. Her heart began to pound and her head throbbed as she stared across the room at the quarreling pair.

Teddy?

How could that be? For ages, she'd assumed that her younger brother was still in Ireland! How could he be there—not twenty feet away—sitting in a working-class pub in Islington, England?

And why? It had been months of silence from him. Worrying, nightmare-provoking silence.

Oh my God! I can't believe this! There's Teddy!

It was mindboggling that she'd finally located him while on assignment for MI5. She could only stare while Theodore Farrington Forbes received what appeared to be a vicious tongue-lashing from some angry Irish colleen.

Lacy was about to take a step forward to make her presence known when she realized, with a shock, that she was in that pub on an undercover mission for MI5, for pity's sake! The boisterous crowds surrounding her had blocked her view, so she peered around the shoulder of a patron throwing back his pint of Guinness. She wondered, for a split second, whether she was actually hallucinating. Squinting through the veil of cigarette smoke, she saw her brother pump his arm up and down, making a rude gesture she'd seen him do many times before.

Yes, it *was* Teddy, his high cheekbones flushed in anger and looking a good deal thinner and like some scruffy, downtrodden dockworker.

Lacy watched, dumbfounded, as he broke his hostile silence directed at the woman sharing his table and shouted something unintelligible at her over the skirling music blaring from the band. Then he dug into his pants pocket and fished out some cash. Jumping to his feet, he threw down a handful of coins on the table and stormed across the room, elbowing his way through a side door and disappearing into the night.

The redhead with whom Teddy had been arguing tossed back what was left in her glass of ale. With the same scowl Lacy's brother had displayed, she made no attempt to prevent his departure and turned her attention to the table next to her. Leaning forward, she whispered into the ear of a large, broad-shouldered man who looked as if he might be employed as a well-muscled stevedore on the Thames waterfront.

Lacy's breath was ragged from the shock of watching the brief encounter between her brother and the flame-haired girl that had taken place across the noisy bar. When Teddy bolted out the pub's side door, Lacy forgot all thoughts of the assignment Lord Rothschild had given her.

God help us, Teddy! What in hell has happened to you?

Lacy swiftly turned on her heel and sped toward the door through which Teddy had vanished. Outside, she saw her younger brother turn a corner onto Queensland Road, and she instantly gave chase.

Dashing within thirty feet of him, she called out, "Teddy ... *Teddy! Wait!*" but he kept striding forward, ignoring her shouts.

She was glad she'd worn a pair of flat-heeled brogues for her venture into a sketchy part of London and began to hurry faster. Within seconds, she came within a few yards of her brother's hunched figure determinedly marching away from her.

"Teddy, it's *me*! Lacy!" she screamed. "I can't believe I've run into you like this! *Stop, goddamnit!*"

To her relief, Teddy finally halted in his tracks and slowly turned around, a look of utter astonishment spreading across his lean, drawn features.

Lacy, stashing her hands on her hips, declared heatedly, "Yes, that's right. It's your *sister* whom you've totally ignored for *months*!"

"Good God, Lacy!" Teddy replied, clearly dumbfounded to see her in Islington of all places. "What in the world are *you* doing here? I thought you were back in the States by now." He glanced over her shoulder in the direction of the pub but didn't say anything further.

For a moment, Lacy's mind went blank. Instinctively, she knew that she'd best not reveal what she was doing on Queensland Road near a pub frequented by potential Irish revolutionaries on her first assignment for MI5.

Groping for a plausible answer, she managed, "I-I got off at the wrong tube station." In a distant part of her brain, she realized that she'd told her first lie as an intelligence agent. "I couldn't believe it when I spotted you!" She stretched out her arms and felt tears springing to her eyes. "Oh my God, Teddy ... *where* have you been all this time? Why haven't you tried to get in touch with me? Even after war was declared, you never wrote me in Boston or New York. You don't even know that the fake poet died last winter and Mother's been—"

"I don't care one damn thing about Remington Rowe *or* June, and I'm glad to hear he's dead!" he said, fists clenched at his side. "And I was sure that if I contacted you, Mother would find a way to try to track me down. You and I both know the only reason she cares about *us* is to use either you or me to get her mitts on the almighty Forbes and Farrington family trusts." Teddy scowled at Lacy with the same ferocity he'd bestowed on the Irish girl inside the pub. "I'm through with everything and anyone having to do with our god-awful families!" he exclaimed, nearly shouting. "I don't want their money, and I *do* want them out of my life! Forever!"

"I don't blame you," Lacy replied in a low voice, "except for Granny Farr."

To her surprise, a faint smile appeared at the corner of her younger brother's mouth. "Of course, except for Granny Farr—and you."

"Mother ordered me back to the States when Rem ... uh—"

"Offed himself in the arms of his latest mistress?" Teddy said with disgust.

At her look of surprise that he'd heard of the scandal, he elaborated, "It was a juicy story in all the papers, even on the Emerald Isle."

"I rushed back to New York on her command, and she'd already buried him, can you believe?"

"Of course I can. She wanted you back for her own purposes, didn't she?" Before Lacy could answer, he held out his arms. "Come here," he said, his voice lowering. A sweet look she remembered from their childhood lit up his face. He enfolded her in a bear hug. "God, it's good to see my guardian angel sister!"

She was touched he referred to all the times she'd shielded him as best she could from the self-absorbed, sometimes cruel adults they'd grown up with. On numerous occasions, she'd even tried to rescue him from problematic situations that were Teddy's own doing. As she embraced her brother, Lacy was shocked to feel how prominent his shoulder bones felt beneath his moth-eaten cardigan. His every aspect spoke of someone with threadbare clothes who'd rarely enjoyed three square meals a day. Whatever world his Irish cronies had inhabited, it must have been far from the milieu of posh boarding schools and glamorous vacation spots of their youth. Gazing at the dark circles ringing his eyes and his unkempt appearance, she felt like crying.

She pulled away from his arms and proposed, "Look, we can't talk here. Why don't you come back to my flat with me and I'll fill you in on my latest adventure escaping from Nazis in Norway. You can have a nice warm bath and let me make you dinner."

"You can *cook*?" he teased. "Well, that's quite a change from the useless nonsense they taught you at all those finishing schools."

"Well, at least I learned to speak French and German," she reminded him, "which we both may find useful in making a living, given the war."

"Well, I failed both," Teddy admitted with a smirk, "although the smattering of German I did retain does have its uses at times."

Lacy found his last statement a bit worrying and wondered what other thoughts were circulating in his brain. She felt him peering into her face.

"Good God, Sis ... I think I should ask you *exactly* what you've been up to since last we met."

Just at that moment, Lacy spotted a lone cab trundling down the street in their direction. Without consulting Teddy, she stretched out her arm to hail it, but before the vehicle could reach her, the sound of a sudden roar drew her eyes skyward. The deafening noise grew louder by the second as she saw that a fleet of approaching aircraft were darkening the horizon. She stared with growing alarm as they began swooping down low over the city. Lacy could just make out decals of Iron Crosses plastered on their wings and tail sections.

"Teddy! Look!" she cried. "Aren't those *German* planes?"

Her brother swiveled his head and stared up at a swarm of twin-engine bombers drawing ever closer. Reverberations of explosions began to rend the air.

"Those are Heinkel bombers!" Teddy declared, and Lacy briefly wondered how he could so handily identify specific planes in a German squadron.

Then her memory flashed on Lord Rothschild's warning that an invasion of the island nation had been forecast to launch anytime. Was this the first foray?

Before she could utter another word, Teddy grabbed ahold of her hand and commanded, "Quick! Let's go! These guys mean business. We'll make a run for the tube station!"

Without a second's hesitation, Lacy joined her brother dashing pell-mell toward the sign outside the nearby Islington Station that read Air Raid Shelter with an arrow pointing downward. Once inside, they speedily descended multiple flights of stairs while the impact of explosions shook the very ground beneath their feet.

When they finally arrived at the tube station's lowest level, Lacy exclaimed between uneven breaths, "I need you to tell me ... what the hell ... *you've* been up to ... baby brother mine!"

Teddy made no answer. With her right hand still held tightly in his left, she glanced at a knot of startled, stranded tube riders standing nearby who appeared not to know in which direction to proceed.

"Everybody, get down on the ground!" Teddy ordered, crouching against the walls of their subterranean retreat just as terrifyingly loud sounds of detonating bombs thundered overhead.

Chapter Twenty

The chill from the cold white wall tiles penetrated the back of Lacy's wool coat during the long hour she and Teddy huddled on the concrete flooring in the nether regions of the tube station. Nearby were other Saturday travelers equally grateful to be sheltered from the bombs pummeling Islington above ground.

The cacophony of explosions finally abated, and while the two siblings waited impatiently for an all-clear siren, Lacy was determined to learn precisely where Teddy had been since they'd last seen each other on a ski holiday in Chamonix, France, eighteen months earlier.

To start off the conversation, she gave a short monologue describing her "serving as an assistant typist to a zoologist, Baron Rothschild," along with her earlier efforts for the Red Cross raising funds for the Finland Field Hospital, which had been followed immediately by the German invasion of Norway.

"No kidding?" he said. "German troops arrived one day later? That must have been a bit dicey."

"It was," she said with a nod, as all the terrifying moments with Pem and Noah flooded back. She looked sharply at Teddy. "I want to write a book about some of the dreadful things I saw the Nazis do on our trek back to Britain."

"Hmmm," was Teddy's only response.

She waited for him to pick up the conversation, but he remained silent.

"So," she said, keeping her tone light, "I've filled you in on *my* exciting months since I saw you last. Now it's your turn to tell me what you and your Irish pals have been up to and why you left Ireland."

Teddy looked at her for a long moment, volunteering nothing.

Lacy demanded, "Well, are you at least willing to tell your older sister what you are doing in such a seedy-looking section of Islington?" Teddy's right eyebrow shot up, but again, he didn't answer. Lacy tried to make him meet her glance. "I take it things didn't work out for you as you'd wished in Ireland? Is that why you're here in England?"

It alarmed her to no end that her brother had been frequenting a watering hole Rothschild judged to be a place where IRA troublemakers gathered. Her MI5 boss's entire mission was to prevent any plots threatening to harm the British anti-invasion effort at home and put a stop to further violent Irish acts of independence.

Could Teddy have become a supporter of such activities?

In a way, Lacy's own rebellious American heart couldn't blame him if he had embraced Ireland's wish for independence, but the Allies were fighting the threat to all democracy that German aggression presented. She could only pray her brother hadn't been brainwashed by Irish militants to commit violence when MI5 intelligence agents believed they were in the pay of Herr Hitler.

Finally, Teddy began, "I'm here in London ..." He then fell silent once more, clearly choosing his words as carefully as she had chosen hers. "I'm here with friends of mine who came over to ... uh ... visit relatives."

He's fibbing without lying ... just like I was.

"Irish relatives," Lacy surmised. "Which relatives? The kind who aren't particularly sympathetic to Britain's war against Germany?" She shifted her tone. "I hope you don't think Hitler and his henchmen will keep their promises and grant Irish independence if the Jerries ultimately conquer Great Britain." She sought to meet his gaze. "*Promise* me, Teddy, you won't get yourself involved in something dangerous ... or treasonous!"

She watched as his mouth formed a grim line.

"You've told me about your typist job for some Jew aristocrat," he countered harshly. "Does that mean you're part of the British toffs now?"

"For God's sake, Teddy!" she exclaimed, her voice echoing across the empty tube platform. "What I am is one of the few members of the Farrington-Forbes family that actually *cares* about your welfare!"

Just then, the piercing sound of the all-clear siren wailed throughout the expanse of underground tile and concrete. Teddy swiftly stood up and pulled Lacy to her feet.

"Well ... you now can head back on a train to wherever you were going," he said, abruptly turning away from her.

"Wait!" she cried, fishing for a pencil and a scrap of paper in her handbag. She could see that he was anxious to escape any more of her questions. "Here's my address on Gower Street. *Please* keep in touch!"

Teddy bit his lower lip while he considered his answer. "I'll try," he allowed reluctantly, extracting the hastily scribbled note from her fingers, "but it's best if you don't wander into this neighborhood again. There are some tough characters around here, and—"

"If that's so, then why are *you* here?" she interrupted. "Where are you living now?" she demanded. "What are you doing here? How can I find you again?"

In answer to her rapid-fire questions, Teddy's expression shifted from a scowl to a familiar, engaging smile that had charmed many a young lady of his acquaintance. This abrupt change in demeanor alone rendered her highly suspicious of what her brother might truly be up to.

"*Teddy!*" she said with exasperation.

"Don't worry so much." With a jaunty wave of the slip of paper Lacy had given him, he assured her, "See? I can always find you on Gower Street, so not to fuss about me, my darling sister. Believe it or not, I'm all grown up now." He offered her a full-fledged grin. "It was great seeing you again, Lacy girl! I've almost missed your mother hen-ing me."

And before she could say another word, he turned and swiftly took the nearby staircase two steps at a time. Lacy watched him push past their fellow refugees from the aerial attack and disappear onto Queensland Road.

Lacy faced Lord Rothschild's desk, which was sandwiched within the narrow confines of Wormwood Scrubs' typical prison cell. Tess was at her desk, typing furiously. Victor closed his second deputy's report about her expedition to Islington and her observations within the pub called Hannigan's. To her great relief, he nodded his approval.

"So, from what I read here," he said, placing the folder in a stack for Lacy to file later, "MI5's sources were correct. Hannigan's is definitely frequented by Irish types that might well be bent on making mischief in Britain."

"*Was* frequented," Tess interjected with a shudder. "Victor, you saw the newspaper pictures. It was leveled by the bombing."

"Perhaps a few less troublemakers for us to deal with," he muttered.

Lacy thought about the redhead arguing with Teddy and wondered whether she and the others at the pub had heeded the warning sirens and taken shelter.

"As for what I saw before the sirens went off," she volunteered, blotting the scene of devastation from her mind as best she could, "I can only report that members of the crowd there all seemed to know each other well, and they did seem ... uh ... to be a rough sort. Then that bomber attack happened, and I ran for the shelter."

Lacy was experiencing severe pangs of guilt for not reporting her unexpected encounter with her brother or revealing how little forthcoming he'd been as to why he and his friends were patrons there. Nor did she disclose that the Teddy and the redhead had quarreled furiously before he bolted out the door.

In retrospect, it had concerned Lacy that the young woman's behavior after Teddy left had indicated that she was very familiar with the heavyset man into whose ear she had whispered. It had looked suspicious, as if he might have been a leader of some sort. But until—more like *if*—Lacy learned more about whether her brother's associates were members of the active IRA, she'd decided to remain silent to protect him from the often-heavy hand of British law when it came to the Irish in England.

"Good work on this first assignment," Victor said with a distracted wave of his hand. He then bent over the next folder he was due to inspect. Looking up, he added, "And I'm so sorry you were caught in that hellfire from the bloody Luftwaffe."

Tess volunteered to Lacy, "You should have heard the blasts that went off that day near Gower Street, but luckily, no damage on *our* block."

Victor had a grim expression clouding his face. "The War Office has adopted the Germans' term 'London *Blitzkrieg*' for what happened last Saturday, and I fear we're in for a lot more of the same. I suspect our enemy is trying to soften us up in preparation for their promised invasion, although our RAF boys are giving them a good aerial thrashing, thank God."

"But the damage all over London has been terrible," Tess protested.

"All the more reason to know where the shelters are as you come and go from here," Victor cautioned his two assistants. "And keep those blackout curtains drawn tight at your flat, you two." Lacy and Tess nodded as Lord Rothschild pointed to Lacy's desk. "There's a pile of German wireless intercepts sent over from Bletchley waiting for you over there, girls. Keep a look out for any mentions of something the Krauts are calling Operation Lena." He glanced at the next file he was due to read, adding, "No rest for the weary around here, I'm afraid."

Returning home from work one week before Christmas, Lacy and Tess had barely closed the door to the Gower Street flat when their roommate, Pat, came running down the hallway to greet them.

"Quick! Get dressed! We're all going to the 400 Club tonight! And you won't *believe* who is going to meet us there."

"The usual crowd, I suspect," Tess replied, tiredly shedding her coat and hanging it on one of the hooks in the hallway. "The Two *B*s —Blunt and Burgess—along with Kim Philby and his pals from MI6, don't you imagine?"

"Hard to believe they've all found a perch in foreign intelligence, isn't it?" Pat said, shaking her head. "I mean, given what pro-Russkies most of them are."

Tess gave a laugh. "My posh Cambridge classmates fancy themselves wildly radical, but when it comes down to it, they're an elite bunch enjoying the usual benefits of the Old Boys Network landing good jobs in the government."

"Oh, bother with all that!" Pat said with a grin. She turned to Lacy, her eyes alive with excitement. "You'll never *guess* who else came by here today!" Before Lacy could reply, she screeched, "That adorable Yank doctor of yours, that Pembroke fellow!"

"Pem is in *London*?" Lacy cried, dropping her coat on the floor. "He came here? To Gower Street?"

"Yes," Pat replied, clapping her hands, "and he's managed to get a room at the Ritz for the night, can you believe? I told him we were all going to the 400 Club tonight. He said he'd meet us there but had some appointments to keep first."

Stunned, Lacy could only ask, "Did he say why he'd come down here?" Silently, she wondered why he'd hardly written to her at all and given her no advance warning of his arrival.

Pat shrugged. "We only spoke a moment at the door. He said he had a lot of things he had to do while here, although what they were, I haven't a clue."

All three women said simultaneously, "Hush-hush, right?"

"What *isn't*?" Tess added with a sigh. She put an arm around Lacy, sympathizing, "Don't be too upset that he didn't alert you he was coming down from Manchester. It's wartime," she reminded both friends needlessly. "Nobody tells anybody *anything* these days, and half the time, the phones don't work and the mail never arrives."

Lacy could only summon a nod, reflecting upon the way she'd withheld from her boss the information that her long-troubled brother had been frequenting a known IRA watering hole. In like manner, Pem hadn't said anything in advance, but here he was in London. The ultimate irony for herself, Lacy mused, was that her signing the Official Secrets Act dictated that she couldn't even tell Pem she'd finally seen Teddy when she and Pem met tonight.

But didn't she have a duty to tell her boss she'd met up with her brother at Hannigan's?

Teddy's my only sibling ... and maybe those are just his pals.

Lacy suddenly felt as if a stone had lodged in her stomach, and she'd never felt lonelier or more isolated in her life.

The taxi, its headlights shuttered in accordance with blackout restrictions, entered Leicester Square and pulled up to the entrance to the 400 Club at Number 28A. Clutching the long skirt of her lavender taffeta evening gown, Lacy was the last to get out of the backseat. She heard, before she saw, the effusive greetings that Charles Pembroke was receiving from her boisterous roommates.

"It's lovely to see you again!" Tess exclaimed.

Pat chimed in, "And how sweet of you to be waiting here to greet us." She flung out a gloved hand in Lacy's direction. "And I bet I know why," she added with a sly smile, stepping back to provide Lacy a path to his side.

Pem had somehow located the black-tie attire required for entrance to the 400 Club and looked way beyond handsome in his evening clothes.

"Lacy!" he greeted her, smiling broadly. "They promised to deliver you tonight, and here you are, looking stunning, as usual. Good work, girls!" he praised her flatmates.

Lacy was suddenly in his arms, the feel of his height and strength enfolding her and filling her with a happiness she'd almost forgotten existed.

"Come on, you two," Pat said with a laugh. "Let's get downstairs to the club before any air raid sirens go off tonight."

Chapter Twenty-One

The group of friends headed to the lower-level establishment known as the nighttime headquarters of London society. The eighteen-piece orchestra that Lacy remembered from the evening of her presentation at court was playing softly, and the tiny dance floor was packed with bodies clinging closely, hardly moving.

As Pat had foretold, the large table at the back had already been claimed by the "usual suspects," as she called the trio of Kim Philby and Burgess and Blunt, along with Victor Rothschild.

To Lacy's relief, after they greeted the group, everyone, including Victor, appeared pleased to see Dr. Pembroke again. Without further conversation, Pem led her to two chairs positioned at the far end of the table. "So we can talk," he whispered.

The moment they were settled after a waiter poured them two glasses of Veuve Clicquot somehow smuggled in from France, Pem squeezed her hand and said, "So you took the job with Lord Rothschild." Taking a sip from her glass, she nodded. Pem said, "I imagine, like the work I'm doing these days, yours, too, is probably very—"

"Hush-hush?" Lacy interrupted with a laugh. "Yes, it is, but since he gave both you and me a general outline of our in-country antisabotage work that day you first met him, you can probably imagine what our unit is doing."

Pem took another sip of champagne. "Since you're working domestically, I'm guessing you're under MI5, right?"

"I never said that," she replied, suppressing a small smile. "So, what about you?" she asked. "What can you tell me about what you're doing at the Manchester hospital?"

"I'm not there anymore," he replied. "Well, not exactly."

He chuckled at her look of surprise and confusion, lowering his voice so as not to be heard above the buzz of conversations swirling around them. With the music playing in the background to muffle his words, he pressed his lips close to her ear, his breath shockingly arousing.

"The hospital administrator found out I was also trained as an architect and designer. Now they've got me designing hospital trains," he whispered back, "or at least improving the terrible ones someone designed during the last war."

"You mean trains that carry actual patients from battlefields? As in Dunkirk?" she murmured, imagining the thousands that had been hurt in that fiasco.

He paused, then whispered again, "Just like with the field hospital designs, I was allowed to combine my medical knowledge with my passion for practical design. I couldn't believe my luck!"

Lacy shook her head. His latest assignment had been so Pem. After arriving in Britain with no visa, the man had landed squarely on his feet doing what he loved.

"So, why did they let you come to London?" she asked.

Pem looked at her without answering at first. After a long pause, he revealed, "Because I'm being recalled to Walter Reed Hospital in the States."

"To design hospital trains for *our* government?" Lacy surmised out loud.

"I never said that," he replied with a deadpan expression, echoing her earlier quip.

"But the US isn't in this war yet, so why are they sending you to Washington instead of keeping you working in the UK?" she protested, realizing instantly Pem's news meant he would be leaving Britain.

"I asked the Brits to contact my former professor at Harvard for any books the medical library might have on our own hospital trains manufactured during the Great War. Apparently, he told important people in D.C. about my design work in the UK, and so, higher-ups on both sides of the Atlantic waved some magic wands, and bingo—"

"The rest is history," Lacy interrupted glumly. "So, you're leaving. When?"

Pem looked down at his champagne glass for a long moment before he met her gaze and said, "Tomorrow night, on a special Pan Am flight taking some bigwigs to Washington."

"Ah, so now *you're* a bigwig," she said, struggling to keep her tone light. "Are you going to enlist in the U.S. Army while you're there?"

Pem seized her hand under the table and held it tight. "Look, Lacy, I've already been ordered not to discuss this with anyone, but I can tell you this much ... It all could be good for us," he insisted. "I imagine I'll be back here in a few months' time."

"To do what, exactly?" Lacy demanded.

"Can't say, exactly."

"*Won't* say," she countered.

Pem leaned forward and whispered into her ear, "Because I *can't* say."

"It obviously has to do with hospital trains," she said flatly. "British and American ones."

"I never said that," he repeated and tried to coax a smile from her.

"And you want to do this? Take risky flights back and forth across the Atlantic?"

Pem paused, and Lacy could see he was marshaling an argument for a decision he'd already made.

"Having the opportunity to be a designer of ... uh ... whatever might be needed right now is a damn sight more rewarding for everyone than watching these poor boys die as a result of their god-awful wounds under the unskilled medical care provided by a doctor as inexperienced as I am."

Pem's beseeching gaze was pleading for her to understand and support his decision, whatever it was. At bottom, she did support what he was doing, but her mind was swirling over the implications for their relationship. Of course, she recognized what an important contribution his design work could be for thousands of people wounded in the increasingly brutal war.

"They're lucky to have you on both sides of the Atlantic," she murmured. Abruptly changing the subject, she asked the question that had immediately popped into her mind as soon as he'd revealed he was returning to the States. "So, I expect you'll be paying a visit to Boston while you're there."

From the moment she had learned he was heading back to America, she'd been unable to keep a vision of Pem's reunion with Eleanor out of her thoughts.

This is so hopeless.

Suddenly, she wanted to dash out of the club, hail a cab, flee back to the Gower Street flat, and pull the covers over her head. Pem was *leaving*. He had huge important tasks ahead of him. They both did.

During war … love and romance with a married man can only end in despair for the other woman, she thought, tears threatening as she fought to retain her composure.

"Lacy!" Pem said, his breath warm in her ear. "I can see on your face you're already giving up on us, but don't do that!" His lips brushed her cheek, bringing her even closer to crying. "I love you. I will show you I can make this right for us! It's just, with the war and all, it can't be done quickly." Abruptly, he stood up from the table, announcing to whoever was paying attention, "It's my last night in London, so Lacy and I will be off. Goodnight, everyone. It was good to see you all again."

Guy Burgess, three sheets to the wind, as usual, looked up from pouring himself another glass of whiskey. "So … the Yank is already tired of our company." He took a swig of the amber liquid sloshing in his glass and glanced at Tony Blunt and Kim Philby. "Well, we're certainly tired of *his*."

"Guy!" Tess admonished him. "Let me order you some food."

As if nothing untoward had just transpired, Blunt and Philby resumed their conversation while Pem grabbed Lacy's hand.

"What a total jerk!" Lacy said under her breath.

"Roger that," Pem replied as he led her toward the door they'd come in. "I've got a room at the Ritz just waiting for us."

They were halfway up the stairs near the street when the sirens began to wail.

"Oh *shit!*" Pem said. He made an about-face and hustled her toward a sign that pointed to a designated shelter beneath the club located in an even lower basement situated below the kitchen.

As they raced down the echoing stairwell, the first of a loud series of explosions shook the walls. Lacy sent up a prayer that her friends had heeded the warning and fled to some other area of the building. Her mind flashed on the moments she and Teddy had hunkered down in the Islington tube station. She felt Pem pull her down to the floor. Arms around each other, they huddled together, dressed in their elegant evening clothes, alongside some of the club's kitchen staff clad in their worn and grease-spattered attire.

For what seemed like hours, the bombs continued to fall. Lacy squeezed her eyes shut, tucked her head under Pem's chin, and held on to him for dear life, terrified the building above them would collapse in a cacophony of sound and fury.

At two in the morning, the all clear finally sounded. Pem pulled Lacy to her feet and rubbed his hands up and down her arms as she shivered in the cold.

"We're *okay*, sweetheart," he assured her, "but that sure was something, wasn't it?"

To steady her nerves, Lacy forced herself to inhale several deep breaths. "This was my *second* air raid, and trust me," she replied, "it doesn't get any better with practice. The German word 'blitz' describes it perfectly."

Pem nodded and then led her up the three flights of stairs, the others who'd sheltered with them following behind. Reaching the street level, relief flooded Lacy when she spotted the group from their table standing on the sidewalk several yards ahead. To her amazement, Deborah Mitford and Andrew Cavendish were also among the crowd milling under the tattered awning of the 400 Club. Earlier, Tess had told Lacy that their fellow debutante Debo had let it be known to her circle of friends that she'd been appalled at her sister Diana's marriage to Britain's most famous Fascist, Sir Oswald Mosely, and that both were in prison.

Losing sight of Deborah and her escort, Lacy heard several women in front of them murmuring, "Oh my God! I can't *believe* it. Look ... half of the street's practically gone!"

Lacy had smelled the destruction before she had a clear view of the 400 Club's exterior. The building had suffered serious damage to one corner, but its broken windows and pockmarked façade were nothing compared to the destruction surrounding them.

"Pem, look at all that smoke and fire!" Lacy exclaimed, pointing to the shells of several nearby structures where dancing flames glowed orange and black behind a few walls that remained standing.

Fire brigades were arriving in droves, their sirens wailing. Stunned survivors were stumbling out of front doors and standing silently in the street.

To Lacy's astonishment, a handsome limousine suddenly appeared from around the corner, dodged a few piles of detritus littering the streets from the bombing, and halted at the curb. Victor Rothschild scanned the area and hailed Pem and Lacy, who were hemmed in by knots of people near the entrance.

"My car was parked in St. James's near my flat," he explained, gesturing for them to join him. As they drew closer, he said, "Fortunately, my chauffeur was due to pick me up and waited in a garage until he could dodge the worst of it. Can I give you both a lift ... and Tess too? Pat found an escort who is taking her for a nightcap somewhere."

Pem indicated a stretch of road littered with more rubble. "I'm staying at the Ritz," he told Victor, "just down Piccadilly here, but do you really think your driver could manage to get past all the—"

Victor interrupted briskly, "The Ritz is less than half a mile. It's no bother. My man, Alfred, will navigate around this mess. Do get in, you two."

Noticing that Victor's car had been fitted out with the required shuttered headlights, Lacy was torn about whether she should disembark with Pem at the Ritz or dutifully bid farewell when the car got there and go home with Tess.

Pem's leaving tomorrow!

Lacy could see that if she went straight home, it would be one way to face the inevitable sooner rather than later. Pem would soon be gone and their relationship increasingly untenable.

Before she could decide, Pem spoke up. "As it happens, I've invited Lacy for a nightcap. Can I entice you two to join us?"

Tess looked inquiringly at Victor, who answered for both of them. "That's very kind of you, but I've had a long week, and so has Tess.

We'll drop you first and just be on our way to St. James's—but thank you so much. Another time, perhaps?"

"Let's plan for that," Pem replied.

Is Tess going to spend the night with Victor? Lacy wondered, shocked to hear the two men figuring out their post-Blitz logistics without consulting either of the women seated in the car.

Tactfully, Pem volunteered, "I'll see that Lacy gets home safely."

What's safe about spending the night with a man I'm not likely to see for months, years—or ever? Lacy wondered, her heart sore.

Within minutes, Victor's limousine pulled to a stop in front of the Ritz Hotel's sandbagged entrance.

"At least tonight's bombing hasn't rained down here," Tess said, peering out the window with a shudder. "Lacy and Pem could have been killed tonight if they'd left the club three minutes earlier."

Pem pulled Lacy close to him, and despite her confusion about what would happen next, she felt relieved to feel his arm around her shoulders. Victor exchanged smiles with Pem as his chauffeur opened the rear door.

"Have a pleasant night and safe travels, Doctor," Victor said, nodding to Lacy, clearly expecting her to exit the vehicle as well.

She'd allowed the decision to be made for her ... and half of her wasn't sorry.

Bidding them goodnight, Lacy could only surmise that wartime seemed to have suspended moral judgments as to the conduct of married men ... and the women who cared for them. Tess's sympathetic attitude about Lacy's relationship with Pem had confirmed her suspicion that her flatmate *was* actually having an affair with their boss.

The car with Victor and Tess hadn't turned the corner and disappeared before Lacy faced Pem, asking softly, "Why are we doing this?"

"Because it's my last night in Britain?" Pem replied, answering her question with a question.

Lacy shook her head in frustration. "You're about to cross the Atlantic at a treacherous time, and if you *do* make it safely to Walter Reed, you're bound to discover that you're a very busy, very married man," she said pointedly. She looked down at her black satin shoes and lowered her voice, struggling to keep her emotions under control. "At this juncture, you and I going upstairs to your hotel room seems pretty pointless—all things considered—don't you think? You're going back to your old life ... And what about Eleanor?"

Her words hung heavy in the chilly air outside the hotel.

Pem didn't answer but gently seized her elbow and guided her into the hotel lobby, deserted at that late hour except for a desk clerk busily consulting paperwork.

"First we have a nightcap," Pem said, leading her behind a tall, potted fern for privacy. "Then we'll have all night for me to convince you exactly why we are doing this."

Chapter Twenty-Two

Lacy stared through the fronds of the potted palm at the desk clerk sitting across the Ritz Hotel's deserted lobby.

"Convince me right now why I should go upstairs with you when you'll be leaving tomorrow! Why is this a good idea ... for *me*?" she demanded, close to tears.

"Because I love you, Lacy! You're the most important person in the world to me!" His grip on her arm tightened. "Leaving you here in London is the last thing in the world I want to do, but the job I'm being asked to do is bigger than you and me. The damn *war* and how it's killing and wounding people is, sadly for you and me, more important than either of us," he pleaded. "I don't want to leave here without holding you all night and making love to you. I want to leave London feeling that what I'll be doing and risking are worth it because *you're* in my life!"

He drew her close, kissed her hard, then pulled away, moisture filling his eyes.

"But Pem—" she began.

"It's *you* I want to survive this for," he interrupted her mid-sentence. "Don't you feel the same?"

By that time, tears had begun to spill down her cheeks and, to her shock, his as well. Perhaps it was the bombs dropping or the searing terror that they might have died in the basement of the 400 Club that night, but Lacy abruptly seized Pem's hand and nodded toward the elevator to their left. The doors had just opened, and the smartly uniformed operator gazed at them questioningly.

Before they stepped inside, she murmured, "Yes, I feel exactly the same. Let's go upstairs."

As 1940 became 1941 in the weeks following Pem's departure for Washington, Lacy found her thoughts constantly drifting to heated memories of her last night with Pem, shadowed by feelings of desolation and a strange sense of abandonment. She tried not to think that Pem was on the same continent as his wife of eight years. And given what both the U.S. government and the British War Office were probably asking him to do, seeking a divorce had to be low on his very long priority list, she concluded.

One evening in late January, Tess put down her spoon beside a bowl of watery cabbage soup and declared, "You've hardly said a word tonight." She paused and laid a sympathetic hand on Lacy's. "Look, you would have heard by now if that Pan Am flight had been shot down."

"So why haven't I had a word from *Pem*?" Lacy demanded. She'd spent the last four weeks trying, as Tess had urged, to keep the faith, but Pem's silence had seemed deafening.

"Half the ships traveling between America and England are being blown out of the water by German U-boats," Tess replied, "and the bags of mail they carried are at the bottom of the Atlantic with them, I suspect. Have you written *him*?"

"Yes," Lacy retorted. "I didn't write him at Walter Reed Hospital because of the secrecy he indicated was involved in whatever he was exactly doing there," she said carefully, "but I wrote to an address I had for him at the Harvard Field Hospital project in Massachusetts."

Tess shook her head. "Who knows if they'll forward it to wherever he was ultimately assigned."

"But I haven't had even a postcard since he left!"

Tess said soothingly, "He's probably constricted by the same hush-hush world we're living in with telephones and cables restricted and the censors making it hardly worthwhile to send *even* a postcard!"

Lacy kept silent about her unhappy and probably neurotic visions of Pem returning to visit Eleanor in Boston. Her throat tight, she said, "I keep repeating like a mantra, 'What do I expect? He's a married man!' At times, our relationship seems hopeless to me, Tess!"

"There's a war on."

"I *know* that!" Lacy shot back testily.

"And if you love someone," Tess added quietly, "it's never hopeless."

Lacy stared at her cooling soup. "With this horrible war, who knows if we'll ever cross paths again?" She swiped her eyes with her linen napkin, muttering, "Bombs falling all over England every night. Entire neighborhoods getting blown up. What chance is there Pem and I will ever be together? Let's be real here, Tess. I haven't heard a single *word*! Maybe it's all for the best."

"Don't be daft," Tess scoffed. "From what I saw the night at the 400 Club, he's mad about you, wife or no wife." She leaned forward, patting Lacy's hand, adding, "No, I rather think with the Blitz and everything else, the normal rules of life, to say nothing of marital decorum, are suspended during wartime. This Eleanor person may live somewhere in the wilds of Boston, but the good Doctor Pembroke is madly in love with *you*."

"Boston's not wild. It's quite civilized," Lacy reminded her, wishing she had as much faith as Tess did that love conquered all, "and so is Mrs. Charles Pembroke the Third of Brookline, Massachusetts. Trust me, we can assume Eleanor Choate Pembroke is *very* civilized."

Tess waved her hand as if Lacy's remarks meant nothing. She leaned forward across their small round dining table and winked. "Now, finish this terrible cabbage soup and hold on to what you know to be true about that lovely man because you never know what might happen next."

Not knowing what might happen next proved to be all too true the very next month. Returning to London after spending a chilly March weekend at Tess's parents' house in Cambridge, Lacy and Tess emerged from the nearby tube station only to confront a sight on Gower Street neither of them would ever forget.

"Our b-building," Lacy stammered, pointing at a smoldering pile of rubble where their townhouse had once stood.

Frozen side by side, the two women stared, stunned to see the devastation the latest bombing had done to their Bloomsbury neighborhood.

"Gone," whispered Tess. "Our entire flat ... is *gone!*"

"And so is half of our street," Lacy murmured.

Tess turned and clutched both Lacy's arms, their gazes meeting. The two of them cried in unison, "*Pat!*"

With Lacy in pursuit, Tess bolted down the block past warning barricades, heading toward the cement stairs that remained the only witness that their home had once stood there.

"Oh my God!" Tess stared into the smoldering ruins and cried, her voice bordering on hysteria, "Pat! *Pat!*"

Just then, a fire warden who had been supervising an emergency unit inspecting the wreckage approached them, his arms waving. "You ladies lived here?" he asked, rushing to their sides.

"Yes," Lacy answered, her arms around Tess to comfort her. "We just came back to London. Our friend ... our flatmate—"

"Not to worry, not to worry," he hastened to assure them. "I spoke to the young lady who said she lived here. She'd headed for the tube shelter in plenty of time to avoid Herr Hitler's latest handiwork. She's fine, bless her. Left the house the minute the sirens sounded, she told me."

"Did she *say* her name?" Tess demanded, wiping her eyes. "Patricia Rawdon-Smith?"

The fire warden nodded. "That's the one. Patricia. She said to let you know if I saw you that she'd be at 'Lord Rothschild's in St. James's, if you please,'" he pronounced, affecting a posh tone. He winked, adding, "Since you girls mingle with the toffs, you're bound to be all right."

Lacy and Tess hugged each other joyfully, and then Tess turned and bussed the fire warden on the cheek, exclaiming, "Thank you! Thank you *so* much!"

Blushing beneath his tin helmet, he admonished them, "Now, don't either of you be going in there to try to find a lipstick or photo album or anything. We're about to close down the street completely until we know the gas lines are shut off and it's safer to breathe the air." He shook his head. "You won't be coming back to live here anytime soon, I'm afraid."

The desolate days grinding toward a late 1941 spring seemed to Lacy to be an exhausting combination of constantly dashing to the nearest air raid shelter, translating German intercepts for Victor for hours at a time, and infiltrating secret meetings of the banned British Union of Fascists to, in Victor's words, "keep an ear to the ground for any potential BUF mischief-making."

And still, she'd had no word from Pem.

The same day that Lacy, Tess, and Pat had found themselves homeless, Victor had promptly offered them a flat within the three floors of the large building he'd leased at 5 Bentinck Street. The owner had allowed him to turn the basement into a well-appointed air raid shelter. Their new quarters were within blocks of the small flat in St. James's that their boss had taken, conveniently close to the MI5 head-quarters.

Victor extended the same generosity to additional Cambridge classmates. "Anthony Blunt and Guy Burgess are also homeless, thanks to the Blitz, but I've given them a place on a different floor, so that should be all right, yes?"

Tess replied, "Perfectly," but Lacy thought to herself, *Well, beggars can't be choosers.*

Lacy didn't consider Tony Blunt as odious as Guy Burgess, but she didn't much like either of their snobbish attitudes toward Americans. Both Burgess and Blunt had signed on with British Intelligence, with the latter having been recruited as a deputy MI5 to one of the higher-ups. On the other hand, it didn't surprise her that Victor had let his Cambridge mates move into his leased property once he'd elected to take smaller quarters in St. James's near his work. His wife had sensibly—and conveniently for Tess—departed London for their country place, away from the nightly bombing.

Later, Lacy asked Pat, "Won't Guy Burgess's notorious carousing, even on the floor above us, become ... well ... a royal pain?"

Pat shrugged. "Possibly, but beggars—"

"Can't be choosers," Lacy finished her sentence. "That's what I figured you'd say."

Soon after the three women moved to their new lodgings, Lacy wearily arrived at Victor's office with little to report after lurking at a ragtag conclave of British Fascists who met in the back room of an antique store. Tess had just brewed tea in their electric kettle and handed Lacy a cup.

"All this group seemed to talk about was their hope the German invasion of their country would come soon, but they divulged nothing concrete because they didn't seem to know much about anything," she said with disgust.

Victor pointed to a file on his desk. "Well, here's something we *do* know. Our code readers sent a dispatch this morning that at least twenty German agents have recently infiltrated England as part of something I mentioned to you before, dubbed Operation Lena."

"Good heavens!" Tess exclaimed, putting down her teacup on her desk to come stand beside Lacy. "Sounds like a mini-invasion has already begun!"

"Did they parachute in?" Lacy wondered aloud.

"Some did ... and some arrived aboard ship," Victor disclosed. "The purpose of this operation seems to be to lay the groundwork for their hoped-for major invasion by finding out where it would be best to land ... map out where our munition storage depots are ... that sort of thing."

Lacy could only imagine what might be ahead with just the three of them in their tiny antisabotage unit trying to cope not only with the homegrown sympathizers but also with actual German spies sneaking onto their shores.

Victor continued, "At the end of last September, two men and a woman landed by seaplane in Moray Firth and rowed ashore in a rubber dinghy. They've all since been apprehended and held in Scotland."

"Well, that was lucky that they were caught so quickly," Tess said.

"Quite," Victor replied. "Recently, the woman has been brought down to London." To Lacy, he said, "I've arranged for you to go to the prison where she's being held and see what you can learn from her."

Me? Lacy thought. She was surprised he'd chosen her over Tess for the assignment. Her heart beginning to speed up, she asked, "You want to know why she and her confederates came here?"

A feeling of dread settled over her. Lacy had serious doubts that she had the skills to force a spy to spill the beans. Victor pointed to the file on his desk.

"Yes, we want to know why she came here and what, specifically, she was sent here to do. Try to find out who she was planning to meet up with—"

"Like what's left of the British Fascists?" Tess interrupted.

Victor gave another short nod, continuing, "—And which locations in England were targets of German reconnaissance or destruction."

"So now they're actually German spies *on* British soil?" Lacy confirmed.

He replied as if her remark was a bit daft. "Only the woman is here. Her two male confederates were hanged, so we want to find out everything we can from the one who remains in our world."

Lacy didn't blame him for expressing sarcasm. She could only wonder why he thought she was at all capable of getting an enemy agent to talk.

Because he has few choices, and my guess is he'd rather spend the day with Tess.

Then another thought struck ominously. What if those secret invaders had intended to hook up with IRA comrades who'd come into England? She still hadn't been able to bring herself to tell Victor about Teddy's likely association with local Irish malcontents.

What if there is some sort of plan for the two groups to—

Victor broke into her panicked musings. "We're not actually sure the woman, Vera Eriksen, *is* German. Perhaps she's Russian or even Scandinavian."

"The name 'Eriksen' sounds Scandinavian," Tess chimed in.

"Well, she's had a number of aliases," Victor informed them, "but word is, she's quite the femme fatale. That's why I'm sending Lacy, with her journalist background, to interview her instead of a male agent I could poach from MI5 HQ."

Like the Russia-loving Guy Burgess, Lacy reckoned, recalling how she'd seen him from a distance in Hyde Park one day when he'd been deep in conversation with a short gentleman in a fedora and black coat. The menacing figure had reminded her of the goons that had followed Pem and her to the Moscow train station.

Now, wouldn't that be a joke, she thought grimly, *if Victor sent Burgess to quiz a spy who turned out to be a Russki in the employ of German intelligence!*

Startling her out of her reverie, Victor announced to Tess, "And as for the plan for you and me today, Miss T, I've just had word that there's some newfangled bomb nobody's seen before that's turned up in a shipment of children's toys."

"Toys? And you're the one expected to *defuse* it?" Tess demanded.

"It's in a transport crate on the receiving dock at Harrods," Victor said matter-of-factly. "Shouldn't take long to defang the thing." He smiled at Tess with a fondness he didn't bother to hide. "Not to worry, my dear. You'll be on the phone three stories up in the director's office taking notes. Then it's my treat downstairs in the tearoom."

Tess nodded, smiling thinly. Victor closed the file on his desk.

"Oh, one more thing, girls," he said, chuckling. "MI5 has taken pity on us. Our little unit is being moved from this prison cell to a small office in St. James's, walkable to HQ."

Tess and Lacy exchanged looks. The 3rd Baron, Lord Rothschild, had waved *his* magic wand and persuaded someone— "probably Winston himself," Tess declared later—to provide their small group with an office closer to MI5 headquarters and practically next door to Victor's newest wartime billet. As a former resident of Beacon Hill, Boston, Lacy knew well that it always helped to have friends in high places.

Their boss rose from his desk and reached for his topcoat. "Chop-chop, ladies. This war waits for no one."

Lacy offered a silent prayer that Victor's fine motor skills as an expert dissector of frog eggs would allow him to neutralize the German's latest lethal device without blowing himself and Harrods department store to high heaven. Meanwhile, she set off to meet a prisoner named Vera. Or maybe Svetlana? Who knew?

Chapter Twenty-Three

Lacy rose from the wooden chair in the prisoners' conference room, indicating that her half-hour interview with the spy who had recently been apprehended was at an end.

"I demand to speak to my contact at MI5!" Vera Eriksen, a lithesome, long-legged, dark-haired twenty-eight-year-old beauty, declared for the third time in her distinct Russian accent. Throughout the interview, she'd repeatedly claimed to have done work for both MI5 *and* the Germans.

Seeing that her interrogator was about to depart, Vera's beautiful mouth settled into a thin line. Her neck was slender and elegant, her waist tiny, and her hands expressive. Lacy could see how she could easily have once been a ballerina with the Bolshoi, as her case file surprisingly stated.

And a diva, most likely, Lacy judged, pausing with a final thought.

"One last question for you," she said pleasantly, her thoughts flying to her brother, Teddy, whose whereabouts and activities remained unknown. "What about the IRA activists roaming about this country? Had you plans to connect with any of them?"

After seeing her brother in Islington, Lacy had determined that she couldn't ask Victor to help find where he lived in England at that point since she'd never summoned the courage to share with her boss her suspicions about the company Teddy had kept.

Vera offered a slight chuckle, filled with spite. "If only you knew what diabolical plans that particular network of Mick malcontents has in store for this country they despise."

Lacy felt a choking sensation squeeze her throat.

Would Teddy actually dare to take up arms against England with his IRA comrades or carry explosives to detonate at train stations and railroad crossings? She could only hope that only the most experienced Irish and Welsh saboteurs would be assigned to cripple larger targets like munition dumps and aircraft factories, and not rank amateurs like her brother and those brawlers she'd seen in the Islington pub.

Suddenly, Lacy longed to breathe in fresh air. She had no need to prolong the meeting with this captured spy, as she could jot down the information Vera had disclosed once she boarded the tube train back to the office. Victor would be quite interested to learn about Vera's hints concerning Germany's future plans to infiltrate England with additional Abwehr saboteurs paving the way for their hoped-for invasion of Britain.

"Well, Miss Eriksen," she said, summoning a pleasant tone, "I'll pass along your request to speak to the person whose code name you gave me, and I imagine someone will eventually be in touch."

"And the two men I landed in Scotland with?" the prisoner asked sharply.

Lacy affected a shrug. "No one told you? Hanged by the neck under our latest antisabotage laws," she replied calmly. The stricken look that spread across Vera's face told Lacy that perhaps the feisty young beauty wasn't so nonchalant a spy as she'd wished to appear. Lacy pushed her chair into the small table. "No doubt you'll be hearing from someone of higher authority soon."

She turned to the guard, who opened the door, and swiftly left the room.

Oh, Teddy ... you are so out of your league with spies like Vera—or Svetlana—or whoever she really is!

All Lacy could do was pray that her brother had stuck to drinking his Guinness and let his Irish friends play the fool for Hitler.

Victor looked up from the report Lacy had written about her interview with Vera Eriksen and nodded his approval. Their newest working quarters weren't as small as the former cell at Wormwood Scrubs prison but were far from spacious, with Tess's and Lacy's desks facing each other on one wall and Victor's on the other.

"Quite an interesting type, this former ballerina," he commented with a wry smile.

"What's happening to her now?" Lacy asked. "Did she really once work for MI5 as she claimed to me?"

Victor merely cocked an eyebrow. Without answering her question, he pointed to the papers on his desk. "You did well on your first foray into the murky world of spy craft. I told HQ it would take a woman to get the best information out of someone like Vera Eriksen, and it seems you have."

Tess rose from her desk and drew near. "Are they going to hang her like the two others who rowed ashore with her?"

In a strange way, Lacy had come away from her time with Vera rather admiring the woman's spunk for having navigated in a totally man's world of international skullduggery. And the thought of her interview with Vera possibly condemning the former dancer to the hangman's noose was more than a little unsettling.

Victor laughed at Tess's question. "Hang her? Good heavens, no. As Lacy has demonstrated, Miss Vera has proven quite useful. She's being sent to the Isle of Man, where scores of our other prisoners of war are being held."

"In other words, MI5 is using her as a snitch against the team she formerly worked for?" Lacy stated, eyeing Victor directly.

So she did *work for British intelligence, and now she's a double!*

"I never said that," he replied with a sly smile. "Meanwhile"—he pulled a file from atop a tall stack— "I have another assignment for you, Lacy. There have been credible threats that the IRA is planning to attempt to bomb one of our munitions or tank-carrying trains being manufactured at"—he consulted the file— "the Birmingham Railway Carriage and Wagon Works. I want you to go up there and take stock of the situation. See if any Irish factory workers there may be tipping off local IRA chaps about gaining access to the plant or the routes the new munition cars will take. If you have time, telephone me with what you find—and then ride one of the trains back from Birmingham."

"Ride a train full of ammunition that some fanatics might try to bomb?" Lacy asked, rattled by his off-hand directive. "And ride it to where?"

"Well, those weapons transports travel from the factory to one of our ports in the south of England, I would imagine," he replied dismissively. "That's where the explosives are being sent before they are ferried to our troops on the Continent. Keep an eye out for anything suspicious you see along the way and report back."

Tess demanded, "And do exactly what if she *does* see something? For God's sake, Victor, at least let her get off the train as it goes through London!"

Ignoring her interruption, Victor said, "Like I told HQ, few saboteurs would suspect a woman has them under surveillance." Lacy could feel him studying her startled expression. "I do want you to know, Lacy, that you are perfectly free to decline any assignment like this that smacks of a bit more danger than you'd prefer."

"A *bit?*" Tess broke in.

Ignoring Tess again, he allowed, "All right ... it's fine if you get off the munitions train in London if you haven't spotted anything untoward on the journey south. I'll get someone from Scotland Yard to ride down to Portsmouth or wherever."

"Victor, *really!*" Tess protested. "No one has the casual attitude toward explosives that you do." She turned to Lacy and put her arm around her friend's shoulders. "Just tell him no. You can poke around the carriage works, but you're not about to ride a train full of ammunition with a bunch of IRA lunatics on board!"

Lacy's thoughts were racing. She had a keen desire to show Victor she was up to the tasks that were being thrown her way, but she also had a deadly fear that she might discover her own brother, Teddy, could be involved in such hairbrained schemes with his Irish cronies. If only she had some way of finding out where he was and ferreting out how he spent his time—and *where*.

She gazed at the file clasped in Victor's hand. If she declined the tough assignments and proved unable to perform what was necessary as an MI5 agent, she'd be jobless, penniless, and in a world of trouble as a non-British citizen in a time of war. On the other hand, if she went to Birmingham's railway manufacturing plant, she might see something that could nip the IRA offensive in the bud before Teddy or any other youthful mischief-maker was ever involved. That way, her place in Victor's unit would be secure.

"I'll do it," she said emphatically, "but I'll exit my railway car in London if nothing suspicious has occurred. Please assign someone else to ride it to the port."

She wondered whether she would be able to summon the same sangfroid that was somehow second nature to Baron Rothschild. Could she coolly board a train packed with bombs, ammunition, and saboteurs who wouldn't hesitate to shoot her dead?

<hr>

Without telling even Pat or Tess, Lacy spent the next Saturday in Kilburn, in Northwest London, peering through the windows of pubs known to be frequented by the county's large Irish community. It was a mere five miles from Islington, and for a moment, she thought she'd spied—through a smoky glass window—the redheaded woman Teddy had argued with at Hannigan's. When she peered in from the door, however, the woman with flaming hair was far more heavyset than Teddy's adversary and definitely older. Discouraged and already exhausted after a busy workweek, she entered the Kilburn station on the Bakerloo line and went home.

The very next Monday, Victor ordered Lacy to head north to assess whether Irish factory laborers at a metalworks that manufactured train cars designed to transport munitions were the likely saboteurs worrying the War Office. She was scheduled to have a brief meeting with the chairman of the Birmingham foundry in the town of Smethwick, about four miles from Birmingham's city center. The metalworks produced not only train cars but also, as of that moment, tanks and a variety of other heavy wartime equipment.

Victor had set up her trip there under the guise of planning to supply the company's on-site cafeteria, along with troop train canteens, with whatever foodstuffs and beverages current rationing policies would permit. She'd asked to meet a representative group of the chairman's workers to learn, as Victor's directive had said, what the men favored when it came to meals and snacks after a hard day's effort.

She boarded an early-morning train and arrived in good time to meet the factory workers after their lunchtime break.

"Even if they're not soldiers," she said to her host, summoning her most charming smile like the actress she had become, "your workers will give me an idea of what active men prefer to eat."

Her reasons for having come all the way up from London seemed a bit thin, but the chairman appeared pleased that the British War Office was paying his enterprise some attention. Within the hour, she was led to a cafeteria, where a long table was filled with men clad in their work gear.

After a number of innocuous questions, she casually asked the group, "Do you have many Irish or Polish factory workers here at this plant? Despite the new rationing laws, even here, the War Office's hope is your company canteen might be able to request things like Irish soda bread or cooked cabbage dishes if there's enough interest in such things," she said, looking at the group expectantly.

A worker in blue overalls with patches of soot on his face spoke up in a distinct Irish accent. "Fat chance we Irish blokes would be treated to such luxuries as real food after a day's work in this grease pit," he declared, anger and cynicism lacing his words. "We're lucky if we get the right money in our pay packets every week."

He looked around at several of his companions, whose nods signaled there were, indeed, disaffected Irish workers at the metalworks. From a few scowls ringing the table, she could see they weren't very happy toiling at the foundry making tanks and railroad cars.

After posing several more questions about food preferences to the surly group, Lacy concluded her bogus interrogation and thanked the men, who shuffled out mumbling complaints under their breath. She felt sure she had enough evidence to report that British security most likely should keep an eye on places employing recently arrived Irish workers. There might well be a need at that plant to ward off any contemplated sabotage plans, especially if more German spies infiltrated the country and joined forces with such seemingly discontented men as she'd encountered thus far.

The junior executive whom the railway works chairman had provided as Lacy's escort seemed oblivious to the blatant hostility she'd just witnessed. He smiled cheerily and guided her outdoors at the mammoth manufacturing complex that spread over many acres of flat land. The late-April showers had cleared, leaving great puddles of water everywhere in the gigantic rail yard.

"Would you like a quick look at the factory's interior design department before you go?" he asked politely. "I think I can find someone to show you drawings of the new dining cars we're installing and how they plan to store their foodstuffs aboard."

Lacy was longing to catch the train back to London, even if it was transporting ammunition. Instead, she politely nodded in agreement and was led deeper into the muddy rail yard.

"I'll introduce you to some of our chaps designing our latest carriages," he proposed. "The government rationing fellows that you report to will want to know the excellent way food can now be stored on board." Looking anxious to return to his regular duties, he declared, "Once you've had a chat and seen our latest schematics, our man there will escort you to your evening train in plenty of time."

From the cafeteria's exit, her guide led her outdoors to where a series of huge sheds housed the various stages of manufacturing heavy metal equipment. Finished train coaches were sitting on sections of rail platforms, while within an open-ended shed several hundred feet away from the cafeteria building, gigantic cauldrons were erupting in flames where molten metals would soon be made into sections of train cars or tanks.

A few hundred meters farther down the foundry's enormous yard, Lacy and her guide approached a long, low-roofed building with a series of taped windows, its foundation surrounded by sandbags. They entered a sliding wooden door at one end of the structure, which Lacy speculated might have once housed horses that pulled factory wagons. In a line of cubicles that she reckoned had been stalls for equines, rows of men in shirtsleeves were bent over spacious drafting tables littered with large sheaves of paper on which they appeared to be sketching.

Her company minder hailed a figure walking toward them from the far end of the large, but narrow and drafty, wooden shed.

As soon as a harried-looking supervisor with a thin mustache and equally thinning hair reached their side, her host swiftly made introductions. "This is Miss Lacy Forbes, here from the London War

Office to learn about how we're to feed not only our workers here at the plant but also the military men on our newest troop trains."

The minder's duties concluded, he quickly took his leave. Before the head of the company's drafting department could even step forward to shake her hand in greeting, a voice vibrating with incredulity called out from one of the stalls.

"*Lacy*? Lacy Farrington Forbes?"

She heard the joy in the voice that had called out, and its loving, familiar tone stopped her in her tracks.

Chapter Twenty-Four

Lacy spun on the heels of her black ankle boots, feeling as if someone had just socked her in the chest. She could barely breathe. Not twenty feet away stood Dr. Charles Pembroke, not clad in a white coat denoting a physician but with his shirtsleeves rolled up and a slide rule in his right hand.

Pem strode to her side and happily posed the question, "Whatever in the world are *you* doing here?"

Lacy was finally able to inhale a gulp of air. She stared at him a long moment, then replied, "Since I haven't heard a word from you since I waved goodbye at the airport, I get to ask you first: Why the hell are you *still* in England?"

Pem glanced at the puzzled expression on the face of the railway company's head of the drafting department and asked him, "Do you think I might be excused early, sir? As you may have concluded, Miss Forbes and I know each other from America. From Boston, in fact. Since she's here, it would be lovely to take her to tea."

Pem's superior frowned slightly, sensing tension in the air. "Ah ... well ... I suppose that might be all right if you'll be ready to display your blueprints of the hospital train carriages by tomorrow, nine o'clock sharp."

"Absolutely," Pem reassured him. "I'll have everything in good order to show your team in the morning."

Well, what do you know? He's been designing hospital cars for both the UK and the US!

"And since you know the young lady, would you be willing to take my place and see she gets safely on her train?"

"Yes, sir!" Pem said eagerly. "Of course, sir."

By that time, many of the architects and engineers in the various former horse stalls had turned away from their drafting boards and were staring curiously at the two Americans facing each other in the middle of the room.

Lacy shifted her gaze from the chief designer back to Pem, whose pleading glance warned her they should take any personal discussions somewhere private.

"Why don't we go to a nice tearoom I know downtown in Smethwick?" Pem proposed, as if sipping a cup of Royal Blend at four o'clock on a Tuesday were a normal occurrence between a pair of Americans in the wilds of the western Midlands.

"Fine," she said shortly, torn between wanting to pummel him for the long silence she'd endured for months and wanting to throw herself into his arms.

Lacy hesitated at the entrance to Pem's small quarters at his rather rundown hotel in the heart of Smethwick.

Leaning against the doorframe, she remarked, pokerfaced, "I doubt your colleagues at the factory would call this place a tearoom."

Pem set his bulky portfolio on the narrow bed pushed against one wall. Lacy assumed it contained the large blueprints of train cars he was due to unveil in the morning. He turned, strode to the door, and seized her hand. "Shall I tell you why I couldn't write you?"

She nodded without speaking as he drew her into the room and shut the door.

He pointed to the portfolio. "My world is now as high security as yours, I suspect. I've been sent to Birmingham on loan from the U.S. Army Medical Corps. You heard the supervisor say that tomorrow, I'm to show my designs for railway cars built as useful vehicles for the war effort."

"Useful how?"

"I shouldn't tell you, but I will. Useful as hospital trains, weapons transports, casualty evacuation cars ... rolling morgues."

Lacy winced. "I see. But couldn't you at least have let me know personally that you made it across the Atlantic without being blown out of the sky?"

In an achingly familiar gesture, she felt the back of his fingers trace the line of her jaw. His eyes were riveted on hers. "No one in America was to know I wasn't still in England, and people in Britain weren't to learn I'd been sent to the US, just that I'd left the Manchester Veterans Hospital."

"You kept no big secret of that," she protested. "You told Victor, Tess, and me that night at the 400 Club that you were headed back to the States."

"And immediately afterward, I disclosed that fact and your names to my superiors. They just laughed. 'No bother,' they said. 'Rothschild's MI5, and so are those females working for him.'" Pem continued, "Like you, I expect, I had to sign documents for the war departments of both countries, promising not to reveal where I was in D.C., for whom I was working, or what I was working *on*. You already knew I'd worked in Manchester as a doctor and that I was returning to America, probably to join the Army Medical Corps. But once I'd left Britain, I was forbidden to contact anyone directly or say anything about what my new assignments were regarding train design for the war on penalty of—"

"I know," Lacy interrupted. "I signed something similar. Even so, why was it all such a secret?" she asked skeptically. "Everyone knows trains are used in wartime for military purposes."

"More than anything else, it was about keeping Congressional right-wingers and influential isolationists in the US *ignorant* of what preparations for a possible war FDR has been making. Roosevelt's inner circle was adamant that no information about these projects I've been doing—for Britain as well as America—be leaked to either the American or British press. America is not a party to the war, remember?"

"How could I forget?"

He grasped her shoulders with each hand and leaned forward, gently brushing his lips against hers. She didn't respond, still rankled by his weeks of silence.

Once Pem released her, she said, "When I never heard from you, I spent a lot of time imagining you finishing whatever your assignment in Washington was and then taking up your former life in Boston, perhaps as a doctor on a military base up there or something."

"You mean you thought I'd been with Eleanor all this time?" Lacy averted her eyes. Pem shook his head. "'O ye of little faith.'"

"Why wouldn't I wonder?" she retorted.

Pem's tone softened. "Of course, you'd wonder, and I'm sorry. I didn't mean to make light of your feelings. But, as a matter of fact, I haven't been to Boston at all, nor have I seen Eleanor even once, although we spoke on the telephone one time." He grimaced and then added, "I think we were both shocked by what little we had to say to one another."

Even about getting divorced? Lacy wondered.

But rather than speculate on that painful topic, she changed the subject, demanding, "And how long have you been at the railway works, may I ask?"

"Just over a month." He clasped her shoulders again. "Believe me, darling, I longed to call you or write, but I'd given an oath not to communicate with anyone other than design colleagues and my immediate military officials."

"So this radio silence from you would have gone on indefinitely if I hadn't run into you today?"

Lacy's emotions were ragged and close to veering out of control. For weeks, she'd worried that his plane might have been shot down and that the news could have been suppressed by authorities. Then she'd grown increasingly more upset over receiving *no* word from him at all since the moment they'd bid goodbye. A part of her recognized she was bordering on being unreasonable, but her ingrained reflexes about trusting anyone with matters of the heart had definitely kicked in.

She stiffened when Pem enveloped her in his arms, and she knew he sensed their reunion in his tiny Birmingham bedroom was not going well.

"Look, Lacy, I totally understand why you're upset—angry, in fact. But it was killing me, too, not being able to be in touch." He leaned closer. "The good news is that I've recently been told that I probably will be allowed to have contact with 'family and close friends' once this phase of my service in Britain is completed—as long as I don't mention I've been helping the Brits convert train stock to wartime use or let slip to any reporter what I've been doing."

He had probably already violated his oath of secrecy just now, and his plea for understanding sounded convincing when they were standing only inches apart.

She asked quietly, "How soon will you return to Washington again?"

"I honestly can't say because I don't know." He paused and then asked, "And, by the way, might I ask what *you* were doing in Birmingham?"

She sighed as a vision of her signing the Official Secrets Act floated through her head. When she didn't answer him, he pulled her close, their lips almost touching.

"You're not supposed to tell anyone *anything* about what you're assigned to do either, am I right?" He promptly threw his head back and laughed, then hugged her tightly. "Nobody would believe the situation the two of us are in, would they?" He appeared relieved. "I was so shocked and completely flabbergasted when you walked into that building today, but I'm so damn glad you did!"

"I very nearly didn't," Lacy disclosed, remembering how she'd followed the company minder to the carriage work's design department only to be polite. "All I wanted was to board a train and get back to London."

"Thank God your impeccable Boston manners prevailed."

Pem drew her even closer. She could almost feel her walls of resistance and self-protection begin to crumble, knowing full well the dangers that would ensue if she allowed them to fall completely. She felt his arousal as he pressed her body against the length of his frame. It felt so wonderful to be in his arms again. Safe and sexy and so *right*.

With a knowing smile, she murmured, "Believe me, it's nice to feel just how glad you are that I'm here. In your bedroom," she added as a rush of unfettered happiness lifted her spirits for the first time in months.

To hell with Eleanor! she thought. Pem felt like hers—and hers alone.

"I want you so much," he whispered, his voice hoarse with emotion, "and I never dreamed I'd get to be with you like this."

Lacy saw something new in Pem's eyes: a shadow of the fear that life was short. In war, you never knew what could be taken away in an instant.

Before they kissed again, she warned, "Listen, Soldier, I have a train to catch before midnight, but *my* good news is ... I want you just as much."

Lacy opened her eyes, uncertain what time it was or how long they'd been asleep. Pem's small room was pitch-dark with blackout curtains blocking out all available light, which meant that she had no idea whether it was even still daytime.

She turned on a bedside lamp and glanced at her wristwatch, then abruptly sat up in bed. Jostled out of the embrace they'd been locked in, Pem rose onto his elbow and blinked.

"What time is it?"

"Very, *very* late," she replied, moving toward the edge of the bed. "It's after eleven o'clock. The train I'm supposed to catch leaves just before midnight!"

"Damn, damn, *damn!*" Pem replied with a long moan. "Come here, you blond bombshell."

He made a grab for her waistline, but she slithered out of bed. She turned quickly to reach for her scattered underwear and the prim and proper dress of a "food specialist" that she'd worn for the meeting at the factory.

"I cannot miss that train!" she exclaimed, frantically stuffing her precious nylons into her handbag and pulling her dark-blond hair into an emergency ponytail. There wasn't time to do anything else but jump into her clothes and speed to the station.

"Right," Pem mumbled, pulling himself to his full height next to the bed. "But what a way to end our— What shall we call the last four hours?" He wore a mischievous grin that bordered on lascivious.

"Let's call it delicious ... although it was sans condoms," she said, a shadow of worry intruding on her fevered recollections of their love-making. Nearly dressed and slipping on her shoes, she blushed to remember how protected sex had been the last thing on her mind once they'd stripped each other of every shred of clothing. It even cheered her to realize the man she loved wasn't carrying condoms in his travel gear as a matter of course these days.

Pem, still naked and a stunning sight to her eyes, strode to her side and playfully trapped her in his arms.

"I did my best to be careful, but you were quite the siren, Miss Lacy." He leaned back, his expression growing serious. "You promise you will tell me if—"

"And you'll do *what*?" she cut him off. "What could you do sequestered up here or buried in secrecy in D.C.?" She struggled to keep her tone light and forced a smile. "I'm fairly sure I'm past the time of the month when this could be a problem, so fingers crossed."

"But *promise* ..."

Pulling away from his embrace, she plunged an arm into one sleeve of her coat while Pem hastened to help her with the other. Then he swiftly slipped into his trousers and shoes and threw his topcoat on without pausing to put on a shirt.

Fortunately, Pem's lodgings were a walkable distance to the Smethwick train station and they arrived in the dark chill of the night a few minutes before midnight. There were only a few railcars lined up on any of the platforms running through the depot. Behind a single locomotive were three railway passenger cars. Attached to the rear of them, forming the end of the train, were a few open-topped, steel-sided wagons. Heavy tarpaulins hid what Victor had told Lacy would contain individual bombs, wooden boxes of ammunition, or other ordnance Lacy preferred to know nothing about.

"Good God!" Pem exclaimed. Lacy could see his gaze had fastened on the rear cars. "This train is also hauling a shipment of weapons or major explosives!"

"How do you *know* that?" she said, feigning disbelief.

"I work at the place where they design and make these types of cars, remember?" He shot her a fierce look. "I don't want you to get on a train like this one!"

"I have to," Lacy stated matter-of-factly.

"No, you don't!" Pem declared. "These always travel at night, if possible, due to potential sabotage along the route by the crazy Irish revolutionaries or the lingering British Fascists that haven't been rounded up yet."

Silently, Lacy added "infiltrating German spies" to the list of possible saboteurs who could blow up such a shipment. She tried to avoid thinking about her impending long hours sitting on a train pulling railcars packed with volatile cargo.

Pem forced her to meet his gaze. "The reason these trains travel in darkness is, of course, to avoid as many civilian casualties as possible should they be attacked. Darling," he pleaded, "stay the night with me, and I'll put you on an early milk train tomorrow—one that doesn't have this sort of moving arsenal!"

"I can't," she insisted. She paused and then found an excuse. "I promised Tess and Victor that I'd return to London for our early-morning meeting tomorrow."

Pem appeared dumbfounded at hearing that, his eyes widening with concern, then anger. "Lord Rothschild has you doing *these* sorts of tasks?" he demanded. "Literally having you ride shotgun on two wagonloads of weapons?"

"I never said that," she retorted, knowing that was exactly what Victor expected her to do. "I just have to be back at work tomorrow."

Chapter Twenty-Five

Before Lacy could say anything further to appease Pem's worry about her boarding a train hauling munitions, a conductor striding toward them shouted, "All aboard! This train is leaving in three minutes! In three minutes, this London-bound train will leave the station!"

Behind him straggled several sleepy-looking passengers carrying all varieties of luggage, wicker baskets, and parcels wrapped in brown paper and secured with string. Pem stood beside Lacy, arms stiff, his hands coiled in fists by his side. She could tell he was more upset than she'd ever seen him.

Once the knot of people passed by, he said, "Oh, dammit to hell, Lacy, I can't believe this!"

She threw her arms around him, whispering in his ear, "You know what they say. 'There's a war on, remember?' If I have any hint there's something amiss, I'll jump off the train at the next stop." She kissed his cheek. "I've got to go. Cable me the next time you fly across the Atlantic, promise?"

His arms relaxed a bit, and then Pem embraced her once more. "I don't believe for a second you'd jump off," he rejoined, his tone aggrieved, "but I suppose I'll just have to assume you made it safely to London if there's no news of sabotage along the way."

"Very much like what I'll have to do—again—the next time *you* fly across the Atlantic," she reminded him, keeping her voice steady.

"Cable that you love me after you touch down ... Roger that?" She kissed him again, adding, "I love *you*, Soldier!"

Pem cocked his head, then heaved a heavy sigh. "This system stinks," he said. Gently, he took the back of her hand in his and kissed it, then briefly held it against his cheek. Lacy sensed he was doing his best to make their farewell something they'd both remember fondly. He leaned closer to cup her face in his hands. "I'm so grateful we had this time."

"Me too," she whispered, already feeling the familiar pangs of desolation at having to say goodbye once again.

And in a train station, of course.

If only she could shake off the many childhood experiences of crushing separations she'd endured leaving people and places she cared about.

"Goodbye," she murmured into his ear, then forced herself to pull away from the circle of his arms.

Before Pem could respond, she hastened up the iron steps into her assigned third-class carriage. Once inside, she was acutely aware of how luxurious her camel coat was compared to the threadbare attire her fellow passengers wore. She dropped onto a pew-like seat next to the only other woman on the train.

"Bless me, but I'm glad there be another lady on board tonight," declared her seatmate, her accent giving away her Irish roots.

"I'm glad too," Lacy agreed quietly, scanning the platform outside the smudged window for a glimpse of Pem.

The older woman nodded in the direction of a gaggle of young men clad in tattered work clothes who were clustered at the other end of the car. One was already dancing a jig in the aisle to a tune played by another on his pennywhistle. The men surrounding them clapped and hooted encouragement while they guzzled Guinness from bottles held in each hand.

"Those chappies'll be drunk before we're halfway to London town," complained the woman.

Lacy stared at the disorderly group, struck by how easily her brother, Teddy, would fit in among them. They were young, rambunctious, and gleefully ignoring their fellow passengers, who undoubtedly wanted to sleep on the way to London. She scanned their faces, wondering whether the lighthearted demeanor of any of them masked the sort of malcontent Victor worried could drive them to sabotage. They certainly didn't seem the sort to be focused on anything but swilling their beer.

Out of the corner of her eye, Lacy saw that Pem had come to stand on the platform outside her window, a frown of worry creasing his brow. A shrill whistle blew, the train gave a lurch, and her rail coach started to move. Pem cast a glance over his shoulder at the two steel wagons attached to the rear of the train. Lacy pictured the tarps covering their deadly cargo, not only to hide it but also to keep sparks along the railroad platforms from igniting the lethal contents inside.

Mentally pushing away thoughts of a possible disaster, Lacy touched her fingertips to her lips and then waved. Just before Pem's figure slid out of view, he patted the side of his chest where his heart was and blew a kiss with both hands.

Lacy swallowed hard to keep tears at bay, forcing her mind to the task of being watchful of her surroundings. She turned away from the empty window to gaze again at the cadre of young Irishmen gathered at the front of their car. They were laughing raucously, trading empty bottles of beer for fresh, full ones.

Not every Irish immigrant is a traitor or saboteur! she chastised herself silently. Surely, Teddy would be smart enough not to be mixed up in something so dangerous as deliberately setting off explosives in Hitler's name?

Then another thought struck.

What if Rothschild had been tipped off about IRA plans to detonate *that* particular shipment of bombs scheduled for a south coast port via London? Would he knowingly have sent her, instead of Tess, on such a dangerous mission, charged with warning the authorities before the miscreants could strike?

Was this *her* last goodbye?

Lacy's apprehension about the cargo being hauled behind her third-class railcar had kept her awake from the moment the train had pulled out of Smethwick. Her back had grown stiff, her bottom sore, and her nerves were frayed after she'd spent hours perched on the bench covered in worn-out upholstery, keeping a vigilant eye on the passengers in her coach.

Within minutes of their departure, her seatmate had covered her head with a scarf and pulled her knitted cap down over her ears to her jawline. These hours later, the older woman was slumped against the train window, dead to the world. It was an amazing feat, considering that the increasingly rowdy passengers who had commandeered their carriage were still swigging their bottles of beer.

Stifling a yawn, Lacy surveyed the motley crew for the hundredth time as the West Midland train rolled along the last thirty kilometers leading to London's Euston Station.

The conductor strode down the aisle, crying, "Watford coming up! Arriving at Watford Station! Please gather all your belongings before you leave the train. Watford Station next!"

Drawing back the train car's blackout curtains, Lacy peered through the morning gloom at the yellow brick depot, the second-to-last stop before London. The merry band of men who'd ridden at the front of the car jumped from their seats and piled out the front exit of the carriage to breathe some fresh air. She noticed that two of the older ones had actually fallen asleep at some point during the night. Rousing themselves, they followed the others outside.

As per Victor's orders, Lacy sprang to her feet and stepped down onto the chilly platform. Hugging her coat's lapels close to her neck, she turned her gaze toward the rear of the train. Her fellow male passengers had surrounded the last car and pushed the tarp aside, with the tallest of the group peering into the shipment of heavy explosives.

"Blimey!" she heard him exclaim. "Will ya look at how much of this stuff we've been haulin' behind us all journey long!"

One of the older men shushed him, and another cuffed him upside his head.

"Shut your gob!" the pugilist exclaimed. His companion gave the snoop a hard thump on his back. "Get back on the train or I'll throw you into one of these wagons—and won't that be fun for the rest of us later on?"

Later on? What will happen later on? Lacy wondered, alarmed.

She quickly remounted the three metal steps of her railcar and sought out the conductor, who was standing in the vestibule, consulting a clipboard. When she'd first boarded at Smethwick, the short, rotund older man in his navy-blue uniform had greeted her with a smile, prompting her to wonder whether he had been informed that "someone from the War Office" would be on his train that night. When she'd identified herself as such, he'd looked surprised to see a woman assigned to that task. Then he had smiled.

"Well, there's a war on, isn't there, pet?" he'd said. "Everybody's got to do their bit, don't we? Don't you worry, though," he'd assured her before returning to his duties, "I'll be lookin' after you with those ruffians ridin' up front."

Given what she'd just seen near the weapons shipment, she tapped the conductor's shoulder to get his attention again.

"The next stop ... Wembley, is it?" she asked in hushed tones. He nodded. "It's urgent you tell the stationmaster there to have some men from Scotland Yard greet our specific car the moment we arrive at Euston!"

The conductor's eyebrows raised. "Something's amiss? I was told we're transporting ... uh ... that c-cargo," he stuttered. "I did note the lads clustered on the back platform, but do you think ...?"

"We can't be sure there's anything's wrong," she replied, keeping her voice low, "but a few of the group were looking under the wheels and peeking beneath the tarpaulins. I didn't dare linger to see if they were doing anything else."

"Well, we can't take a chance of rolling into Euston Station with some detonators or timing pencils strapped to the axles, can we now, love?"

Lacy realized, then, that the conductor was obviously well versed in what the "enemy within" could do to set off a shipment of high explosives.

Just then, the two men who'd chastised their comrade near the ammunition wagons came through the vestibule, their expressions subdued. Lacy wondered whether the pair were mulling over some task an IRA higher-up had ordered them to accomplish. Or had they already done mischief, timed to ignite the cargo once it was inside a major London train complex? It had happened before ... up in Manchester, Lacy remembered Victor telling her.

A whistle blew. The conductor glanced down at the face of his pocket watch. "I don't have time to go into the depot here," he said, a worried frown creasing his forehead, "but you can bet I'll have a quick word by phone at the next stop."

"It's the last before we get to London, yes?" Lacy confirmed.

The conductor gave a quick nod, and they exchanged solemn looks. He then swiftly jumped down onto the platform, calling out that the train was leaving forthwith. In a trice, he was back onboard.

Thank God there's one more stop before London.

But would there be enough time to summon Scotland Yard?

Her stomach in knots, Lacy returned to her seat, sinking down next to her companion, who had remained asleep. A few minutes after the train resumed its journey, the two men who had chastised their mate rose from their seats. The tallest one was clutching a canvas satchel tightly in his arms. Both men disappeared into the lavatory at the end of the car.

Lacy stared at the door they'd gone through. The same two men who had been napping prior to the stop in Watford hadn't been carrying a satchel at that point—but now one of the pair was. She could only wonder whether *this* was the appointed moment, in the privacy of a toilet stall, when they would prepare the fuses timed to set off the explosives. Victor had warned her that such devices allowed the scoundrels to get well away from the scene before the devices ignited.

A voice in her head urged caution.

What if these roustabouts are merely factory workers going to the loo to pee and have a shave before arriving in London, plain and simple?

Was it fair to assume, merely because they were a disorderly bunch of ill-mannered types, that they were prepared to kill a bunch of innocents in the name of Irish independence? If Scotland Yard rushed in and those men had done nothing wrong except stay up all night drinking Guinness and peeking under a tarp out of curiosity, she'd surely be sacked from MI5 as "that idiot American lady" who couldn't distinguish a homegrown terrorist from a lamppost.

During the next leg of the journey to London, time ticked by with agonizing slowness until the train slowed down once again and stopped in Wembley. Lacy watched while the two men with the canvas bag instructed their companions to stay seated. Then the pair left the carriage car, along with the conductor, who was seeing to the needs of the new passengers boarding the train.

Frozen on her uncomfortable bench seat, Lacy observed the conductor quickly duck into the ticket office where a telephone would be available to call London law enforcement. Unable to sit still, she got up and entered the vestibule, peering around the train car's doorway to see what might be happening near the two freight cars. She could catch only a glimpse of a pair of work boots peeking out from beneath one of the metal transports filled chockablock with military ordnance.

Lacy took a deep breath and tried to *think*. Wouldn't the average observer from MI5 surmise the suspect was in the act of attaching his death device to one of the axles bearing the weight of all those bombs? Why did she doubt herself so?

Just as she was about to turn back into the car to avoid being seen, the one Irishman came around the munitions car and assisted his companion out from under it. Lacy swiftly retreated to her assigned seat and had barely sat down when the two Irishmen scrambled onto the train and strode down the aisle toward their fellow travelers.

Mere minutes later, she heard the conductor shout, "All aboard! Next stop: Euston Station, London! Euston Station next!"

The passengers who'd remained on the train during the last stop began to prepare for their pending arrival.

What if those two men up front are amateurs like Teddy? she fretted, her heart pounding with each turn of the train wheels. *What if they set the timers wrong? What if—*

As the horrifying possibilities bubbled in Lacy's mind, the backyards of outer London were floating by. Gazing blankly at laundry flapping on lines, she wondered whether the drying knickers would be the last sight she'd ever see. The woman next to her stirred and opened her eyes.

"Well, blessed Saint Mary, just look where we be! Almost in London!" She smiled at Lacy. "Did you get some sleep too, dearie?"

Lacy shrugged and bit her lip as the train entered a dark tunnel leading to Euston Station and eventually came to a halt with a jerk inside the terminal. She winced and squeezed her eyes tightly shut, every muscle tensed for what might happen next.

Chapter Twenty-Six

Lacy felt a hand on her arm. "Are you all right, dearie?" her seatmate asked.

She hadn't realized she'd kept her eyes shut tight. Her seatmate had already drawn open the blackout curtains. Through the window, Lacy saw a crowd of uniformed officers, along with several stern-looking men in overcoats whom she supposed were plainclothesmen from Scotland Yard. The next thing she knew, men in blue uniforms were swarming onto their train car, grabbing every male passenger within sight, and rousting them down to the platform. In short order, they were lined up facing the car they'd just arrived in.

"Hands on the side of the carriage, and be quick about it!" bellowed one officer.

"Oh, goodness me," Lacy's seatmate exclaimed, staring out the window. "What's amiss, I wonder?"

An additional team of police rifled through the men's pockets while other officers dragged out their luggage and began a thorough search.

But are they inspecting the two rear wagons? Lacy agonized, unable to see from inside the train what was happening at the end of it and wondering whether she should just make a run for it.

The conductor suddenly appeared by her side. "An inspector from the Yard wishes to speak with you, miss," he informed her, pointing toward the far end of the car. "He's waiting at the foot of the stairs."

Lacy's fellow traveler stared, open-mouthed, as Lacy made her way down the aisle and stepped off the train, her legs feeling rubbery.

"Miss Lacy Forbes?" a plainclothes detective asked briskly.

"Yes, sir," she identified herself, her head beginning to ache from tension and no sleep.

"Excellent job, miss."

Lacy could only stare and follow the finger he was pointing toward the rear of the train. A man clad in dark oilskins and goggles was standing next to the last car. He handed his partner a small round alarm clock and a square of something that looked like a pound of butter with skinny wires dangling from it. In his other hand, he held several red cylinders the size of Winston Churchill's favorite cigars.

Pointing toward the last car, Lacy blurted, "That's dynamite, isn't it?"

"Indeed, it is. And the putty to go with it. Set to go off six or seven minutes from now—in time for those traitorous Micks to make a beeline out of here." He added, "Herr Hitler won't be pleased to learn we stopped 'em, but your Lord Rothschild certainly will."

Lacy sagged against the side of the car, feeling the periphery of her vision blur gray. The inspector grabbed her elbow to steady her. "Just give me a minute," she murmured.

"I don't blame you for feeling a bit woozy, miss ... riding on this train all night, knowing those explosives were behind you and those louts were on board." He cocked his head toward the ammunition wagons. "If their plan had worked, we'd all be digging out of a mighty large pile of rubble."

If we'd survived to dig out of anything.

The usually somber Lord Rothschild was all smiles when Lacy walked through the door at the St. James's office the next morning. Tess jumped up from her desk and gave her friend a hug since she hadn't been on Bentinck Street when Lacy had dragged herself into their flat.

If she'd expected an apology from Victor for assigning her to ride on a train he knew was a likely target, she wasn't offered one. He did, however, make clear that he was pleased with her decision to have the conductor notify the authorities to summon the bomb experts, which had saved the day.

Was this MI5's way of testing the guts required to be one of their agents?

If so, Victor's attitude of business as usual signaled she had passed with flying colors. Lacy wondered whether she should be angry or glad he'd put her to that test. It occurred to her that in the business of fighting a war, fate could rest with people and personalities she couldn't control.

Victor's smile vanished as he pointed to a report lying open on his desk. "It turns out that detonating that load of weapons on the train in Euston Station wasn't the only mission on the minds of those Paddies you were traveling with," he said. "Besides the two operatives we caught red-handed, the other men we apprehended in that group had tins of petrol, matches, rags, and empty beer bottles in their satchels—all equipment clearly aimed at igniting Molotov cocktails around London."

Tess, who'd been listening attentively to the previous conversation between their boss and Lacy, once again rose from her desk. "Lacy was also exposed to men planning to hurl Molotov cocktails? It's a miracle our friend here came back in one piece!"

Lacy had only recently learned that term for such improvised incendiary devices, which had been named after a Soviet foreign minister in the 1930s and used in warfare for the first time in the Spanish Civil War. Shocked by Victor's recent revelation, she also realized she now had *two* secrets she'd kept from her employer: that her brother had been associating with suspicious-acting Irish citizens in Islington and that she'd met up with Pem in Birmingham the previous day and learned some closely-guarded secrets about the British-American war effort!

Tess vigorously shook her finger at their boss. "Given what you put her through, you at least owe Lacy a lunch at the Savoy."

Lacy found herself studying Victor's reaction to Tess's admonishments. Her flatmate was his lover, his confidante, his right hand. It occurred to Lacy that those were most likely the reasons he'd been more willing to risk his second assistant's life than that of the woman he so clearly cared for. Then again, she reminded herself, their boss took Tess with him on most of his bomb defusing assignments.

Face it, Lacy, antisabotage work is risky for anyone involved.

She, Tess, and Victor had all volunteered for a unit in MI5 that dealt with unknown people without uniforms willing to kill civilians anytime, anywhere. The truth was those on the train and in the station all survived by sheer luck, thanks to the railway conductor and the prompt response from Scotland Yard. Clearly, Victor had put them all on alert, doing what he could to protect her and those around her. The thought that Teddy could be part of the world that had almost ended her life was sickening.

Perhaps this is the moment I should tell Victor…

Yet, Victor had looked out for Tess's life, not hers, on that assignment. Shouldn't she do the same for her brother by not turning him in but, instead, using whatever means she had to find him and stop him from hurting others—or himself?

Victor jolted her thoughts back to the present. "I do, indeed, owe both of you a lunch at the Savoy for all your hard work this week. Unfortunately, I can't join you." He pointed to a stack of files towering on his desk. "I have all these to go through, plus I have an appointment to see Winston this afternoon." With a wave of his hand, he gestured toward the door. "But, yes, after what Lacy's endured, lunch there is definitely in order today. You two go, and I'll call ahead to put your meal on my tab." He waggled his finger at Tess as she had at him just moments earlier. "But I expect you both back at your desks checking the translations of the latest German transmissions by two-thirty at the latest—and only one bottle of champagne between the two of you, understand?"

Tess put her arm through Lacy's and replied with a saucy smile, "The rationing's got so bad, we'll be lucky if they'll have even a glass of Chateau Plonk on hand. But thank you for treating us to lunch, Victor." She turned to her office mate. "More than champagne, my friend, I expect you need a good stiff tumbler of Scotch! Let's be off before our revered employer changes his mind and puts another pile of love notes from the Krauts on our desks."

In the weeks that followed Lacy's return from Birmingham, Victor fell into the habit of treating his two assistants to lunch at the Savoy quite often. Lacy couldn't begin to count the number of reports for which she and Tess had double-checked the translations from German to English. She hadn't had a free moment to do anything about tracking Teddy's whereabouts since Victor had sent her on numerous forays to record the extent of bomb damage around London.

"I need these details to put into my reports on sabotage perpetrated by insiders, compared to the ongoing aerial bombardment," he'd explained.

One evening a month later, Tess startled Lacy by announcing they were to go to dinner, rather than lunch, at the hotel's other restaurant, the Savoy Grill. When Lacy asked her why dinner, why the Grill, Tess declared with a mischievous smile, "Prepare yourself ... I have a surprise for you."

By the end of the day, Lacy was exhausted, didn't feel well, and wanted to beg off, but Tess wouldn't hear of it, declaring they'd take a taxi directly from work. They entered the dining establishment that was far less formal than the Savoy's large River Restaurant, where debutante balls had often been held prior to the war. There, waiting to be seated, was their flatmate, Pat, accompanied by their fellow deb, Deborah Mitford.

Lacy had heard from Tess that Debo was seriously being courted by Lord Andrew Cavendish, the son of the current, "very Anglican" Duke of Devonshire. Andrew was also the younger brother of Billy, whose love affair with the Catholic U.S. ambassador's daughter and Lacy's friend Kick Kennedy continued to cause ripples on both sides of the Atlantic.

The minute the group of young women were seated at their table, Pat exclaimed to her roommates, "I had fingers crossed you could meet us for dinner tonight because our friend Debo here has a big announcement to make. She didn't want to share it until you were all gathered together."

Lacy and Tess looked expectantly at the youngest of the six Mitford sisters, who smiled broadly and declared, "Andrew and I are getting *married*!"

"So we can say it's official! Golly, how exciting!" Tess exclaimed, and they all clapped their hands with excitement.

"Wonderful!" Lacy chimed in, fighting to maintain a happy smile in spite of sensing an ominous churning in her stomach she hoped was due to the mere stress of her MI5 activities and the bombs that fell over London nearly every night.

"Tell us *when* and *where*!" Pat urged.

"April nineteenth," Debo replied, her eyes shining with happiness. "Andrew's a second lieutenant in the Coldstream Guards now, so it won't be a grand wedding at all. We're set for Priory Church at St. Bartholomew's." Her radiant expression sobered. "As you well know, I have my five sisters to deal with, so I can't ask any of you to be *in* the wedding party as I so wish I could," she apologized, "but I hope you'll sit right up front in the bride's family section that I'm reserving for my dearest sister debs!"

Just then, the waiter arrived with an ice bucket, a bottle of champagne, and a large plate of oysters.

Tess announced to the group, "I ordered these as soon as we came in. Victor said this happy gathering is on him, so let's make the most of it!"

The mere thought of slimy crustaceans sliding down her throat was prompting Lacy's stomach to turn over on itself. "Please excuse me," she mumbled, struggling to her feet. "I need to go to the ladies' ... be right back."

As she turned to make a dash, she noticed Pat and Tess exchanging glances. Surely, they must have noticed by then how often their flatmate had suddenly rushed off to the bathroom, especially right after breakfast.

But this is dinner, Lacy thought, dismayed at the thought of what her recent attacks of indigestion might mean.

It had been some six weeks since Lacy had spent that passionate night on Pem's narrow bed in Smethwick. Among the Bentinck Street flatmates, complaining about "the curse" was a common joke—but Lacy had been noticeably silent on the subject since her return from her Birmingham train adventure.

Retching into the Savoy Hotel's very elegant commode in the ladies' restroom, she knew that was the final confirmation of what she'd feared after her missed menstruation that month. She'd recently disclosed to a Red Cross nurse she knew that she might well be pregnant—and she was mortified. Her three friends sitting in the swank

Savoy Grill had long shared with each other the most current methods to avoid finding themselves in the family way.

What an absolute fool I was that night.

Struggling to breathe evenly to calm her racing heart, Lacy cupped her hand on her abdomen. Yes, she cursed herself for acting with such abandon with Pem, yet she felt a sudden rush of love and a strange awe and wonder at the evidence that they might have created a life together.

Her brief moment of elation was immediately followed by an avalanche of worries that smothered the moment of joy. She sagged against the toilet stall's marble walls, stifling her sobs.

Oh God, the war ... Pem ... my job ... and what about Teddy? What about money? She had a sudden vision of Granny Farr presiding over sherry hour in her parlor on Beacon Hill. *The shame of it in her eyes! How will I possibly cope?*

She was the first to recognize that she had only herself to blame. From day one, she'd known that Pem was married, with a wife living in Lacy's hometown! There was no one who could help her decide on what she should do next.

Everything from there on out was up to her.

Chapter Twenty-Seven

In the end, Lacy couldn't face her situation alone. She broke down the minute she, Tess, and Pat closed the door after returning home from dinner at the Savoy. Having forgotten all about Debo's upcoming wedding, the three made for the front sitting room, double-checked that the blackout curtains were closed, and turned on a few lamps. The trio formed a tight circle around the glowing small pile of coals in the brazier as they warmed themselves in their drafty Bentinck Street flat.

"You never told us you'd even *seen* Pem up in Birmingham!" Tess began.

"I couldn't," Lacy said, reaching for the handkerchief Pat handed her. "Neither of us could—or should—have told anyone. It was an absolute fluke that Pem and I ran into each other at all in that gigantic factory." Lacy blew her nose and looked from Tess to Pat, adding, "Pem's signed the same sort of security documents Tess and I have. I'm not even allowed to tell you what he was doing up there."

"Well, your trip to Birmingham happened little more than a month ago, so at least you're not that far along," Tess said, "but how do you feel about it? And how do you imagine Pem would feel?"

"If I were married to Pem and there wasn't a war going on," Lacy replied, tears brimming in her eyes again, "I'd be over the moon, but ... it's impossible! And I don't have any idea how Pem would feel.

Maybe, if he knew, it'd be a complication in his life right now that he'd hate!" she cried.

"You don't think he's that kind of a rat, do you?" Pat declared, adding, "Of course, I only have my ex-husband for reference."

Tess declared, "Pem's a doctor, and he seems like such a decent fellow from what we've seen. Do you really think he would end the relationship if he knew he was going to be a father?"

"I don't *know*," Lacy wailed, "but how in the world could I have a baby *now*? We're all holding our breaths to see if the Germans are going to invade England, for God's sake!"

"So you're thinking you can't have it?" Tess asked quietly.

Lacy could only give a slight shake of her head.

Pat suggested, "We could try the scalding hot bath routine and have you jump up and down a lot."

"Oh, for goodness sake, Pat!" Tess complained. "Those are old wives' tales. She needs to find a doctor who'll ... take care of it," she finished with her usual practicality mixed with a look of sympathy cast in Lacy's direction.

Lacy saw that her friends had more than an inkling of the conflicted emotions whirling in her brain while she considered the reality of an unplanned pregnancy at a time when the whole world was on fire. Was it even fair to bring a baby into a world that was falling apart? Getting blitzed nearly every night?

And then there was the practical side. She didn't even know for sure where Pem was so she could write and tell him. And how could she support herself and an infant without a job? She was sure she'd be let go at MI5.

"Please don't tell Victor about this," Lacy pleaded.

"I won't," Tess replied, "but if you decide to have the baby, you can't keep it a secret forever."

Pat nodded in agreement, refilling Lacy's teacup and handing it back to her with a salt cracker. "When are you going to let Pem know?" she asked.

"Even if I knew where he was, what could he do?" Lacy demanded, suddenly aware of the pain and petulance in her voice. "Rush to London to make an honest woman of me? He's *married*. More than likely, he's probably two thousand miles away from here by now, doing some hush-hush job he can't even tell his *wife* about."

Lacy broke down in earnest, burying her face in the handkerchief Pat had loaned her.

"Well, he could still be up in Birmingham, so track him down!" Tess advised bluntly.

Lacy looked up and shook her head. "I had the distinct feeling he was soon headed back to D.C." She swiped the cloth under both eyes, declaring, "And besides, wherever he is, no one like us is supposed to know! What's the use of trying to tell him anything?" The severity of the situation felt as if she were being buried under a pile of rubble. "Besides," she cried, "I've known him for nearly two years, and he's still married to Eleanor, isn't he? What's he done to change that? Nothing! That looks to me that this is the particular path he's sticking to."

"That's because there's a war on!" Tess said, her exasperation evident. "The civil legal system is moribund during times like these. Ask Victor," she declared and then looked as if she regretted her candor. Softening her tone, she said, "Pem loves you, Lacy. I'm certain of it."

"But a baby?" Lacy cried, her emotions running wild. "Pem and Eleanor have never had children in eight years of marriage," she said. "Doesn't that pretty much tell you that neither of them wants any?"

"You don't know that!" Pat protested. "I'm the only one of us that's been divorced," she declared, "and I didn't want to have children with ... with my ex. But that didn't mean I don't want to have little ones someday. Assuming this war ever ends and enough good men survive it."

At Pat's gloomy words, the atmosphere in the room grew even more somber, the only sound issuing from the steadily hissing fire.

Finally, Lacy spoke up. "Look, the more we talk about this, shouldn't I just face it? My relationship with Pem—and now ... *this*—make everything truly hopeless."

She paused, seeking a way to reveal yet another secret she'd been keeping for several days. Finally, she revealed, "I-I've found a Red Cross nurse working in London who I knew when we sailed to Norway with the field hospital I was involved with." Her thoughts flew to the dangerous journey she, Pem, and Noah had endured getting in and out of Scandinavia and then fleeing from the Nazis on all those trains. "She says she knows a doctor who could ..."

Lacy allowed her words to hang in the air, silently recalling the uncomfortable conversation she'd had with Jayne Girard, with whom she'd shared a stateroom on the *Drottningholm*.

Pat said, "So you were pretty sure you might be pregnant before today?"

"Last week, it began to sink in that I might be, and I got in touch with her."

"And you're going to get rid of it?" Tess demanded. "Just like that?"

Stung, Lacy's eyes filled with tears. "Not just like that!" she retorted shrilly, her cry full of the torment ripping through her heart. The life blossoming inside her was part of Pem too, and she missed him so. A secret fear was that a U.S. Army captain in the Medical Corps evacuating casualties on the front lines might not survive the war. The tiny spark of life inside her might be the only part of him she would ever have.

Striking back, she cried, "Do you think I haven't agonized about this?"

"Of course, you have," Pat said, shooting a disapproving look at Tess.

Lacy could feel the moisture sliding down her cheeks. She stared at her hand with the sodden handkerchief balled in her fist. "Having a baby out of wedlock with a married man during wartime is bad enough, but I'm not even allowed to contact him here or in D.C. because I'm not supposed to know *where* he is—and the truth is I *don't* know for sure where he is! If I write him at Walter Reed Hospital or in Birmingham, the censors are bound to report it to his superiors. This is just plain crazy!" She looked up, and her view of Tess and Pat swam before her eyes. "Come on, now, tell me you don't think I'm in an impossible situation. It's *absurd*." She blinked away her tears and beseeched her two friends, "What would *you* two do if you were in my place?"

Pat and Tess exchanged glances, their long silence nearly deafening in the sitting room.

After a moment, Pat said softly, "If I were pregnant, I'd hope you'd stand by me while I faced what you're facing."

Tess looked apologetic for her implied criticism that Lacy was making a hasty decision. "And if I were in your shoes, I'd hope my good friends would go with me to the ... procedure," she added, reaching out to cover Lacy's hand with her own.

Weepy and relieved to hear their support, Lacy offered a watery smile and said, "Well, that's it, then. My Red Cross contact said she'll make the appointment for later this week."

"That is, if you're determined to go through with it ..." Jayne had added with a troubled expression.

Lacy couldn't forget that Pem had pleaded with her to let him know if—

She forced herself to block that thought. What in God's green earth could he do about it even if he *did* know she was pregnant? Wasn't it better to have the abortion sooner rather than later, before the precious product of the love they had for each other became even more real to her—and threatened her sanity?

And my sanity is definitely on the line.

Tall and exuding a no-nonsense demeanor, nurse Jayne Girard slipped a white armband with its distinctive Red Cross symbol on Lacy's sleeve. "Wear this, and let me do the talking," she advised as they headed down the stairs to the tube station that would take them to Islington. Like Jayne, Lacy had donned the uniform she'd worn on the ship that had transported the two women and the rest of the field hospital team on their ill-fated voyage to Norway. The Red Cross nurse had vetoed Tess and Pat accompanying them to the doctor's office.

"Two Red Cross women will not attract attention, and that's exactly what we want."

The thought of having to go to Islington, of all places, prompted Lacy's spirits to sink even lower, especially when Jayne told her that the procedure to end her pregnancy would take place at three o'clock in the afternoon in that borough north of the Thames where she'd run into Teddy at Hannigan's.

"Unfortunately, you're most probably just outside the legal limit of seven weeks pregnant," Jayne explained, referring to England's 1929 Infant Life Preservation Act, which criminalized "the deliberate destruction of a child capable of being born alive" *after* seven weeks of gestation. "Most women, like you, don't even know they've conceived until well into the second month. At that point, it practically takes an Act of Parliament to get a doctor to agree to perform the procedure."

They stepped onto the train and took seats beside one another.

As the tube train gathered speed, Lacy asked above the clatter, "How do you know this doctor we're seeing?" She attempted to make her question sound casual. It was anything but.

"I don't. Know him, I mean. I know a nurse who knows ... *of* ... him."

"Oh." Lacy paused and then ventured, "Is he considered ... reputable?"

Jayne looked at her intently. "You know that old saying? 'Beggars can't be choosers?' It was the best I could do," she said, and Lacy heard defensiveness in her tone. "I felt I owed you since you got me and our field hospital team out of Sweden on that ship barely a step ahead of the invading Germans. One of the British doctors I met on board finagled my getting off in Italy with him, and we made it back to England even before you did."

Lacy merely nodded, grateful for Jayne's help but numb to her chatter about her recent engagement to her rescuer from on board the Swedish ship. Lacy hadn't been at all happy to learn that the seedy part of Islington was home to less-than-respectable doctors willing to make extra money ending unwanted pregnancies.

It would be in Islington of all places!

In the wake of her only other visit there, Teddy had made no attempt to contact her. The few inquiries she'd had time to make about him had turned up no clue as to where he was or what he was doing. She was counting on the chances of her encountering him in Islington a second time being almost zero, thank heavens.

Jayne led the way up the tube station steps and into the main thoroughfare. A block further down, she pointed to a tarnished brass plaque tacked onto a down-at-the-heels building. It had no doctor's name engraved but merely said Surgery, which Lacy had learned meant only that the building housed a medical office. She'd thought both Tess and Pat had looked relieved when Jayne had insisted they not accompany her.

Addressing the flatmates just before leaving Bentinck Street for the appointment, Jayne had advised, "Don't think you're letting Lacy down. You two will have plenty to do looking after her when we get back."

Lacy had felt anxious at hearing Jayne's words, which had sounded quite ominous. She began to wonder about how many things could go wrong. Any operation could be dangerous, and she dreaded to contemplate the whispered tales of coat hanger abortions performed in back alleys. At least Jayne had located a proper doctor and was herself a nurse.

When she and Jayne had arrived at their dreaded destination, Lacy stood back a step while Jayne knocked on a door that was sorely in need of a new coat of paint. Within seconds, a woman opened it a crack. Recognizing their uniforms, she opened it wider and bid them to enter. Lacy and Jayne found themselves in a small waiting room with dingy walls painted a mottled, sickly green. A few uncomfortable wooden chairs were scattered about, but no tables or reading matter were in evidence.

"Have a seat," the receptionist said perfunctorily. "I'll tell her you're here."

"*Her*?" Jayne echoed.

"Doctor Jones's nurse will explain ... and then you can decide."

Confused, Lacy asked, "The doctor is a—"

"No, a man," Jayne corrected, casting a look of irritation at the receptionist's retreating back.

Before Lacy could ask another question, the nurse appeared. Her uniform was rumpled, and a pack of Craven A cigarettes peeked out from her skirt pocket. "Dr. Jones was called away," she announced. "I didn't know how to reach you."

"How soon can we reschedule?" Jayne asked crisply.

The nurse paused a long moment, gave a glance at their uniforms, and responded, "Hard to say," before adding confidentially, "But you know we nurses do most of the dirty work for these procedures, don't we, just?" She paused, then said casually, "*I* can do it if you like." The woman cast a cursory glance in Lacy's direction. "That is, if you'll pay the same fee."

"You know perfectly well that you're not licensed to perform this operation," Jayne retorted.

Dr. Jones's nurse volleyed back, "And surely you know how difficult it is to get anyone to perform it *at all* these days." She shrugged.

"I can do it now, or you can make an appointment for ... whenever." Her fingers were stroking the cigarette pack in her pocket. "It may be a while, though, as I believe Doctor has been called to report to the medical recruiting office or something."

Lacy had a gut feeling the woman was lying, but before either woman said anything further, Lacy blurted, "Look, let's get it over with." She looked at Jayne. "Will you stay in the room with me?"

Jayne's lips formed a straight line, and she shook her head. "No, and I recommend you do *not* do this, Lacy."

"What choice do I have?" she protested, hearing her voice rise in distress. She took a step toward Dr. Jones's nurse while pleading with Jayne, "Will you at least wait for me here?"

Jayne hesitated before answering. Clearly, most abortions in Britain often skirted the law, but a person unlicensed to do the procedure put everyone involved at risk. Jayne avoided looking at the other nurse.

"You know, Lacy, I could lose my license and be fired from the Red Cross and sent back to the States if anyone found out I countenanced a nonphysician performing this procedure."

Just then, a siren began to wail. All three women exchanged startled glances and grimaced.

"Oh, for God's sake! Not an air raid *now*!" Lacy groaned. "Not again! It's still daylight!"

The sirens grew more shrill and more insistent.

"It's the East End," the nurse replied, alluding to the many industrial targets the Germans had hit during their months of bombing London.

Jayne said urgently, "Clearly, they haven't finished shelling all their targets. Let's go!" she commanded, turning to leave. "The air raid shelter's nearby."

"So is our basement!" the nurse declared over the howl of the sirens. "We have a surgery down there. Kill two birds with one stone?"

Lacy couldn't believe the woman's nerve. *She must really want my money*, she thought, fighting off a feeling of panic at the notion of undergoing surgery in the middle of an air raid.

"Lacy! Come on!" Jayne cried.

"What's the difference?" Lacy shouted over the piercing decibels, her voice strident with a sense of futility she'd never felt before in her life. "Either I die on my way to an air raid shelter, or my baby dies in a basement. It's all the same."

"Well, make up your mind," Dr. Jones's nurse said impatiently, retreating toward the door she'd entered through. "As you said before, it's your chance to get it over with."

Jayne's dark expression mirrored her unhappiness with the entire situation. "Do whatever you think is best, Lacy," she declared, tight-lipped. She then strode out of the room, calling over her shoulder, "If you make it through all this and can walk, meet me in the tube station when it's over. I'll wait there *one* hour after the all clear blows."

Nurse Jayne Girard bolted for the front door that would lead her outside and to the underground refuge from the bombs that were whistling to earth. By the time Jayne had disappeared through the front door, sirens had reached an ear-splitting pitch. Like a sleep-walker, Lacy numbly followed Dr. Jones's nurse, who was ten feet in front of her, bolting down a long flight of stairs.

Chapter Twenty-Eight

"Fully awake now, are you?"

Lacy opened her eyes and groggily peered at her wristwatch. "I'm awake, sort of," she said. "Is it ... over?" A wave of emotion swept over her, and her throat clogged with unshed tears.

Oh, Pem ... I am so sorry.

The thought of what might have been ... *who* that tiny embryo, no longer protected by her body, might have been ... left her emotionally paralyzed. She could hardly breathe. And yet, she knew, given her impossible circumstances, it would have been sheer lunacy to bring a life into a world amidst a war like the one that had been raging in the skies above the operating table.

"Time you were up and out," the nurse said briskly. She was no longer wearing a mask and had shed her rubber gloves. She helped Lacy sit up and handed her a sanitary pad. "Here, you will have some bleeding, so put this on—and be quick about it! I have to clean up here before Doctor comes back."

Lacy's head was literally spinning from the aftermath of the anesthetic as she followed the nurse's bidding and prepared to leave.

"Righteo," the nurse said briskly. "Off you go now," she added and, with her next breath, stated the amount she expected Lacy to pay.

Tucking the proffered pound notes into her bra, she steadied Lacy on her feet. Slowly, they mounted the stairs to the ground floor.

"I don't think I can walk to the tube by myself," Lacy murmured, sagging against the wall. Her stomach was in turmoil, and she was afraid she might faint.

"Oh, all right," the nurse grumbled. "I'll help you across to the station."

The two women slowly walked through the office and out onto the street.

"Do you ... uh ... substitute for Dr. Jones quite often?" Lacy asked, feeling a hundred years old with each step. Praying for a "yes," she hoped that the woman had performed abortions in Dr. Jones's absence more than a few times.

"I do them whenever the opportunity arises," the nurse replied and then winked. "I'm the scheduler too, so tell your friends." A sly smile crossed her lips. "It all works out rather well for the patients as well as me." She gazed up at the late-afternoon sky and then down the street. "Luckily, no bombs landed near here this time," she said before confiding, "Our neighborhood pub got hit a while back."

Lacy remembered the first day of the Blitz the previous September when Hannigan's had gotten blown flat. How much had changed since Victor had sent her on that first significant assignment. How complicated life had become.

Nodding goodbye to her unenthusiastic escort, Lacy clung to the stair railing as Dr. Jones's nurse darted across the street without a backward glance. The second Lacy took the first step down to the deserted lower level, her assaulted midsection began to contract painfully. Inhaling deeply to clear her foggy brain, she concluded that the air raid's all clear signal had probably awakened her from her drugged, unconscious state.

Gingerly descending the final steps to the train platform, Lacy continued to feel woozy from the ether and more than a little nauseous. She slowly made her way down the rest of the distance and felt relieved beyond measure when she spotted Jayne sitting alone on a bench beside the platform, reading a newspaper.

"Ah ... there you are," Jayne said, setting the paper aside and rising to her feet. Lacy surmised that her face must have looked pale and wan, for Jayne swiftly stepped forward, took Lacy's arm, and led her to a train that had just pulled in. "Are you in pain?" she asked with a concerned expression.

"What kind of pain?" Lacy replied wearily. "Physical, mental, or emotional?" Then she collapsed on a train seat just as the doors slid shut.

Before her eyes closed, she saw that a gush of blood had run down her legs and was pooling on the floor.

———

Lacy sensed people in her bedroom, but the agony searing through her abdomen absorbed all her concentration.

"She's got a very high fever," she heard Jayne murmur. "I think you'd better call a doctor."

"What about the one who did the procedure?" Tess demanded. "Can't you get a hold of him?"

Lacy heard Jayne lower her voice, and then the door closed and a muffled but heated conversation began raging in the hall.

———

Lacy had no memory of being transported to a hospital, nor was she aware of having had a second surgery, this one performed by a doctor whom Victor Rothschild knew. She only comprehended that her abdomen felt as if it had been run over by one of Britain's A22 tanks.

A few days later, when visiting hours were allowed, Tess and Pat walked through the door.

"Am I being sacked?" Lacy asked Tess before she'd even arrived at her bedside. One of the nurses had related to Lacy the drama of her arrival, with Baron Rothschild no less directing the entire staff. "Tess, I begged you not to tell Victor!"

"No, you're not being sacked—yet," Tess retorted. "And let me tell you, Victor's medical man saved your life. Fortunately, he also knows to keep his mouth shut."

Lacy tucked her chin beneath the sheet and said nothing more.

"You could have *died*," Pat exclaimed from the foot of the bed. "Victor was as worried as the rest of us." She leaned closer and lowered her voice. "But we didn't dare tell him some quack nurse perforated your uterus with some sort of sharp—and probably unsterile—instrument. That's surely why you went septic."

Tess warned, "As it is, Victor wanted to report that Jones fellow, but we fibbed a bit and told him you went to a doctor's office somewhere on your own and we didn't know the MD's name. And by the way," she added testily, "Pat turned out to be a blood match for you and gave you a pint, along with others. And in addition to finding a doctor to repair the mess you were in, Victor was the one who got you the latest, rather miraculous medication, penicillin."

Lacy continued to remain silent, too tired and miserable to do anything else.

Pat tried to lighten the tense mood invading the room by chirping, "And lucky you, it's only recently been prescribed for sepsis."

Tess, still clearly worried and out of sorts, declared, "Yes, Lacy Forbes, you *are* one lucky lady! I hope you realize that."

Lacy didn't feel at all lucky and, in fact, was battling a shroud of gloom that had settled over her from the moment she'd awakened in Dr. Jones's basement. She had to struggle to make a show of gratitude toward her friends.

"Please tell Lord Rothschild how much I appreciate what he's done," she managed to say in a monotone that she realized didn't *sound* very grateful. "What you *all* have done," she amended, knowing on some deep level that she did, indeed, owe them all a lot.

Later that afternoon, a nurse informed her that the botched abortion had caused a significant loss of blood. "We had to tap into the blood usually reserved for patients fresh from the battlefield."

The woman's disapproving tone left Lacy with the feeling that she'd probably deprived combat soldiers of desperately needed care for their wounds.

The following day, Victor's doctor entered Lacy's hospital room and stood beside the bed. The surgeon looked very thin in his white coat, which he'd left unbuttoned. His hair was salt-and-pepper gray, and his dark eyes, framed by grizzled eyebrows, searched her face. Gazing up at him from her pillow, Lacy imagined Dr. Roger Taylor was just beyond the age to be sent to the front lines to serve in the medical corps, and she was thankful that someone of his experience had been called in on her case.

"You had us rather worried, my dear," he said. "How are you feeling today? Still tired, I suspect."

Lacy nodded in agreement and waited for him to shame her as his nurse had done.

Instead, he was kindness itself and took her hand in his. "I'm glad to see your color has improved," he commented, taking her pulse with a quick glance at his wristwatch. "The penicillin has done wonders to clear up the infection." Still holding her hand, he said gently, "I can imagine how ... difficult all this has been for you. I'm pleased to see the progress you've made ... but I'm afraid it's rather uncertain what your long-term prognosis might be. If the damage done to your body might prevent future pregnancies."

Dr. Taylor's words hit her hard, and she couldn't manage a response. She was aware of how intently he was watching her reaction to his alarming news.

"You're not married, I understand."

"No," she murmured. "Not remotely."

"Well, then, there will be time for your body to continue healing, and we can hope for the best ... down the road."

"And the odds are ...?" she pressed, then wondered why she had bothered to ask.

"It's impossible to say at this point, but I felt I should tell you that there could be future adhesions that might make conceiving ... difficult."

"I see."

Was it some sort of punishment? Some part of her wondered whether it was exactly what she deserved. *She'd let that Dr. Jones's nurse ...*

"I'm very sorry you've had such a tough time," Dr. Taylor said quietly.

"So am I," she replied, looking past the surgeon's shoulder.

In her continuing silence, he patted her arm, then turned to leave. As he did, Lacy faced her head toward the wall and waited several seconds for the door to close, longing for sleep. The problem was that her fevered dreams in the hospital were filled with wailing infants and patients in nearby beds, writhing in pain. Just as she imagined she had been.

The following afternoon, Pat burst into Lacy's hospital room and shared the news. "The doctor told us you'll be released in a day or two."

Tess, following right behind, declared, "Just in time for Debo's wedding." She set a newspaper for Lacy to read on the bedside table. "And Pat and I used some of our ration points to buy you a new dress! You still have your long white gloves, yes?"

Lacy wasn't sure exactly where she'd stored them but nodded in the affirmative.

Pat added excitedly, "Debo said to tell you she's absolutely thrilled you'll make it to see her tie the knot with Andrew!"

Lacy felt the first small scintilla of pleasure she'd experienced in a long time at seeing that the friends she'd met those last few years truly seemed to care about her. She was grateful, too, that her flatmates appeared to have made allowances for her ill grace regarding all the efforts Victor and the two of them had made on her behalf during her convalescence. Like everything else, fine fabrics were restricted commodities during wartime, and she was touched by Pat and Tess's very generous gift. She summoned an appreciative smile and tried to join in on their animated chatter about Deborah Mitford's upcoming nuptials. Even so, she was relieved when, a quarter of an hour later, the stickler-for-the-rules nurse on duty that day ushered her two best friends out of her room.

As Lacy watched them leave, voiceless cries caught in her throat in spite of their kindness.

But don't you see? A new dress can't make up for this awful emptiness.

She heard the door to her hospital room close, powerless even to form a complete sentence to express the latest wave of bereavement she felt or explain her ever-present crushing sense of loss. Of Pem. Of their baby. Of any contact with Teddy or Granny Farr. Even contact with a mother who had abandoned her children at every turn.

But who are you to ask for pity? she scolded herself silently. *Are you any better, Lacy Forbes? At least June let you live ... Pem will think you're a monster.*

Lacy once again turned toward the wall, unable even to cry anymore. Plunging her head deeper into her pillow, she dreaded the dreams that were sure to return that night—ones populated by lost, abandoned infants haunting her troubled sleep and more than likely disturbing it for many nights to come.

Lacy was well enough on April 16 to sit in a front pew on the bride's side of St. Bartholomew's Chapel, one of many witnesses to the joining in matrimony of Deborah Mitford and Lord Andrew Cavendish. How much life had changed since that night three years earlier when she, Debo, and Kick Kennedy had all entered the Buckingham Palace ballroom for the presentation ceremony to the King and Queen. And how could Lacy ever forget her memory of the scene around the table at the 400 Club, meeting Pat, Victor, his wife Barbara, and Tess for the first time? And later that same evening, she'd had that encounter with Burgess and Blunt, Cambridge University classmates who'd spent the entire night making rude remarks about Americans and Jews.

Lacy begged off joining everyone for the reception at the Mitfords' Rutland Gate, which wasn't far from the American embassy residence where she and Kick had set out with Debo for their royal presentation.

"I'm feeling a bit wobbly still," she prevaricated.

The skeptical glance sharp-eyed Tess gave her showed that at least one friend doubted that was her real reason for heading home.

"The Mitford place took a bad hit just a few days ago," Pat related, alluding to the location of the wedding reception. "Half the windows on one side were blown out, but apparently, they've filled the frames with armloads of camellias donated by the Duke and Duchess of Devonshire."

"It's a scene not to be missed!" Tess commented, arching an eyebrow.

Lacy again made her apologies and was able to hail a cabbie outside St. Bartholomew's Church, deeply grateful she could, indeed, miss it all. Marriage celebrations were the exact opposite of what she felt like joining. Climbing into the taxi, she felt very *un*married, having not heard from Pem since Birmingham.

Chapter Twenty-Nine

In the weeks following Lacy's second surgery and the Mitford-Cavendish wedding, she had been amazed at how incredibly kind and considerate Victor had been. He seemed to appreciate her need to keep busy with the kind of assignments that required strict attention to detail. Occasionally, she would force herself to face the blank piece of stationery sitting on the small desk in her bedroom where she'd attempted to write Pem about all that had happened since they'd last been together. Each day she didn't receive any word from *him* made it even harder. Her heart told her she should surely tell him about the pregnancy, but then it hardened with questions that governed all.

Why hasn't he found a way to confirm he arrived safely in D.C. … or made sure, after Birmingham, that she—?

During working hours, she kept her mind focused on double-checking the German translations of intercepted transmissions sent over from Bletchley that Lord Rothschild put on her desk. When she seemed stronger physically, he assigned her the job of coordinating with Scotland Yard in their investigations of London bombing incidents to determine whether any of them had been caused by ground-level sabotage rather than enemy aerial attacks.

"I'm collecting data on the number of these kinds of in-country incidents," confided Lord Rothschild, "so I want you to be sure to get all the details you can gather from the local constabulary's search and reporting teams."

The work required careful gathering of evidence and then intense concentration to assess it all. Victor's assignments had become a real boon, as Lacy hardly had a second during the day to think about the sadness that descended in waves when it was time to sleep.

In early May, Victor surprised both his assistants by announcing, "I've arranged for you ladies to be fitted with ATS uniforms today."

Lacy looked at Tess questioningly, mouthing the letters "A.T.S.?"

"That's the Auxiliary Territorial Service," Tess replied promptly. "Basically, like the chaps', the uniforms are army-issued khaki-colored woolen tunics with nice brass buttons. The skirts for the women are stick-straight and fall below the knee." She looked at Victor with a pleased expression. "Finally! We're in the army, just like *you*," she chortled. "It's about time we were recognized as such! Will we also be eligible for military medals and pensions?" she teased.

Before he could answer, Lacy asked, "Will they let *me*, an American, wear a British uniform?"

"If *I* say so, they will. Here," said their boss, handing Tess a slip of paper. "Take yourselves to this military tailor shop. They're expecting you. My order for your uniforms and the address are right there. Be back at the office in an hour."

Tess excitedly tucked his instructions into her purse. "By the way, Colonel Rothschild, sir," she asked with mocking deference, "what rank are we to be?"

Victor revealed one of his rare smiles. "I've told them to issue you badges of subalterns. If you both behave, you might one day be promoted to junior commanders."

A few days later, Victor sent Lacy out to make another acquisition.

"Your file says you worked for American newspapers, yes?"

"Yes, the *Baltimore Sun* in the London bureau and the *Boston Globe* in the States the year before I came back to Britain."

"Did you ever take photographs in those jobs?"

Lacy paused, remembering how she had used her small Kodak camera

when sent out on silly assignments about teas and charity events.

Whatever Victor was hinting at, however, sounded intriguing, so she quickly answered, "Oh, yes, I've shot film on stories I've covered."

"Good! I want you to go to this address and pick up a Leica camera confiscated from a German spy we arrested recently." Lacy knew that both motion picture and still Leica cameras, made in Germany, were some of the best in the world.

I sure hope I can figure out how to use it.

Victor informed her, "It's a series two, nice and small, and it takes sharp pictures. Be sure to have the boys at Scotland Yard thoroughly demonstrate how it works." He pointed to the directions he was handing her. "I've arranged for payment through my bank, so purchase plenty of film to go with it."

"And what sort of pictures will I be taking?" Lacy asked, wondering whether she was about to become a full-fledged undercover spy for MI5.

"Bomb sites," Victor said. "You won't just write reports. From here on out, you'll illustrate them with close-up photographs for our files."

Lacy kept hoping that Pem would find some way to contact her, but the weeks passed by with no word from him whatsoever. It bothered her to no end that she hadn't a clue where he was or when she might hear from him. Didn't he ever think about their last night in Birmingham?

In her few private hours, she fought against dwelling on her decision to end the pregnancy, but as Pem's continuing silence stretched to months since they'd last been together, her spirits began to sink to new depths.

If he truly cared, he'd manage somehow to get in touch, she thought, resentment starting to fester whenever she allowed her thoughts to drift in that direction. And, as per usual, the other section of her brain declared, *There's a war going on, stupid!*

Another thought began to plague Lacy. Even if he *did* contact her and she revealed she'd been pregnant and put an end to it, wouldn't Pem, a doctor who'd pledged to "do no harm," consider her a dreadful human being?

Everything between us now has changed.

In her effort to stop dwelling on her harrowing experience in Dr. Jones's Islington basement, she began to obsess, instead, about what had certainly proven to be the futility of conducting a love affair with a legally unavailable man during a war.

With each passing week, Lacy forced her thoughts to devise some way to put Pem out of her mind. With fierce determination, she began to plot two strategies: finding out where her brother, Teddy, was and concentrating on doing the best job for Lord Rothschild she possibly could. Perhaps if she could stay focused on those dual goals, she could blot out the persistent feeling of abandonment and the simmering grief that lay just below the surface.

When Tess asked her one warm spring day whether she'd heard anything from Pem or let him know what had happened, Lacy experienced a sudden flare of anger and hurt burning furiously in her chest.

"Actually," she began with a steely effort to keep her tone devoid of emotion, "I've not had one word." She paused, the familiar feeling of gloom descending once again. Then she looked at Tess directly to underscore what she was going to say next. "As a matter of fact," she declared, an iron shield beginning to encircle her soul, "I've decided that 'must move on' is going to be my mantra from here on out." She inhaled a deep breath before she added, "So, when you get a moment in private, please tell Pat that I'd greatly appreciate it if we three didn't raise the subject of Pem anymore."

"Lacy," Tess said, her tone full of sympathy, "I can understand why not hearing from him is terribly difficult, but you just don't seem yourself. Not since ... well ... since you came home from the hospital. My mum once told me that she felt rather *depressed*, I guess one would call it, after a baby of hers was stillborn a few years before I came along. Gloomy all the time, she described it. Thinking no one cared about how terribly sad she was feeling. Perhaps—"

"No!" Lacy interrupted, desperate not to reveal how totally broken she'd actually felt.

I've managed to present this defense my entire life, so why stop now?

"I'm *fine* now. I just don't want to deal with this anymore! Pem has decided to get on with this life, no doubt, and now I want to get on with *mine* ... that is, if I manage to survive this war."

And most days, she was able to convince herself she'd chosen the best—perhaps the only—sane course.

———

One morning soon after Lacy had made her pronouncement about Pem, Victor was already at his desk when his two assistants arrived at their St. James's office. "Have you heard about King's Cross?" he asked as soon as they'd come through the door.

"What?" they chorused in unison, hanging their coats on the coat tree.

"I'm amazed that the explosions didn't wake you last night, even from Bentinck Street."

"Oh, we hear something practically every night," Tess declared. "Just not what got bombed if it wasn't us."

Lacy added, "It sounded about a mile or so away. As soon as the attack started, we dashed down to your basement bomb shelter and spent the night there."

"So, King's Cross Station got hit?" Tess confirmed. "How badly?"

"I want Lacy to take her camera to go have a look and make a report."

Lacy felt a stab of alarm. "Are you thinking such loud explosions could be *local* sabotage?"

Each time she'd been sent to survey the work of the IRA bombers or the nefarious activities of other in-country malcontents, she'd felt sick to her stomach at the notion Teddy could have been involved.

Shaking his head, Victor told them, "It definitely wasn't locals. It was aerial bombing—and rather large scale, all right—but only on a single target this time." He pointed to the file he was about to hand Lacy. "Our RAF boys have been giving it right back to the Krauts all these months of the Blitz. Churchill thinks massive bombings like the one on King's Cross may be Hitler's last hurrah before he turns his attention to attacking Russia with any weaponry of his we haven't yet destroyed." He turned to Lacy. "Ask the search and recovery lads today to detail to you *exactly* what munitions were dropped on the station—as well as the size and number. The PM wants to compare our data with that of previous big hits around the country. He thinks it may well indicate the attacks are actually diminishing."

"Or," Tess declared, "it may tell us Hitler's got an endless supply of armaments to keep hurling at us!"

"My dear, it could turn out to be precisely the opposite," Victor countered.

Puzzled by Lord Rothschild's comments, Lacy asked, "Why does Mr. Churchill think Russia is an easier target for Hitler than *we* are?"

"Russia's air force is not impressive," Victor replied. "If the King's Cross attack used fewer munitions than big attacks on British targets earlier in this war, it might show Hitler is actually easing off on us a bit because he believes switching his attack to his former ally, full force, is a better use of his limited stockpile of thousand-pound bombs."

"Ah ... I see," Lacy murmured. "Single targets. Fewer bombs aimed at those targets. Either he's running out of the big stuff, or he's going to commit what he's got stockpiled to conquering Russia."

"Or both," said Victor. "Your observations, documented by that camera of yours, might help Winston discover if his theory is correct." He pointed to another folder in his tall pile. "Tess, you and I have an appointment this morning to meet with the sketch artist who'll be drawing the schematics of the last bomb we defused. The Munitions Board has been clamoring for the details. You've got the notes you took that day, yes?"

"Of course!" Tess grabbed her clipboard and her coat. In less than a minute, she and Victor were at the door, Tess asking him with a saucy smile, "And lunch, afterward, at the Savoy?"

"I think the Ritz might be a pleasant change. Anthony Blunt thought he might join us."

When the office door closed, Lacy felt frustrated. She never could understand why Victor and Tess continued to honor their Cambridge University ties with Blunt and Burgess. Both were known as serious drinkers. They were also homosexuals, one discreet, the other quite notorious. It was well known that the other tenants in Victor's building had vociferously complained that Blunt and Burgess's flat had become a "male whorehouse," with men in flamboyant clothing and shrill voices coming and going at all hours.

Lacy didn't give a hoot about what their sexual preferences were, but couldn't such men be blackmailed by their enemies? Her thoughts drifted to the scene she'd happened to witness a week earlier. Burgess, working for MI5 as so many of Victor's Cambridge classmates were, had been sitting on a bench in Regent's Park in the middle of the day. He'd been deep in conversation with the same man in a fedora, speaking with a Russian accent, whom Lacy had spotted talking with Burgess in Hyde Park the previous year. When Burgess's companion had faced a certain way, Lacy had gasped at seeing a wine-red birthmark on his cheek.

My God! Could that be the same fellow who tailed Pem, Noah, and me to the train in Moscow?

How many fedora-sporting Russians with red birthmarks on their faces could there be? Victor's fellow members of The Apostles, a Cambridge secret society, Burgess and Blunt had long embraced far-left politics, but Russia had backed Germany since before the war had even begun in '39. Lacy couldn't help but wonder why the War Office had recruited "the Two *Bs*" to work anywhere near British intelligence agencies.

Reflecting upon the scene at Hyde Park, Lacy heaved a resigned sigh and stowed her Leica, her notebook, and the file Victor had given her about the King's Cross bombing into her satchel and prepared to leave for the bomb site. Musing over the conversation between Victor and Tess she'd just heard, she judged her superior's political views to be far more measured and moderate than those of his more radical classmates. Victor Rothschild was a scientist to his core. He judged things by the facts, not philosophy.

Yet ...

Heading for the door, Lacy couldn't help but wonder why those old school ties kept Tess and Victor so loyal to their Bentinck Street neighbors, especially given the highly secretive nature of Victor's MI5 antisabotage work aimed at preventing the enemy within from striking in support of Germany. And why anyone would trust the Russians—even if currently their Allies— was beyond her.

Did Churchill and the higher-ups in the War Cabinet know what close company the group kept with one another? Lacy had no reason to doubt Tess's or Victor's loyalty toward Britain, but she often wondered whether her boss ever considered how he and Tess might be tainted with guilt by association concerning Burgess and Blunt.

I sincerely hope Victor and Tess know what they're doing.

But Lacy had long since recognized it was best to keep such opinions to herself. She hiked her camera case more firmly on her shoulder and closed and locked the office door behind her. Under her breath, she mumbled the line from Tennyson's poem, "Ours is not to reason why ..."

Chapter Thirty

Lacy stared up at the enormous gap in King's Cross Station's steel-and-glass ceiling. She'd spent the morning and much of the afternoon chronicling the horrific destruction throughout the location and could hardly credit Victor's hinting that Germany's nightly bombings might soon be aimed at Russia instead.

Gingerly climbing up a mound of rubble heaped on top of one of the train platforms, she focused her camera lens on what remained of two massive, chained-together one-thousand-pound bombs that had demolished most of the station's roof and exploded the entire west side of the building. She swiftly grabbed a few shots of the repair crews already busy at work.

"Tell Lord Rothschild we hope to have the station operational in eight days' time," declared the station master, who'd served as her guide. "Apart from the roof and wall, the most serious damage was to Platform Three," he explained as Lacy snapped some wide-angle photos of the large crater. "Worst of all," he noted with dark humor, "those big bruisers exploded the beer vaults below." He winked. "But tell His Lordship that trains will be running out of here in a week or so."

By the time she'd returned to the office, Victor had left for an afternoon meeting at MI5 HQ.

"So, how bad was it at King's Cross?" Tess asked as Lacy hung up her coat and set her Leica on her desk.

"Pretty horrific. Even though the bombs fell in the wee hours, twelve people

died." What she didn't tell Tess was that right as she had been about to leave, the crew had uncovered another body that she'd watched being removed. "I'll be convinced the Blitz is over when the sirens stop wailing every night."

To all of Britain's relief, the sirens did, indeed, mostly stop during May of 1941. Just as Victor had reported and Churchill had forecast, Hitler's Blitz campaign against Britain tapered off to a few sporadic attacks in favor of his opening salvos dropped on Russia.

"So, let's get this straight," Lacy declared to her colleagues. "Russia's now officially on *our* side, despite what they did to the poor Finns and all the other countries they've oppressed around the Baltic?"

She could only think how pleased their upstairs neighbors, Burgess and Blunt, must have been that Russia had switched allegiances. Even so, she wondered how Victor felt about the virulent antisemitism practiced by their recently acquired Russian allies.

By early summer, even the newspapers were declaring the Blitz was over.

"But still," Victor complained, "these damned *in*-country troublemakers continue to cause mischief ... which it remains our job to prevent."

He pointed to a list of incidents with probable attribution to either British Fascists or IRA operatives doing damage in England.

On a Saturday in July, Victor's warnings proved only too true. A sharp series of rings alerted Lacy that someone was at the flat's front door. She was still in her night clothes, feeling dog-tired from the week's work climbing over the rubble to photograph the aftermath of a series of suspicious incidents around London where local infrastructure had been attacked.

The doorbell continued to ring insistently as she scrambled into a dressing gown. She was alone in the flat. Tess was spending the weekend with Victor at some hideaway of his. Pat, too, was away, having left early to spend the day with her new beau, Richard Llewelyn Davies, a young architect who, amazingly enough, specialized in designing hospitals, a profession akin to Pem's.

If Pem were still here, I bet the two of them would become great friends.

She chastised herself roundly for even imagining a life with Pem that included not only her but also her cherished circle of friends. His long silence had made that out of the question.

Remember your mantra! Must move on!

The ringing doorbell was replaced by a sudden pounding on the front door, interrupting her thoughts, which had begun to spiral down in their usual, depressed fashion. Startled by the intensity of the blows against the wood, Lacy sped down the hallway and peeked through the spyhole. With a gasp, she had to grab hold of the front doorknob to steady herself. Allowing a few seconds to take several deep breaths, she flung open the door.

She could hardly believe the sight of her sandy-haired brother standing in the corridor, one bloody hand cradled against his other arm. How had he even known where she was? He'd had only her Gower Street address from before their flat had been bombed out.

"Oh my God, *Teddy!*" she cried, taking in the shocking sight of him. "What's happened?"

"A-an ... accident."

His voice was raspy and raw, his face drained of color. Blood had soaked the front of his threadbare shirt and tattered tweed jacket and dripped down onto one scuffed shoe. The well-fed, robust frame that had once enabled him to excel at downhill skiing at fancy alpine resorts was now emaciated and stooped over at the waist.

"An *accident*?" she exclaimed. "How did you know where I live?"

"Gower Street neighbor ... not bombed out," he struggled to tell her. "You left ... this address."

"Well, thank heavens I did," she exclaimed, gesturing for him to come in. "What in hell happened? Where *were* you?"

"A-accident ..." he repeated, barely above a whisper, before stumbling into the foyer and collapsing on the floor.

Lacy knelt down beside him and peered at the limb he had

wrapped in some sort of rag soaked through with more blood. His eyes fluttered open, and he whispered, "It went off just as I let go."

"*What* went off?" Lacy demanded, a feeling of dread invading her stomach, which was a strong signal that she might well understand what "it" was.

The bloody hand was Teddy's right. It had all the hallmarks of the kind of injury documented in the many reports that crossed her desk. IRA bombings of London's rubbish dumps, post office trash bins, electric transformers, and the left luggage departments of train stations often did lethal damage to the perpetrators before the amateur saboteurs could leave the scenes of their crimes.

"Where did this happen?" Lacy persisted. "And when? It looks as if you've lost a lot of blood."

"In ... a call box. On Wimpole ..."

"You tried to blow up a *telephone* booth on Wimpole Street?" she asked in horror. "Was anyone else hurt?"

"N-no ... just ... me, but ..."

She watched Teddy struggle to find the words to explain—or probably justify—what he'd done, but before he could summon a further response, Lacy left him where he was on the floor. She dashed down the hall to find some clean rags or a bath towel to sop up the blood and bind his hands more firmly so he wouldn't bleed to death.

At least I know the basics of first aid, she thought, searching frantically for the right material. Thank heavens Red Cross workers had taught all of the Finland Field Hospital support team members the fundamentals before they'd sailed from New York. As Lacy grabbed some Turkish towels from the linen supply and sped back to the foyer, she worried that her brother's injuries might well require hospitalization. How would she answer the hard questions sure to be asked about how Teddy's hand had come to be so mutilated?

Kneeling beside him, she demanded, "How often have you set off explosives like this?"

He didn't open his eyes but mumbled, "First time ... a test ..."

"A test of what? You wanted to see how many people you could kill inside a telephone booth?" she said sarcastically.

Eyes still closed, he whispered, "A test of me."

"Oh, wonderful! To be accepted by those supposed friends of yours, you had to prove yourself?" Lacy shook her head in frustration.

"This isn't a fraternity initiation, Teddy. Innocent people could have been killed. And you can't have thought doing Hitler's bidding like this was going to make Northern Ireland an independent country? The Fuhrer is a monster and will certainly double-cross people like you who are risking their lives so foolishly."

Teddy's lids flew open. "Silly debutantes like *you*," he said with a nasty edge to his voice, "know nothing about politics and world affairs."

"Oh, for goodness sake!" she retorted, completely out of patience with him. "You're not even Irish. We Forbes immigrated from *Scotland*!"

Teddy fell silent as she gingerly began to unwrap his hand and put the bloody rags to one side.

"And as for knowing about politics and world affairs," she snapped in her big sister voice, "you might be very surprised to learn how much I *do* know about the nasty universe you've been inhabiting."

Lacy swallowed hard when she saw three fingers were missing as Teddy's blood pooled on the parquet floor. Glancing down at his face, she saw that his eyes had rolled back in his head and his body had gone limp.

Dear God ... how much blood has he lost?

"Oh, Teddy," she murmured, "all this to blow up a British call box? Half of London has been leveled to ashes," she declared, sopping up the blood with the towel, "and you thought this would amount to more than a hill of Boston baked beans?"

But Teddy didn't hear what she said because he'd truly passed out this time. Now, Lacy's biggest fear was that he might have found her too late.

Once again, Victor came to the rescue. He arrived less than a half hour after Lacy's call from the same hospital she had been admitted to after her botched abortion and engaged the same Dr. Taylor to attend to her brother's injuries. She'd employed her MI5's "Assistant" voice to ring every place she imagined Tess and Victor could be and finally found them at a country cottage on one of his estates.

"I am *so* sorry for calling you away from your weekend ... uh ... getaway," she apologized, both embarrassed and concerned about what Victor and Tess must have been thinking. They were all standing outside the recovery room where Teddy was resting after his surgery. With a worried glance through the glass window at her brother's still form, Lacy said, "I know that I should have told you the minute I saw my brother in that Islington pub with all those suspected IRA sympathizers, but—"

"He's your baby brother," Victor cut her off. "I can understand you wanted to protect him, but, Lacy, this is a serious breach of security."

"I realize that," she replied. "I'll understand if you want to sack me, but I didn't want him to bleed to death, so I brought him here and called you."

"I have a sister like you," Victor said quietly, "and I hope she'd do the same for me ... but we have a problem. Hanging is the penalty for sedition."

"He could be *hanged*?" Lacy felt her throat tighten. "Like those German fellows who entered Britain with that spy, Vera Eriksen?"

"Yes. It could very well happen if the police can link him to the explosives found in the call box. What did he have with him when he arrived at the flat?"

"Nothing ... Just the clothes on his back and less than a farthing in his pocket."

"Do you know if anyone else was hurt by the explosion he caused?"

"He said no."

"Do you think anyone saw him coming in the building on Bentinck?"

Lacy thought a moment, then replied, "I don't know for sure, but there was no one in our corridor, and everything seemed pretty quiet on a Saturday morning."

"All right," Victor said decisively. "Perhaps there's no evidence as to what he was up to." He looked at her sternly. "I have trusted you, Lacy, and you've let me down."

"I know," she replied, feeling miserable. "I kept telling myself I didn't know for *sure* that he'd been caught up in doing any destructive mischief and was just worried about the company he kept."

Victor gave a faint nod, his expression grim. "You've been a valuable asset in my unit, but if this got out ... that my own assistant harbored a brother busily sabotaging public spaces in Britain, our goose would be cooked." He paused, and Lacy could see he was considering several alternatives. "Have you any idea how often he was put up to carrying out orders like this?"

"He said it was his first time—a 'test,' he called it, to prove himself to the group."

"Ah," Victor said. "But first attempts can do plenty of damage to innocents, as you and I have both seen all too often."

Lacy studied his face as he mulled over the fact that at least it had been Teddy's first attempt at sabotage.

"I know it's no excuse, but this stupidity was driven more by my poor brother's obvious desire to belong to *something* than a lethal protest against Mother England."

"His stupidity, as you describe it, could have killed or maimed people who have nothing to do with the struggles in Ireland. Children playing nearby—"

"Oh, do I realize that," Lacy interrupted with a shudder, "but please, Victor. My brother had such a screwed-up childhood, he would never have lit the fuse if he'd seen any kids nearby!"

After a long pause, he declared, "I am going to send Tess to the call box your brother attempted to blow up to survey the scene. If she can confirm no one in the area got hurt and that there's no damning physical evidence or witness to link this to your brother, her report will thereby conclude very little."

"Oh, Victor, thank you! I'm so grate—"

"Hold on a minute," he interrupted. "If there's a report that anyone else got hurt or conclusive physical evidence linked to your brother, there's nothing I can do. He will be charged with sedition, and *you'll* be lucky, as an accessory, merely to be deported yourself."

"An accessory?" she repeated, stunned.

Victor nodded, then continued, "You might well be deemed one. If Tess *doesn't* find a problem for us there, however, then I'll have him arrested here at the hospital as an alien without proper documentation and have him deported rather than interned here in Britain at His Majesty's expense. We'll send him back to America on the next military flight, courtesy of some U.S. Army contacts of mine."

"Can you do that?" Lacy wondered aloud and then looked around to see whether anyone outside the hospital recovery room had heard her. "America's not in this war. I didn't know there were regular U.S. Army flights back home."

"Well, now you do," he snapped, "so I expect you not to mention it to anyone, along with what I propose to do about your brother."

Lacy was silent for a long moment, having heard the deserved rebuke in his tone. Teddy *could* have killed innocent people, but from what her brother had said, she was fairly certain that Tess would find no evidence in the call box to link Teddy to anything. Taking a deep breath, Lacy began to feel a tiny bit calmer. She was intensely touched that Victor would even consider making a sub-rosa arrangement to save her brother's life—an action that could ruin *his* career and reputation, yet he was willing to risk it.

Teddy would have lost his entire hand but for the surgery performed by the same skilled Dr. Taylor who had saved her life. Her brother had remained sullen before his operation despite all the kindness shown to him. It occurred to her that perhaps he was as damaged psychologically as he was physically by the life he'd been leading. Victor's decision to send him back home, if he could, was by far the best of many unfortunate options, and she was grateful beyond words that he might get a break.

Lord Rothschild pointed through the hospital's glass window into the recovery room. "If it proves possible for me to do this, in whose care should we thrust this troubled brother of yours?"

"Our grandmother," she said decisively. "Cecilia Farrington, in Boston, would take him in hand, and I can assure you, she would see that he behaved."

Victor nodded. "If we are able to release him, I will pass along that information to the officials who will ensure that he's delivered to her door."

Lacy sought Victor's gaze. "I can't thank you enough for your doing this, Victor," she said softly.

"It still depends on what Tess finds in the call box," he warned.

"I understand," she said, nodding. "I know you don't have time to hear the reasons Teddy chose this path, but at heart, he's just …"

"A wounded bird?" Victor asked.

Lacy wondered how often Victor himself had been hurt by slurs and bullying. Perhaps he had been raised by parents who'd shown him little affection in the same way Teddy had.

"Wounded, for sure," she repeated, "and now his shattered hand."

"Well, if all goes as we hope, at least that hand will keep him out of *all* armies, including the IRA and America's, if it comes to that." Victor regarded her intently. "Are there any other secrets you've been keeping from me that you need to confess?"

Lacy's heart gave a lurch. She knew it was time to give Victor an honest answer.

"Yes, there are, but I can't tell you *what* they are."

Chapter Thirty-One

"You can't—or won't—tell your commanding officer what secrets you've been keeping from me, even when you're given a direct order to do so?" Victor said, and she heard the edge of distrust in his voice again.

Lacy swallowed hard and replied, "Sir, there are some things your Official Secrets Act and America's version of it forbid me to say."

Only the sound of nurses bustling up and down the corridor filled the frosty silence between Lacy and Lord Rothschild.

Desperate to break it, she blurted, "What I've kept from you doesn't relate to *anything* that affects our work. What I can tell you, though, is that I saw Pem—Dr. Charles Pembroke—when I was in Birmingham. It was completely by accident, but I should have told you immediately that he instantly recognized I was going to ride a munitions train back to London." She sought Victor's gaze, pleading with him to understand. "Please believe me when I assure you that I told him *nothing* of my assignment, but—"

"No doubt he was distressed that your superiors were putting you in harm's way like that?" Victor interrupted.

Lacy raised an eyebrow, answering promptly, "Yes. He assumed I was in Birmingham on orders from you, but I got on the train anyway without telling him I was boarding the car to do surveillance."

Victor shrugged. "I knew all about your seeing him there and that he was undoubtedly the father of the child … you lost."

Lacy smothered her surprise at hearing that and could sense he was watching closely for her response. "Tess told you," she declared, struggling to keep her answer as undramatic as possible, although her temper flared at learning Tess had gone against her word. "She'd said she wouldn't."

"She had to when she begged me to find a doctor for you when you were so ill. But it didn't take a genius for me to guess how you'd become pregnant. I knew about Charles Pembroke's top secret posting at the train factory in Birmingham."

"Of course, you knew," Lacy echoed glumly, well aware that MI5 higher-ups like Victor appeared to be all-knowing, all-seeing all the time!

He shrugged again. "My meetings at HQ, you know," he offered, confirming her suspicions. He patted her hand. "Let's just agree from here on out that whenever your conscience pricks you about something, you tell me about it." A faint smile appeared before he added, "Or tell me as much as you can, and I'll decide if you should be sacked for holding back."

Grateful to receive such a generous reprieve, Lacy nodded vigorously to underscore her acceptance of their agreed-upon way forward.

Victor directed her, "Now, the minute Teddy Forbes regains consciousness, go in there and tell him to keep his mouth shut and obey the young lieutenant I've assigned to guard him." He turned to leave, then turned back, "And give your grandmother's name and address to the officer. If Tess can find nothing incriminating, we'll get word to Mrs. Farrington that her grandson is on his way."

Relief flooding her entire body, Lacy moved toward Victor and impulsively hugged him in thanks, exclaiming, "Now I totally understand why Tess ... well, you know ..."

"Puts up with me?" Victor said, his lips revealing his amusement as Lacy stepped back. "I imagine it's quite similar to how that fellow, Pem, puts up with *you*. You bright young things can be quite bothersome at times, you know."

When Victor said Pem's name aloud, Lacy found she couldn't summon an apt response. Instead, she faced the door to the recovery room. "I'll stay here until my brother wakes up and then let him know that his days in the junior ranks of the IRA are over."

As Lacy had hoped, Tess found nothing but a dented, barely blood-spattered red call box on Wimpole Street and no reports of witnesses or injuries. *Only Teddy's,* Lacy thought sadly. Lucky for him, the explosive detritus had been whisked away—probably by his accomplices—with no incriminating trace of who or what had caused the vandalism.

As a result, within days, Lacy and Teddy were given a uniformed escort to Heston Air Park, a military airfield eleven miles outside London. Lieutenant Moffett, the young officer from the hospital, was at the wheel and assigned to ensure that Lacy's brother was "strapped into his seat on the plane, and the doors closed for takeoff," as Victor had ordered sternly before they'd left London.

Sitting beside Teddy in the backseat of the car, Lacy eyed her brother's hand, still a ball of bandages, with his right arm in a sling. He seemed otherwise unhurt—except for his pride and the recent, strict restrictions on his freedom.

Noting her gaze, he declared under his breath, "I wanted you to help me, not have me deported."

Lowering her lips to his ear so their driver couldn't hear, she whispered harshly, "I wanted you not to *bleed* to death! Deportation was not my intention, but it's certainly a solution."

"It's not the one I wanted," he retorted, his words laced with resentment.

Speaking in undertones, she said with little sympathy, "You could have killed an innocent person who merely wanted to make a call in that telephone booth that you intended to blow up, and to what purpose?" She could barely keep her anger and frustration under control. "Even if Hitler wins this war, Germany will never give Ireland the freedom they've promised! Just look what they've done to Poland and all the other countries in their path!"

"Our people had it on good authority there'd been protocols exchanged."

"Not worth the paper they were printed on!" she shot back, glaring at him. "If any other of your compatriots had set a bomb in a place that could have killed civilians, they would have been *hanged*! You were just damned lucky you had the brains to arrive at my door.

Be a little grateful you were merely ordered deported back to the States and weren't designated an enemy alien and executed."

Teddy remained silent and stared morosely out the window as their car sped through Fulham and other bombed-out sections of western London. It vexed her to no end that he didn't seem to grasp how much trouble he'd been in.

"Honestly, Teddy," she said, unable to hide her irritation, "getting you deported instead of hanged was the best that I could do to literally save your neck!"

In a burst of pent-up anger, Teddy said between his teeth, "Your Lord Rothschild saved me, not *you*, so don't try to claim the credit."

"He's not *my* Lord Rothschild, and I have no idea *who* actually did what to save your skin," she fibbed. "All I know is it pays to have friends in this world, and I suggest you begin making some better ones when you get back to Boston."

Even as Lacy bid him farewell at the rain-soaked airstrip, Teddy expressed only grudging acknowledgment of how fortunate it was that he wasn't going to be locked up in a British jail for the rest of his life—or executed under wartime legislation. As the two siblings stood in silence, their Royal Army escort approached and announced it was time for Teddy to board the flight.

"Take care of yourself, will you?" Lacy pleaded softly, her heart sore that her little brother had become such a lost soul.

"Hard to do that with three fingers blown off, wouldn't you say?"

He raised his injured arm and then winced. He looked so forlorn, she felt a rush of sympathy for him. In the years leading up to the war, she'd done her best to try to make up for the total lack of parenting he'd suffered as a child. She understood more clearly now that those deficiencies had been a major reason he'd been drawn to the camaraderie and "family feeling" the Irish revolutionaries he'd met drinking in East End pubs had offered the lonely boy ... then barely a man.

"Look, Teddy ... I am so sorry this happened to you," Lacy said, seeking to hold his glance. He merely nodded in recognition that she'd softened her tone toward him. She offered a small smile and bent forward to brush her lips briefly on one side of his cheek. "Fly safe and take good care," she murmured. "Just rest and get well at Granny Farr's until you decide what's next."

The large military plane's engines coughed and its propellers began to whirl loudly barely twenty yards away.

"And what should I tell Gran *you're* doing over here?" Teddy shouted in her ear as he accepted the food parcel Lacy had prepared for his transatlantic journey.

"Like I said, Lord Rothschild is a zoologist, and I do typing for him when not volunteering with the Red Cross in London," Lacy replied, offering the same cover story she'd given to Teddy when they'd run into each other in Islington.

"Time we get you on board, Mr. Forbes," Lieutenant Moffett intervened, pointing toward the plane.

Lacy's spirits rose as Teddy suddenly leaned forward and gave her a hug. "I guess this is it," he said, his voice gruff. After a moment, he added, "Thanks, Sis."

Lacy clung to him longer than she should have, then finally replied, "Love you, Squirt," using the name she'd given him when he was a kid. "Let Granny Farr help you find a new path ... and please give her my best love."

"I will," Teddy replied, "and stay safe yourself."

He glanced at the overcast sky, and Lacy knew he was thinking that the world he was leaving remained a dangerous one for his sister. He made another sudden move to embrace her one last time, leaving her with a blessed sense of relief that no true ties between them had been irreparably severed.

She watched him mount the steps into the plane in front of his escort, whose duty was, literally, to strap him in his seat. She squinted through the soft rain beginning to fall and said a prayer to no deity in particular that Teddy's plane would cross the Atlantic undisturbed by any marauding *Messerschmitts*.

The young lieutenant soon emerged from the plane's gangway and came to stand by her side. "All cleared for takeoff," he reported as the lumbering aircraft pivoted and began to roll down the runway. They watched as the plane became airborne and then disappeared into the low clouds looming overhead.

Within the hour, Lacy was back in London. Mounting the steps to the entrance of the building of flats that Victor had leased out to so many of his friends and coworkers, she began reliving her brother's bittersweet farewell.

Before she inserted her key into the building's outer door, she noticed a cable message was stuck in the postal slot, addressed to her. She tore it open. Had something happened to Granny Farr? Was her mother summoning her home again, employing heaven only knew what invented excuse?

With shaking hands, she pulled the cable out of the envelope.

HARVARD FIELD HOSPITAL FINALLY TO OPEN EARLY SEPTEMBER IN SALISBURY. STOP. DOC YOU KNOW SUPERVISING THE JOINT. STOP. SEE YOU SOON. STOP.

The cable wasn't signed, but Lacy's heart jumped at the thought Pem would be back in Britain in a few months' time. The army was sending him directly to Salisbury Plain, but obviously, he would eventually get leave to come down to London. For a brief moment, she allowed her spirits to soar. Pem was coming back to England! It would be hard, but perhaps it would be easier to tell him in person what she hadn't been able to commit to a letter.

But then what? We start all over again?

Coming instantly to mind was Tess's accurate evaluation of the civil judicial system in times of war. Divorce proceedings, Lacy could only imagine, were as low a priority in the courts in America as in Great Britain. And besides, Pem was on full-time duty for the U.S. Army Medical Corps. The fact that he'd designed the Harvard Field Hospital back in '38 probably meant the army had likely tasked him with overseeing its construction in the UK. Undoubtedly, his latest duties in D.C. had required eighteen-hour days. Despite some fairly compelling reasons for what had transpired, Lacy had to face the very real truth that he'd never made the time to contact her in the intervening months before dispatching the dramatic cable she held in her hand.

As so often happened with Lacy when it appeared she was about to be let down and assume the worst in people, a small voice spoke quietly in the back of her mind.

A war is going on, Lacy. There may be extenuating circumstances.

Like Tess kept telling her, "mail sinking in ships torpedoed by the damned German U-boats, government censors throwing letters in the bin, and who knows what ..."

And had *she* written to tell him she'd been pregnant?

No.

But then, before she could bring herself to once again cut Pem some slack, the anguish she'd experienced during such a long silence from him rose up. Chances were great that he'd never taken leave to go up to Boston to sort out his personal life with Eleanor before coming over there again.

Like telling her he wanted a divorce.

Lacy's repressed resentment had begun to bubble up and churn into a toxic brew. The truth was she'd had absolutely *no* communication from him since Birmingham, end of story! *And now* this, she fumed, staring at the rather flippant cable. The horrible experience of the doctor's office in Islington flashed before her. For sure, Pem would be sad about the lost pregnancy. Even angry at her for not trying harder to let him know. But what had *he* done to make sure she was all right after they'd made love with no protection? Had he written? Found *some* way to call or send word he was worried about her welfare since they'd been together in Birmingham?

Not a thing until today!

Once again, she was the one left to cope on her own. What more evidence did she need that she was—and would always be—the one left waiting and *wanting* in a relationship with a married man? Those last, endless months had destroyed any illusions she might have had of some fairy-tale ending. The war couldn't be the only reason for their broken connection.

If he could send a cable today, why not before?

And since he was returning to England, was he just assuming, despite his long radio silence, she'd still be eager to pick up where they'd left off?

Where we left off? she thought bitterly. *I was* left. *Period*!

For a long moment, she stared at the cable, then crumpled it into a ball and stuffed it into her coat pocket. She fought the sense of dread at the thought of ever telling Pem she'd been pregnant with their child —and could likely never carry a child again.

One thing is true, she thought grimly. *If I refuse to see him, I won't have to reveal a thing.*

CHAPTER THIRTY-TWO

Lacy couldn't quite bring herself to throw away Pem's cable, so she stuffed it under some winter clothes in her Louis Vuitton footlocker at the bottom of her bed. It was mid-September before she heard anything more from Pem, and then it was merely a postcard with a picture of the Washington Monument in D.C. on it that he must have found at the bottom of his briefcase, but the postmark was from the UK.

Sadly, I can't make it to London
anytime soon but will be in touch.
XO CMP

"That's *it*?" she declared aloud. After months of silence, she'd received a cable saying Pem was coming back to England and then that one-sentence excuse? No asking how she was or how she *was* after their night in Birmingham?

Out of sight, out of mind?

Her anger gathering steam, Lacy suddenly had the thought that perhaps Pem just considered her his U.K. girlfriend at that point.

She showed the postcard to Pat when she arrived home from work. "Can you believe this? We can only assume that Pem's been over here a while," she said, feeling her blood pressure soaring, "and this is what I get?"

Pat took the card from Lacy, fingering a corner. In a tone Lacy recognized was meant to be soothing, Pat replied, "I'm sure he'd call you if he could. You know how disjointed the post has been since the Blitz. He might have written before this, but perhaps it got lost in transit or he said something in other letters the censors didn't like and his letters were held back."

Shades of Tess's exact words, Lacy fumed silently.

To Pat, she retorted, "After I was with him in Birmingham, he never even bothered to tell me he'd arrived safely in D.C. or asked how I'd been since … since we last saw each other," she said, feeling her chest tighten at the thought of the doctor's basement operating room. "He just let me know that he was coming back to the UK, and then *this* arrives," she rejoined, pointing to the postcard.

Given her hard-won resolve during the lengthy silence when it had appeared her relationship with Pem was over, she was once again sorely tempted to throw the card directly in the trash. Instead, she tossed it beside the crumpled remains of his only cable in the bottom of her trunk.

He ignored me at the worst time in my life. He deserves the same treatment.

And besides, I'm busy, she told herself. There were suspects to interview. Bomb sites to examine and photograph. Explosives to witness Victor defuse. The longer the separation from Pem with no contact, the easier it would become to put him out of her mind.

Almost.

As she'd done as a child at boarding school when her name had rarely been shouted out at mail call, she hardened her defenses. Given all she'd gone through during her short pregnancy, Pem's two brief communications—seeing that he'd finally sent them—were too little, too late.

One evening weeks after the postcard had arrived, Lacy returned from work to find a note addressed to "Lacy Fobes"—her name misspelled—pushed through the front door of their building.

Pem asked me to tell you
he hopes to be in touch soon.

The short missive was signed "—a friend" by whoever had delivered it. Lacy stared at the uneven handwriting, hurt and frustration boiling in her chest. Pem couldn't even be bothered to write a note to her *himself*? And not one word asking her how she was or telling her *when* he hoped "to be in touch"! Storming into her bedroom, she opened the top of her footlocker, threw the scrawled note on top of the postcard of the Washington Monument, and slammed the lid shut.

As the weeks rolled on, no further communications from Pem arrived at Bentinck Street. Lacy could hardly admit to herself how devastating it felt to no longer have even that link. As the new silence between them lengthened, there were days when she thought of writing him a short note officially breaking things off. *Would he bother to respond?* she wondered. The few times she sat down with a pen in her hand, she couldn't get the words right and, in frustration, determined that silence on her end was better. As even more time elapsed, she was forced to assume that Pem didn't really care or had finally figured out that she had decided it was over between them.

Fortunately, Lacy hadn't much time to dwell upon what felt like a permanent breach. Earlier in August, the internal reports of the Allies' disastrous raid on Dieppe in France kept everyone in Victor's office up to their eyeballs in checking the translated German intercepts that came in day and night.

Known as Operation Jubilee, the Allies' assault along the French coastline had turned out to be devastatingly misnamed as it had been anything but jubilant.

"The reports I've been reading are *so* grim," Lacy moaned, handing the latest one to Tess.

"What the hell went wrong?" Tess asked Victor.

He rose from his desk and pointed to a map tacked up on their office wall. "Well, for starters, it turned out to be a poorly conceived, overly complex plan. The after-action report says there wasn't enough fire support from both aircraft and artillery. Even worse, the troops sent into their first real battle were inadequately trained." Victor resumed sitting at his desk, a scowl on his face. "The entire mission was intended to test our forces' ability to launch amphibious assaults against German-occupied Europe, but it's been an unmitigated catastrophe."

Tess held up a typewritten list of the casualties. "Six *thousand* of our men died," she said, "including hundreds of Canadian infantry and British commandos."

"Oh God ... That's horrifying," Lacy responded, lifting a sheet of paper from atop her desk and pointing. "And just look at the number of Royal Navy ships and aircraft that were destroyed, as well as our loss of pilots! We all were so hopeful this assault would mean we had started the push to reclaim France."

Victor turned to a pile of reports on his desk, noting grimly, "The only good thing one could say about Dieppe is that we've been taught some valuable lessons about attacking from land and sea."

"Valuable and expensive lessons in every way imaginable," Tess said sorrowfully. "The operation's colossal failure, though, makes one wonder if we'll ever be able to claw back the Continent from the damn Germans!"

Lacy merely nodded in agreement and tackled another batch of German intercepts sitting on her desk. It was the only way to stop thinking about Charles Pembroke III and the lengthening silence between London and the Salisbury Plain.

After the Dieppe disaster, the months leading up to Christmas 1941 melded one into another until, late in the afternoon on Sunday, December 7, the flatmates on Bentinck Street had their world turned upside down yet again.

Lacy, Pat, and Tess had just finished their afternoon tea when Tess turned on the wireless. The atmosphere in the sitting room crackled with the shocking news of an all-out Japanese attack on a large American fleet anchored in Pearl Harbor, half a world away.

"All those thousands of poor sailors and civilians," Lacy said softly. "Sitting ducks on a quiet Sunday morning."

"Don't you imagine your president will have America join us now?" Tess speculated.

"He'd better," Pat observed grimly.

"FDR? He will," Lacy agreed with Tess. "Or our west coast is likely to experience a Japanese-style blitz all its own."

The day after the surprise assault in Hawaii, Britain and America declared war on Japan. On December 11, Germany declared war on the United States. By New Year's at the dawn of 1942, everyone was wondering what to expect next from Hitler, Churchill, and FDR.

Sitting at home, with rationing stricter than ever and no parties arranged by anyone that year, Tess looked over at Lacy as midnight neared. "I know we're not supposed to mention a certain doctor of your acquaintance," she said, "but aren't you at all curious what he's doing up in Salisbury now that America has officially joined the Allies?"

A few days earlier, Lacy had broken down and told Tess and Pat about the cryptic message from a supposed friend of Pem's left at the downstairs door.

"At least he had someone take the trouble to bring you a note," Tess had said with her usual practicality.

"And then nothing!" Lacy had countered. "Here he is in England, and ..." Her voice had choked, and she hadn't been able to say another word.

Pat wondered aloud, "Given what happened in Pearl Harbor, do you suppose Pem was called back to the States to set up field hospitals in the Far East Theater before he could even get leave to come see you in London?"

Lacy supposed it was possible. "But wouldn't he have sent word?"

Or did he just not care?

Tess set down the cup of tea she was using to toast in the New Year and asked quietly, "Despite his recent cable and those two notes, I'm betting you haven't told him you were pregnant, have you? You've just let everything drift."

Lacy took a sip of her tea and didn't answer.

Tess pressed, "How could you write back and not mention what happened?"

Lacy lowered her eyes to her lap and balled her fists. The atmosphere in the sitting room was suddenly stifling. "I didn't write back."

"*What?*" Tess and Pat chorused.

"Not at *all*?" Tess pressed. "Even though you could send word to Salisbury?"

Finally looking up, Lacy saw both questions and condemnation in her roommates' expressions. "Don't either of you understand? I just can't deal with it!" she burst out tearfully. "I don't have it in me to have some huge drama with Pem, 'Mr. Married Man,' after months of his silence *before* they brought him back to England! I just can't get past the fact he never wrote me after we were together in Birmingham!" she declared angrily, her voice shrill in her own ears with the grievance she simply couldn't seem to let go of. "He just didn't bother. Can't you see? I can't stand to play the role of his sometimes U.K. girlfriend anymore!"

"But, Lacy, perhaps he can't—" Tess began, but Lacy overrode her.

"And now that America's in this goddamned war and Pem's apparently over here, he *finally* got around to getting in touch just before his plane landed, and then he never came to London to see me." She set down her cup of tea in its porcelain saucer with a clatter. "No, thank you!"

"Well, why haven't you written to tell him how upset you are?" Pat demanded. "When I kept badgering Richard that he didn't stay in touch enough, he got angry and told me to grow up. I've finally realized that these aren't normal times, as he so rightly pointed out. Everything's all screwed up." Pat leaned toward Lacy and took her hand. "He said something that really stuck with me ... and that was that if we truly care for one another, we just have to *trust* each other."

Tears edging into the corners of her eyes, Lacy replied, "I tried to put something about ... Islington on paper, but I sounded like such a pathetic creature, I balled up the letter and threw it away."

"Then don't be so hard on yourself—or Pem!" Tess protested. "Like Pat said, these *aren't* normal times. You don't know *why* he might have had to remain silent all this time. He may have had serious reasons, and heaven knows all forms of communication are totally shambolic these days." Her expression carefully composed, she added, "And since *you* were the one who stayed silent when you knew you were pregnant, maybe he just assumed that you were fine."

Pat, who had been listening to the back-and-forth, spoke up again. "Look, I'm someone who's dealt with a genuine jerk ... my ex-husband." To Tess, she said, "The fact is Lacy hasn't heard from him, and so we don't really know if he's being a jerk or *isn't* being one." She reached out and took Lacy's hand. "For sure, neither Tess nor I want you being set up for more heartbreak, but maybe you shouldn't shut the door completely."

Tess nodded her agreement. "Until you know the true reason for Pem's long silence, we just don't want you to cancel your own happiness."

Pat looked relieved that Tess had joined her in a gentler approach. "Think about it, Lacy. All of us have been under a lot of stress, and that probably includes Pem. Just a couple of days ago, I demanded to know why Richard hadn't called me in ages. After my basically berating him again, he finally shouted at me that he's under orders not to breathe a word about what he's been up to in recent months and refused to say another thing because—"

Tess broke in, "Exactly! It's war, Lacy! Nobody knows for sure what's really going on. Don't you think you might be so emotional about all this because of all the physical difficulty you had after the—" Tess halted her mild harangue, prompting Lacy to jump to her feet.

Hoping to swiftly end the discussion, Lacy proposed, "Let's just agree with Pat that, yes, we're *all* under stress. We've our jobs—which are completely crazy with all the secrecy we've been sworn to—plus coping with the constant bomb threats and months of air raids that sent us down to the basement practically every night last year. On top of everything, my brother was barely saved from hanging! For me, at least, it's all just *too much*!"

And before either Pat or Tess could reply, she bolted from the room.

<hr>

The first weeks of 1942 were some of the darkest, most depressing Lacy had ever experienced. Since communication from Pem had ceased entirely in the wake of her own silence following his arrival in Britain, she tried to tell herself each day that it was by far the best solution she could have hoped for. After her emotional explosion on New Year's Eve, Tess and Pat had remained blessedly silent on the subject of Dr. Charles Pembroke.

However, just before Valentine's Day, another cable was delivered to their door.

ARRIVING SOON. STOP. PREPARE FOR SERIOUS POWWOW. STOP. PEM

"What does it say?" Tess demanded, watching Lacy grimly stuff the rectangular yellow piece of paper in her pocket.

"Has someone died?" Pat asked, placing a sympathetic hand on Lacy's arm.

Without answering, Lacy turned toward the hallway that led from the vestibule.

"It's from Pem, isn't it?" Tess called after her. "Well, you have to face him sometime!"

Ignoring her words, Lacy slammed her door and shut herself in her bedroom.

The following afternoon, a Saturday, Pat Rawdon-Smith was the first to reach the flat's front door when the bell rang. Earlier, Tess had set off to see what could be had at the shops nearby, and Lacy was in her room with the door closed.

"Why, Pem!" Pat exclaimed to the tall figure in a U.S. Army uniform. "It's been *such* a long time. How wonderful to see you! Come in."

Pem stood in the corridor outside their flat with two dozen red roses in his arms. "Lovely to see you again, Pat," he responded. "These are for all of you," he said, handing the bouquet to her. "Happy Valentine's Day—almost."

Pem removed his hat and held it in the crook of his arm. Pat received the flowers, smiling politely, her voice overly bright as her friend's lover entered the flat. "You Yanks are amazing. How in the world did you manage to find these?"

Then she forced a laugh. "Better you don't tell me." She pointed to the insignia of two snakes wrapped around a staff with wings on either side of his lapels. "And it's *Captain* Pembroke now, I see.

Congratulations." She called over her shoulder, "Lacy! Come see who's here, and look what beauties he's brought us!"

Pat bid Pem to follow her into the sitting room. Selecting the leather club chair, he said, "By the way, Pat, I've encountered quite the coincidence."

"You have?" she replied, taking a seat on the sofa, roses in her lap. "What about?"

"It's rather amazing, in fact. For the last while now, I've been assigned to coordinate efforts to redesign U.S. and British Army hospital trains with an architect specializing in British military hospitals. A fellow named Richard Llewelyn Davies." He winked. "I believe you're acquainted."

"How extraordinary!" Pat exclaimed. "You know Richard?"

"I've been working closely with him for months now."

"He never breathed a word!"

"Neither of us were allowed to ... until just this week. Our joint team created the specifications for our state-of-the-art American hospital cars to fit onto *your* railroad tracks." He smiled faintly, adding, "Although I think you call tracks 'platforms' here. The prototypes we made in the United States are going to be duplicated here in Britain. Now that America has joined the Allies, there's no need to be so hush-hush about the project."

"So, was your supposedly being in the Midlands somewhere since September merely a cover story?" Pat speculated with a faint frown.

"You never heard me say that," Pem answered in code for "yes."

"You and Richard must both be quite pleased with yourselves!" Pat replied, the look on her face reflecting her own admiration and pride in her new beau's contribution to transporting injured soldiers away from the front lines.

By that time, Lacy had arrived at the sitting room doorway and was sensing that all the blood may have drained from her face. From her bedroom, she had instantly recognized Pem's deep voice, and while coming down the hall, she had paused to listen to his and Pat's conversation. To Lacy, their cordial exchange had made it seem as if Pat had welcomed Pem as though life were normal and she'd never been pregnant. As she listened to them, she had no idea how to even find the words to describe everything that had happened since she'd last seen Pem in Birmingham. She'd felt so abandoned by his subsequent silence, yet she couldn't imagine how to defend why she hadn't written to him at all. With each passing moment, her stomach in turmoil, she became even more upset at the sight of his tall, handsome figure clad in his U.S. Army Medical Corps uniform. Complicating the situation even more in her mind was the fact that he was apparently working closely with Richard Llewelyn Davies, Pat's new main squeeze, an architect with a calling astonishingly similar to Pem's, yet Richard hadn't even revealed that to Pat either.

Lacy tried to focus on their conversation as Pat exclaimed, "That's so amazing that you know and work with Richard! I met him ages ago as a deb, through the Cambridge Apostles crowd and all ... but we've only recently been seeing each other."

Lacy fought off a renewed sense of panic when Pem glanced over his shoulder and saw her standing just outside the room but not advancing inside. She had absolutely no idea what to say first. What would *he* say after all those months of silence?

She saw Pat's gaze shift from Pem to her and back to Pem. After a long pause and sensing the tension, Lacy's flatmate hastily rose from her seat. "Well, I'll just get these gorgeous blooms into some water," Pat proposed, nodding at the roses she held in her arms. "It'll ... uh ... give you two a chance to ... talk," she finished lamely before heading down the hall toward the kitchen.

Lacy and Pem fixed their eyes on each other, and neither uttered a word while they both waited to hear the kitchen door close. Lacy had no choice but to take a seat on the sofa, a good ten feet away from their visitor.

The second she sat down, Pem demanded without preamble, "Why haven't you answered my cables or any of my notes? Surely, one or two must have gotten past the censors."

"I received the pitiful few you sent, yes."

"Pitiful? Wow, that's quite a put-down, Miss Forbes."

A suffocating sense of gloom was descending on Lacy in waves. Thinking of his rare, lackluster communications stashed at the bottom of her trunk, she felt compelled to defend herself for not having written him since she'd ended her pregnancy. In response, she made a guess at what was probably obvious.

"Nowhere did *you* write me, cable me, or call to say you'd 'sorted things out with Eleanor,' as you used to say ... and that you were no longer married." Lifting her chin, she declared, "After your deafening silence on that and all other subjects, I gave up trying to understand why. Finally, I decided it was time we just put a period at the end of the sentence on this impossible situation." She rose to her feet. "I do apologize. I should have just written you back to say it was over."

Pem leaped from his chair, blocking any attempt by her to exit the room.

"Oh, no, you don't! You can't just walk out." She could see he was infuriated in a way he'd never been before. "You can't be the one to leave first. You're going to hear me out *and* tell me what's going on!"

"And just what will I hear from you?" she said, a nasty edge bleeding into her voice. "That you've wanted to initiate a divorce, but with your duties and all and the US finally becoming an ally in this blasted war, you just couldn't manage to—"

"I *was* going to say something like that, yes," he exclaimed, "and it's true! It's been a hellish time for us both, I suspect, but that doesn't mean that I don't want to be free to be with you as soon as it's possible!"

"Isn't that what all married men say?" she shot back. "'Oh, dear me,'" she mimicked mincingly, "'so sorry ... I was awfully busy, you know. There just wasn't time to file the divorce papers or write you a real letter!'"

"But Eleanor was—"

"I don't want to hear it!" she cut him off. "I'm *done* with this misery! I'm done with excuses. Can't you see? I'm done with *you*! Please just leave."

Pem threw his hat on the other end of the sofa. "No! I won't leave!" he yelled. "Not until you tell me what in hell is going on with you. I'm sorry it took me this long to come see you, but both Richard and I were under strict orders not to contact anyone outside our unit until the last of the hospital prototype cars made it across the Atlantic. For a long stretch before Pearl Harbor, we weren't even allowed to write anyone about *anything*. The hospital cars were unloaded in Liverpool last week and sent to the Birmingham Rail Carriage Works, where hundreds like them will be manufactured."

"So you weren't even in Salisbury?" she demanded.

"Richard and I had to keep mum since our collaboration began long before the US joined the Allies. For months, everyone on both sides of the Atlantic had to *think* I was assigned to the Harvard Field Hospital in Salisbury, but most of the time, I was in either D.C. or Birmingham."

Her breath caught at his mention of Birmingham. "There's always a reason, isn't there?" she snapped. "*Always* a reason."

Pem gave her a stare as if he hardly recognized her. "Lacy, what has happened? Why has everything changed? You're so brittle, so distant and remote. Not like yourself at all! You look positively depressed."

"Thanks for the compliment!" she retorted.

He took a step closer. His voice gentle, he said, "Darling, for months, everything I was assigned to was basically a dark ops. When I got to D.C. after Birmingham and our project was immediately declared top secret, I had the pilot cable to tell you that I'd landed safely. I realize you didn't hear from me as often as I wished, but you never answered even once! *Why?*"

"I never received a cable from any pilot," she retorted, making it clear that she suspected he was inventing an excuse.

"The pilot showed me the receipt for the message he sent," Pem insisted.

"Well, it never arrived."

Looking away, she couldn't bring herself to meet his eyes. The sight of him. The intensity in his voice. His pleading blue eyes. His obvious confusion tugged at her heart, but swirling at the back of her black thoughts was the truth that he was still married and that she didn't have the strength or courage to make the confession about her pregnancy that she knew she should.

"I've had a job to do too, you know," she said, defending herself. "Full of stress, just like yours. We've been bombed out of one flat, and we're living in the basement of this one most nights because of the Blitz. I translate endless German messages—a language I *hate*! I go with Victor to help defuse explosives disguised as children's toys and chocolate bars. My brother was deported this year, and"—she looked up— "and you're still married to Eleanor, remember? I'm just exhausted from it all."

Pem's look of concern nearly undid her resolution to finally and unequivocally end it all between them.

"Why wouldn't you be exhausted, sweetheart," he said, taking a step toward her, his voice full of compassion. "You've had so much to deal with, as we all have in this damn war, but can't you give me a chance to make you see—"

"You've had many chances to tell Eleanor how you feel," she interrupted, suddenly filled with horror and dread at the idea of relating what had happened in that Islington basement.

Pem was still married, so it didn't matter either way what she had done, did it? The strain of the last few months felt as if it were swallowing her whole. Anger was her only shield.

"Your silence after Birmingham just about killed me," Lacy declared, her voice vibrating with emotion. "First you say you're on your way over here ... followed by a lousy postcard saying you couldn't come to London. Then *nothing* but a misspelled note you got *somebody else* to write!"

"I wanted to write more often, but didn't you get—"

"I just can't be the other woman anymore!" Lacy cried, balling her fists by her sides. "We've reached a dead end, Pem, so please don't sing the 'after the war' siren's song to me."

Pem's expression revealed both confusion and emotional fatigue, and Lacy sensed it was akin to her own. "My marriage died a long time ago," he said, his voice low, a complete contrast to her outburst. "I've wanted to take steps to end it officially, but like you ... a lot of, well, *life*—and my job—keep getting in the way. I thought you'd understand that."

"'There's a war on,'" she interrupted, mimicking the oft-quoted bromide.

"Lacy, what is *wrong* with you?" he demanded. "The war *is* the reason I wasn't able to—"

"Nothing is wrong with me!" she retorted, her voice blaring full blast. "What's wrong is *us*! And I'm just as much to blame as you for allowing this to happen in the first place. Let's just agree not to write or call or make any more attempts to contact each other. It's just too painful."

Lacy had begun to feel as if coping with their relationship was akin to all the air strikes they had endured, being hammered by one thing after the other—the war, the difficult pregnancy followed by the abortion, Pem making no attempt to get divorced, and even the trauma of what had happened to Teddy and his involvement in the IRA's attacks on England. For Lacy, there was just too much damage to build anything back. She'd barely managed to crawl out of the rubble, and confessing about the child they'd created together felt like one more blow she couldn't withstand. Building a wall between herself and the pain of inevitably losing Pem felt like the only thing she could lean on. If it crumbled too, what would be left of her?

Pem's darkening expression told Lacy her words had put him in a state of shock that was slowly turning into anger. Before he could mount another defense, she cast her final volley. What she was about to say felt like a matter of her own survival.

"There is no other way to say it, Pem." She paused, then declared, "This is *my* call. I can't do this anymore. It's over."

Chapter Thirty-Three

Lacy's last words declaring she was finally calling it quits with Pem rang out above the sound of the front door opening. Tess appeared at the entrance to the sitting room. In her hand was a string bag full of whatever groceries the three women's combined ration points could purchase.

Catching sight of Pem, Tess exclaimed, "Oh, what a wonderful surprise! I wondered when you'd grace our shores once again. Welcome!" Then she took a closer look at Pem's livid expression. Her friend shifted her startled glance to Lacy and instantly absorbed the high-velocity tension reverberating around the room.

Ignoring Lacy, Pem grabbed his khaki hat off the sofa, then turned to Tess, who had been joined at that moment by Pat, who'd heard the front door open.

"Sorry to be so abrupt," Pem said tersely to Lacy's flatmates, "but clearly, it's best if I leave. *Now*."

When he reached the front door, he turned and gave a slight shake of his head, as if he couldn't believe what had transpired during the last ten minutes. Then he was gone.

For a good fifteen seconds, silence hung in the air.

Tess finally broke it with, "Good God, Lacy! Will you please tell Pat and me what that was all about?"

Pat said dryly, "I don't think you want to know."

"So, did you finally let him know what happened to you?" Tess demanded. "Was he angry because of the abor—?"

"No," Pat interrupted, answering for Lacy. "That wasn't it because she never even told him she'd been pregnant, did you, Lacy?" she continued, her tone accusing. "You apparently simply ordered him to— What is it you Yanks say? 'Get lost' without letting him know what happened to you. To both of you."

Tess turned to face Lacy with an incredulous expression. "You just sent him packing? You never even had the courage to explain you've been in an all-consuming state of *depression* ever since you went to Islington to have the—"

"What are you, Tess, some psychiatrist?" Lacy shouted. "Just stop it! Both of you! It's so easy for you to judge. To pronounce your sanctimonious opinions. To give *advice*. You have no idea what it's been like for me."

"Yes, I do," Tess countered quietly. "I love the Third Baron Victor Rothschild, remember? He's married. He and Barbara have the children I long to have with him. So, actually, I *do* have some idea what it means to care for someone who's unhappily married." She gave Lacy a steely look. "But for me, the answer is you love the man no matter what, and, at the very least, you tell him so."

Lacy's mind was so fixed on her own grievances that she could summon no fitting retort. She was mentally exhausted by the disaster that involved not only Pem but also a schism that she felt widening between her and her two best friends. All she could think to do was spin on her heels and storm down the hallway, slamming her bedroom door behind her.

Lacy tried to convince herself that shoving that door closed had felt good. Powerful. She'd finally put an end to the slow-motion misery of having fallen in love with Pem despite the warnings that had rung in her head from the very first day they'd met in Boston.

Anyone with half a brain should have known it wouldn't end well.

For several moments, she stood rooted to the carpet with the scene she'd just caused flashing through her mind as if she were watching an overwrought melodrama. She forced herself to inhale several deep breaths while trying to ignore a single thought that kept bouncing back.

What if Tess is right?

According to her, if you loved someone, you loved them. Period. And you told them so.

War or no war, the sane part of Lacy's brain knew she should have told him everything ... including that she'd been pregnant. But how could she ignore the fact that—war or no war—Pem remained married and had done nothing to change that?

An obvious answer was what Pat and Tess had maintained—that perhaps it *had* been too crazy a time for him to initiate a divorce. And what if Lacy's immediate reaction to getting that first postcard from Pem saying he wasn't coming to London to see her had just been a throwback to all the times her "nearest and dearest" had let her down? She'd been a lonely, emotionally bereft child repeatedly banished to a strange, new school in a country whose language she had to learn. Pem's silence, whether intentional or not, had certainly ripped the scab off *that* wound.

The self-inflicted loss of Pem felt as if it were crushing her. He'd been the only man in Lacy's life who'd seemed to truly *know* her, care for her as the person she was, and understand her and the deep scars she'd carried from her insane childhood. The war, of course, had only amplified those problems and put incredible stress on them both. And then the loss of ...

She couldn't even complete the thought. Yet, the silences from his end, whatever the cause and despite his explanations, had nearly destroyed her.

Lacy could almost hear the steely tone Tess would have used in response to her self-pity. *"Wouldn't Pem expect you to tell him right away if you'd created a life together?"*

Instead, what Lacy had done was make him the villain in the drama when he didn't even know she'd carried their child. She'd just felt scared, then aggrieved, then abandoned. Driving *her* silence had been her guilt about ending the pregnancy.

She began to pace back and forth near the bottom of her bed. It was hard to admit, even to herself, that she hadn't seemed able to shake a leaden feeling of gloom since becoming so sick following the abortion. It was depressingly similar to how she'd felt when her appendix had burst in the Swiss surgeon's hands as he was removing it. They'd notified June that her young daughter was quite sick afterward, but no one had come to see her in the hospital. At the moment, Lacy felt just like she had back then, the offspring of wealthy, self-centered parents too busy to care.

But Pem isn't at all *like them!* the rational part of Lacy's brain insisted. *Tess is probably right*, she acknowledged silently. *I probably do need to see a psychiatrist.*

Pem's few communications tucked beneath winter clothing in her traveling trunk beckoned as if they were sending out radio signals. Lacy knelt at the bottom of her bed and opened the footlocker's lid. The first thing her fingers touched was the balled-up note Pem had somehow managed to get a friend to deliver during the time "everything … was basically a dark ops," as he'd said. Slowly, she smoothed the creases of the first cable she'd received and confirmed that it *wasn't* the one Pem insisted that his pilot had sent to confirm he'd landed safely in D.C. The weeks that had passed between that lost cable and the hand-delivered note from Pem's friend added up to months!

And, of course, she'd assumed the worst.

With a sinking feeling that she had been more than unfair to Pem, she stumbled to her feet, only to stagger toward the bed and fall in a heap onto the mattress. *Of course* Pem had been concerned she might have gotten pregnant from their wild night together. But when she had never written back, just as Tess had asserted, *he'd* assumed she was fine.

Normal people understand letters and cables get lost in wartime, but not me!

Lacy sat up on the bed, feeling a powerful urge to try to find where Pem had gone and somehow make it right with him. Then she leaned against the headboard, acknowledging that one undeniable fact continued to govern everything.

Dr. Charles Pembroke III is still a married man, and he's taken no steps to change that in three years.

What if, unlike so many other situations in Pem's life, *undoing* his mistake of marrying a woman because of family pressure couldn't be fixed merely with his easy charm or charisma? It would take effort and be a major disruption in his life.

Did he think the upheaval was worth it? And even if he did,

would Pem want to marry her if he knew she might never be able to have children? Then again, did he even *want* to be a father? In eight years of marriage, he and Eleanor had chosen not to have any children, but Lacy knew now that *she* desperately wanted to be a mother if it were still possible. Were those the sorts of serious hurdles that she and Pem could never overcome?

Lacy rolled onto her side, hugging her pillow to her chest. She had no idea where Pem was due to be assigned next, seeing as the hospital railcar project was launched and no longer a secret. Yet, every move either one of them made from there on out would be governed by the demands of the secret government nondisclosure agreements they'd signed for their war-related jobs.

It is what it is, she thought, dry-eyed by then. *I've done what I've done. I've ended it.*

The only way forward was, as Tess had advised, at least to acknowledge to herself that despite all that had happened, she loved Pem. She truly, deeply loved and admired him—and earlier that night, she'd ruined everything. As of this dreadful moment, her choice was simply to "keep calm and carry on," however wretched it felt to be her own sorry self.

PART THREE
THE DARKEST NIGHTS

CHAPTER THIRTY-FOUR

The rupture between Lacy and Pem seemed permanent as the winter of 1942 ground on. Lacy tried not to look through the post that Tess left on the front hall table every day for the three women to paw through.

Fortunately, the rift that had developed between the flatmates wasn't long-lasting. To Lacy's relief, Tess quickly made overtures to put an end to the bad feelings that had erupted in the wake of Pem's visit to Bentinck Street.

After a few days of frosty exchanges between them, Tess met Lacy in the kitchen early one morning when the latter was boiling water for their breakfast tea. Tess swiftly strode to the cupboard and pulled out the big Brown Betty teapot they always used.

"Honestly, Lacy," she said, scraping the soggy tea leaves from the previous day they were forced to reuse, "what we've all been living through has been ghastly but especially for you. I'm truly sorry it's been so rough." They both watched as Lacy poured hot water into the pot Tess held and gave the recycled tea leaves a stir with a spoon. "I've been thinking a lot," Tess continued, "and I believe I better understand now how hard everything's been for you."

Lacy brought down three cups from the shelf and placed them on the counter in the tiny kitchen. "Thank you for ... saying that," she murmured. "It couldn't have been easy for you either, caring for Victor."

Tess poured the first cup, handed it to Lacy, and gave a small sigh. "At least I get to see him most days and know where I stand as we carry on in this mad thing we're doing together."

"But how can you bear the fact that he makes no move to get a divorce?" Lacy asked quietly. "He and Barbara barely tolerate each other, yet he's done nothing to change his situation, has he?"

"I have to trust that he will file the papers when it's possible," Tess replied with a shrug. "I want the kind of relationship my parents have, so I'm willing to wait until the war's over and see if I'm destined to have it."

"If it ever ends," Lacy murmured glumly. "The war, I mean."

Tess poured herself a cup and one for Pat, who entered the kitchen just then.

"I heard you two from the hall." Pat put an arm around Lacy and gave her a gentle squeeze. "I'm sorry, too, for everything you've been through, Lacy. As far as I can see, it's been our friendship that's helped the three of us survive the hellish nightmare of the so-called home front."

Lacy looked from Pat to Tess, the balm of relief pouring through her, and replied softly, "Our friendship is what's kept me afloat, for sure."

She'd lost her chance at love, but knowing she still had people like Tess and Pat in her life felt as if she'd been thrown a life preserver when she was drowning in a violent sea. In fact, Lacy suddenly realized that the camaraderie and support she'd experienced on Bentinck Street had surprisingly bestowed upon her a chosen family. It had been the only sustaining element in her life during all the months of the war's turmoil, uncertainty, and danger.

Tess and Pat had become more like her sisters than flatmates or friends.

Lacy raised her teacup, which she then gently clinked against the edges of the other two. "Here's to us," she said.

"To us!" chorused Tess and Pat.

Nothing much changed in the lives of Victor's tenants on Bentinck Street during the first half of 1942, although headlines screaming about Allied losses to German U-boats greeted them every time they walked out of their door for work. Victor had trusted them with the early knowledge that thousands of American troops were arriving daily and setting up bases all over Great Britain.

The three friends avidly followed the news about the Americans' first bombing raid on Germany in May. One morning in June, Lacy and Tess arrived at work to take in the sight of Victor with his head in his hands as he stared down at a thick report. His gaze reflected deep consternation and distress of a kind Lacy, for one, had never witnessed in him.

"*What*?" asked Tess, rushing to his side.

"We've just received intelligence that the mass murder of Jews by gassing is going on at a Nazi camp called Auschwitz, near Krakow in Poland."

"*Gassing* people to death? Oh God, Victor ... I'm so sorry," murmured Tess.

"I've apparently lost some family members in other branches of the Rothschilds," Victor said, "but we won't know how thorough Hitler's been until—or if—this bloody war ever comes to an end."

Tess threw her arms around him, the two of them oblivious to their friend's presence in the room. Lacy's thoughts had fled to Noah, and she prayed that the SS hadn't sent him to Auschwitz.

In spite of Victor's vast wealth and status as a member of the distinguished banking family—and membership in the British aristocracy—Lacy had long noticed the veiled slurs cast by others and witnessed the barely disguised distaste for him as a Jew. She'd despised hearing the slights and outright insults, some of which had been delivered even by supposed friends like Guy Burgess and the subtler Anthony Blunt. Victor's male tenants on Bentinck Street were happy to accept their landlord's largesse, but those two particularly had displayed the same antisemitism that Lacy witnessed simmering just below the surface among many of the smart set she'd known during her debutante years. Hitler's gassing of the Jews seemed to her just a horrifying extension of the same phenomenon.

The one bright bit of news was that on June 25, General Dwight Eisenhower arrived in London and "set up shop," as the newspapers reported in bold headlines.

"I like Ike," Lacy declared, pointing to the newspaper she'd been reading that announced the American general had been appointed supreme commander of the Allied Expeditionary Force. She smiled, adding, "My Grandmother Farrington always calls him by that name and says he's an absolute dear."

"Your family *knows* him?" Tess asked, impressed.

"Granny's father was a general too and taught Ike at West Point."

Victor looked skeptical. "A U.S. general … known as a 'dear?'" He heaved a sigh. "Well, let's pray your Ike is a match for an enemy that kills women and children using poison gas."

During the last few months of 1942, Lacy succeeded in purging most —but not all—thoughts of Pem to the far recesses of her mind. Her days were full of disruptions caused by a cascade of events that were taking up every waking hour of the MI5 group in St. James's.

In November, their office was kept busy following the U.S. invasion of North Africa.

One evening, Pat came into the kitchen after a rare telephone call from Richard. "He couldn't say anything about where he was or what he was doing, but it was clear to me that he's still in England." As she resumed her seat at the table, she said to Lacy sympathetically, "Let's hope the same is true for Pem."

Lacy set down the fork she'd used to push their sparse dinner around on her plate. She could only nod her agreement, clinging to the hope that the U.S. Army Medical Corps was employing Pem's architectural and design talents rather than his therapeutic skills and that he wasn't tending to the wounded somewhere in Africa.

Meanwhile, the Germans, having occupied northern France, made a swift move mid-November to fully control the entire region from the English Channel to the Mediterranean.

"Our side certainly deserves to have a win one of these days," Tess declared, her downhearted tone reflecting the mood they all were feeling.

As the year neared its close, Tess and Lacy arrived at work the blustery week before Christmas Eve. They shut the door to the office just as Victor was returning the receiver to the telephone on his desk.

"Take a seat, you two," he bid them, rising from his chair and walking toward them on the other side of the office. Lacy could sense he was upset, but his tone was even as he announced, "The British foreign secretary will tell the full House of Commons today that mass executions of Jews are going on in Nazi prison camps all over the Continent, not just at Auschwitz."

"It's about time they faced what we already suspected," murmured Tess.

Victor looked at Lacy. "You should be proud that a U.S. spokesman just declared in a news conference that the US vows to avenge those deaths."

In the early months of 1943, Victor shared with his two assistants reports that more names had joined the list of Nazi death camps: Treblinka, Mauthausen, Buchenwald, and Ravensbrück.

"We know that others exist," Victor said grimly, "but just not where."

Lacy's spirits sank even lower at the thought of what Noah would have endured if he'd been sent to one of those charnel houses, which was more than likely.

When word arrived via a classified channel that twenty-seven merchant ships had been sunk in the Atlantic between March 16 and March 20, Lacy said under her breath to Tess, "Those seamen weren't combatants! Neither was my friend Noah. It scares me how much I *hate* the Nazis!"

Being cleared to read MI5's daily dispatches chronicling the long list of German atrocities had the effect on both Lacy and Tess of rendering totally surreal the prewar world of parties and debutante balls the women had known.

"Those bouffant white evening gowns and long white gloves seem even more frivolous to me now than they did in '38," Lacy said with a sigh.

"They *always* seemed silly to me," Tess replied, "although we certainly had our amusing moments during the house parties and those nights at the 400 Club."

"Well, thank God the damned German Blitz appears to be over," Lacy said. "How can I ever forget the night I ended up waiting for the all clear in the lower basement at the 400 Club, along with the entire kitchen staff, with Pem in top hat and tails and me dressed in a silk evening gown!"

She could almost feel Pem cradling her in his arms as they huddled on the floor.

Strangely, Lacy and Tess were reminded of that world in June. One spring evening, Pat arrived home from work with a few wilted carrots and half a chicken in her satchel. Unpacking her latest treasures, she declared, "I bring you the amazing news I heard from our sister deb Diana Barnato that Kick Kennedy has returned to London."

"You're joking!" Lacy exclaimed. "I figured the Kennedys wanted to keep her as far away from her Protestant great love as possible," she added, referring to the Catholic Kennedys' well-known opposition to even highborn Brits like the Duke of Devonshire's son, Billy, who followed the Church of England.

"How'd she manage to get over here in the middle of a war?" Tess asked.

"She'll let us know when she arrives here for drinks on Saturday. But poor Kick!" Pat joked. "She had to share the *Queen Mary* with some eighteen thousand American soldiers on board!"

Lacy laughed. "Clever girl! I saw a picture of the ship. It's not quite the luxury liner the *Queen* once was now that it's painted gray from stem to stern."

Within days of Kathleen Kennedy's arrival, she had been to visit an entire retinue of debutantes she'd come out with at the ceremony at Buckingham Palace. She complained when she came to Bentinck Street, "If only the parents would let me live in a flat like *this* instead of making me stay upstairs at the fusty old Hans Crescent Club."

She sat on their sofa, sipping a coveted thimbleful of sherry Pat had poured in celebration of their friend's return. She was clad in the same Red Cross uniform Lacy had from her days traveling with the Finland Field Hospital team. Kick's hostesses were amazed to learn that old Joe Kennedy Senior, who'd famously opposed America joining Britain's fight against the Nazis, had allowed Kick to enlist as a greeter at the London club, which had been refitted as a Red Cross social gathering place for American GIs.

"It's a grim sort of watering hole," Kick reported, "located behind Harrods department store in Knightsbridge. My job is talking to homesick soldiers all day, helping them write letters to their moms and sweethearts, and playing cards and Ping-Pong, for goodness sake, for hours on end!" she grumbled. "It's beastly boring when all I want to do is be with Billy!"

Billy, of course, had been Kick's great passion in the whirlwind days of the young women's court presentation and was clearly the inspiration for her joining the American Red Cross abroad. William, officially the Marquess of Hartington, and heir to the Duke of Devonshire, was also their friend Debo's new brother-in-law since she had recently married Billy's brother, Andrew Cavendish.

Kick moaned, "It took Billy two *weeks* to get leave from his training in Hatfield to come see me. And can you believe it?" she groused. "I'm allowed only one and a half days off a week. It's been practically impossible for Billy and me to see each other at all!"

Lacy felt a pang of something close to outright envy at recalling her own sense of yearning to see Pem those long months after their rendezvous in Birmingham. She tried to push such thoughts aside and struggled to focus on their guest. Kick spent the next minutes declaring that both the directress of the soldiers club and the "equally difficult" program coordinator were driving her nuts.

Waiting for Tess to fill her glass with a drop more sherry, Kick testily dismissed the former woman as "a sort of pushy lady" and the latter as "a Jewess who's very jealous of me."

Seemingly oblivious to how that exchange might strike Tess—whose lover happened to be the best-known Jew in Britain—Kick put her sherry glass on the side table. "Since I don't want to lose my London perch," she declared, "I've decided to put up with the place and the undesirables who run it, at least for now."

After their guest departed, Tess commented dryly to her flatmates, "I have a feeling the goal of the daughter of Lacy's former ambassador is to snare a future duke rather more than do her bit to support America or her Allies."

"Apparently so," was Lacy's sour reply.

"Well, if she outfoxed her father to get here," Pat declared, "I'm betting it won't be long before she becomes the newly minted Marchioness of Hartington—and a future duchess."

Kick's return to London had the effect of energizing the covey of former debs to assemble whenever they could at several of their old watering holes that had escaped the London Blitz. Like Lacy, Tess, and Pat, many of the young women were holding important jobs that greatly restricted the leisure time they'd enjoyed back in 1938 as members of Britain's upper crust back.

At one of the few get-togethers Lacy had time to attend, she'd learned that a deb she knew, Sarah Norton, was working at top secret Bletchley Park, the requisitioned estate where code breakers toiled to unravel encrypted German transmissions twenty-four hours a day. Another deb, Helen Vlasto, had joined the Royal Navy's VADs, "the Voluntary Aid Detachment," Tess explained for Lacy's benefit, adding, "She's working as a charge nurse."

One day in July, Diana Lyttelton, who'd made her debut with all of them, met the group for lunch on a break from the War Office's all-important Map Room, announcing the news, just made public, that the Allies had landed in Sicily.

"Well, here's some other news," Pat revealed to Kick and the others. "Diana Barnato just got certified as an ATA *flyer* ferrying fighter planes to various air bases around the country. She's even been given officer rank!"

Later, when the three flatmates arrived back home, Pat noted slyly, "After all that conversation of which debs are doing amazing jobs in this war, don't you think Kick became unusually quiet during the lunch?"

"I noticed that too," Tess said with an arch of her eyebrow as they all hung up their coats. "I guess you could say the debs we knew best are doing a lot more than just playing Ping-Pong, that's for damn sure!"

Chapter Thirty-Five

The subsequent months of 1943 were a blur for the three residents at Number 5 Bentinck Street. Lacy and Tess had never been busier responding to every type of in-country threat Hitler's Abwehr spy agency could devise. When the Allies began bombing both Rome and Hamburg in July, scores of Italians and even expat Germans living in England required MI5 operatives like Victor's two deputies to be sent all over the countryside to interrogate them regarding their loyalty to their host country. If Lacy or Tess detected something fishy, they could recommend that the foreigners be put in detention camps in Scotland or on the Isle of Man "for the duration."

"I just hope we're being fair," Lacy fretted to Tess as the two rode back home on the train after an interviewing session at a prison north of London. "I sent a German couple to a camp outside Glasgow today. I'm pretty sure that they were both reporting to a spy we haven't yet caught. Their answers simply didn't match up. But what if I'm wrong?"

"Better safe than sorry," Tess replied. "At least they're not being sent to a place like Auschwitz."

The next morning, Victor pointed to the latest stack of folders on his desk. "We're going to have to double our scrutiny of every single Italian seeking refuge in the UK who declares opposition to Mussolini," he announced sternly. "We're already finding that many who are claiming asylum here were out-and-out collaborators!"

"Do you think there's a renewed push on to send over more enemy infiltrators?" Lacy asked, accepting her share of folders that would determine her activities for the rest of the summer.

"I'm afraid so," Victor said with a weary sigh. "It's not just the enemy within, as so many are fond of saying. Now we've been assigned to round up enemy *newcomers* posing as hapless refugees."

Tess, pointing to the pile Victor had placed upon her desk, declared, "Ready, steady ... GO!" and opened the first folder, pen in hand, poised to write the questions that could ferret out the next in-country spy or saboteur.

One day in the first week of September, Victor walked into the office with a broad smile and news that took Lacy and Tess completely by surprise. "The Allies have just accepted the Italian surrender!"

"No!" Tess said, delightedly clapping her hands.

"What happened to Mussolini?" asked Lacy.

"Rescued by the Germans, we're told."

Three days later, however, German troops occupied Rome, crushing the jubilation they'd all felt so briefly. And by the end of the month, Victor's little MI5 group was even more disappointed. Hitler's forces had reestablished Mussolini as the leader of the Fascist government.

"I don't know about you," Lacy commented to Tess across their two desks, "but this seesaw is really getting to me." And for the thousandth time, she wondered where Pem's U.S. Army Medical Corps unit had been sent.

The news became even more chaotic when the Allies entered Naples in October and word of an enormous British air raid on Berlin followed in November. In December, the Allies' new partner, the Soviet Union, launched an offensive on the Ukrainian front.

The only benefit Lacy could see in the deluge of good and bad news and their office scrambling to respond was that it had kept her mind off the subject of Dr. Charles Pembroke.

Mostly.

That same week in December, Lacy awoke in the middle of the night when, despite her best intentions, her first conscious thoughts were of Pem.

Where is he? Is he safe? Did they send him to Italy to evacuate our wounded troops ... or is he back in D.C.?

Disturbing her sleep even more at the dawn of 1944 were the horrific reports of Allied casualties from the fighting at Anzio, a region some sixty kilometers south of Rome.

Consulting a top secret report from the front, Victor relayed the grim news the following morning. "American casualties in Italy are thought to be somewhere between eighteen and twenty-four thousand."

Stunned by the enormity of the number, Lacy asked, "What about Allied *deaths*?" Dreading his answer, she envisioned the hospital trains Pem had designed, every bunk occupied with wounded soldiers calling out for help from an exhausted staff of doctors and nurses. "Do we know yet how many died?"

Victor consulted the file. "It's estimated to be about seven thousand Allied troops."

"Seven *thousand*," Lacy repeated softly, considering how so many American families would soon be plunged into mourning. Her next thoughts were to wonder whether Pem and Richard Davies had, indeed, been assigned to Italy. Pat had heard nothing from Richard for weeks.

"And the Krauts?" Tess asked, her voice laced with anger. "What are the stats for them?"

Victor consulted the folder labeled *Anzio – Your Eyes Only* once again. "The German forces suffered around five thousand killed and more than thirty thousand injured."

"And the Brits?" Tess followed up quickly.

Victor paused as he stared at the report. Finally, he answered heavily, "British forces have suffered an estimated *thirty-six thousand* injured or missing and seven thousand dead."

As the sheer numbers of dead and injured sank in, Lacy's worst unvoiced fear shifted from *Where did the U.S. Army Medical Corps send Pem?* to *Is he even alive?*

As the beginning of the fifth year of the war rolled deeply into the winter months, the flatmates on Bentinck Street grappled with significantly less food in the shops and fewer gatherings organized among the former debs.

"Half the country estates where we attended weekend house parties have been requisitioned by the military," Tess noted, handing Lacy the plate that she'd just washed after a quiet evening at the flat. One bright ray of hope in all the gloomy news had been some fresh, persistent rumors.

"There is something big afoot, don't you reckon?" Lacy asked Tess, drying the wet plate. She reminded her friend of the German transmissions that had crossed their desks all week. The dispatches seemed to be expressing a high level of anxiety about *where* Hitler and his advisors were speculating that an Allied assault might take place if one was in the offing.

One morning soon afterward, Tess demanded of Victor, "Is it *true*? Is there actually a large-scale invasion planned for sometime later this year?"

Lacy chimed in boldly, "Let's hope it's based on the lessons learned from the Dieppe fiasco."

Victor looked from one to the other and shrugged without answering.

"Oh, don't be coy," Tess said, her exasperation showing. "Is there even a *remote* possibility that an invasion is going to happen this year?"

Victor continued to gaze at both his assistants with his typical bland expression. Finally, he responded, "You never heard me say that."

On a cold February afternoon, the phone in their unit rang while Victor was away at a meeting. Lacy jumped up from her desk to answer it. Hanging up after jotting down a quick message, she said to Tess, "Scotland Yard wants Victor to call them right away."

"Oh boy," Tess replied briefly, returning to the files piled beside her.

Soon after Victor returned from MI5 headquarters, he put down the phone receiver at his desk and advised his two assistants, "I want you both to dress warmly tomorrow. We three are taking the train to Kettering."

"Where's that?" Lacy asked.

"A couple of hours northwest of London in Northamptonshire," Tess informed Lacy, then asked Victor, "And why are we going there?"

The leader of their unit opened a desk drawer and pulled out a small, gun-metal gray carrying case that Lacy knew all too well contained the dissecting tools he'd formerly employed as a zoologist at his lab in Cambridge.

His tone surprisingly droll, Victor declared, "A crate of onions that needs attending to is sitting in a field outside that very village."

"*Onions?*" Tess exclaimed. "You're joking?!"

Both Tess and Lacy knew what Victor always meant when he said something "needed attending to." There was a bomb, newly discovered, that no one else knew how to defuse.

Eyeing the scientist's tool kit, Lacy murmured, "An unusual-looking device has been found in a crate of *onions*?"

"That's right, ladies. Courtesy of the Jerries dispatching it from Spain, or so I've just been told. It's of a type that the local constabulary doesn't recognize, so they called Scotland Yard, and—as per usual—the Yard called us, as Lacy relayed to me just now. Bring your camera, if you please," he directed her, "and, Tess, you're in charge of carrying the field telephone. Be sure the crank to charge it up works," he advised her. "Meet me at the St. Pancras rail station tomorrow, eight a.m. sharp. With any luck, no explosives will go off before we get there."

This time, the tension surrounding defusing the unusual device nestled in the crate full of onions planted by Germans had been worse than ever. Victor always shrugged it off, but Lacy wondered how many more such adventures, as he called them, the three of them could take—without him getting killed and the two women going mad.

Lacy set to work helping Victor arrange the standard procedure with the field phone placed on a nearby cart and connected to Tess, who would take Victor's dictation of each move he made from a nearby hotel. Then Lacy pulled out her Leica and began taking the prerequisite photographs to document the procedure.

She snapped a series of close-ups of Victor's fingers pointing to the detonator and wires protruding from the bomb. With each move, Lacy felt every muscle in her own body tensing. Once Victor gave her the familiar nod of his head to remove herself a safe distance from his operation, she marched across the frost-covered field to join the village bystanders.

Standing next to a waiting ambulance positioned there in case the worst happened, she held her breath as she lifted the pair of binoculars hanging around her neck and stared at Victor's figure bent nearly double over the crate. As the moments ticked by, she felt a familiar panic rising from her gut to her throat. *What is he doing now? How much time is left for him to render it harmless?* she wondered, her anxiety becoming excruciating. Any second now, one wrong move and—

After some ten agonizing minutes, a shout went up from the crowd surrounding her. The ambulance driver, pointing a finger toward Victor, yelled, "Look! Milord's holding the damn bomb over his head!"

Lacy squinted through her binoculars' long-distance lens to see that the device she had just photographed in the crate was in Victor's hand, its wires dangling harmlessly as he waved it triumphantly in the direction of the onlookers.

"Blimey!" exclaimed a man clad in overalls standing a few feet from Lacy. "That's one toff who's got some big bollocks!"

Lacy felt a rush of relief that Victor had cheated death once again, followed by the sensation that she might well faint. The farmer who'd commented on Victor's show of courage with such rustic gusto grabbed her by the elbow to steady her.

"Don't blame you, miss," he said, shaking his head. "That Lord Rothschild is one Jew with nerves of steel."

On the train heading back to London, Lacy sat alone, gazing at the passing scene, while Tess and Victor found a quiet corner in another car. Moodily, her gaze took in fields with grazing sheep and then the backyard lines of laundry that invariably greeted passengers along the routes that led into the train stations of England's capital city. Evidence of the Blitz bombings was everywhere, including piles of rubble where row houses like hers on Gower Street had once stood. She could see the carcasses of rusted, burnt-out autos and craters twelve feet wide that made some streets impassible until crews could come to fill them in. As evening began to fall, the scene out the train window deepened her gloom.

Victor and Tess were going to dinner somewhere. Once back at St. Pancras Station, Lacy headed for the nearest underground and at her stop, began to walk back to Bentinck Street. It was a relief to get some air and clear her brain of the anxiety that lingered after such a stress-filled day.

Two blocks from the flat, Lacy pulled up short. On the corner opposite her stood wavy-haired Guy Burgess, holding a briefcase. She stared as he swiftly exchanged it for a similar one passed to him by a short figure dressed in a black trench coat and a felt fedora. It was too dark to see whether the recipient had a birthmark on his cheek. Neither man exchanged a word.

What if it's the same guy I saw him with in the park those other times?

Thankful that night had fallen, Lacy ducked into a doorway until she saw Burgess proceed in the same direction she was going. He was obviously headed toward the building where they both lived, with the briefcase he'd swapped clutched in his hand.

What the devil did Burgess pass on to that man? she wondered.

The scene she'd just witnessed was far more worrisome than even the accusations that Burgess and Blunt were running a "male whore-house" out of the flat Victor had lent to them. She'd heard the slan-derous whispers about some of the raucous parties that were occasionally still held by the homosexual members of the Cambridge crowd.

Lacy remembered vividly that day when Victor had said to her, "Are there any other secrets you've been keeping from me that you need to confess?"

For a certainty, the same might be said of Guy Burgess, she fumed. *And he's switched from MI5 to MI6 now, for God's sake!*

If he were an actual Soviet agent, he could, at that moment, be passing on national security secrets to the Russians, not merely internal governmental tittle-tattle.

But would Victor dismiss an eyewitness to his Cambridge mate's suspicious behavior? If she described what she'd just seen, would Burgess's fellow graduate be angry at her or simply write her off as a homophobe? Or had Victor known all along Guy Burgess could be a double agent of some sort?

Suddenly, she was struck by an even darker thought.

Could Victor be one himself, and if so, working for whom?

What if he were aligned with Guy Burgess or Tony Blunt and a few other Russia-loving Cambridge grads working for various British intelligence agencies?

Immediately, she rejected that speculation. Victor had just, that very day, risked his life to protect his country and its citizens from a bomb that could have maimed or killed him. Surely, he wouldn't have done that if he were working for Stalin, the notoriously brutal dictator, to bring on the downfall of Britain.

A crushing fatigue descended on Lacy as she put the key in the front door of her flat. What a day it had been, topped off by Guy Burgess acting in a highly suspicious manner on the same day that his classmate, Victor Rothschild, had risked his life defusing high explosives.

Unexpectedly, Lacy's thoughts drifted to Pem—his good sense and solid judgment. And she wished for all she was worth that he were there to talk to and compare notes.

Chapter Thirty-Six

The next morning, Lacy and Pat had breakfast in the flat after spending half the night in the basement of their building due to ear-splitting air raid warnings that had gone off before midnight.

"I thought the Blitz was officially declared over," Pat said sarcastically with a yawn as she poured herself her morning tea.

"Tess must have ended up at Victor's place after their dinner," Lacy noted, pushing back from the kitchen table to prepare to head for work. Just then, the phone rang in the foyer, a rare occasion at such an early hour. "I'll get it," Lacy offered, walking swiftly to catch it on the third ring.

A voice said, "Greetings from the Ritz Hotel."

"Tess?" Lacy said, alarmed. "Are you all right? What are you doing there?"

"While we were at dinner, Hitler reduced Victor's flat in Saint James's to rubble, to say nothing of Wilton's, his favorite restaurant around the corner."

"I take it you were luckily dining somewhere else last night?"

Pat, having heard Lacy's alarm, had joined her in the foyer.

"Yes, at a place near St. Pancras when we got off the train. We were starving."

Covering the mouthpiece, Lacy said, "Victor and Tess just missed being killed! Victor's flat was demolished while they were having dinner near St. Pancras!" She turned back to the phone. "But you're all right, yes?" she confirmed.

"We're living in the lap of luxury," Tess said cheerfully

"We were just saying that we thought the Blitz was over," Lacy noted glumly.

"Oh, Victor says it's just another warning from Herr Hitler not to launch any invasion." Tess paused and said something muffled to her lover. "All right, then ... we just didn't want you to worry. See you at work."

Following the bombing of Victor's flat, Lacy's boss took up residence at the Ritz, a location not too far from their MI5 office that, fortunately, had not been damaged by the latest aerial barrage. In the wake of Tess and Victor's close call, Lacy felt more on edge than ever and found it hard to get a good night's sleep.

However, in late April, she and her flatmates enjoyed a cheerful diversion from the stress of sporadic but continuing air attacks in London when a fat envelope arrived, hand-delivered to their home.

"No one but close family is invited to Kick and Billy's wedding next month," Pat explained, waving an invitation to a postnuptial party in honor of the newlyweds at the home of Lady Hambleden—whom none of them had ever met. Pat grinned, noting, "Don't you think the card's beautiful calligraphy on this stiff bond looks frightfully smart on our mantlepiece?"

Lacy peered over Pat's shoulder, noting, "So, they're getting married at the Chelsea Registry Office on Saturday, I see."

Pat nodded. "Plans were speeded up. Billy is due to ship out any day now, although to *where* is anybody's guess."

"Like half the men we know," Tess said glumly, and Lacy felt the same.

The rumors that "something big" was about to be launched while Hitler was battling Russian troops on several fronts in Eastern Europe had grown even more deafening. Reports had been circulating within their MI5 unit that hundreds, perhaps thousands, of British and American troops on bases all over the UK were being moved *en masse* to points in southern England.

Clearly, everyone working in intelligence felt something was about to happen, but exactly *what* was a closely guarded secret, even from officers *in* MI5.

"Kick's wedding is on May sixth, is it?" Tess asked. "If there is something big afoot, it would appear that Lacy's American friend has snared her heir to the Dukedom of Devonshire just in the nick of time."

Lacy, recalling Kick's antisemitic remarks the day she'd come to their flat for sherry, wondered whether Tess and Victor would attend the party for the couple. She also questioned if Guy Burgess, Anthony Blunt, and the Cambridge Apostles were on the guest list.

Yet, on the day of the event celebrating the wedding, everyone from Victor's Bentinck Street flat was present at the elegant reception. Some two hundred guests drank champagne as if there wasn't a war going on, utterly ignoring for a few hours what appeared to be an imminent Allied invasion about to be launched across the Channel.

The question was *from* where *to* where.

Billy looked very smart in his military uniform, and Kick, of course, was all smiles in a pale, knee-length dress and matching floral hat. On cue, the guests threw rose petals at the bride and groom as they left for a reportedly very short honeymoon at the young Marquess's family mansion, Compton Place, in Eastbourne.

Commencing June 3, Lacy, Tess, and Victor were practically sleeping at the undamaged St. James's office as they scrambled to keep up with the intercepted German transmissions that were flying back and forth between the upper echelons of the Nazi hierarchy and being distributed to their MI5 unit. Lacy reconfirmed a decoded, translated German transcription sent over from Bletchley to the Admiralty and on to Victor. In it, a member of Hitler's brass was questioning whether the long-anticipated invasion of France by Allied forces was truly about to begin at Calais.

As they had every morning that month, the three roommates had risen early on the June 6th and been glued to the wireless long before dawn had broken, desperate for the latest news. At work, Victor remained on the phone most of the day, jotting down notes but refusing to say very much other than, late in the afternoon, "The Allied landing of our troops in France *is* ongoing."

Early on the morning of June 7, Victor pointed to a square on his desk calendar, announcing with a wave of a printed dispatch that had just been delivered to their door, "The War Office reports that yesterday, we sent some one hundred and fifty-six thousand Allied soldiers across the Channel to the beaches of Normandy."

"So! It was Normandy ... not Calais," Lacy breathed, silently wondering where Pem was at that very moment.

"And the casualties yesterday?" Tess asked, her voice tense.

Victor's expression grew even more somber as he consulted the paper in his hand. "On the first day alone, there've been about ten thousand Allied casualties, with more than four thousand troops known to be dead."

Lacy murmured, "Well, Pat told me this morning that Billy Cavendish received firm orders to head over there next week." Despite Kick's unwelcome remarks about Jews, Lacy found herself feeling sorry for the new bride.

Victor stood up from his desk, seizing a wooden pointer. He bid them to have a look at the map of the European continent affixed to the far wall, aiming the tip of his tool at the landmass marked "France."

"If we succeed in pushing past these cliffs on Omaha Beach here," he declared, tapping his pointer, "and manage to scale the other assault points, eventually putting our troops on the road to Paris," he elaborated, again pointing his stick at the map, "our MI5 antisabotage unit has been assigned to liaise with Eisenhower's supreme headquarters as soon as it's safe to do so."

"In Paris?" Lacy murmured, awestruck.

"Yes, in Paris, and that includes both of you."

Lacy and Tess looked at each other, turned away from Victor's map, and embraced.

"Once we get to Paris, our first order of business," Victor explained, "will be to organize our people to detect and neutralize lethal booby traps that retreating German armies are bound to have set for our advancing troops."

"We three are the bomb defusing detail?" Lacy asked, her voice almost a squeak.

Victor nodded nonchalantly. "It would seem so ... at least early on."

"Well, bomb disposal duties do take a bit of the shine off this visit to *La Belle France*," Tess remarked with a straight face.

"Golly," Lacy said, thinking back to the field outside Kettering where she'd watched Victor defuse the bomb burrowed inside the onion crate. "That's some assignment they've given you, milord."

"Given *us*," Tess reminded her.

"We'll just be sent out on the tricky ones, but we'll have help," Victor said, retracting the pointer and leaning it against the wall. "Our regular bomb squads will also be deployed over there, but my other job—and yours too, ladies—will be to recruit and train scores of the French to do this work in many, many places." The corners of his mouth turned up slightly. "And I intend for us to beg hospitality at the very nice Paris house of my cousin, Baron Elie Robert de Rothschild, on Avenue Marigny. Fortunately, he managed not to get killed when he was imprisoned and somehow gained his release recently."

Victor looked from one assistant to the other and gestured toward the ever-present pile of folders on each desk.

Tess spoke before he could. "We know ... 'Chop-chop, ladies,'" she quipped, "'the War Office needs us to finish these right away.'"

"That's right," Victor said. "We want to be ready to depart for Paris at a moment's notice."

Chapter Thirty-Seven

The MI5 trio housed at the offices in St. James's awaited orders to head for Paris, but none came in June. Less than a week after D-Day, Lacy was startled awake at 4:25 a.m. on June 13 by the sound of more sirens blaring than she remembered ever hearing during the full-on Blitz.

She met Tess in the hallway, and the two of them dashed into the sitting room to peer out the window.

"Did you hear explosions or anything?" Lacy asked.

"No, all these sirens woke me up," Tess replied, racing to the wireless and setting the dial to the BBC.

Within minutes, the deep voice of the presenter intoned, "A large rocket, some forty-five feet long, struck Grove Street, with at least six people killed, some thirty people injured, and at least two hundred left homeless. The projectile was launched from an as-yet undisclosed location along coastal France, with a range of some one hundred and fifty miles. According to monitored enemy news outlets, German broadcasts are calling it a V-1 or 'revenge rocket' unleashed on Britain in response to the recent Allied invasion."

"Forty-five feet *long*?" Lacy exclaimed, stunned by the sheer size of the weapon. "What's Victor going to do about defusing ones that landed but may not have gone off?"

Tess groaned. "I have an awful feeling they *all* go off when that much weight slams to earth."

Later that same day, when they arrived at their office, Victor informed them—to their great relief—that the V-1 rocket threat would be dealt with by an entirely new anti-armaments department. "We're still assigned to head for France after the mop-up from Normandy to Paris is complete."

Meanwhile, the pilotless, winged revenge missiles, powered by pulsejet engines, began pummeling London in earnest, giving off no other warning of their imminent arrival than a characteristic buzzing sound just before they plowed into the earth.

"Calling them *doodlebugs* makes them sound cute," Lacy said, shuddering, "and they're anything but."

"Well," said Tess, "we'll just have to get used to sleeping in the basement shelter every night and pray we get sent to Paris soon."

Lacy thought her nerves couldn't take one more night of German buzz bombs. At last, in late August, Lord Rothschild announced their antisabotage MI5 unit of three would finally be departing for France following the exciting news of the Allied liberation of Paris on the 24th.

"The Germans are headed east, at last!" Lacy exclaimed.

Tess had the bright idea of Victor asking for her and Lacy's fellow debutante, Diana Barnato, a pilot in the Air Transport Auxiliary, to fly them to France—which, with a wave of his hand, he arranged.

Arriving at 23 Avenue Marigny, they discovered that conquering American troops were already ensconced at the Rothschild mansion belonging to Victor's cousin. The Yanks had taken up residence there shortly on the heels of the fleeing German occupiers' departure from the same premises.

Within only a few days—and with the okay of General Eisenhower, Lacy suspected—the Americans were billeted elsewhere, and Victor declared the Rothschild family establishment the official headquarters of his "small but mighty" antisabotage division of MI5.

"I've offered a few rooms in this vast manse to some other smaller entities run by British officers I find both worthy and amusing," he informed his two assistants, requesting they tell the cook he'd rehired from his cousin's former retinue to prepare dinner for ten. Somehow, the beleaguered chef located the food necessary to feed them, "probably on the black market," Tess said, lips pursed with mild disapproval.

Once Victor's cousin, Elie Robert de Rothschild, recently released from captivity in Colditz Castle, saw the improvements in their mutual standard of living, he seemed happy to leave Victor in charge.

Within a few days of their arrival, Lacy and Tess not only went out with Victor every time bombs were suspected to be buried in the most unlikely of places but also found themselves in the Rothschild kitchen, supervising a staff thrilled to be back working for the renowned banking family. As the last days of summer rolled by, more luncheons and dinners were added on and the residence became a very popular place to be invited to dine. Guests, assorted dignitaries, and former acquaintances of Victor's wandered in day and night.

In the mansion's wood-paneled library, Victor, Tess, and Lacy—all three of them attired in full military uniform—held weekly bomb defusing seminars for a host of former French gendarmes and Allied soldiers assigned to learn Victor's "tricks of the trade," as he casually told the assembled groups. As American and British troops were pushing eastward in pursuit of the retreating Nazis, the enemy continued to lay booby traps in their wake as they headed deeper into their home territory. Victor's "bomb brigades," as he called his trainees, were needed everywhere.

By mid-September, horrifying reports from liberating troops began reaching Victor's desk. They related ghastly discoveries made at Nazi concentration camps scattered all over formerly occupied territories.

"Just last July," Victor disclosed, his hand resting on the latest report, pain etched on his face, "the Soviets entered Majdanek outside of Lublin in Poland, and what they found ..."

Lacy could tell he was unable to finish his sentence. Tess looked over his shoulder at the report that had caused him such distress.

Gently removing it from his hand, she quietly read aloud, "Majdanek began as a forced labor camp, but at liberation, it was clearly a place where death to its inmates came in gas ovens, as well as by typhus, beatings, lethal injections, and forced drownings in sewage pits." Tess reared back and stared at Lacy. "What kind of monsters *are* these Germans?"

Victor pointed to another dispatch delivered that day. "At least a hundred and fifty thousand prisoners were brought to Majdanek," he said. "Mostly Jews, of course. Their conditions are just as indescribable."

Lacy's stomach turned over at the thought that Noah might have been sent to a place like Majdanek. The chances he'd have ever survived were nil. She absorbed the agony reflected in Victor's expression, wondering whether he would ever again be able to assume the life of a wealthy, privileged young scientist that he'd enjoyed before the war.

Lacy and Tess exchanged worried glances, both aware that those firsthand testimonials detailing such sickening human cruelty would haunt all three of them to the grave.

Just then, one of the newly engaged servants knocked on the frame of the library door. "My Lord," she said, speaking French, "the Mademoiselles Tess and Lacy have a visitor. May I show him in?"

"Who is it?" Tess asked, as fluent in French as Lacy was.

The maid looked sheepish. "It was a difficult name, and I'm afraid I didn't quite understand the gentleman. He's an officer, I think. Something to do with medicine, perhaps, by the looks of his lapels. The snake wrapped around a staff?"

Tess stared at Lacy, exclaiming, "I think Mademoiselle Lacy should be the first to greet our visitor."

Rushing out of the room, Lacy nearly collided with the figure standing in the foyer.

"Ah! So glad I found you at home," declared a clipped British accent. "Is Tess here too? I come with greetings from your flatmate and *my* brand-new fiancée, Miss Pat Rawdon-Smith!" he announced with a flourish. "She's sent me here to extend to you both her dearest love and to tell you of our recent engagement."

Richard Llewellyn Davies, looking trim in his Royal Army Medical Corps uniform, extended a friendly hand.

Lacy turned away from him and burst into tears.

Tess, who'd followed her into the foyer, swiftly stepped forward and seized the hand of the architect specializing in designing hospitals. Then she and Richard both glanced in Lacy's direction with looks of concern.

"We thought it might have been Dr. Charles Pembroke surprising us," Tess said smoothly, "but, Richard, how marvelous to see you! Huge congratulations on your engagement to our girl! We couldn't be more thrilled, could we, Lacy?"

Lacy swiped her hand under her eyes to brush away her tears. "Th-that's wonderful, Richard," she said sincerely, trying to mask the trembling in her voice. "Truly, I couldn't be happier for you both." And she was.

It's just that, for a second, I thought ...

Captain Davies appeared mildly bewildered by the roller-coaster reception he'd just received. He offered a nervous smile, revealing, "As it happens, Lacy, I have a message from Pem for you today. As I think he told you both in London, he and I have been collaborating quite a while, supervising the manufacture and now the deployment of hospital train cars that are so needed by our Allied forces since the invasion last June."

"Ah, so *that's* what brings you both to Paris," Tess responded. She pointed to the door behind her. "Come on through, why don't you? We can talk much more comfortably in the front sitting room."

Numbly, Lacy followed their lead, but all she could absorb was the fact that after a rupture of two years, Pem had sent her a message, albeit through an intermediary. Her thoughts flew in all directions as the three of them sat down in the grand salon—Lacy and Tess on a brocade sofa, Richard in a leather chair.

Before Lacy could react to the news that Pem was in Paris, Pat's fiancé volunteered, "As you might suspect, our U.S. and British joint medical units are about to leave for the front. We'll be following our armies as they move east, coordinating the transportation of injured soldiers away from the battle lines in the Netherlands and, ultimately, from Germany."

Lacy swallowed hard at hearing that Pem and Richard would be extremely close to active war zones. Still struggling to regain her composure after her emotional outburst, she felt Richard's gaze assessing whether she'd gotten a hold of herself.

Apparently, he assumed she had, for he jokingly said, "As a matter of fact, Lacy, I think Pem would be quite pleased if he'd witnessed your disappointed reaction to the mere *sight* of me." Digging into his pants pocket, he pulled out a slip of paper. "When I told Pem this morning that Pat knew where both of her best friends were staying in Paris, he asked me to give you this."

Lacy rose from her seat and took the note from Richard's hand. Unfolding it, she read,

If you're willing, meet me at café Les Deux Magots,
6 place Saint-Germain-des-Prés, 6th arrondissement,
this afternoon at four.
—Pem

Chapter Thirty-Eight

Lacy dressed in the one decent outfit she had remaining in her wardrobe after five years of war. It was navy blue, with a dark-blue-and-green tartan collar and cuffs and a trim waistline that emphasized her slender figure. She brushed her shoulder-length dark-blond hair vigorously and swept it up into a chignon with care, then pinched her cheeks, as rouge was nowhere to be had those days. As she gazed at herself in a mirror in her assigned bedroom in Lord Rothschilds' borrowed mansion, she knew Pem was bound to notice how much skinnier she was due to the years of restricted rations —that was, until she'd arrived in Paris.

Happy that she'd brought the cotton frock with her to France, she decided it might calm her nerves to walk across the River Seine at the Pont Alexandre, a bridge that led directly into the Saint-Germain district. She'd eaten at Café Les Deux Magots many times when she was a student at the Sorbonne. She'd always relished the notion that Hemingway used to write sitting at one of the small tables when he frequented the place in the 1920s and had even used it as a setting in *The Sun Also Rises.*

When Lacy entered the café under its green awnings, her heart began to pound as she gazed around the restaurant. Pem had chosen a table for two in the far back corner, and his captain's hat was resting on a woven raffia-backed chair nearby. He must have been watching for her because he rose instantly as soon as she'd crossed the threshold and made her way toward him.

The majority of patrons had chosen the cluster of small round tables outside on the sidewalk. It was a clear day, with a hint of autumn in the air. Convivial chatter and the clink of glasses rang in her ears.

Lacy had tried to plan what she would say when she first saw Pem, but as she approached his table, her mind went blank, her heart racing. He was in his khaki captain's uniform, his blue-black hair glistening, and he was as handsome as ever.

Standing his full six feet, he gestured with one arm for her to take a seat beside him. As she sat down, she placed her pocketbook next to his hat on the chair, where the two personal items coexisted peacefully side by side.

"I'm glad you came," he said. Eyes as blue as she remembered locked onto hers. "I-I wasn't sure you would."

"I wasn't sure either," she replied with a nervous laugh. "But I kept wondering why you'd reached out after all this time, so I came to find out."

"I only learned today that you were in Paris."

"Richard Davies?" she confirmed, nodding. "A rather amazing coincidence, isn't it, that one of my two best friends is marrying your opposite number in the rather specialized world of hospital trains."

"Richard got pushed into it since the brass knew he designed hospitals, so why not hospitals on wheels? The same thing happened to me when our top guys found out I was a doctor who was also trained as a hospital architect specializing in industrial design."

Each of them forced a smile. Lacy fiddled with a crease in her skirt.

Pem cleared his throat and said, "Richard just proposed to Pat last week when he was briefly on leave in London. She told him that you and Tess were over here, working for Rothschild on whatever in the world he's doing for MI5."

"And living in the mansion on the Marigny owned by one of his cousins," she replied with another small laugh. "Once they get it all cleaned up, now that the Germans and the Yanks have cleared out, it's going to be pretty posh."

The two fell silent, neither one, she imagined, knowing what to say next.

Pem turned and hailed a passing waiter.

Then, to Lacy, he said, "My French is lousy to nonexistent. Would you be willing to ask the *garçon* for two Kir Royals?" he proposed, referring to glasses of champagne topped with crème de cassis.

Lacy nodded and spoke to the waiter in rapid French.

"*Mais oui, Mademoiselle*," he replied promptly. "*Tout de suite.*"

When the waiter departed to fill the order, Pem said, "I want to raise a toast."

"To what?" she asked, hardly able to conceive what the two of them, sitting side by side like his hat and her purse on the chair, had to celebrate.

"A toast is in order ... to me." He was staring at her so intently, Lacy felt as if his gaze had glued her to her chair. Pem said, "You see before you an officially divorced man."

Pem had declared his shocker quietly, but his words drilled through any ability Lacy had to keep the sense of detachment she'd been struggling mightily to maintain. She sat back in her chair, the raffia weave pressing into the thin material of her dress.

"Well ..." she said finally. "That's not exactly what I expected to hear today."

"Why not? I told you the last time I saw you that I wanted to be free ... to be with you. I know you told me in London two years ago not to write or call you, but at least I ... I wanted you to know I'd followed through with what I said I'd do ... when I had been able."

Pem was a truly honorable man, she reflected, someone who did what he said he would do, even when he had no guarantee of the outcome.

After a pause, he continued, "Believe it or not, the split was mutual."

"Just like your agreement not to have children was mutual?" she asked, keeping her tone neutral as if she were only mildly interested in his answer.

Cocking his head to one side as if he were puzzled by her question, he said, "Well, here's irony for you. Turns out that during most of my assignments back and forth between England and D.C., Eleanor was having an affair with a doctor at the hospital where my father works."

Lacy sat back in her chair. "Did *she* tell you that?"

"Oh, I got the message loud and clear when I took the train back to Boston to finally sort out the mess we'd made of our marriage."

"Didn't it upset you to find that out?"

Pem gave a quick shake of his head. "It startled me, for sure, because Eleanor had always seemed to care more about how things looked than how things actually were." He chuckled. "I arrived at the house late," he related, "but she got out of bed, put on her dressing gown, and calmly told me she was in love with this guy I'd done my residency with."

"Was she pregnant perchance?" Lacy asked in a sharper tone than she'd intended.

Pem paused before replying, "No. But she told me that night that she hopes to be, and so does the new doc in her life."

Lacy shot him a look of disbelief. Getting a divorce from a wife of eight years was really *that* easy for him?

As if reading her thoughts, Pem continued, "At first, she didn't admit the affair, and ... neither did I come clean about *you*."

Lacy briefly glanced around the restaurant, playing for time before she replied to that startling revelation.

Pem didn't wait for her response. "We two sat in the kitchen, talking till two in the morning, and *finally* had the first honest conversation in our entire relationship." He stared out across the restaurant as if witnessing the scene all over again. "After quite a bit of wrangling as to who was to blame for the tangle we were in, we ultimately agreed that we were and always had been completely unsuited for each other. That we had married under family pressure from both sides ... and because—back then as an 'aging deb,' as she put it—she'd pushed for the wedding, too. She and I had both gone along with everybody else's plan."

Lacy was spellbound by how honestly Pem admitted his own passive acquiescence. He'd clearly done some soul-searching as to what part he'd played in the mess of their marriage, and she couldn't help but admire him for it.

Pem continued, seeking her gaze, "I admitted to Eleanor how I'd given in to being hounded by my parents *and* her into the practice of medicine when I really loved architecture and industrial design ... I loved creating and building." He smiled faintly. "When I said that, Eleanor confessed that all *she'd* ever dreamed of was having an ordinary life, being married to a normal doctor like her father and like this George Chapman fellow, and she'd resented my taking another path."

"And how did all that strike you?"

"As I listened to her, Lacy, I could see that for *her*, wanting the same life her mother had chosen was a perfectly reasonable way to want to live."

"But it just wasn't the way *you* wanted to live?"

"No, it wasn't ... and not with her."

Just then, the waiter appeared with their Kir Royals. Pem hesitated to speak again until the server set down their champagne flutes and drifted away.

"The truth is," he said, raising his glass in a silent toast, "Eleanor and I were both relieved we could part ways with no hard feelings."

"How convenient that must have been for you two."

Pem shook his head. "Not convenient at all. It was *hard*. Hard to tell each other the unvarnished truth ... and hard to tell our parents we were calling it quits."

Lacy instantly regretted the spiteful tone that had just come out of her mouth. As they gently touched the rims of their glasses together, she nervously sensed that Pem was studying her closely.

"It sounds to me, though," he said quietly, "that the hard feelings are on *your* side."

Lacy stared into her glass, her eyes fixed on the bubbles rising to the top. "I guess I do still have hard feelings ... and the reasons I do are partly my own fault."

"What do you mean?" Pem asked, looking genuinely puzzled.

"I finally figured out that you had, in fact, made some attempts to communicate with me after we ... after we were in Birmingham."

Pem abruptly set down his glass. "So, you *did* receive my messages —but you never answered them?" he asked, incredulous.

"What was there to answer?" she said sharply. "A cable saying you were coming to London and a postcard saying you couldn't make it."

"And that was it? That was all you ever received from me?"

"Well, there was a note with my name misspelled saying you'd try to get in touch 'sometime.'" She met his glance. "I never received the cable you said the pilot sent me about arriving safely in D.C. The postcard didn't show up until *months* after you left. Then the note you had someone deliver said nothing of substance. I felt hurt and angry about your long silence, so I threw everything into the bottom of my trunk and made no attempt to write you."

"That's *all* you ever received from me?" he repeated. "You never got the long letter I had a cousin send secretly, despite strict orders not to communicate with anyone during that time? I sent it because I wanted to be sure that there were no dire circumstances for you after … Birmingham."

Lacy could only stare at him, absorbing his last words as if they'd been spoken in a language she didn't understand.

Finally, she stammered, "N-no … and you never mentioned *that* letter the last time you were in our London flat."

"I started to that day, but you hardly gave me a chance to say anything. If you remember, you cut me off mid-sentence and said it was 'your call' and we were through."

Forced to acknowledge silently what Pem said was true, Lacy replied, "Well, I never got anything from you asking me if … well … if our night together had—" She swallowed hard. "I interpreted that as meaning you just didn't—"

She couldn't complete the sentence, but Pem did it for her. "Care?" he asked, incredulous. "I risked a court martial writing you at that point in my project when I was under orders to contact *no one*."

"And *I'm* telling you that whatever you wrote never arrived!" she insisted.

Pem stared into his champagne. "I chanced it because I wanted to be sure that you didn't get pregnant."

Lacy took a tiny sip from her flute and set it down.

"Well … I did."

"Become pregnant?" He stared at her waistline, trim in her blue cotton dress, a belt cinching around her narrow middle. "We made a baby together, and you didn't *tell* me?"

"I hadn't *heard* from you in months, Pem! I had no idea, for sure, where you were!" She looked around to see whether her outburst had attracted attention.

Pem grew very quiet before finally asking in a low voice, "And then you did … what?"

The buzz of happy, recently liberated Parisians sipping their wine contrasted with the long silence before Lacy answered his question.

At length, she repeated his question. "What did I do when I realized I was pregnant?" The time had come, at last, to tell him. "I soon started being very sick to my stomach every single morning." She looked off across the heads of the diners as those first days of shock and terror came rushing back to her. "At first, I told no one. I felt so alone and miserable."

"And then …?"

Lacy sought his glance, his understanding. "I was scared."

He pushed away his champagne flute. "I can imagine." Then he said, "You thought you hadn't heard from me … so … you had an abortion."

His sentence hung in the air between them.

A few more seconds passed, then Lacy replied, "I did. In Islington. At seven or eight weeks."

When he looked up, she saw the moisture that had gathered in his eyes. His next words shocked her.

"I can understand why you felt you had to end the pregnancy, but I just wish you'd had more faith in … us."

Lacy felt her own tears clogging her throat. "I broke it off with you because I'd been devastated at not having heard a word from you after Birmingham. The Blitz, here, made everything—and especially *our* situation—feel hopeless. You were married and stationed God only knew *where*. You'd never wanted children, and I—"

Pem sat back in his chair, shaking his head in denial. "I didn't want to have children with *Eleanor*!" he protested. "I knew from my wedding day we were wrong together and shouldn't inflict our mismatched misery on an innocent child."

Pem's expression grew sorrowful. He reached for her hand. "I would *never* have abandoned you … or our child. If you'd told me, I would have urged you to go ahead and have the baby. I would have come to you as soon as I could. After our big fight and you broke it off, I knew I couldn't live in the marriage I was in, even if you and I never saw each other again."

Pem's gaze was boring into Lacy, and she braced herself for what she knew was coming.

Pem shook his head. "Why didn't you have the decency to tell me the truth about what was going on with you when I saw you last in London? That was *my* child too! You're always so sure no one will stand by you or demonstrate loyalty toward you, and then you prove that's *true* by driving them away!"

"But you'd said you didn't *want* children!" she insisted brokenly.

"You assumed that's what you *heard* when I told you I didn't want to bring a child into my marriage with Eleanor," he countered. "Of course I'd want to have a child with *you*. Why do you always assume the *worst*, even with me?"

Lacy felt the tears streaming down her face and was glad they were sitting in a dark corner of the café.

"I don't know," she whispered.

"Don't you think you should find out?" he asked sharply.

"I know it's no excuse," she began, "but I think part of what happened to me is that my head's been screwed up from the incessant air attacks, the stress of my job helping Victor in his crazy bomb defusal. And ..." She looked away. "And I've had this horrid, lingering guilt about allowing the abortion ... to go forward. I couldn't face you with what I had done."

Slowly, she related most of what had occurred that day in Islington, including the bombing raid while she was in surgery. Even so, due to the darker corners of her trauma, she couldn't quite make herself come clean about the involvement of Dr. Jones's nurse and the basement operating room.

"I only seemed to be able to fight this dark depression I've been feeling since then by trying to ignore it and concentrating, instead, on my duties at MI5."

Pem gazed at her a long moment and then said with a sigh, "Ah, my poor darling ... what a terrible time of it you must have had. I'm so sorry ... so very, very sorry you had to go through all of that alone."

He gently put two fingers under her chin, forcing her to look him in the eye.

"Listen, Lacy! Here we sit in liberated Paris. Predictions are Germany's beaten. Hitler will be forced to surrender soon. It'll take some time for this damn war to be officially over, but look at it this way! You and I have been given a second chance! We'll get married. *Tomorrow* if you want to." He threw back his head and laughed. "I bet your Lord Rothschild can wave his magic wand and help us do that. We'll start a family, and—"

Stricken by Pem's excited proposal, Lacy shot her hand out, her palm against his chest as if to push away his words, his very self.

"I'm pretty sure it's too late to be sorry," she whispered as a wave of deep sadness swept over her, one so powerful, she could hardly speak.

"What do you mean, 'too late?' It's *not*, Lacy, if you don't want it to be!"

She could see that exasperation was creeping into his tone.

"It is," she insisted. "It's probably too damn late for any second chance."

Chapter Thirty-Nine

Suddenly, Lacy wanted everything between her and Pem to be laid out on the table at last.

"It's very likely too late for me ever to have another baby," she confessed. "I had a terrible infection after ... after ..." She couldn't finish her sentence.

Pem leaned back in his chair, staring at her. She could see him mulling over her previous description of what had transpired in Islington.

"You didn't have a doctor do it, did you?" he said quietly. "You went to some backstreet butcher who killed our baby and probably maimed you in the bargain." He stared at her as if seeing her for the first time. "Jesus, Lacy! How could you do that? I don't fault your decision to end the pregnancy, given the complications between us, but how could you do that to *yourself*?"

"I *went* to a doctor," she protested, "but ... he wasn't there when I arrived, so his nurse—"

Cutting her off, his dismay evident, he declared, "You were that anxious to be done with it? You went through with it anyway? You let someone not qualified to—"

"No, you don't understand!" she whispered hoarsely, his rational accusations cutting her to the core. "The doctor was called away! I *told* you, there was an air raid that day. Bombs were falling above the basement operating theater, for God's sake!" Righteous anger churning in her gut, she rasped, "I cried over that lost soul and still cry at night, but I got sepsis! I nearly died! And now, since I probably can't have children, I suppose that doesn't fit your *new* plan, does it?"

"Lacy, be fair! It upsets me so much to hear what you went through, but letting a—"

"But *what*?" she cried, feeling as if her entire life were plunging off the rails like a train car with broken axles. "Now I'm damaged goods? Not what you want, either?"

Her mind was on fire recalling the terror of going down those steps to the doctor's basement surgery with the world exploding overhead. Jayne Girard had refused to stay with her! She had been totally alone, abandoned by everyone, including Pem. Suddenly, she could feel the mask being pushed against her face and smell the ether ... remembering blacking out, then waking up in that makeshift operating room, knowing what she'd done to the life she'd wanted to protect so much.

Pem was staring at her, his eyes brimming with hurt and confusion. "Try to understand it from my side," he said. "I trained as a doctor. I know how dangerous that procedure can be without a practitioner who knows what he's doing. It horrifies me that you might have been mutilated, allowing what that nurse did to you!"

"You're totally right," she said, a cool, fatalistic sensation filling her chest. A feeling that had been so familiar in her childhood. She was on her own. No one was there to take her side. "I was a thoughtless idiot. But let's face it, Pem. It is what it is. I did what I did. I can see that life with me—but without the children you want—won't be the *easy* road to marital bliss you might have had in mind."

The old shield of steel that had always protected her from the worst of life's body blows slid into place. Pem would never forgive her for what she'd done, regardless of the circumstances under which she'd done it. Better to face that then and there. If Pem was accustomed to things always working out to his liking, it wasn't going to be like that with her.

The annoying voice living in the back of her brain reminded her things hadn't been so easy for him either, what with his battling a father bullying him into medicine. Despite that, he'd earned and paid for his architect's degree, to say nothing of risking his life on the front lines of a war, trying to save injured soldiers. But overriding those thoughts, the front of her brain shouted that it was more than likely she couldn't have children, and she could only imagine the pain that would cause them both as the years went by.

"God knows, Pem, you'd probably prefer to tread a simpler path. The one with me, I'm afraid, would be solidly uphill."

"You're not being fair," he said quietly. "You're telling me how I feel, and you're totally wrong."

"Maybe you think I'm wrong, but here we are in Paris with a war still raging," she countered, with a sense that numbing ice was flowing in her veins. "You and your hospital trains are moving toward the front lines, while Tess and I will be helping Victor to defuse more bombs and booby traps till the Germans surrender—if they ever do. What do you calculate are the odds that both of us will *survive* this goddamned war?"

"I pray we both do," Pem replied, his voice low.

The guilt she'd harbored for so long for submitting to Dr. Jones's nurse's persuasion to "get it over with" felt like it was about to smother her. Lacy shook her head. "I doubt you're ever likely to excuse the decisions I made that day. It's stupid for us to make plans at this point."

"Lacy, please *don't*—"

"Don't you get it, Pem?" she cut him off, wishing she could jump in the Seine. "This feels hopeless. It always *has been* hopeless, so let's just—once and for all—save ourselves the misery and call it quits."

Pem shook his head like a man defeated in the match of a lifetime. He slowly withdrew a 100-franc note from his wallet, set it beneath his champagne flute, and rose to depart.

"See?" she whispered between her teeth. "You're *leaving*. What a surprise."

Pem turned to face her directly, towering above her, handsome as a movie star in his uniform, with the medical insignia a golden glow on his lapels.

"Yes, I am going to go," he confirmed softly. "I've run out of ways trying to convince you that I'm not the mother who constantly pushed you away when it suited her. I'm not your alcoholic father who left his little girl to drink himself to death. Nor am I even your batshit crazy stepfather who shot himself in the head and took his mistress with him." He raised both hands in frustration. "You've had some horrific things to deal with, but by now, you should have figured out that I'm the guy who *doesn't* leave. I hate that you had to go through being pregnant without me and got sick afterward and had to mourn our baby alone."

He bent forward and lowered his voice even more, moisture rimming his

eyes. "I wish everything could have been different, Lacy, and I understand now

why it wasn't. You didn't hear from me enough or get the support you deserved. You faced a horrible choice, made all on your own. But *I'm* the guy who kept coming back to you—over and over. Even today."

Lacy felt his despair and her own at seeing him about to leave. In his actions, she perceived his determination to put an end to the unhappiness she was causing them both.

"Every time I come back," Pem said, as if pleading with her to understand something she had never been able to grasp, "you always find a reason to push me away. You always expect the worst." He seized his hat. "Hey, I guess I'm more of a doctor than I thought," he said, his voice verging on bitter. "I thought love would heal that wound, but it clearly hasn't. My diagnosis? Maybe it can't."

In a familiar gesture that made her heart nearly slow to a stop, he bent toward her and brushed the back of his fingers along the side of her cheek. "You take good care, you hear me? I've got a hospital train to catch."

Lacy watched him thread his way through the cluster of small tables and disappear down the Boulevard Saint-Germain. She remained frozen in her chair, his words ringing in her ear.

"Every time I come back, you always find a reason to push me away."

She'd just done that. Again. Hurting herself and hurting the man she loved beyond anyone she'd ever known.

And the worst of it was, she absolutely didn't know *why* she'd done such a terrible thing.

Lacy returned to the mansion on Avenue Marigny, her thoughts of what had just happened with Pem revolving in an endless loop.

I love and respect Pem so much ... and yet, look what I've done.

She had a horrible feeling that, especially during times of severe stress, she was driven by forces she simply didn't understand. He had tried his best to make her see he wasn't like any of the people who had hurt her and Teddy over the years. In her deepest soul, she'd known that was true, yet ...

"You always expect the worst ... you always find a reason to push me away."

And so she always had.

Once at the mansion's front entrance, she passed through the carpeted foyer and headed directly for her assigned room on the second floor. Quietly closing her door, she flung herself on the tapestry counterpane.

Within seconds, there was a rap on her door. "Lacy?"

It was Tess, who had evidently heard her come in and followed her up the stairs. Lacy rolled over onto her back and sighed. "Yes, it's me. You can come in."

Tess closed the door behind her and strode over to the bed. "Well?" she demanded. "What happened? Was Pem at the café?"

"Pem's leaving for the front, along with Richard Davies."

Tess waved her hand. "Yes, Pat told me all that in a letter that came just after you left—and all about her getting engaged and that Richard might try to see us if he had time. I mean, what happened with you and *Pem*?"

"He told me he's divorced now."

"Really?" she exclaimed. "That's amazing! And during wartime. Not any easier in America than in Britain, I imagine."

"It was amicable, he said."

"Double amazing. *And ...?*"

Lacy pulled herself to a sitting position and leaned against the tufted headboard. "With us? Not so amicable."

Tess's face fell. "How upset was he when you told him about—?"

Lacy quickly interrupted. "He was upset and sad, but it's much more complicated than just that."

"What was complicated about telling him the truth? And that

you love him?" Tess asked with a frown. "You told me you'd say all that."

Lacy had no words to describe how her entrenched, warped beliefs that she couldn't seem to let go of had brought her and Pem to the impasse they'd reached at the café. Even worse, she'd never gotten to the part where she was able to tell him how much she loved him, how she admired him for the way he'd ultimately held to his belief that his path was architecture and design. She'd never confessed that she desperately wanted him in her life. And then she'd gone and ruined everything.

A headache was starting to pound.

"I don't know, Tess. I've made a hash out of everything."

"And he's left now?" Tess said, sitting down on the edge of the bed.

"Soon ... if not already."

"And you feel ... what?" Tess asked, putting a sympathetic arm around Lacy.

"*Terrible*!" She began to cry. "I don't think I've ever felt this awful in my life."

"Then you've got to tell him so. You've got to find him before he leaves."

It took a single phone call from Victor but several hours of waiting to discover that the next hospital train due to leave Paris was scheduled to depart from the Gare de l'Est rail station at eleven o'clock that evening.

"It's ten-fourteen," Tess declared, breathless from running up the stairs to Lacy's room. "Get your coat on!"

"Oh, Tess, what if Pem doesn't want to have another go-around with me?"

"Well, better to find out now, don't you think?" she demanded. "He's headed for the front, working in a major war zone. You don't even know if he'll come back. How will you feel if he doesn't and you never told him that you obviously can't live without him?"

"Aren't you laying that on awfully heavy?" Lacy snapped.

"You bet," cried Tess. "Come on! I'm going with you!"

"Okay, Miss Bossykins ... but this is on you if it doesn't work out!"

Lacy plunged her arms into her coat sleeves, and the two ran down the stairs and out the front door.

<hr>

It was ten minutes to eleven when Victor's driver pulled up in front of the train station's arched, colonnaded entrance. Dashing from the car into the station itself, the two women paused to catch their breath. Inside the massive cavern of Gare de l'Est, trains were heading for Switzerland, while Allied troop trains lining other platforms were destined for the Netherlands and Germany.

"Victor said to ask the ticket master what trains the hospital cars are attached to," Tess advised, pointing to a bank of windows on the other side of the hall. "Follow me!"

With soldiers, Red Cross nurses, and Parisians newly liberated from their German oppressors jamming the platforms, they'd just reached the ticket office when a voice called out.

"Tess? Lacy? What are *you* two doing here?"

Both women whirled around to take in the sight of Richard Llewellyn Davies with a huge duffle bag slung over his shoulder.

"We're trying to find Charles Pembroke before his train leaves!" exclaimed Tess.

Lacy knew from Richard's expression that they'd come too late.

"His hospital cars were attached to a troop train that left forty-five minutes ago," Richard revealed, looking at Lacy sympathetically. "My lot are scheduled to go out at eleven, so I'm afraid that I can't stay and talk for long."

"Why two trains?" Tess asked with a worried glance in Lacy's direction.

"Security," he answered. "If the damn Jerries try to dive bomb one train on our way toward the front lines, mine becomes the backup. If both trains make it, we'll have twice the space for all the casualties that are expected in the next big advance eastward."

"Don't the hospital cars have big red crosses painted on their roofs and sides?" Lacy demanded.

"Makes no difference to the Nazis, we've been told. They'll bomb the train anyway." He glanced up at the huge clock looming over the platforms and said, "So sorry, dear ladies, but I've got to go!" He smiled and hiked his duffle higher on his shoulder. "Give my best to Victor," he said to Tess, and to Lacy, he added cryptically, "I'll be sure to tell Pem you made every effort to see him off."

"And we'll tell Pat we saw *you* off," Tess said. "All good luck, Richard."

"Yes," Lacy quickly chimed in, fighting bitter disappointment that they hadn't gotten there in time. "Take good care and travel safe."

Richard's expression turned somber as he replied, "Thanks. I've got the distinct feeling that we're going to need a bit of luck this next little while."

Lacy and Tess waved him goodbye and then exchanged glances. Just that morning, Victor had apprised his two assistants of the launching of Operation Market Garden in the Netherlands, an Allied action aimed at clearing a path through to Germany. The first wave of joint American and British forces had set off in early September, and Lacy wondered whether that was also Pem and Richard's assigned destination before the Allies pushed on to Germany.

Tess put her arm around Lacy's shoulders. "Well, it's back to defusing bombs for us, I guess, but at least you tried." She gave a light tap on Lacy's chin. "I have no doubt that Pem will eventually hear of your effort to say goodbye." Then Lacy's friend gave her one of her hard no-nonsense looks. "When you see him next, you can make your amends."

But will I ever see him again? Lacy wondered. *Will he even make it through the coming battles*? Nothing was ever certain in a war, nor did things seem to go smoothly when it came to her and Pem.

"It's getting late," Tess said, nodding in the direction of the huge clock high on the station wall. "Let's head back."

The second Lacy and Tess stepped inside his cousin's mansion, Victor called to them from the library. Obediently, they crossed the threshold into what had become their MI5 Paris office to see Victor surrounded by floor-to-ceiling bookshelves, standing beside his desk and looking grim. He had his hand resting on an old-fashioned black telephone with its receiver cradled on a brass hook.

"In a minute, I'll ask you whether you caught up with Dr. Pembroke, but I've just received some very sad news about one of our friends."

Lacy wondered how much more bad news she could withstand after not seeing Pem before his train had left. Gazing at Victor's melancholy expression, she felt her heart give a lurch, sensing instinctively that the next words from his mouth would be terrible news.

"Our friend, Billy ... Lord Hartington ... your friend Kick Kennedy's recent bridegroom. He's been reported killed."

CHAPTER FORTY

"Billy's dead?" Tess cried. "Oh, God, *no*!" Lacy, tears welling, turned to stare at Tess in shock. "When?" Tess demanded as the two women clung to each other in the doorway. "Where did it happen?"

"A messenger brought this report after you left for the station, and I confirmed it just now by phone. Billy's Fifth Coldstream battalion was one of the first units advancing through the Netherlands," he explained, glancing down at the dispatch. "The division's armored tanks faltered when they came up against some earthen walls the Germans had laced with trees and brush roots. Apparently, those same tanks didn't maneuver well in the brackish marshlands in that region. As a consequence, Billy's battalion was shelled in Démouville but eventually proceeded to the village of Heppen." Victor paused, squinting at the sheet of paper he was holding in his hand. "Oh, good Lord!"

"What?" demanded Tess.

"There's an addendum at the bottom here. Officers are not required to adhere to strict battledress in the field. Since it had been raining and dusk was coming on, Billy was wearing a white macintosh."

"A raincoat?" Lacy asked, translating British English for herself.

"Yes, along with pale corduroy trousers, it says here, which, apparently, made him an easy mark for the German sharpshooters perched on roofs above the town square."

"His bright colors made him stand out," Tess murmured, advancing into the library and sinking into one of the leather club chairs. "So they got him."

Victor consulted the report again, as if to be sure he was relaying the incident to them accurately. "Shot in the head."

"Oh *no!*" they cried in unison.

Lacy came to stand beside Tess's chair. "Poor Kick," she murmured. "They'd only been married five *months!*"

Victor pointed to the dispatch once more. "The commanding officer of the Guards is calling their subsequent capture of Heppen the key to the whole operation to extend a bridgehead closer to Germany for the final push."

"That's something, at least," Tess muttered.

Victor cautioned them, "They've a long way to go, and the fighting's been horrendous."

"How ghastly for the Duke and Duchess of Devonshire as well," murmured Tess.

"And think how much longer this damn war is bound to last," moaned Lacy, a wave of fear and worry sweeping over her at the thought of Pem and Richard heading east that night. Her thoughts drifted to the families reacting to the news of Billy's death.

With Billy gone, Andrew Cavendish and Debo are destined to become the future Duke and Duchess.

Lacy had always liked the kind, brave Billy Cavendish. Now he was dead—killed, like so many other young men willing to put their lives on the line to fight Hitler.

Lacy felt tears spilling down her cheeks at the thought that Pem and Richard hadn't volunteered to bear arms but rather to bear hospital stretchers. But just like regular soldiers, they were heading for the front lines, risking their own lives to make sure wounded men made it into well-designed and operated ambulance trains to be transported to safety. At that moment, both architects were following the same path toward Germany that Billy and the Allied troops had taken.

A kind of regret Lacy had never experienced before nearly strangled her. She *had* to understand why she'd pushed Pem away earlier that day ... why she had a sick predilection to always expect the worst of people, regardless of who they were or how they'd behaved. *Why,* though she was long past her childhood, did she continue to paint all humanity with the same black brush whenever she hit bumps in the road?

Whether she and Pem ever saw each other again, she had to find out.

Lacy mutely nodded at Tess and Victor, made her way out of the library and up the stairs to her room, and flung herself on her bed.

Kick Kennedy's Billy is gone forever, she mourned, staring at the ceiling. The bride's debutante days of waltzing in her flowing white gown and long white gloves with the man who'd so briefly been Kick's husband were never to come again.

Lacy buried her head in the bed's feather pillow that Rothschild's housekeeper had unpacked. Against its soft linen, she prayed, *Please, please, please keep Pem and Richard safe.*

Lacy did her best to make peace with the fact that she hadn't arrived at the train station in time to see Pem before he'd left and that the entire mess was her fault—as well as the war's. She cried only at night, softly into the luxurious feather pillow on her bed. During the day, she struggled to maintain an American version of a stiff upper lip and threw herself into helping Victor however she could.

Just before they'd received the news of Billy's death on September 10, yet another of Germany's offensives had begun in the form of new, even more powerful German V-2 rockets flung at Paris, in Porte d'Italie, and London, on a street in Chiswick.

"Good Lord!" Lacy exclaimed, handing the latest report to Tess. "These damn things are forty-five feet long, like the others, but the V-2 versions have a two-hundred-mile range and are traveling at eighteen hundred miles per hour!"

"All I can say," Tess replied wearily, "is that the Allies better get to Berlin soon and stop this madness."

By Christmas, six months after D-Day, Victor's MI5 unit in Paris, in Lacy's view, had evolved from one preventing homegrown sabotage into a "teach our side how to defuse bombs" platoon in liberated Paris. As the days wore on, it became clear that lethal devices planted by the retreating Germans around the city and across Europe were hidden in all sorts of dangerous places.

Right after New Year's, Victor declared, "Just as in England, there are enough buried munitions in France alone to keep twenty times the number of people we've trained busy for years and years." He waved the latest dispatch from London that had arrived that morning. "The good news, ladies, is our fearless leaders at the War Office have determined that we've done the best job we could over here. They say it's time for our antisabotage unit to come home."

Tess gave a cheer, but Lacy couldn't help but wonder whether Pem and Richard would ever hear those words: "Come home."

———

For Lacy, returning to Britain offered no respite from the anxiety that anyone, including her, could fall victim to the vicious V-2 rockets the Nazis kept flinging across the English Channel. In late January of 1945, when she, Tess, and Victor arrived back at the St. James's office, the terrifying V-bombs continued to pummel both France and England. By the time the last revenge rocket fell on Hughes Mansions in East London at the end of March, Lacy was wondering how much more their nerves could take.

Pat, as expected, had heard nothing from Richard on the eastern front, which meant Lacy had had no word about Pem either. The two women had made a practice of declaring aloud that hospital trains were doing the "work of the angels" and would somehow be protected from harm.

"What else can we do?" Pat said, giving Lacy a hug each time they said their mantra.

So carry on they did.

In April, Victor sent Lacy, camera in hand, to photograph the V-2 rocket damage suffered to an entire wing at the Royal Hospital Soldiers' Home, along with several other damaged sites all over London, and investigate what Victor had taken to calling "odd incidents." Those were explosions that may or may not have been last-ditch acts of war at factories and power stations.

"Most are simply German armaments that are taking their own sweet time detonating," Victor declared. "People step on them, or a tractor rolls over one buried in a field."

Meanwhile, their office was privy to reports of the furious fighting taking place on the Continent, including the successes of the Allied troops pushing through the barriers to invade Cologne, establishing a bridge across the Rhine.

Then a blow fell that left Lacy, especially, feeling that for every glimmer of hope that the war's end might be near, yet one more shock would bring her to her knees.

Tess had just turned on the wireless to listen to the BBC evening news when, instead of a broadcaster's voice speaking, funereal music was playing, its somber tones creating a sense that the three room-mates were in a church.

They huddled around the radio as a voice intoned, "Franklin Delano Roosevelt, the thirty-second president of the United States, died suddenly of a cerebral hemorrhage this twelfth day of April while taking a restful break in Warm Springs in the state of Georgia."

Lacy cried out, "Oh *nooo!*"

"That is so sad," Pat said, looking over at Lacy sympathetically.

"He didn't live to see that this war looks to be almost over," murmured Tess.

All Lacy could think of was Granny Farr using her magic to somehow persuade the powers that be who were close to FDR to obtain the necessary paperwork that allowed the Finland Field Hospital team to set sail for Norway. The president of her country, who'd shouldered so many burdens, big and small, was dead, and she could hardly bear it.

How deeply Gran must be mourning his death tonight, she thought, mentally carving more room to grieve for the president in the wake of all the deaths everyone had endured during the war.

Two weeks after Roosevelt's passing, Tess hung up the phone on their boss's desk and declared, "That was Victor. German forces on the Ruhr have surrendered, and—"

Tess had tears in her eyes, her voice choking. Lacy dreaded that she was about to announce something terrible that would cancel the latest good news of the partial surrender.

"*What?*" she demanded.

"Hitler committed suicide."

"Hitler *killed* himself?" Lacy was stunned into momentary silence. Finally, she managed to ask, "When? Where?"

Tess began to smile. "April thirtieth, Victor said. The führer shot

Eva Braun and himself in the head inside his bunker below the Reich Chancellery in Berlin."

"No!" Lacy cried, jumping to her feet and clapping her hands, thinking *Shades of Remington Rowe and his lover*. "There've been rumors before. How do we know that's true? For *certain*?"

Tess declared excitedly, "The War Office just found this out from transcriptions Bletchley intercepted from a Hamburg radio station. An announcer interrupted their normal programming yesterday to announce that Hitler had died that afternoon."

Lacy glanced up at the wall calendar. "Today is May second," she murmured. "The bastard's been dead for two days now."

Tess waved around the phone receiver. "Victor had to go meet with Winston, but he was also just officially informed that German troops have surrendered in Italy!"

Lacy pictured Pem and Richard hearing that news, but then she wondered whether they would even know about those shocking events if they were still under fire somewhere.

Where *was* Pem?

And when will it all really *be over?*

After word of Hitler's suicide was made public, news from all fronts swiftly filtered into their three-person office. Confirmation arrived that the Soviets had stormed into Berlin on April 21, and seven days later, that Mussolini and his mistress had been shot by partisans in a village on the shores of Lake Como while trying to flee to Switzerland.

Tess read from a message delivered by hand to their door, "They were executed by machine gun in front of a villa, then their bodies were taken to Milan and hung upside down."

"Fine with me," Lacy replied, contemplating how different a woman she'd become since the days when she'd begged people to fund a hospital in Finland dedicated to *saving* lives.

Then, on May 7, Victor burst into the office with a bottle of champagne and roses. "It's official!" he shouted, which was a very uncharacteristic change from his usual, self-contained demeanor. "German forces have offered an *unconditional* surrender to the Allies!"

Tess jumped up from her desk and threw her arms around him. Lacy, too, ran over and relieved her boss of the champagne and bouquet, singing with glee, "'Ding, dong, the führer's dead!' We won! We *won!*"

Victor immediately sobered, gave a swift kiss to Tess's forehead, and said, "But, sadly, the war in the Pacific is far from over. And back here, there's just been terrible news from the U.S. Seventh Army when they liberated a death camp called Dachau nine days ago. Reports are it was ghastly beyond anything one could imagine."

Had Noah been sent there? Lacy's heart cried out.

Lacy set Victor's celebratory gifts on his desk and could sense there was

more bad news coming. He took up his wooden pointer and indicated the map.

"The American Army has also come across additional concentration camps in Gusen and Mauthausen." He fell silent a moment and then added, "There were nearly one hundred thousand prisoners locked behind barbed wire at Mauthausen alone."

"Oh, dear God!" Tess cried, pacing in front of Victor's desk. "Who knows *how* many people they interned or murdered during this terrible war!"

"Mauthausen ..." Lacy repeated softly, searching her memory of the years she and Teddy had spent at grim boarding schools in Austria and Germany. "How far is that camp from Vienna?"

Victor raised his pointer once again. "It's in Austria, about two hundred kilometers from Vienna and about the same distance from Munich, Germany. A lot of people on both sides of the border would have known what horrors were going on there."

"How bad was it when the army reached the camp?" Tess asked quietly. Both women knew how the news about the horrific treatment of Jews in those camps streaming out constantly hit Victor like physical blows.

In response to Tess's question, he leaned his pointer against the wall and sank into his desk chair. "The reports are that there were dead bodies piled up everywhere on the grounds and thousands of skeletal survivors behind barbed wire," he said in a low voice, "without food or medicine. From what I've been told, conditions were indescribable."

Lacy turned to Tess and murmured, "Do you suppose Allied hospital trains will be sent to those places to bring back survivors needing emergency care?"

Victor had obviously overheard and gazed at her intently past the perpetual file folders piled high on his desk. "I asked about that, actually." He paused, as if gathering strength to speak further. "From what we're learning daily, the planners at 10 Downing Street tell me that it's likely every one of the prisoners who somehow survived these charnel houses will need medical care. I imagine the worst cases will come out first. And, yes, most probably by trains pulling hospital cars to ports on the Channel, and then hospital ships will bring some of them here."

By mid-June, the MI5 unit in St. James's knew that the Allies had taken over Berlin and divided up Germany, overthrowing the Fascist government.

Near the end of July, their world turned upside down once again. Victor entered the office on the 26th with the latest *Times* rolled under his arm announcing, "Churchill's lost the election. Brits are tired of the war and tired of him."

"The ingrates!" Lacy snapped.

Tess shrugged. "People are sick of rationing. Fed up with the toffs able to buy goods on the black market versus the rest of us." She looked at the 3rd Baron Rothschild and smiled faintly. "You're not in the true toffs category, even though you are very rich."

"And bought food on the black market in Paris," he said dryly, adding, "but look how it helped restore the French economy."

In early August, the entire world was rocked back on its heels with the solemn announcement that the United States had dropped their atomic bomb on Hiroshima.

"That should finally stop the bastards in their tracks," Victor declared the next morning.

Reading a few paragraphs of the newspaper account, Lacy

murmured, "This was no ordinary bomb, Victor. Estimates are perhaps it killed some eighty thousand *civilians*, but the death toll is expected to go much higher. Maybe even double when all the bodies are found."

"Well," he replied harshly, "you Americans lost thousands the morning of Pearl Harbor. Lots of friends of mine died on Burma Road and God knows how many family members in German concentration camp ovens."

Lacy could only wonder what men like Pem and Richard, who'd spent those years trying to save people, thought of the horrifying destruction to human life that one atomic bomb must have caused.

Chapter Forty-One

Not surprisingly, Pat was the first to have word about where the hospital trains that Richard and Pem had collaborated on had been deployed.

"Your guess was right. They were evacuating the sick from the concentration camps," Pat told Lacy, rushing into the front sitting room after waving the letter that had been left in the slot at their building's front door earlier that Saturday morning. She called down the hallway, "Tess! Come in here! I've just gotten my first letter in ages from Richard!"

Lacy heard Tess open her bedroom door and call, "I'm still in my dressing gown. Just give me a moment."

They'd all slept in late that morning after the long, grueling early-summer months when "Top Priority" had appeared on scores of decoded transmissions. Many concerned German security forces whose captured documents had given Victor and his assistants a clearer view of what MI5 had been up against in trying to keep former Nazis and spies out of Great Britain during the last paroxysms of war.

Victor had warned his two deputies, "We can expect to see some of these nasty characters trying to seek safe harbor outside Germany as Nazi higher-ups are constantly being captured and imprisoned, claiming they 'knew nothing.'"

Recalling Victor's words, Lacy waited impatiently for Tess to reach the sitting room to hear Pat read Richard's letter.

"Here I am!" Tess called excitedly, hurrying down the hallway.

They huddled around Pat on the sofa while she read her fiancé's lengthy missive confirming that hospital trains had been bringing back civilians as well as wounded Allied soldiers.

We've had the very unsettling assignment
of transporting men, women, and children
—some of them incarcerated for years—
who were barely alive. Many perished
before we could even move them to receive
the kind of expert medical care they so
desperately needed. I cannot and will
not describe to you what these journeys
out of Germany and Austria have been like,
but just know how I long to see you, my darling—

Pat halted reading as a blush bloomed on her cheeks.

Tess gave her a hug. "Feel free to read the rest in the privacy of your bedroom!" she teased.

Listening to his words, Lacy could only assume Richard would have mentioned it if Pem had asked him to send her a message or, worse, if he had been injured during those tumultuous last days. Most likely, Dr. Charles Pembroke was, indeed, alive and—unlike Richard, who had sent an immediate love letter to Pat—had made no attempt to contact her.

What did you expect? Now it's up to you to figure out why you let this happen.

At Lacy's request several weeks previously, Victor had quietly located what he'd called a "mental health specialist" on Harley Street for her to speak to. Since that first appointment, she reminded herself, she'd been making some progress in trying to understand the negative impact of her "quite complicated childhood," as the doctor had described Lacy's formative years to her. More importantly, he was helping her devise strategies to change her behavior whenever situations threatened to trigger responses like those she'd had in her relationship with Pem.

Struggling to maintain her composure after hearing Richard's letter, Lacy rose from her seat. "I'll just go and make tea," she volunteered.

She was pouring hot water into the Brown Betty when she heard footsteps running down the hallway. Pat burst into the kitchen, waving Richard's missive, with Tess following close behind her.

"Lacy! Lacy! You will not *believe* what's happened."

Lacy cupped her hands around the teapot's plump sides, needing its warmth. *Had* Pem sent her a message through Richard?

"You know that doctor you told us about after the Nazis overran Scandinavia?" Breathless from sprinting down the hall, Pat announced, "Richard and Pem *found* where he'd been taken!"

For a few seconds, Lacy felt stunned. "Noah Fischer?" she exclaimed. "They found *Noah Fischer*?"

Before she could ask anything further, Pat pointed to her letter and exclaimed, "Yes, that's him! 'Doctor Noah Fischer of Cambridge, Massachusetts.' He's *alive*! He was at a camp halfway between Vienna and Munich!"

"Mauthausen? In Austria?" Lacy interjected quickly. The camp Victor had mentioned before, located not very far from where she and Teddy had once been sent to school.

Pat peered at the sentence she'd been reading. "Yes! That's the one. 'Mauthausen.' Pem apparently recognized him right away. Richard says the guy's survival story is incredible, and he'll tell us everything when he gets back here."

Tess turned and gave Lacy a hug. "That's wonderful! By your description, your friend always sounded like such an amazing person."

"He was. *Is*," Lacy corrected herself, still trying to absorb the fact that Noah was *alive*. "In fact," she said, her voice choking, "Pem and I both consider him one of the best people either of us has ever known."

She could only conclude that by some miracle, Noah had endured the very worst humanity could inflict on another human being—and survived.

Pat continued excitedly, "Richard's letter says that he and Dr. Fischer are due to arrive on a boat train from France in about a week," before adding for Lacy's benefit, "and since your friend is a civilian and a Harvard-trained doctor, Richard and ... uh ... Pem pulled some strings and arranged for him to go straightaway to the Westminster Hospital in Chelsea."

Tess looked at Lacy with a grin. "Chelsea? He'll practically be our neighbor!"

Pat immediately looked apologetic, hastening to say, "Richard didn't mention if Pem was going to be on the same evacuation mission, but he said that Pem specifically wanted Richard to convey to you, Lacy, that Noah Fischer was found alive at a prison where they think some ninety *thousand* inmates died during these last few years! Apparently, the poor man is very ill."

After all this time, Pem sent me a message, Lacy thought.

But only through Richard. Still ... that was something.

Two days after the first atomic bomb was detonated, Lacy could hardly believe the news that the United States had dropped a second one on Japan, that time on the city of Nagasaki.

While Tess and Pat rejoiced at the news, Lacy experienced a kind of revulsion she doubted she could ever explain to her friends. Her Leica had chronicled the enormous destruction the German's thousand-pound bombs and vicious V-1 and V-2 rockets had done to Britain. She'd photographed the human remains of arms and legs buried in the ground and snapped shots of air raid wardens sobbing against the remains of buildings minus their roofs or windows. The thought of the blanket devastation that America's two atomic bombs must have inflicted on all those civilians made her sick to her stomach, even though she acknowledged that it would probably bring Japan to its knees—and thereby save Allied lives.

Tess, sitting at the kitchen table, looked up from the newspaper account, announcing, "This second one killed some forty thousand civilians, and probably more will die eventually from radiation sickness, they say. They're predicting Japan will surrender at any moment now."

Pat, drying dishes at the sink, said, "Well, that's one way to end a war."

It is, Lacy thought bleakly. *A brutal way, matching the brutality of our enemies.*

Lacy barely had time to process the momentous news of Japan's expected surrender because later that week, Richard Davies was suddenly back in London. When Pat returned from their overnight reunion at the Ritz, she arrived with the news that Dr. Noah Fischer had been admitted onto the third floor of Westminster Hospital on Fulham Road in London.

Pat came into the foyer as Lacy gazed into the hall mirror, setting her cloche hat on top of her head. "Richard said to tell you he'll meet you at Dr. Fischer's hospital room, 352, on the third floor." Pat paused for a moment and then continued, "He also told me to say that you should prepare yourself for a shock."

"I guess I'm prepared," Lacy replied, meeting her gaze in the mirror. "Victor was sent some of those images that the photojournalist Lee Miller shot at one of the concentration camps when our GIs arrived. The prisoners who were still alive looked like walking skeletons. Poor Noah is probably in similar shape."

"Richard also warns that the nurses won't let you stay long."

"I don't care if they only let me stay five minutes," Lacy said, grabbing her handbag from the hall table. "When those Nazi thugs hauled him off the train in Romania, I thought for sure I'd never see him again." She swiped at the moisture that had gathered in the corners of her eyes. "I just want to convince myself it's really true that Noah Fischer isn't dead."

"Yes, he's in Room 352," confirmed the white-capped woman at the nurses' station on the third floor of Westminster Hospital. "Mr. Davies told Dr. Fischer you were coming, Miss Forbes, but I'm afraid you can only stay about fifteen minutes. He is still very weak and needs rest."

Nodding, Lacy took a tighter hold of the bag of braided Challah bread she'd picked up at a Jewish bakery to smuggle into Noah's room. She turned away from the reception desk and headed down the corridor, looking for Room 352.

The door was open about a foot. Lacy halted and stared at the emaciated figure in the bed whom she hardly recognized. Noah, who had never been a big man, looked almost cadaver-like, his cheekbones protruding, his cheeks hollow, and his eyes mere sockets with dark circles in stark contrast to the chalk-white pillow on which his head was lying.

Lacy knocked softly on the door. Richard Davies was standing next to the bed. He turned and motioned her to enter. Slowly, she walked toward the other side of Noah's bed. She felt like crying at the sight of his gaunt condition but somehow summoned a smile to her lips.

Noah was the one who cried as she approached, reaching his matchstick arms out to embrace her. "Lacy ... I-I can't believe it's you," he said, tears spilling down his cheeks.

"I can't believe it's *you*," she choked out, setting her bag with the bread on his bedside table. "When they took you away from that train ... I was afraid that after all this time, you were—"

"Dead? That they'd killed me? That's exactly what Pem said when he first saw me," Noah replied, patting the side of his bed for her to sit next to him.

Stricken at hearing Noah mention Pem's name, Lacy reached for the young doctor's bony hand, which was even paler than the white bed sheets.

Richard looked down at the patient and prepared to depart. "It's Lacy's turn, so let me leave before they declare visiting hours are over," he said, smiling. "I've been invited to dinner at your place, Lacy, so I expect I'll see you a little later."

For a long moment, she and Noah merely held hands. Finally, he said, "I'm alive today, you know, solely because I was the only doctor who survived the four-day trip in those cattle cars. Once we got to Mauthausen and they realized I had my medical bag still with me, the Germans put me in charge of all the dying prisoners. For nearly five years, I tended as best I could to my fellow inmates in that hellhole. I had little medicine, no supplies, and only prisoners to help me. Doing that work, though, was the only reason the camp commandant didn't send *me* to the ovens."

"I've seen some of the photographs," Lacy disclosed quietly. "I doubt, though, anyone who didn't live through what you did could ever understand the horrors you've seen."

"But I *lived*," he said with surprising fervor and immediately fell into a paroxysm of coughing, his thin chest beneath his hospital gown heaving as he sought to catch his breath. Lacy hastened to put a glass of water from the bedside table to his lips. When he recovered, he told her, "I have to wonder *why* I survived when so many didn't."

"Luck," Lacy declared grimly. "We've survived thus far purely as a matter of fate," she asserted, thinking of her close calls on the munitions train, the bomb defusing assignments, and the fluke that she had happened to be out of London when their Gower Street flat had been bombed during the Blitz.

Lacy asked, "Have you been in touch with your parents yet?"

Noah remained silent, then finally replied, "My father passed away two years ago, but my mother, as you can imagine, said that her prayers had finally been answered." Noah sighed and smiled faintly. "While I've been in this hospital bed, I've had a lot of time to think about why I was spared. I've decided the reason I made it through when so many didn't is that now, I'm supposed to help other Jews who somehow endured the nightmare too. If I can figure out how to get to Palestine, I want to go there to help establish a place for surviving Jews and offer medical care." He gave Lacy a wry look. "If I am any example of the support they'll need, they're going to require a lot of it. My mother wants to meet me there."

"Oh, Noah ... I was hoping I could take you back to Boston when I return."

He looked at her oddly, asking, "Is that your plan now? Going back to Boston?"

Lacy shrugged. "Frankly, I'm not sure about much of anything concerning my future until the war is officially declared over, but I can't lose you so quickly now that I've found you again."

"What about Pem? Are you willing to lose *him*?" he asked with a steady gaze.

Unnerved by his question, Lacy remained silent for a few beats before she asked, "Is he back in London? Have you seen him?"

"He and Richard brought me here."

"He must have known I'd come see you right away." She made a pointed glance around the hospital room. "I don't see him here."

Noah's gaze was unwavering. "Answer my question. What about him?"

"How much do you know about our sorry story?" she asked.

"All I can say is that he looked pretty miserable when I asked him about you just as you do now because I asked you about *him*. What gives with you two?"

"Pem is another thing I'm not sure about. *Yes*, I'm in love with... *love* him," she declared, answering Noah's piercing stare. She shook her head and blurted a confession, "The last time I saw him in Paris, I-I really made a mess of things on my side, but it's too long a story for visiting hours."

Noah grimaced. "I can give you the same short version as I did to him: cut the crap! We've got this one life, you know? Don't waste a second of it. I knew you two were a perfect match that first time we all met for lunch in Cambridge when we decided to work together on the Finland Field Hospital."

"You thought that? Even though he was married?" Lacy marveled. "My Grandmother Farrington said the same thing the day she and I met Pem at some Beacon Hill charity do."

"Well, he's not married *now*." With a glimpse of his former wry humor, Noah said, "I ask you, what other man in this crazy world could handle an American debutante doubling as an MI5 operative for the Brits in the world's bloodiest war?"

"You aren't supposed to know anything about that! MI5, I mean."

"Oh, Richard and Pem told me everything about you and Pat and your other friend, Tess. We spent hours together on that hospital train. To hell with that...Secrets Act? What else were we going to talk about except all the people we know and care about?"

"How would you describe Pem's attitude toward me these days?" she asked quietly.

After all, Lacy assumed Richard had told Pem she'd tried to catch him to apologize for her distorted view of things before his train left Paris for the Eastern Front that night. Yet, Pem had been in London, and he hadn't gotten in touch.

Noah's eyes fluttered shut. Lacy wondered whether he was searching for what answer to give her or merely exhausted from all the company that day.

After a few seconds, he said softly, "He just said you'd called it off;

then he told me that he did as well, but, Lacy ... if *you* were the one who made a mess of things, go fix it!"

Just then, the door opened wide and the nurse Lacy had seen earlier announced firmly, "Time for your medicines and a nap, Dr. Fischer." To his visitor, she said, "You'd best let him rest now."

Lacy nodded, bent down, and kissed Noah's forehead before stumbling out of the room in a daze.

If you're the one who made a mess of it, go fix it!

Chapter Forty-Two

Lacy made her way down the hospital corridor toward the elevator, deeply regretting that she hadn't pressed Noah for a way of contacting Pem. Neither Noah nor Richard had even mentioned where their friend was stationed. She was only too aware that it definitely was her job to "fix it," but for all she knew, Pem could be back in D.C. by now.

Lacy's mind was filled with images of Noah's thin, weak condition as she rode the elevator to the ground floor. Crossing the lobby, she pushed open the hospital's double doors, her thoughts preoccupied with the weighty conversations she'd had with both Noah and the doctor on Harley Street in the last weeks. So many astonishing events had transpired since she and Pem had last seen each other in Paris. They'd lived in very different worlds since they'd parted. Her psychiatrist had warned it would take time to sort it all out.

If we ever could ... or if Pem even wanted to.

Outside the hospital, she was barely conscious that the August air had cooled and held a hint of autumn as golden light filtered through a few tall trees in the nearby park. Reaching the curb of Fulham Road, she absently glanced across the street and froze. On the corner stood a tall, familiar figure in a military uniform, his captain's hat sitting rakishly on hair the color of coal. Flowers in his hand, he appeared to be about to cross the street, heading in her direction. Lacy could only stare.

Go fix it! a voice cried out in her head.

Stepping off the curb, she lifted her arm to wave and shout a greeting. Then she heard the sudden screech of brakes and saw the flash of a lumbering black taxi approaching the hospital entrance mere inches away.

She tried to jump back, pushed her left hand against a fat headlight, and then ... remembered nothing more.

Through a fog of pain, Lacy heard Pat say, "Richard, I came as soon as you'd called the flat!" There was a gasp, followed by, "Dear God! What happened to her?"

"She stepped off a curb and was hit by a taxi that was just pulling up to the hospital."

"Forgot to look left on Fulham Road?"

"Something like that."

Lacy wanted to tell Pat that years ago, she'd had it drilled into her head by her English nanny to look both directions when crossing a street in London, but somehow, she couldn't move her lips. The only sound she was capable of was a low moan because the pain in her ribs and her leg was excruciating.

"Better get the nurse, Pat," Richard said in a hoarse whisper. "Lacy's due for surgery in an hour, but she probably needs more medicine right now for the pain."

The next thing Lacy felt was a sharp stick in her arm, followed by ... blessed unconsciousness.

The tunnel was long and as dark as ink, with a tiny pinprick of light at the end. Lacy kept staring as the light moved closer, and then the railcar she was riding in emerged into a train station, its roof blown away and a huge crater on the other side of the tracks. Human remains were scattered everywhere, so she averted her eyes. Through the window of the carriage car, she spied Pem standing on the platform as if he might be there to greet someone, his uniform crisp, his captain's hat perched at a jaunty angle. Lacy pounded on the glass to try to get his attention, but the car slid slowly by, and all she saw was her mother, June, turning her back and walking away with a man on each arm. The trio was taking cautious steps to avoid the debris left by the bomb, whose fat nose was just peeking above the rim of the hole it had dug upon impact.

Lacy suddenly wondered where Teddy had gotten to and looked frantically around the railcar, but he was nowhere to be seen. She pressed her face against the window, straining to see whether Pem was still standing on the platform as the train seemed to be turning, heading for the crater where the bomb had burrowed into the earth, still treacherous, still capable of killing and maiming.

"Pem!" she screamed. "Pem, here I am!"

She felt the front of the carriage coming off the rails and the entire car tilting to the left, the front of it about to slam into the bomb.

"Pem!" she cried once more before everything went dark.

Lacy opened her eyes. Her back was propped up against a pile of pillows, with more pillows cushioning part of a heavy cast on her left leg. The plaster encasing the extremity stretched from her thigh to her toes, and at her ankle, it was suspended on a pulley system attached to a frame around her bed.

"Well, well, sleeping beauty," said Noah, clad in a bathrobe and sitting in a wheelchair beside the bed. "You certainly are looking a bit more like yourself."

Lacy smiled wanly, then winced. Her ribcage hurt like hell. "I'd say the same thing about you," she replied. "When did they let you out of your hospital bed?"

"Today's the first day, and I insisted they wheel me down to see you."

Noah closed the book he'd been reading, apparently having been sitting there for quite some time waiting for her to wake up. "We have something to celebrate."

"That we're both banged up in the same hospital at the same time?" she retorted.

She'd felt fully awake only since the morning and had fallen back to sleep three or four times since. Her nurse had told her she'd been either asleep or drowsy, first with anesthetic after surgery, then with pain medication, and "away with the fairies" on and off for nearly four days.

Noah informed her, "After your collision with the taxi, they brought you back into the hospital. You were immediately given pain meds until a surgeon could be found to put your left thigh bone back together."

"Oh God, they must have thought I was one of those stupid Americans who—"

"They did," Noah interrupted, teasing her. "And then your two broken ribs on your left side required more serious analgesics until the pain lessened."

"The doctors may say the pain's reduced," Lacy replied, "but trust me, it's still there."

"You were obviously still out of it last night," Noah said, pointing to an unopened bottle of champagne resting on her bedside table next to a vase full of slightly wilted roses. "You didn't drink any of that lovely bubbly."

Puzzled, she asked, "What do you mean? And why the champagne?"

"Last night, at midnight, all hell broke out all over the hospital and someone left this for you. The Japanese just agreed to an unconditional surrender!"

"No!" declared Lacy, wincing again because of her swift intake of breath. "All that happened after I walked in front of a taxi?"

"It did, indeed," Noah said, grinning broadly. "My dear Lacy ... the war will officially be over when our General MacArthur and the Japanese foreign minister sign the agreement—with any luck—on September second."

"What day is it?"

"August thirteenth, I think." Noah glanced at the door to Lacy's hospital room and said with a laugh, "I've asked the nurse to bring in a few glasses so we can have a toast together, but I'm not positive she approved."

"How are *you* feeling?" Lacy asked. "Your color has certainly improved."

"And so have my spirits." He paused for a moment and then added, "*Your* spirits should be soaring. I've never seen so many friends check in on someone, including Lord Rothschild, who has been very concerned about you. The nurse told me that one by one, people would arrive and peek in on you to be sure you were okay, and then some would come down to my room. On one of Richard Davies's visits, he brought the Baron to see me."

"What did you think of Victor?" Lacy asked, curious at learning that the two Jewish men she knew best had finally met.

"I liked him enormously ... and ... well, one conversation led to another, and he's offered to arrange for me to go to work for a group that is being funded by a relative of his to provide medical care in British Palestine."

"Oh, Noah ... that's wonderful! I'll hate that you'll be so far away, but I know it's what you want. You'll be the best thing that ever happened to that corner of the world!"

"I'll be working to help to set up hospitals and clinics throughout the region."

Lacy was about to screw up her courage to ask whether Noah knew what Pem's future plans were, given that the war was nearly over. Before she could get the words out, however, in walked Richard and Pat. Her flatmate's arms were laden with more flowers, while Richard was carrying a large wicker basket "with your favorites from Fortnam and Mason's Food Hall," he declared with a flourish.

"The shelves are still pretty sparse," Pat warned, "but I did get a tin of Scottish smoked salmon and some lovely scones." She gave Lacy a gentle kiss on the forehead. "You look as if you're feeling much better today." She set her vase of flowers next to the roses and the champagne bottle.

"I am a bit improved, but if I cough or laugh, my poor ribs bite me."

Pat pointed to Lacy's cast suspended from the bed frame. "Nurse told me they're soon going to give you a walking cast with half a tennis ball glued to the bottom of your foot so with crutches, you can begin to get out of that bed."

Lacy grimaced, pointing to her ribcage wrapped tightly in bandages. "Oh, that should be fun. I hope they wait on the crutches until my ribs are glued back together." Her eyes were drawn to Pat's hand boasting a lovely engagement ring with a diamond of impressive proportions surrounded by a circlet of smaller gems. "Whoa! What do we have here?"

Pat thrust out her left hand and looked up at Richard, smiling. "It took my darling fiancé a while to pry this out of his grandmother's vault, but isn't it smashing?"

"It's absolutely lovely," Lacy said softly.

Pat then reached into her handbag to display a small sheet of stiff bond paper embossed with beautiful calligraphy inviting the bearer to a wedding ceremony scheduled for the following June.

Richard teased, "We figured we'd allow time to save the necessary rations to serve Veuve Clicquot champagne and Russian caviar to sustain the Cambridge crowd."

"And I hope you and Tess will serve as my bridesmaids," Pat said warmly, pointing once again to the cast on Lacy's leg. "You should be good as new by then, they told us."

Noah nodded and said, "I know this woman. Lacy will be back on two feet sooner than any of her doctors predict."

But Lacy's thoughts were bittersweet.

Noah's leaving. Pat and Richard are officially engaged. No doubt soon, Tess and Victor will be too, their futures mapped out now that the war is finally ending. ...

Lacy's future was one big blank. She struggled to summon a smile. "Of course, I would be honored to be one of your bridesmaids, Pat ... if I'm still in Britain, that is." She looked down at her hands clasped tightly together on top of the bedclothes. "Noah just told me that Japan has surrendered, so now that the war is about to end, who knows what's in store for a gal who crashed into a moving taxicab."

She noticed Pat and Richard exchange glances. Lacy couldn't tell whether they were looks of concern or disappointment that she might not be part of their wedding party.

Just then, Victor and Tess appeared at the door, also bearing gifts. Victor had several books in his arms, and Tess had brought a suitcase that Lacy imagined contained some of her clothes and personal items gathered from their flat.

"So, you *are* awake," Tess exclaimed, striding toward Lacy's bed.

Coming up behind her, Victor noted there was no room on her bedside table and placed the books on the window shelf. "You gave us quite a scare, young lady," he admonished but with a smile. "I knew you were courageous when you rode that munitions train but doing battle with a London taxi ..." he teased. "That's quite something else."

"Now, Victor, stepping off a curb without looking both ways could happen to anyone," Tess protested loyally.

"But mostly to Americans who often forget we British drive on the left," he said with a sideways glance at Lacy. "But the good news, I understand, is that Pem assured us that your leg will soon mend and your ribs—"

"*Pem*?" Lacy repeated with a swift intake of breath. She immediately cradled her hands against her ribcage and waited for the pain to subside.

A deep voice from the corridor outside the room boomed, "Did someone just take my name in vain?"

In the next instant, Charles Pembroke's tall frame filled the hospital room's doorway before he strode inside.

Right on his heels, a starchy, gray-haired nurse bustled in behind him, declaring sternly, "These are visiting hours, not party time. Miss Forbes has only been well enough to sit up and sip tea today." Lips pursed, she announced, "I'm very sorry, but only *one* visitor at a time is allowed."

Victor stepped forward to intervene. "Surely, Nurse, you can let us stay five or ten minutes—"

"Sorry, Lord Rothschild," she said, cutting him off mid-sentence, "we can't allow this." The shocked expression on Victor's face indicated that being countermanded so abruptly was an experience quite new to him. "Hospital rules, I'm afraid," declared the nurse. Her gaze swept the assembled group. "Well, now … as I say, only *one* visitor is allowed. Who is it to be?"

Everyone in the room except Lacy pointed an index finger at Pem and chorused, "Him!"

"All right, then," the nurse responded briskly. "All the rest of you, out you go." To Pem, she declared, "And Dr. Pembroke, I presume you will know when it's time for Miss Forbes to rest." She indicated the chart attached to the foot of the iron bedstead. "The schedule ordered for her pain medication says she's due for an injection in about a half hour. If you're not still here, I'll see she gets it."

"Oh, I'll be here," he assured her as the nurse headed for the door, pushing Noah's wheelchair ahead of her while literally shooing Lord Rothschild and the rest of Lacy's visitors out the door.

"Shall we all repair to the hospital canteen?" Lacy heard Victor inquire.

As the last person disappeared into the corridor, Pem turned to Lacy and said, "I'm the guy who never leaves, remember?"

"Don't be ridiculous. You've left many, many times," she replied, "but the good thing is you always come back." She pointed to her elevated leg encased in its cast. "I take it you were my doctor?"

"Heavens, no!" he said, shaking his head with a smile. "I *consulted* with the talented Dr. Roger Taylor, who, I understand, has operated on you ... *twice*, he told me, and on your brother, Teddy, once. He proudly declared that he's practically become the Forbes family surgeon." He pulled up the chair that had been pushed aside for Noah's wheelchair and drew it closer to the bed. "Richard and I called Victor as soon as you had the accident, and Victor brought Dr. Taylor in to do the hard stuff. I just played bedside nursemaid."

"Did Richard also tell you I tried to find you at the train station in Paris before you deployed to Germany?" Lacy asked and realized she was holding her breath.

"That he did."

"But you never wrote."

She began to silently debate whether she even had the energy for this conversation, then heard the echo of Noah's words: "*Fix it!*"

"No, I didn't write ... for two reasons," Pem replied. "We were loading patients, nonstop, out of the concentration camps, and ... I'd already found writing you wasn't very effective, as I remember."

Lacy knew they were both thinking about Pem's rather flippant first cable, the postcard, and the lost letters, plus the pilot's cable and Pem's long letter about Birmingham that she'd never received.

"And even when you returned to London with Noah, you never got in touch?" she asked, wondering whether she really wanted to hear his answer as to why.

But regardless, and even though her heart was sinking, she knew she had to make amends to Pem whether or not he accepted them. There was a chance he was at her bedside merely because he felt sorry for what had happened to her.

Pem leaned forward in his chair. "No, I hadn't been in touch, but I was going to track you down after Noah gave me holy hell the first day I visited him on the third floor. He said my waiting for you to reach out to me was just plain dumb. That I should just tell you ..." He paused before continuing, "Tell you that life was short and *my* life didn't make a bit of sense without you in it."

A blessed relief washed over her. "Oh, Pem ..." Lacy murmured, "neither did mine make any sense at all." She gingerly extended her arm toward his chair. With the greatest of care, Pem enfolded her hand in his.

"Richard informed me what day you were due to visit Noah for the first time. That afternoon, I'd stopped to buy flowers," he said, pointing to the slightly wilted red roses on her cluttered bedside table. "I was heading back to the hospital to try to catch you here when that taxi—"

"So it *was* you!" Lacy exclaimed. Startled, she had a sudden memory of seeing Pem across the street, about to walk over toward the entrance to the hospital. "You were coming back to find me the day I collided with the taxi?"

He nodded, continuing, "From across the street, I heard the squeal of brakes, and I saw that big black cab run into someone who'd stepped off the curb right in front of the hospital building. I ran over to help and couldn't believe it was *you*."

"And it was *you* who I was waving to when I stupidly stepped off the curb without looking!" Lacy exclaimed and then complained, "Oh, ouch! I shouldn't get so excited. How long does it take ribs to heal?"

"Two or three more weeks," he replied. "That is, if you follow doctor's orders."

"Well, I guess that gives me time to tell you a lot of things I think you should hear."

Chapter Forty-Three

Lacy remained silent for a long moment, focusing her eyes on the starched hospital bedsheets.

Cautiously inhaling a shallow breath, she finally said, "It's just that ... that last day in Paris, I rushed to the train station because I wanted to tell you—" She was suddenly at a loss to marshal an apology for the many things she'd said at the Café Les Deux Magots that she so deeply regretted. Recalling her series of sessions on Harley Steet, she repeated her psychiatrist's final words to herself.

You can do this.

Pem leaned forward and softly stroked the inside of her wrist with his thumb. "Tell me what?"

Lacy swallowed hard. "I wanted to tell you—I *want* to tell you that it's taken me a long time to realize that I have had a very warped sense about a lot of things."

"Like what?"

"Like ... that I've held on to the false belief that I can never count on anyone when things go awry." She sought his eyes, adding, "And ... and this belief has crippled me in so many ways, I think. Even in the face of evidence to the contrary, as with you, Pem. I've had a terrible lack of faith in people who *do* deserve my trust."

Pem remained silent, listening intently.

Lacy heaved a small sigh. "It's taken a war and all the pain of what we've both gone through to make me see how lucky I was to find myself in love with a guy like you—even if you were married," she added with a wry smile. "A guy who seemed to like me the way I am ... who cared about the things I care about. Who was sexy and kind and thoughtful ... but when things got dicey in my world, as you may have noticed ... I tended to go AWOL."

"Yup, I noticed."

She sought his gaze, adding, "Like when I thought you didn't care enough to write me after Birmingham or take the legal steps to ... well ... you know ..."

"Get a divorce?" he prompted.

"Well ... yes. When it seemed to drag on and on, my almost automatic reaction was to immediately hide in a dark place and declare it hopeless as a means, I guess, of putting an end to the pain of abandonment I was feeling."

Pem didn't take issue with what she'd said, but his next words bore witness to how long and hard he'd been thinking about the reasons their meeting at the Paris café had gone so wrong.

"Look, Lacy," he said softly, "I can see now how you could feel it *was* hopeless for us at times. I was, in fact, married to someone else and slow to admit my part of why my marriage didn't work ... and slow to try to rectify things, both for you and for Eleanor." He gave a small laugh. "Trust me, getting a divorce during a war is no easy matter, but I managed to do it with no small help from Eleanor." He hesitated. "The pile of communication screw-ups didn't help, did they? Cables not delivered and letters that went astray or were sunk by a U-boat or were held back by a military censor or whatever the hell happened to them. You lost contact with me at the worst possible moment when you were pregnant. None of that was anybody's fault but the damn Germans." He leaned closer. "It was awful that you had to face all that alone while I was bound for months by the Secrets Act not to let anyone but a very few people know where I was—or what I was doing."

"But, as always," Lacy insisted, "I could only imagine the worst instead of realizing there could be *many* other reasons I hadn't heard from you. I've come to understand that was a damaging holdover from how Teddy and I were treated growing up." She stared at their joined hands. "But I *am* grown up now, right?" she asked with a rueful smile. "And I've been trying to change that unhealthy thinking." She looked Pem directly in the eye. "I love you. I know I can trust you. And I've longed to be the woman in your life for a very long time now."

Pem's eyes burned into her. "Brava, Lacy."

"But there's still something else."

"And that is?"

Pem's voice had regained the guarded tone she remembered from their tense discussion at the café in Paris.

Lacy swallowed hard. "And that is ..." she ventured, "what about having children, Pem? Are you sure you wouldn't one day—even if you kept it to yourself—regret or even resent the fact I may not be able to have any? And *why* that has come about?"

His answer was immediate. "No. I would not regret or ever resent it," he declared firmly. "Of course I'd love for us to have a family one day, but having you in my life is what I want the most. But *only* if you feel the same way. We're both in it—or we're not."

Lacy nodded solemnly. "I feel the same way about having you in my life, with or without children of our own."

"From what I've seen in this war, there will be many small children abandoned and alone. How do you feel about that?"

"I would want to marry you first," she teased and then grew serious. "My deepest wish is to bear a child with you ... but I say we consider adoption an option too."

Pem leaned over, gently raised the palm of her hand, and kissed it. "Agreed on all subjects." Meeting her glance, he said, "And I promise you, you'll never be left alone at the train station or anywhere else."

Lacy felt tears gathering in the corners of her eyes as she recalled the terrible recurring nightmare of seeing Pem through the railcar window.

"You're right, you know," she confessed. "I think I used the 'it's hopeless' excuse not so much because you were married but because I lacked the courage to accept your love as real or lasting. I suppose my insane childhood conditioned me to assume, as you suggested at the café, that it was best to bail out first before anyone else could or, in one way or another, leave me metaphorically at a train station. *You* were the one who had faith that maybe ... just maybe ... I'd eventually come to my senses."

"Oh, from the day of your run-in with that taxi when you were out of your head for a while, I was completely *convinced* you'd come to your senses."

"Huh?" Lacy said, furrowing her brow in confusion. "That logic sounds crazy."

"You were unconscious by the time I reached the curb, and you didn't even know I was there that day. Then you went into surgery for your broken leg, and the painkillers kept you totally loopy for a long time because your broken ribs hurt so much." He pointed to his chair. "When I sat right here beside your bed for hours and hours, you kept calling for me by name. I told you over and over that I was right here, but you still kept crying out as if you saw me but couldn't get to me."

Lacy shuddered slightly, explaining, "I kept dreaming I was on a train moving slowly through a station somewhere in Europe and you were standing on the platform. I kept pounding the window for you to notice me, but you couldn't hear, and the train moved past, and I was left all by myself in the railcar, having no idea where it was going." Her voice choked. "It was awful."

"Oh, darling Lacy, believe me, I *heard* you, and I knew then that you love me as much as I love you." He sought her gaze. "But can you trust it? Truly *believe* what we have together is real and lasting?"

Lacy raised Pem's hand to her lips and kissed it as he had hers. "I'll grant you, it took a while—and a little help from a friend on Harley Street," she replied, a faintly mischievous glint in her eye, "but, yes, I do trust it. Absolutely."

"Then marry me," he declared.

"Yes, if you'll marry *me*, despite my crazy, mixed-up family."

Just then, the nurse poked her head into the room and scolded, "You're still here, Dr. Pembroke?" She bustled into the room. "Time for Miss Forbes's injection. Do you wish to give it, or shall I?"

"Oh, definitely *you* do it, Nurse." He rose, bent over the bed, and kissed Lacy gently on the lips. "I have a cable to send to Cecilia Farrington of Boston, Massachusetts, to let her know her favorite granddaughter is officially engaged," he declared with a flourish.

Lacy and her grandmother had exchanged a few letters since the war in Europe ended and prior to her being hit by a London cab.

"Knowing Granny Farr," Lacy said, closing her eyes to avoid seeing the nurse approach with a syringe in hand, "she won't be surprised at all."

Her eyes suddenly opened widely before the nurse could poke her arm or Pem reach the door. "Can we spend our honeymoon at the Palazzetto da Schio in Venice?"

Pem turned and took a step toward the bed. "I've already written your friend, the Contessa, and inquired if our room with the four-poster bed overlooking the Grand Canal might be available."

"Pretty confident son of a gun, aren't you?" Lacy shot back.

"Yup. And after I send the cable to Granny Farr, I'm heading for Garrard and Company to see what rings they have in stock."

"Garrard, the *crown jewelers*?" she marveled. "The debs will definitely approve." Her eyes starting to droop, she asked, "How long will you be gone?"

Her almost-fiancé grinned at her from across the room and wagged a finger at her. "Repeat after me: 'Pem's the guy who always comes back.'"

Lacy closed her eyes, murmuring, "Always comes back ..." Her eyes suddenly popped open again. "For the duration, right?"

As if to his commanding officer, Pem saluted.

"Yes, *ma'am*! For the duration."

Epilogue

The day after Lacy's cast was removed, she and Pem were married at the Chelsea Registry Office and left immediately for their honeymoon in Italy, where they luxuriated in the silk-draped four-poster at the Palazzetto da Schio overlooking the Grand Canal. Upon their return to London, much to the shock of the newlyweds, Lacy soon began to experience every sign that she was pregnant.

One morning as spring 1946 was about to turn into summer, she said to Pem, "I'm mildly embarrassed to find myself a bridesmaid in *two* weddings scheduled a month apart. Maybe Tess and Pat are too nice to suggest that 'Lacy the Blimp' should retire from their nuptials. What should I do?"

Pem looked at her calmly. "Ask them."

The next day, when all three former flatmates met for lunch at the Savoy Grill, Lacy moaned, "By June fifteenth, Tess, I'll look like one of those big, fat dirigibles over London that used to ward off German war planes. I'm saying this to both of you as your dearest friend," she said earnestly, "please believe me that I'll completely understand if you'd rather I not—"

"Nonsense!" Tess cut her off. "You and Pem ran off to the registry and got married with only Pat, Richard, Victor, and me as witnesses." She pointed to Pat across the starched linen tablecloth. "The two of us definitely want you to have to endure the agony of all the gown fittings and wedding madness our mothers insist we go through, right, Pat?"

"Absolutely!" their friend replied. "And besides, having a pregnant attendant at our respective weddings will be good luck. Thanks to the blasted war, we're all such ancient brides, I'm afraid we'll *need* a bit of luck to start having babies ourselves." She smiled across the table at Lacy. "You give both of us hope."

Lacy marveled that, except for the Russians laying claim to many of the countries that the Allies had liberated, peace had been in place for half a year by then. She glanced down at her blooming midsection and felt a familiar rush of tenderness toward the life inside whose feathery movements brushed against her battered uterus. Each morning, she woke up haunted by the fear that something might still go wrong. Then she forced herself to remember the words of her doctor who'd done the surgery when she'd been fighting sepsis.

"I told you that you *might* encounter difficulty conceiving, not that it would be impossible," Dr. Taylor had said with a rather self-satisfied expression while confirming she was, indeed, pregnant so soon after her honeymoon. "One can now assume that I stitched you up quite handily, with no subsequent adhesions."

Lacy gazed around the luncheon table at her two best friends just as Richard and Pem appeared at the restaurant's entrance. Tess spotted them first and gave a wave, declaring, "Victor, sadly, can't join us to finalize plans for Richard's groomsmen's dinner the night before their wedding."

The 3rd Baron Rothschild had recently rejoined the Department of Zoology at Cambridge University. Tess had disclosed that the engaged couple had finally reclaimed Merton Hall from Victor's former wife, Barbara. It was an ancient building that some believed had been the birthplace of the university. Victor, as Tess had described it with a laugh, "has reconnected with his eccentric passion studying and dissecting frogs' eggs, sperm, and their interactions."

Lacy laughed too. "He probably understands better than I do how in the world I managed to get pregnant so quickly!"

Pat raised a glass. "Good heavens, Lacy ... *all* of us are perfectly clear on how you got pregnant."

Lacy felt her cheeks burning by the time the two men reached their table and sat down, their waiter promptly pouring them coffee.

Pem bent toward his wife, gave a gentle pat to her midsection, and placed a kiss against her cheek.

Richard spoke up. "Before we tackle the weighty subject of my groom's dinner this Friday, I'd like to announce that Pem here has just been invited by my architectural firm to join me in designing the renovation of the heavily damaged Royal Hospital Soldiers' Home in Chelsea!"

Pat clapped her hands. "How wonderful! Congratulations, Pem!"

"That's the place where an entire wing was demolished by a V-2 bomb right before the war ended," Lacy said with a shudder, recalling her own association with the deadly "last-ditch" weapons the Germans had rained down on London near the war's end. "Victor sent me there to photograph the damage, and it was truly horrific!"

Pem nodded. "Richard was kind enough to persuade his colleagues that they need a doctor on the team to help them plan the best way to rebuild it so it's state-of-the-art."

"A doctor *and* an architect," Lacy said proudly and then threw her arms around her husband of seven months. Turning toward Pem's benefactor, she said, "Honestly, Richard, you've absolutely saved us from having to have this baby in Boston and miss Tess and Victor's wedding in June."

Pem spoke up, "We've wanted him—or her—to be born in Britain and thus have dual citizenship because without one of us employed here, we've been told we'd have to leave soon."

Tess scoffed with a loyalty Lacy found touching, "Oh, Victor would *never* have let Immigration order either of you out of the country."

Lacy and Pem had already received a great deal of similar Rothschild largesse, having become residents of Ranger's Cottage, located on a small section of a former estate Victor had sold while retaining the three-bedroom abode for use by family and friends.

Tess looked from Pem to Richard, exhorting them earnestly, "Your friend Victor is going to need all the support he can muster from you two men during the week of *his* wedding."

Victor had gone through a very acrimonious divorce soon after the end of the war. Ultimately, he'd been granted a final decree in an undefended petition on the grounds of Barbara Rothschild's adultery.

Lacy was pleased for Tess's sake that her former boss was free to marry her friend, but privately, she'd protested to Pem, "What about *Victor's* long-term, extramarital relationship during our MI5 days? Everybody knew about it, and Barbara's the one blamed, although everybody *also* says she cheated first."

"Surely, by now," Pem replied wryly, "you can't be surprised the British court ruled in *Lord* Rothschild's favor." He paused for a moment. "The same ruling came down for me in Boston."

Lacy shot him a disgusted look, but before she could remark further, he said with mock solemnity, "The old boys' network!"

The old boys' network was in full top-hat-morning-coat-and-cravat splendor at both Pat's and Tess's weddings. Richard, Lacy had learned, had also been a member of the Apostles secret society while a student at Cambridge. Without the slightest sense of surprise, she took in the sight of Guy Burgess, Tony Blunt, Kim Philby, and their crowd raising their champagne glasses on high at both receptions.

Here Guy Burgess is an honored veteran of MI5 and MI6, with no questions asked.

Jolting Lacy back to the present, Pem took her in his arms to join Tess and Victor's celebrants on the dance floor. They'd executed only a few steps to the music when a sharp pain suddenly stabbed Lacy in the abdomen. She clung to Pem to keep from doubling over. Then, to her dismay, she felt a rush of water flowing down her silk-clad legs, soaking her satin slippers.

"Oh no!" she whispered into his ear. "My water broke! It's too soon!" she cried.

"Only two weeks early," Pem assured her, although Lacy could read the concern in his expression. "Let's just quietly leave the reception and get you to the hospital."

Lacy struggled to swim to full consciousness, the pristine white walls of her room at Westminster's General Lying-In Hospital flowing in and out of focus as she pried open her eyes. It felt as if her midsection were on fire, trussed in bandages. Everything ached.

Her fingers plucked at the smooth sheets pulled up under her arms, her mind clouded with a horrible dream. Once again, she'd been inside a wood-paneled railcar with Pem standing outside on the platform, oblivious to her pounding on the window glass to try to get his attention. Struggling against the memory, her bleary eyes swept the hospital room. Why was she there? Where *was* Pem?

She heard the scrape of a chair and turned her head, relief flooding her at the sight of her husband rising to his full height.

"Well, there you are!" he said, looking relieved as he took a step toward the edge of the bed. "Welcome back, darling, but this business of being out like a light is getting to be a rather concerning habit of yours."

Her brain fog began to clear, and she suddenly remembered. "The baby!" she cried. "Did I lose it?"

Pem clasped her hands, a smile spreading across his unshaven but dear, dazzlingly handsome face. "He arrived safely in your surgeon's hands about four hours ago."

"*He?*"

"Yes, all seven pounds and fourteen ounces of him," Pem assured her. "You're not disappointed the baby isn't a girl, are you?"

"I just wanted whatever it was to be ... to be *alive*! I'll save my long white gloves for our next one."

Lacy detected a flash of disquiet on Pem's face. "You had him by cesarean section," he disclosed. "Dr. Taylor insisted on being called in to assist."

"No wonder my belly's on fire," she breathed. "But the baby's all right?"

"Ten fingers and ten toes," Pem reported, the joy on his face reassuring her far more than his words. "I'm sorry to report, though, that what hair he's got is bordering on black, like mine, but he has a perfect nose, just like yours."

Lacy gave a squeeze to Pem's hands. "We've made a child together, can you *believe*? A second chance. And by some miracle, he's all right!"

Lacy tried not to think of the life lost in the basement operating room in Islington. Pem had forgiven her. It was time she forgave herself.

Her husband said, "They'll bring him to you now that you're awake."

"How long have I been out since the delivery?" she asked.

"Nearly five hours, but it seemed like forever," he said, grimacing. "But at least it gave me time to cable Granny Farr. I asked her to notify everyone else."

"Not that my mother, June, will take much notice," Lacy replied, hearing the edge to her voice, "other than to be annoyed that there's one more heir making it harder for her to attempt another raid on the Forbes and Farrington family trusts."

Lacy saw that her bitter words had shocked Pem.

"You don't think she'll be affected by the fact she has her first grandchild?"

Lacy sighed, remembering how her Harley Street doctor had warned her about wishing for a better past. The antidote, he'd advised, was being grateful for the life she had in the present.

"My mother wasn't affected by giving birth to her own children," Lacy disclosed, "other than as a means, she *thought*, to lock in the Forbes and Farrington money. She never seemed to understand that Boston family trust lawyers are even tougher than she is."

Lacy and Pem had already discussed putting the majority of the money eventually due from her trust funds into a separate trust for any children they might have plus using another large amount to fund resettlement efforts for war refugees.

Pem settled back into his chair drawn up beside the bed. Remaining silent for a long moment, he finally said, "Since your mother now lives in D.C., I've been thinking we might consider returning to Boston at some point once the Royal Hospital project winds down ... that is, if you agree."

Lacy could sense he was watching carefully for her reaction. She replied, equally cautiously, "Well, it would be lovely to see Granny Farr and Teddy more often. If we stick to Boston and New York, we'll likely avoid World War Three."

Hearing her answer, Pem said, "Like Granny Farr, my parents are getting older. I feel I owe them to be near, at least for a while. And even if I join an architecture firm or open one of my own, Harvard has already offered me a job teaching hospital design in the architecture department, so we'd make a decent living."

"Your father won't start pestering you to return to medicine?" she asked.

"Oh, I think by now, he's finally decided that my 'combination career,' as he's taken to calling it to his friends, makes him proud. He's shown photos of the hospital trains to all his friends."

"But what about all our friends *here*? And what about all the work that needs to be done rebuilding this country?" Lacy pressed, mildly unsettled by the exploration of where they might go next.

Yet, her two former flatmates were married and starting their own families by then too.

The six of us will always have great times together, Lacy thought fondly, *but our closeness will probably never be quite the same.*

Friendships forged under fire like theirs, though, would be hard to duplicate in Boston.

"We'll always maintain our friends here," Pem assured her. "I expect we'll spend time on both continents. We can come back to Britain whenever Richard wants me for one of his projects, but ..." He regarded her closely. "Will being back in the States put you under a lot of pressure to keep June at arm's length?"

Lacy sought Pem's glance, explaining, "I don't wish any harm to come to my mother, but I can't change the way I feel toward her. Since I accept *she's* unlikely to change the harmful way she behaves toward me, Teddy, and many others, my plan is just to keep a safe distance, and I may need your help with that."

"You've got it," he said promptly.

She smiled up at him from her hospital bed and admitted, "I figured you might eventually want to return to America, so ... actually ... I've written to my old boss at the *Boston Globe*—just as a feeler. I gave the managing editor a brief summary of what I did as a quasi-photojournalist for 'the war effort,' as I put it, and hoped for the best."

Pem looked first surprised and then pleased. "And? Did you get a response?"

Lacy smiled. "Yes—and a prompt one, much to my shock. My cranky editor, Eddie Shaw, said he liked the photos I'd sent him and he'd hire me to do freelance pieces in Boston *or* London." She laughed. "He also proposed I write his editorials for him, which he hates to do."

"That's great news!" Pem enthused.

Lacy paused for a moment and then said emphatically, "And I also want to write that book I spoke about years ago and tell the story of our escape from the Nazis invading Scandinavia, especially now it has a happy ending with Noah's survival."

"You absolutely must write it, darling," was Pem's wholehearted endorsement. "You hadn't signed the MI5 Secrets Act yet, so you can tell the entire, grisly tale of those six months prior."

"I'm so glad you feel that way since you'll be in it."

"As long as you let me review whatever you say about me," he laughed.

"We'll see ... but you'll be reassured to know that I never betray my sources."

She realized with a start that she wanted to interview all the team members who had gone with them as part of the Finland Field Hospital. There were some wonderful doctors and nurses she'd known besides Noah, and it could be fascinating to track them down and hear their stories about what they'd done after fleeing the Nazi takeover in Europe. She'd even try to locate Jayne Girard, the Red Cross nurse with whom she'd never spoken after that day in Islington.

Perhaps Pem and I will discover some good friends on both sides of the Atlantic, she mused.

Just then, the door to the room opened and she heard wheels rolling along the floor.

"There's someone anxious to see you," a cheery orderly from the hospital nursery declared, swiftly placing a bassinet next to Lacy's bed. "May I present Master Pembroke?"

Pem circled around Lacy's bed as the nurse lifted up the baby, who was tightly swaddled in a sapphire-blue blanket. "Let *me* hand him to her," requested Pem.

"Are you sure?" the orderly asked, clearly doubtful a man could do it properly.

"Quite sure," Pem said. "My wife's midsection is very sore, and this way, she can see him and touch his face, and we'll test if it hurts her to hold him."

"I want to nurse him if I can," Lacy declared.

Pem said to the medical attendant, "Would you ask the lactation specialist to come back in ten minutes, please, so she can help Mrs. Pembroke with feeding?"

"Yes, sir," she promptly replied, obviously accustomed to following doctor's directives.

The door closed behind the woman, and Lacy laughed. "You may be an architect, but clearly, you've learned how to boss the hospital staff around."

Grinning without comment, Pem leaned close to the bed to give Lacy her first look at their baby. His eyes were closed and his face cherubic, with long black lashes and a pink bow mouth.

"He's perfect!" she said, awed. "No pointy head or bruises from labor."

"He didn't travel down the birth canal, lucky little fellow." Pem cast Lacy a look of sympathy. "Not so lucky for you that he was coming feet first, which is why they decided to take him by cesarean."

"I don't care," Lacy replied, gently running the back of her finger along the baby's cheek. "He got here safe and sound, so it's all worth it."

Pem ever-so-gently lay the infant on her chest with his little head tucked under her chin. "You were so superstitious about choosing names before he was born," he said, "but we have to fill in the birth certificate later today. Have any thoughts?"

Lacy wondered whether Pem felt pressured to carry on the Pembroke tradition of naming the first boy "Charles," which would saddle the tiny creature with a very long moniker, given he'd be the fourth Charles Pembroke in a row.

Lacy stared down at her son's head, acutely aware that the tiny human pressed against her chest was a miracle. So was the fact that the heroic Dr. Fischer was on his way to British Palestine, courtesy of Victor Rothschild's contacts in high places.

Lacy asked softly, "Pem ... how would you feel if we called him 'Noah'?"

Pem flashed her a smile that lit up eyes as blue as the blanket keeping their son warm and cozy.

"Oh, thank God you didn't want to make him a quattro!" he laughed. "My parents are bound to blame you for not naming him 'Charles Marchand Pembroke the Fourth,' but to me, 'Noah Pembroke' sounds exactly right."

Lacy grew silent for a moment. "Then you owe me one," she said slyly, "because I think we need to add the Farrington name so Granny Farr won't blame *you*."

To the delight of both parents, the name duly engraved on the hours-old British-American dual citizen birth certificate read "Noah Farrington Pembroke"—as would his many passports to come.

AUTHOR'S NOTE

As with my three previous American Spy Sisters novels, *The Spy Wore Long White Gloves* is a work of *fiction*. And like the others, it was inspired by a number of real-life American women who worked for Britain's intelligence agencies even before the United States joined the Allies in WWII.

In a most curious and circuitous way, Book 4 is about a Boston debutante who finds herself working for MI5's antisabotage unit on the home front in Great Britain during the war years 1939–1945. This novel was informed, in part, by the life of a woman whom my late father-in-law, Howard Cook, spoke of with stars in his eyes whenever he said her name: "Polly Peabody ... of the Boston Peabodys."

Howard met Polly and her brother, Billy, when they were fourteen years old at a summer camp in the French Alps run by an American schoolteacher for wealthy, mostly American children of expats living in Europe in the 1920s and '30s. Somehow, a picture of Polly and Howard at about age fourteen standing together inside a glacier in Chamonix ended up in our family collection, but I never knew much more than that about Polly, other than *her* branch of a Boston Brahmin family had been considered "wildly bohemian" by Howard's straitlaced parents. With a house in Normandy full of artists and writers, Polly's mother and stepfather were notorious for placing their children, buck naked, on the backs of local donkeys and wagering on their races during raucous house parties, encouraging the beasts and children to compete on a homemade track. Howard once wistfully related to me that "Polly was very beautiful and highly intelligent." I've always kidded my husband that his dad's nostalgia whenever he spoke of her most likely reflected a tale of the one who got away.

Years later, during research for this series of novels, I was startled to see the name "Polly Peabody" in a superb nonfiction work, *Americans in Paris: Life and Death Under Nazi Occupation* by Charles Glass, published by Penguin in 2010. How many Polly Peabodys from Boston could there have been in France during the World War II period, I wondered. Thanks to Google, I soon located a limited edition book by Polly titled *Occupied Territory*, which was published in London just prior to the Pearl Harbor attack that brought the United States into WWII. In it is her firsthand account of her post-debutante life raising money in 1938 America for a field hospital deployed to Scandinavia. The bulk of the memoir chronicles her subsequent dangerous and bizarre journey, first by plane from Sweden to Moscow and then by train, auto, boat, and plane again, as she zigzagged across Europe to London, barely escaping the invading German Army in the process of conquering the entire Continent.

At the end of Polly's memoir is a plea to American isolationists in early 1941: "I would answer [them] that I have seen Germans goose-stepping down the Champs Elysées and I know the meaning of a Europe lined with grey uniforms ... I know that their aim is not only London but New York as well [and] add my appeal to Americans to give their all that the menace which threatens them as much as it does Europe, *that a world ruled by force alone* [italics added], may be lifted from the hearts of men."

Digging a little more, I found a magazine article in which Polly's granddaughter drops a hint about her grandmother's life once she stepped off that final "escape train" in London a year before America joined the Allies: "We all think Granny [later became] a spy."

That was it. That's all I knew ... until I began to delve even deeper.

Chasing down leads these last two years revealed more of Polly's background but little else about her plausible life as a French- and German-speaking intelligence operative for Britain. Brazenly, I've invented her stand-in, Lacy Farrington Forbes, to show what she *might* have done, based on extensive research and intelligent supposition. But just so you know, Dr. Charles Pembroke III, who shares the harrowing fictional journey with Lacy, is a completely fictitious (and, to me, delicious) character. Sadly, real-life Polly subsequently had several failed marriages in the wake of her traumatic childhood and wartime experiences.

MI5's wartime files still have areas that remain off-limits. My father-in-law and his contemporaries have long since passed away, and even the biographer of Polly's rather extraordinary parents—her mother, Caresse, and stepfather, Harry Crosby—died a few years ago. What I *have* learned, however, was enough to conjure an almost-true tale of what it was like to be a female secret agent on the English home front battling in-country sabotage in Great Britain's darkest hour during the Blitz and while V-bombs showered down over the country.

I was also intrigued to discover that a number of debutantes, including some Americans, were highly valued recruits who performed secret intelligence work for both British and American agencies. This was often due to their finishing school proficiency in spoken and written French and German following their education in the "womanly arts of gracious living" on the Continent.

So, Polly Peabody, a Boston deb, was my jumping-off point and inspiration. Equally important was my asking the question, "What did British and American women Allies do in WWII?"—a query that led me to books and documents chronicling the rigors endured by female civilians and military volunteers in wartime Britain. I also immersed myself in records concerning the strength of the Nazi movement in England and America, the role of the IRA and involvement of Hitler in the S Plan that targeted Great Britain early on, and the not-so-subtle antisemitism in Britain at that time, to say nothing of Victor Rothschild's amazing dexterity (and luck) when it came to defusing the deadly incendiary devices the Germans lobbed into British territory.

Speaking of Lord Rothschild, his small MI5 unit did, indeed, include two female deputies: Tess Mayor, portrayed fictionally in my book, and Theresa May. In my novel, Lacy Forbes stands in for Miss May, but Lacy's fictional life and adventures are clearly her own.

For readers interested in learning more facts about the amazing historical couple Victor and Tess, I've created a selected bibliography that provides a list of nonfiction works relating to their lives as well as books about debutantes of the WWII era who appear in these pages.

Other volumes on the list are nonfiction accounts of the lives of Kathleen "Kick" Kennedy; the Mitford sisters; "the most beautiful spy," Vera Eriksen; and "the Two *B*s," Guy Burgess and Anthony Blunt, along with a number of nonfiction tomes detailing the Cambridge Five spies and the activities of MI5 and MI6 during WWII. (Lacy's security concerns about Burgess and Philby are well founded: Guy Burgess fled to Moscow in 1951, and Kim Philby followed in 1963.)

In 2024, brand new evidence of Anthony Blunt's treachery came to light. In addition to being a member of MI5, he became Keeper of the Queen's Pictures for years after the war. Eventually, Blunt was not only revealed to have been a wartime Russian spy as one of the Cambridge Five, but also suspected of forwarding detailed information about an operation called "Market Garden." Launched by the Allies in September of 1944, this mission involved airborne and ground forces aimed at creating an invasion route into northern Germany designed to shorten World War II. Because the Germans had allegedly learned of the operation through Blunt's disclosures, the Allies' plan to capture key bridges in the Netherlands was seriously compromised, resulting in the deaths and injury of some 17,000 Allied soldiers.

We are left wondering exactly *who* among the "Old Boys Network" in the upper ranks of MI5 and MI6 in those days *knew* about the traitorous activities of Blunt and the Cambridge crowd. In my novel, I wrote about this aspect of British intelligence agency history from the point of view of a contemporary intelligence operative, Lacy Forbes. I placed her as a fictional observer working in the midst of these men who was privy only to limited knowledge of what they might have been up to.

For years after the war, Lord Rothschild was whispered to have been the "fifth man" in the Cambridge Five. That dishonor was later positively bestowed upon Cambridge classmate John Cairncross. Prime Minister Margaret Thatcher spoke in defense of Lord Rothschild's loyalty to Britain in Parliament, firmly discounting the rumors with the facts, but the insinuations against "that Jew" were never quite quashed. One wonders, in our current world of social media, what other false conspiracies could have been hatched.

Based on my extensive research, I am convinced Victor Rothschild was, in fact, one of the great heroes who remained true to Britain despite enduring both subtle and overt antisemitism, even among his aristocratic peers. His lover and later second wife, Tess Mayor, who was not Jewish, was his loyal supporter and brave deputy. During the war, she worked by his side in both England and France whenever "new devices" turned up—ones so problematic that even the veteran bomb squads turned them over to the team of Rothschild and Mayor to defuse.

It might be interesting for readers to note that Kathleen "Kick" Kennedy's presentation before King George VI and Queen Consort Elizabeth took place largely as depicted in my novel. In 1938, Ambassador Joseph Kennedy's wife, Rose, sponsored another American that deb season: Miss Rosmond Harris Seidel, daughter of the VP of the International Association of the Petroleum Industry. Since *The Spy Wore Long White Gloves* is, in fact, fiction, I felt perfectly free to exchange the fair Rosmond for my heroine, Lacy, who—as I've said—is a composite character based on the lives of several highly privileged young Americans who, like Polly Peabody, were brought up primarily in Europe in the 1920s and '30s.

The character of Dr. Charles Pembroke III, Pem, is based on research I sought on the U.S. Army Medical Corps, as well as the true-to-life efforts of Harvard University to create the Harvard Field Hospital in Salisbury, England, before and when America joined the Allies. As a graduate of Harvard College, I am well aware of the Harvard Graduate School of Design, the Harvard Medical School, and the many bold initiatives that have been launched by talented alumni/ae who pursued joint studies in related fields—as did Pem when he saw a way to combine his love of architecture and design with his training as a medical doctor. In seeking information about battlefield injuries during WWII, I explored the fascinating world of hospital/ambulance trains and how they were put to use as the casualties of war began to amass.

As for my depiction of Boston's first families and my fictional Farrington-Forbes tribe, I owe my sense of what that era was like primarily to my longstanding friendship with fellow Harvard graduate Ellie Cabot, a reluctant debutante who invited her eighteen-year-old pal to her coming out ball at the Myopia Hunt Club in Beverly Farms, Massachusetts, my freshman year of college. Ellie provided me with not only a beautiful blue satin ballgown but also my first pair of long white kid gloves. However, any errors in my depiction of this milieu are clearly my own.

The story of Lacy's stepfather killing himself and his lover in the spring of 1938 after Lacy's debut at court is based on the true scandal of Polly Peabody's mother and stepfather, Caresse and her second husband, Harry, nephew of the powerful banking tycoon J. P. Morgan. A self-published poet, Harry Crosby shot himself and his lover, Josephine Bigelow, on December 10, 1929. He was found dead in a bed with a .25 caliber bullet in his right temple, and she lay beside him with a matching wound in her left temple. I used this tragic incident as the reason Lacy was suddenly called back to New York and then fled to the protection of her grandmother, Cecilia Holmes Farrington, a charming, well-connected Boston doyenne who would do anything to help "the one grandchild who'd amounted to anything."

For travelers to Venice, please be aware that there really is a Palazzetto da Schio in the Dorsoduro section (not facing the Grand Canal, however), which welcomed me when I was researching another one of my novels. Elizabetta and Anna da Schio (the Anna portrayed fictionally in *this* novel) were wonderful hosts, and my stay there was a highlight of several trips I've made to Venice.

And here's a final note in the spirit of correcting the record. True-life characters Pat Rawdon-Smith (who is depicted fictionally but *was* Tess Mayor's flatmate on Gower and Bentinck Streets during WWII) and Richard Llewelyn Davies were married in 1943, *not* 1946 as in the novel ... but this storyteller claims the right to change their wedding date for dramatic purposes! However, one of those quirks that can make a historical novelist wake up perspiring in the middle of the night is the fact that Richard did not hyphenate his names, "Llewelyn Davies," until *after* the war when he became Baron Richard Llewelyn-Davies. Such are the pitfalls American writers can fall into. There are undoubtedly others, but I have many friends and experts to thank in my author's acknowledgments who've at least tried to steer me clear of them, so read on!

Author Acknowledgements

I began writing this novel at the tail end of the COVID-19 pandemic. For me, that event allowed me to dive into another time and place while those endless days crawled by when so many of us were confined to quarters. By Book 4 in my American Spy Sisters series, I was immersed in all things WWII, especially the Resistance in France. I wasn't sure I had another book on that war in me until I ran across information about the British intelligence warriors who fought to keep the British home front safe from German invaders and in-country traitors undermining their country of origin.

I enlisted a number of friends and experts to look over certain aspects of the novel and am deeply indebted to Susanna Jennens, Randolph Kent, and Laura Sandys in London for sleuthing out wayward Americanisms and mistakes a Yank is likely to make when writing about wartime Britain.

Also high on my gratitude list is Dr. Roger Taylor for allowing me to borrow his name for the Forbes family doctor and for checking the aspects of the novel that deal with medical, hospital, and wartime medicine. Palliative Care Charge Nurse Alison Thayer Harris was my consultant on automobile-pedestrian injuries as the plot developed and helped me pinpoint what injuries were likely to occur when one stepped off a curb into the path of an oncoming London taxi.

Thanks are also due to architectural designer Carol Kavalaris for evaluating sections that have to do with architects, architecture, and the related world of interior design. Additionally, I owe my gratitude to several insightful readers for offering me feedback on plotting and pace in earlier drafts: Sausalito Books by the Bay store owner Cheryl Popp, authors Diana Dempsey and Allona Kagan, and avid readers Maria Paterno and Marian Taylor.

Holding my hand and offering chapter-by-chapter advice based on their years of experience as novelists are my critique partners,

Cynthia Wright and Kim Ostrom-Cates. Like the characters Lacy, Tess, and Pat, we trio of multi-published authors have supported each other as "The Plotholes," a group of friends and colleagues who exchange chapters of our works-in-progress and provide honest feedback. We've also weathered the publishing storms of the last thirty years, thanks to our durable friendship and sharing not only writing but also coping skills.

Before, during, and after the "COVID years," my Sausalito Dog Walkers group (and their pets) offered this author respite from the "darkest hours" every Tuesday, Thursday, and Saturday. Our 2.7-mile morning treks up and down village hills with our canine posse, including my COVID pup, Viscount, Lord Dashwood—though you may call him Dash!—featured an always welcome 8:30 a.m. stop at Poggio Trattoria with its outdoor tables under the heaters, even in our sometimes foggy summers. My thanks to all the companions and the wonderful morning crew serving the coffee.

The book you're seeing on your e-reader or the print copy you're holding in your hand is a collaboration with Oliver-Heber Books and its remarkable publisher, Tanya Anne Crosby, and her daughter Alaina. These two, along with their amazing staff, are another small-but-mighty outfit that makes the long haul to produce a novel completely worthwhile. I offer my heartfelt thanks and admiration, as always, to OHB's Kimberly Cates for her discernment in editing the final manuscript, designer Dar Albert for one of the best book covers, *ever*, and to Kim Maniquet for her proofreading.

Despite input from the previous list of generous, highly informed editors, readers, and friends, errors can always make it into the final draft of a published work. Any that remain in this one are my own.

And finally, I owe my unbounded gratitude to my wonderful and loving husband of half a century and my partner in all domestic and professional endeavors. I thank you not only for your mots justes but also for an editorial sensibility that has never steered me wrong. Like Pem is for Lacy in *The Spy Wore Long White Gloves*, Tony Cook is the man I love and can count on, no matter what—and we can still laugh along the way.

Ciji Ware
Sausalito, California

Selective Bibliography

What follows is by no means a list of every book or document I read during the research phase of this novel but rather a curated selection that might further inform readers interested in the subject of the British home front during WWII and the heroes and heroines who protected it—including young women who once wore long white gloves.

Baring, Sarah, *The Road to Station X – From Debutante Ball to Fighter-Plane Factory to Bletchley Park, A Memoir of One Woman's Journey Through World War Two.* Sapere Books, 2000

Conover, Anne, *Caresse Crosby – From Black Sun to Roccasinibalda.* Capra Press, 1989

de Courcy, Anne, *Debs at War – How Wartime Changed Their Lives.* Weidenfeld & Nicholson, 2005; paperback, 2022

______ *1939: The Last Season.* Weidenfeld & Nicholson, 1989; paperback, 2022

Fessler, Diane Burke, *No Time For Fear – Voices of American Military Nurses in World War II.* Michigan University Press, 1996

Foley, Michael, *Britain's Railway in the Second World War.* Pen & Sword Books, Ltd., 2020

Hemming, Henry, *AGENT – The Lives and Spies of MI5's Maxwell Knight.* Public Affairs, Hachette Book Group, 2017

Howard, Michael S., *Jonathan Cape, Publisher.* Penguin Books, 1977

Hutton, Robert, *Agent Jack – The True Story of MI5's Secret Nazi Hunter.* St. Martin's Press, 2018

Kitty, Alexander, *A Different Track: Hospital Trains of the Second World War.* Heritage House [reprint], 2023

Lambert, Anthony, *Britain's Railways in Wartime.* Historic England, 2018

Leaming, Barbara, *Kick Kennedy – The Charmed Life and Tragic Death of the Favorite Kennedy Daughter.* St. Martin's Press, Thomas Dunne Books, 2016

______ *The Kennedy Women,* Villard Books, 1994

MacIntyre, Ben, *Double Cross – The True Story of the D-Day Spies*. Bloomsbury Publishing, 2012

Major, Susan, *Female Railway Workers in World War II*. Pen & Sword Books Ltd., 2018

McKinstry, Leon, *Operation Sea Lion – The Failed Nazi Invasion That Turned the Tide of War*. The Overlook Press, 2014

Miller, Joan, *One Girl's War – Personal Exploits in MI5's Most Secret Station*. Brandon Book Publishers, Ltd., 1986

Modin, Yuri, *My 5 Cambridge Friends – Burgess, MacLean, Philby, Blunt and Cairncross*. Trafalgar Square, 2000

Nicholson, Virginia, *Millions Like Us – Women's Lives During The Second World War*. Penguin Books, 2011

O'Connor, Bernard, *Operation Lena and Hitler's Plots to Blow Up Britain*. Amberley Publishing, 2017

Peabody, Polly, *Occupied Territory*, The Cresset Press, 1941

Richardson, Kristen, *The Season – A Social History of the Debutante*. W.W. Norton & Company, 2020

Rose, Kenneth, *Elusive Rothschild – The Life of Victor, Third Baron*. Weidenfeld & Nicholson, 2003

Taylor, Eric, *Front-Line Nurse – British Nurses in World War II*. Robert Hale, 1997

Thompson, Laura, *The Six – The Lives of the Mitford Sisters*. St. Martin's Press, 2015

Tremain, David, *The Beautiful Spy – The Life and Crimes of Vera Eriksen*. The History Press, 2019

Walker, Diana Barnato, *Spreading My Wings – One of Britain's Top Women Pilots Tells Her Remarkable Story from Pre-War Flying to Breaking the Sound Barrier*. Grub Street, 2003

West, Nigel, *Cold War Spymaster, The Legacy of Guy Liddell, Deputy Director of MI5*. Frontline Books, 2018

www.pinterest.com/cijiware Picture Files for Am. Spy Sisters Books 1, 2, 3 & 4

MORE SPELLBINDING WORLD WAR II ADVENTURE AND INTRIGUE IN THE AMERICAN SPY SISTERS SERIES

Book 1: *Landing by Moonlight*

Book 2: *A Spy Above the Clouds*

Book 3: *The Safety of Strangers*

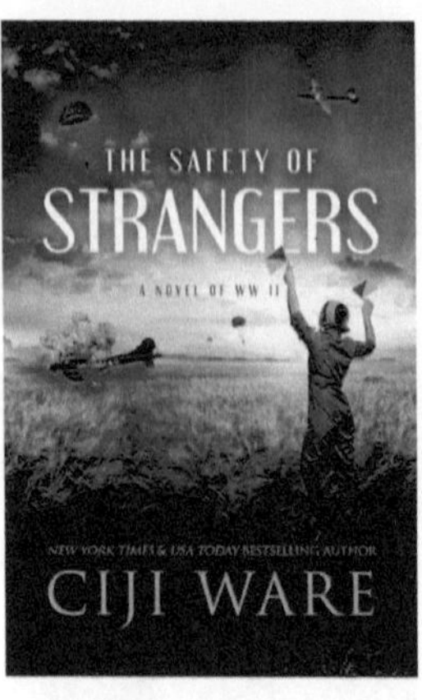

Book 4: *The Spy Wore Long White Gloves*

Don't miss any of Ciji Ware's WWII romantic thrillers!

Books 1, 2, & 3 in the series are inspired by the exceptional women who volunteered as secret agents and 'in-country' operatives for Allied Intelligence to fight the Nazi invasion of France, some joining even *before* the United States entered the war after the attack on Pearl Harbor.

Landing by Moonlight's **CATHERINE THORNTON** in Book 1, a Washington D.C. debutante, is flung in her parachute through the moonlit sky back into France from a low-flying British Halifax after sneaking into an enemy's embassy and stealing the naval operations codes for the Mediterranean fleet. Once recruited as a secret agent and inserted into the

French Riviera, Madam "Colette Durand" is definitely not prepared for the trial-by-fire to come.

A Spy Above the Clouds' **CONSTANCE "VIV" VIVIER-CLARKE** is a poor-little-rich girl from New York whose stepfather sells ball bearings to Hitler's war machine, leaving Viv to her own devices. These include failing out of her Swiss boarding school, being fired by her celebrated Olympic ski coach for lack of discipline, and defying her socialite mother to become an ambulance driver in Paris. Her next outrageous move is enlisting as an Allied secret agent and courier-on-skis, ferrying messages and weapons to the Resistance in the enemy-infested French Alps.

As readers learn from the exploits of **BROOKE BRADLEY de VARNEY** in *The Safety of Strangers,* war changes those who participate in it, regardless of which side they may be on...and "therein lies the tale..."

The Spy Wore Long White Gloves' **LACY FARRINGTON FORBES** never wanted the life of a debutante. But after a family tragedy pulls her back to America from a post-deb whirl in London on the brink of WWII, she trades ballrooms for battlefields—volunteering with the Red Cross to raise funds for a field hospital near the Russian-Finnish front. Dodging bombs, booby traps, and military regulations amidst the Blitz destroying England from the air, this unlikely "Deb at War" is forced to reconcile a tangled web of duty, honor, loss and enduring love while the fate of nations hangs in the balance.

"*New York Times & USA Today* bestselling author and Emmy Award-winning former broadcast journalist **Ciji Ware** once again displays her extraordinary talent for weaving historical fact into compelling historical fiction..."

ABOUT THE AUTHOR

New York Times and *USA Today* bestselling author and Emmy Award-winning former broadcast journalist Ciji Ware has published fourteen historical and contemporary novels, a novella, and two nonfiction works. Her numerous honors and awards include the Dorothy Parker Award of Excellence, a Silver Gavel from the American Bar Association, a DuPont Award for Investigative Journalism, and designation as a Fellow of the Society of Scottish Antiquaries (FSAScot) for her historical novel *Island of the Swans*. She was named to the Martha's Vineyard Writer-In-Residence program and, in 2012, shortlisted for the WILLA (Cather) Literary Award for *A Race to Splendor*. A graduate of Harvard with a degree in history, Ware is the first woman graduate of the college to serve as president of the Harvard Alumni/ae Association, Worldwide. The author lives in the San Francisco Bay Area with her husband "of long duration" and—when not writing—takes ballet barre through the San Francisco Ballet School's Zoom classes, performs in amateur theatricals, and walks just under ten miles a week with the Sausalito Dog Walkers in the hills of her maritime village.

Also by Ciji Ware

American Spy Sisters

Landing By Moonlight

A Spy Above the Clouds

The Safety of Strangers

The Spy Wore Long White Gloves

Hidden Heroines Historical Novels

Island of the Swans

Wicked Company

A Race to Splendor

Time-Slip Historical Novels

A Cottage by the Sea

Midnight on Julia Street

A Light on the Veranda

Four Seasons Contemporary Novels

That Summer in Cornwall

That Autumn in Edinburgh

That Winter in Venice

That Spring in Paris

Contemporary Novella

Ring of Truth: "The Ring of Kerry Hannigan"

Nonfiction

Rightsizing Your Life

Joint Custody After Divorce